THE DRUMS OF DOOM

Erik DJ O'Brien
26 June 2021

ERIK D.J. O'BRIEN

STRATTON
PRESS
Publishing Life

THE DRUMS OF DOOM

Stratton Press, LLC
1603 Capitol Ave, Suite 310,
Cheyenne, WY 82001
www.stratton-press.com
1-888-323-7009

ISBN (Paperback): 978-1-64345-503-7
ISBN (Ebook): 978-1-64345-739-0

Printed in the United States of America

The Duaredheim Staff Saga includes

Kur's Rage
The Drums of Doom
The Last Admiral
The Ice Moon

For Carolyn

The author extends his sincerest thanks to the editor, Angela James of Stratton Press, and his family editors: Kevin and Lucia O'Brien and Tommie Magazu, who is immortalized in this work as the Wizard Zu.

Within these pages, Sir John Anderson of Monson,
Knight of Renown,
lives forever.

Preface

This is the second book of the Duaredheim Staff series, and the continuation of book 1, entitled *Kur's Rage. The Secret Way* or *The Catacombs of the Lych King* may have been more fitting titles, but I chose instead to name it *The Drums of Doom.*

Kur's Rage was the product of over ten years of labor, and its sequel has been an ongoing project since 2004. *Kur's Rage* introduced many characters, Tempus, and a broad spectrum of deities worshipped by its inhabitants. *The Drums of Doom* continues the adventure, and I waste little time in reintroducing established characters. However, at the request of my dedicated audience, I am including a broad cast of characters as an index to this book. I will try, as best that I can, to provide the tools necessary to discover the proper pronunciation of the more difficult names, including brief descriptions and the significance of the characters. Reintroductions notwithstanding, character traits, appearance, and personality should all shine through, as I dutifully put them all through the meat grinder.

I designed *The Drums of Doom* in such a way that it mirrors our own troubled times. The Earth itself, at least as far as we Humans are concerned is in dire peril. We see these dangers every day, on television, in newspapers, in the health of our children, and in the drastic changes to our climate. Religion, the spirit's salvation, created to bring humanity closer to the divine, may instead bring about our ruin. Technology may redeem us, and yet it too is a double-edged sword. In this electronic age, we can communicate across the globe in an instant, and yet we may all be lonelier than ever. All these same troubles exist on Tempus, to one degree or another, and as such, I believe that they add a much greater scope to my tale. Realism and fantasy combine to make the story believable. The motivations of the characters lends grievous consequence to their failures, and I pray that the story will keep you glued to your seat from cover to cover.

The first chapter contains a Declaration of Freedom and a Constitution for the New Republic that could be misconstrued as rebellious in nature. In fact, it is a bold tribute and a powerful reminder of the personal sacrifice and incredible courage exhibited by the Founding Fathers of the United States of America. The Declaration of Independence was itself an act of ultimate rebellion carried out by the bravest of men, who could find no other solution to the problems of their day. If not for their insight and their vision, this would not now be "the land of the free, and the home of the brave." Many delegates and signatories signed the Declaration of Independence. In remembrance, I would like to name some of the Founding Fathers, George Washington, Thomas Jefferson, John Adams, James Madison, Alexander Hamilton, John Hancock, and Benjamin Franklin. These were men whose hands we will never grasp, into whose living eyes we will never stare, and yet their words stand immortal.

The Drums of Doom is foremost an epic fantasy adventure designed to create provocative, entertaining, and exciting images in the minds of its readers. Parallels between our world and the world of Tempus exist solely to add depth to the story and its characters, and not to suggest solutions to the troubles of our times. I do, however, reserve the right as a free citizen, to poke a little fun at it and perhaps to suggest, oh so humbly, that our only chance for survival is to believe that we are all one. One what, you might ask? One everything, I would answer.

My special thanks to all my noble friends who have contributed characters and ideas that helped to make this work complete: Tommie Magazu, Richard Wolfe, Robert Jackman, Edward Brangan, William O'Laughlin, Joseph Garside, and Peter Bell, to name but a few.

In book 1, the characters thwarted their nemesis. Prevailing against all odds, they won for themselves the gem of the staff, a critical component of the Duaredheim Staff. Following the enchanted pull of the locating scepter, they now descend into the uncharted depths of Underearth. Climbing into a world of eternal darkness, their courage is sorely tested.

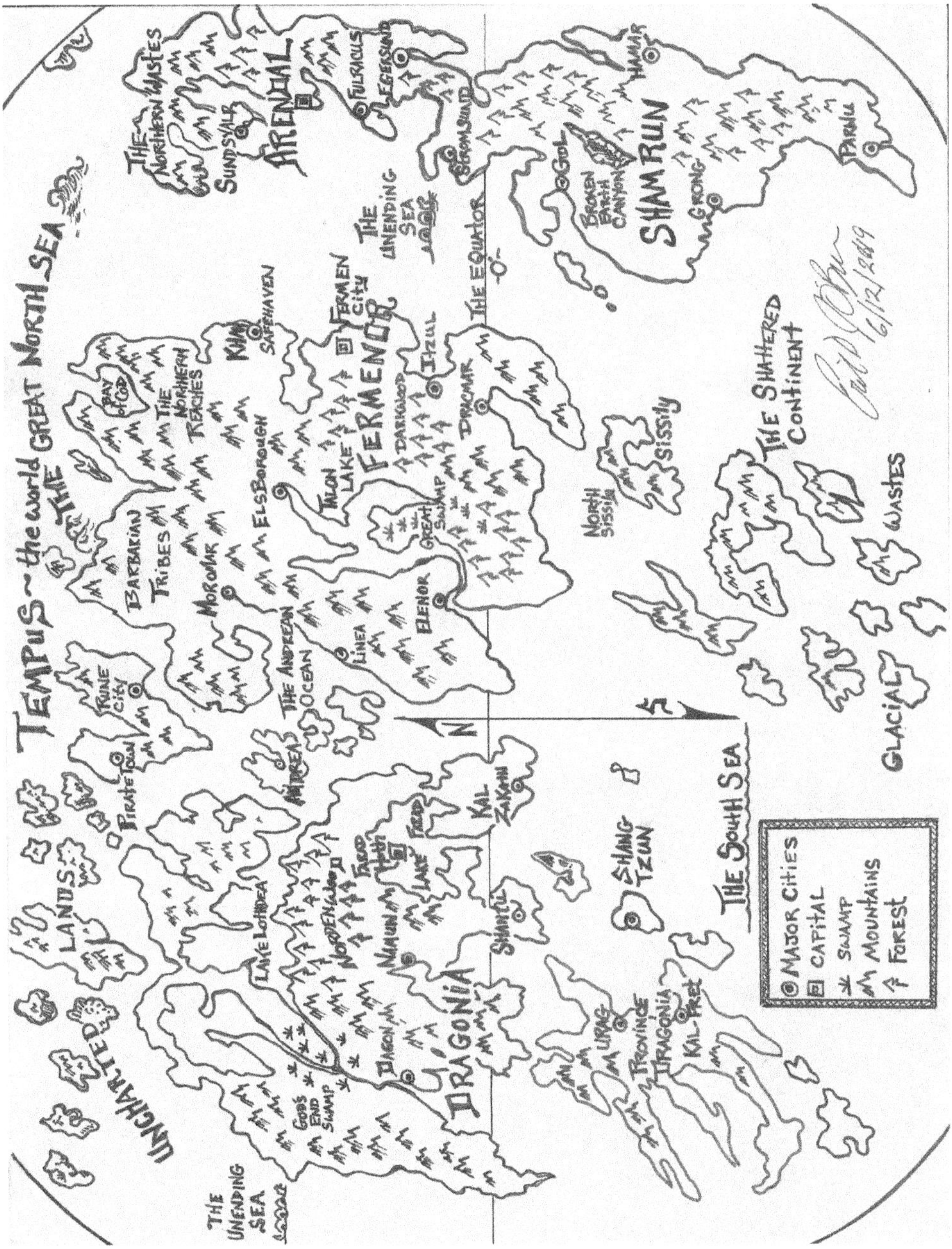
TEMPUS ~ the world
THE GREAT NORTH SEA
UNCHARTED LANDS
THE UNENDING SEA
THE NORTHERN WASTES
SUNDSVALL
ARENDAL
FULRACUS
LEGESSUND
HAMAR
BARBARIAN TRIBES
THE NORTHERN REACHES
BAY of COD
SAFEHAVEN
MOROMAR
ELSBOROUGH
THE ANDREAN OCEAN
RUNE CITY
PIRATE TOWN
LINEA
ELENOR
TALON LAKE
GREAT SWAMP
DARKWOOD
FERMEN CITY
THE EQUATOR
BROKEN EARTH CANYON
GOL
SHAMRUN
GRONG
PARNU
DRAGONIA
GOD'S END SWAMP
KAL ZAKOTH
SHANG TZUN
NORTH SISSILY
SISSILY
THE SHATTERED CONTINENT
THE SOUTH SEA
GLACIAL WASTES
MAJOR CITIES
CAPITAL
SWAMP
MOUNTAINS
FOREST

THE NORTHERN REACHES
TUNDRA
THE GREAT PYRAMID
RED ORCIN TRIBES
DREADMOORE FOREST
TEMPLE
THE DRAGON'S RIDGE MTS
ABANDONED Pit % MINE
OCEAN RIVER
StrongHolt
Hidden Valley
CULTIVATED LANDS
FOREST OF THE ELVEN LORDS
TRIBAL ELVEN KINGDOMS
Trail of the Red Orcin War Party
KORUN-DORR
BARBAROUS TRIBES
The Crooked River
DRAGON'S Foot LAKE
OGRE FANG MTS
JACKALS
Troll Falls
NORTHERNMOST BOUNDARY of SAFE HAVEN
ACORN GROVE
SEERESS
GREEN WOOD
To the Sea
MINING/LOGGING ROADS
To HIGHLAND PASS
NORDTOWN VILLAGE
0 15M
N
W
E
S

PROLOGUE

Shortly after Leander set sail for the lands of Fermenor in the year 2020, the Druids of Arendal completed their greatest temple. The Ice Moon was at its peak. The winter solstice had come. They hurled the last pail of excavated earth, saved for that very occasion, to the four winds. The following chapter is the tale of how they built it.

The Henge of Stone

High kings ruled the lands of Arendal, and the Druids worshipped it. Revered from Egersund to Sundsval, they erected their holiest temple on a high plain by the sea. It was sacred ground, where their ancestors first landed on sailing ships from a forgotten country. The highest-ranking priest of their order was the Arch Druid. He was old, but not overly so, and his hair was white. Tall and square-shouldered, he carried himself with the vitality of a much younger man. His hands were calloused and strong from farming, and his eyes were gray like the sea beneath a storm. Respected and sought after for his wisdom, his visions had helped his people prosper. The designs for his ultimate tribute to the heavens had come to him in a dream. They would build a monumental Henge of Stone.

In his youthful travels, he had found the perfect source of sandstone, which they called Sarcen stone, along their northernmost shores. The form and grain of the stone was perfect, and the location of the quarry, so near to the sea, provided him with the means to move it. His followers had grown restless and complacent. He needed a goal to unify them. During the Harvest Festival, he related his vision. Some claimed that his dream was an impossible task. Others relished the challenge and flocked to his call. When their morale faltered, he would point out how far they had already come, and bolster their hope anew. Twenty years of toil and this is how they accomplished the impossible.

First, the Arch Druid had to find the perfect site, and so he chose the place of their ancestors' landing, on high ground near the sea. The remnants of their ancient temple still stood there. His own father's father had told him that it was once a ring fort built by the Tribe of the Gael, the ancestors of all the Druids. The pilgrim Gael had excavated two great bermes of earth in a wide circle spanning a central moat. Within the innermost ring, a sphere of timbers had once stood. In those ancient times, all manner of barbarians and fearsome creatures roamed the land, and they needed it in order to defend themselves. They called their Ring Fort Eirelot.

The site of Eirelot was no accident. The countryside was a mostly flat expansive plain. Approaching enemies were visible across great distances. The Druids also knew that a powerful nexus of energy existed there. It was the perfect site to nurture and protect the pilgrim Gael. He had seen the place in his dream and the foundation of his vision.

The Henge would preserve their history for all time, and in order to accomplish it, his people would have to accomplish four impossible tasks. The first was to build a mound of earth over one hundred fifty feet across and some fifteen feet in height, with a great gently sloping ramp rising to its top. There were many reasons for this. The soil provided support for each standing stone, allowing them to be erected in a perfect circle, leveled, mortised, and finally capped with curved lintel stones joined by tongue and groove. It would seem a tremendous feat, but it was done yard by yard, one bag of earth at a time, by people with one unifying goal.

The second impossible feat was up to the Arch Druid himself to accomplish. Over the course of an entire year, he charted the passing of the sun, the moons, and the stars in the Heavens, and carefully marked the orientations of each upon the hilltop. Working his way around the perimeter of the mound, he marked where each pillar of his monument would stand in relation to the stars. Each standing stone of his monument would mark the annual progression of the Heavens and allow the prediction of lunar eclipses.

The third task involved even greater toil. His masons labored in the north, notching the Sarcen stone of the quarry walls in a precise fashion, and when winter came, ice froze in the cracks that they had made, and nature accomplished much of what they needed done. Using this raw material, they cut and shaped gigantic pillars of some twenty feet in length and six feet in width, most weighing over twenty-five tons, laid them on logs, and rolled them with the help of oxen to a nearby tributary. There, they fashioned rafts of sufficient size to carry their prize, and punted them down river to the sea. In the same manner, they towed their pillars north and rolled them up the sacred hill.

When each stone arrived, his excavators dug enormous pits, well plumbed and of the exact depth and width necessary to accommodate the standing stones and their footings. They then lowered the Sarcen stones into the pits one after another, plumbed, and backfilled until each pillar stood tall and level within its hole. Erecting them in a perfect circle of some one hundred and eight feet in diameter required the placement of seventy-four stones arranged side-by-side and three feet apart, so that they each would carry half of the load of the capstones that would span them. When every pillar was in place, their topmost surfaces were chiseled smooth to the perfect heights and mortised so that their lintels would seat firmly atop them. Connected by tongue and groove joints, they meticulously carved them to form a perfect circle. The mound of earth provided the perfect surface to carve each one and set them in place, one after another.

When every feature of their labors had been completed, inspected, and judged to be in perfect congruence with the stars, Tempus, and the elements, they excavated the sacred hill, and that was the fourth insurmountable task. When their toils were complete, only the Henge of Stones remained, standing tall for the centuries to witness them. It was a miracle, crafted with the highest respect for their world and the greatest of personal sacrifices.

When the Arch Druid's dream finally stood tall for all to see, there were few nonbelievers left among them. The Henge became a center for worship, holier even than their greatest temples of the past, and their village prospered. Kings and queens from the surrounding lands donated handsomely for burial sites near the sacred monument. Their sons and daughters would often be married there. They routinely held holy ceremonies celebrating the solstices and all the great celestial events. The stone monument became a symbol of perseverance and pride that would carry their culture through the centuries. Generations of worshippers, visitors, and observers would walk among the stones in silent awe because the Henge demanded reverence. It was a lasting testament to the accomplishment and respect that can come from one Man's dream and that is the miracle of Eirelot.

—Antineus Morlinar
Chronicler of history

Vlad's Declaration

Captain's log
Seventh day of Sanguis, 2032

We set sail from the shores of Dragonia with high hopes. The ocean has been for the most part calm, but now we have entered the treacherous waters of the North Sea, and great mountains of ice float all around us. Time, so often a rare thing, is now a bounty, and we, the newest members of the Drakkar Noire, waste none of it. Together with the help of my comrades, we have begun the framework for a new world order.

The Declaration of Freedom

When the gods and government of a nation so profoundly fail the people, it is the supreme duty and moral responsibility of the afflicted to correct it. Should a nation's government abandon its citizens, and due course of law be found to be impotent in the face of the established order, then revolution is the only solution. Insurrection, being by definition the most severe reaction to desperation, cannot be undertaken lightly. This Declaration of Freedom cites the following abuses and injustices perpetrated on the people of Dragonia by their Queen, Goddess, and government:

The five-hundred-year war against the nations of Fermenor has continued to rage despite Parliamentary decree, military advisement, lack of enemy aggression, or a formal declarations of war; for wrongfully perpetuating, the illusion of an "enemy empire" and fabricating evidence designed to continue the war ad infinitum.

The armed forces, ever the pawn of their government, have suffered countless abuses. These include the use of the army to quell insurrection, apprehend suspected outlaws, extortion of taxes by might of arms, and the genocide of several barbarous tribes.

The Queen has systematically reduced the navy, created for conquest and defense of the shores, to a role of piracy, smuggling, and perpetuation of the slave trade.

Dragonian citizens have no right to free trials and can be accused, convicted, and sentenced within minutes, the most common verdict being death.

Dragonian citizens naturalized through immigration or surrender must abandon their faiths and convert. Resisting infidels are publicly humiliated and tortured; those admitting blasphemy, executed.

The Queen routinely ignores laws passed by Parliamentary decree. Parliament itself no longer exists to debate on matters of national importance, but rather is an illusion of legal equality designed to quell rebellion and subjugate the people.

For the Queen's enactment of foreign policies preventing free trade with other nations, and thus perpetuating the decline of national economies.

For the indentured servitude of the peasant classes, the legalized slavery of prisoners of war, and the general acceptance of a society ruled by terror and domination.

For the immoral invasion of private homes for the purpose of quartering soldiers, collecting taxes, search of evidence, or other more nefarious ends. Linked to this is the complete unaccountability for atrocities committed by such soldiers against the people.

What are clear are the totalitarian rule of the Queen, rulership through fear, and the complete lack of individual freedoms.

For these reasons and others so vile they were banned entry into this document, we hereby formally declare our intention to secure the freedom of Dragonia's people. Therefore, as not to revolt without a clear intention of goals and purpose, we have penned the following Constitution of the Republic.

The Constitution of the Republic of Dragonia

We, the champions of the New Republic, do hereby draft this document, declaring that from this day and forever after that, the people of the republic shall never fear their gods or their nation. The New Republic shall eternally establish that all people are born with certain natural rights and that these rights shall be inviolate.

Among these, freedom shall be the indisputable right of the people. Moreover, these freedoms shall include, but not be limited to, freedom of worship, freedom of faith, freedom of opinion, including the freedom to voice that opinion in lawful assemblies, freedom to own lands, freedom to vote in public elections (with this freedom pertaining to all including those without titled lands), freedom to bear arms at all times and in all places sufficient to secure one's own defense, and the general freedom to go where one wills unless those travels should trespass on another's freedom.

The people shall be guaranteed the absolute right to a free trial, be they citizen or immigrant. All matters of law shall be presided over by a law giver appointed by the local community in free election. Only an impartial jury consisting of peers of the accused shall decide final judgments. Levying of criminal reparations owed to victims shall take place according to Brehon Law. Only in circumstances where no other recourse can secure the safety of the people shall the punishment be death.

The people will secure the abolition of slavery throughout all of the lands of the republic. This abolishment shall also include those trapped by indentured servitude and held in needful poverty by their indifferent masters. It shall also be the responsibility of the enslaved to reveal their servitude, and like prisoners of war, it shall be their constitutional right to escape. Such acts of revolt and uprising shall not constitute a crime against master, nation, or God, and as such will be un-punishable by law.

The military shall exist to defend the nation against foreign aggression, and to protect the people against unlawful insurrection and uprising within the republic. Attempts by religious zealots or wanton despots to usurp local rule, or disassemble the lawful government of the republic defines illegal insurrections. Rescue, homeland defense, and the lawful apprehension of fugitives constitutes the legal basis for the formation of local militias. Vigilantism, having no place in a civilized nation, shall be unlawful and punishable by law.

Hunting, trapping, and fishing for the purpose of subsistence is the legal right of the people in all of the wild lands of the republic. Landowners shall reserve the right to allow or disallow the use of their property by outdoorsmen. Trespassers are accountable for poaching and any damages to private property or citizens.

Amendments to this constitution require a majority vote of Parliament. Careful consideration must accompany each amendment; new polices holding Freedom in the highest regard.

Amendments may only add to the Constitution, and may never negate the Laws and Rights penned in this document.

Enemies of Freedom shall be enemies of the Republic, and such foes may constitute the necessity of a Declaration of War, its proclamation requiring a majority vote by Parliament. No one Leader shall ever lawfully declare war against another People or Nation in the New Republic.

From this day forward, the Republic of Dragonia will be a cradle of civilization, a country where the meek shall be able to walk from coast to coast whosesoever they will, without fear for their safety or their lives. It shall be a community of equals, born with the freedom to pursue their individual dreams, pioneer uninhabited lands, and worship what gods they will.

Acknowledging the existence of powers and laws greater than those of mortal kind, and fully knowing that our lives are likely forfeit, our bodies destined for torture and execution, we, of the Drakkar Noire do hereby ratify this document with our signatures penned below,

Vlad Leu Sherroan
Darik Al Luan
Elrick Du'Raneurden
Shiran Coldrun
Andreul Do'Nurum
Dorlin Varul
Olak Tempestus
Draco Pertinax
Monica El Far

Ariana Queensdaughter

> The above signed individuals bear witness to this document on this day, the seventh of Sanguis in the year 2032, before all the gods and the heavens above. To these qualities in the highest we shall ever aspire, until the people of Dragonia are free, to the last man, woman, or child, and unto our last breath, so we solemnly swear.

"Why did you sign your name so boldly, Vlad?" Monica asked.

"So that the Queen will be able to read it," Vlad said, "all of the way from her throne at Farad Hoth!"

"But not yet, I hope," Draco said. "I should like to live for a little bit longer."

"No, not yet," Vlad said, "not until we are ready. Until then, we must be nothing more than loyal followers of the Queen. We shall spend the rest of the voyage memorizing this document word for word, so that as long as one of us lives, so too shall our dream. Our secrecy must be absolute, or we will all surely be fed to the Great Spider."

"To the New Republic," Elrick said boldly, steadfast in the face of such terror.

"To the New Republic," they all replied.

Here begins *The Drums of Doom.*

One-Eyed Jack's

From the Journal of Kalor the Enchanter
Entry 596, Ice Moon, Day 11, 2147

Six months had passed before I saw the three lads again. They had gone off to Harg Pass to guard the Gnoll Hills as I had done so long ago, and after facing many hardships, they once again longed for the peace and adventure of my story. In fact, Kur's son Kragon was himself a corporal in his third year of service, and he was doing quite well by all accounts. In addition, like his father, he was fast becoming a master axman. Rumors were once again spreading that the Red Orcs were stirring again in the north, but who was leading them and what their purposes might be was unknown. The King summoned Dartin and I in the hopes that we might be able to provide some answers for him. My scrying crystal was now as much a part of me as my own body. It was an extension of my will, and through it, my eyes could see into dark places far across the world. However, so far, I had been unable to find the Orcs' leader, nor any other force that might be uniting the tribes again. I searched into every dark tunnel that I knew, but I could find no such agent of evil. I feared that *He* had returned.

Spring had come to Waysborough at last. As usual, I awoke to the cock's crow to tend to my small animals and complete my day's studies. Raven was squawking at me, demanding release from his oval cage. He was a good bird, but like most of his kind, he had a penchant for stealing shiny objects, like my spectacles, magic rings, and similar baubles, things of little use to a crow but critical to a wizard. Nevertheless, on this sunny Woden's day, I dared to let him fly free about my library and out into the courtyard. When my morning rounds were completed, I told Prehd, my young assistant, to watch the shop while I was away. Prehd was very young, and he just happened to be a Gnomish foster child like me. I had come to calling him Techno after my own predecessor in Chaos Magic, and I often had to scold him for stealing. More often than not, the objects of his thefts were pastries from the town square. *Oh well, boys would be boys.* I guess that I should not have told him that part of my story.

I was leaving for the tavern with purpose, for I had seen my three young listeners ride into town, and I knew that they had just arrived on their first leave. I remembered our first meeting like it was yesterday. Promises are promises, and I longed to tell them more of my story.

The cool spring air smelled like hope and new life. It was the perfect day for a reunion. It was the perfect day for memories. With my energy restored, I found a new bounce in my step that I thought I had lost. I strode down the road to the inn, and up the steps I went. Passing through those barroom doors brought my memories back in a rush. It was a strange feeling, much like the familiarity of home. I had to hold back the rushing tide of memories of people and times long past. The weight of it on my shoulders was like a living thing struggling to hold me back. Only my belief that there was still good in the world allowed me to win the battle and walk on. Waysborough was still a peaceful place, and the patrons of One-Eyed Jack's were honest, hard working, and bonded by friendship.

Looking across the tavern's hall to my table, I saw that the young lads had already sat down to lunch, and Sonya had joined them, just like old times! Between them, where the sun fell from a nearby window, stood my empty chair. It had long legs with spindles for footrests and a seat that sat me Man height. A frosty mug of ale rested there, waiting for me, and beside it laid a small pouch of Trem weed. It seemed that they still wanted to hear the rest of my tale after all.

"Nice to see you, Kalor," they said. "We hoped that you'd come by today."

"Now, Pauli," I said, "you don't think that I'd miss a chance to finish my story, do you?"

We spoke of simple things for a while, like people who have long been apart but whose love for one another remains undying. After we exchanged tales of the adventures that we had had since our last meeting, I began my tale anew…

The Secret Way

The shaft descended deep and dark, far beyond any reflected glimmerings of the sun. In case the rusty iron rings of the ancient ladder should fail them, they tied safety lines between themselves, using the techniques that Kur had taught them. However, even after rigorously testing the ancient rings for safety with sharp kicks and mighty pulls, the old Dwarven smith-craft still held, strong and firm beneath their weight. Down, ever down they climbed, rung after rung, into the wet cold of Underearth. To a Dwarf, it was home, and the music of the stone vibrated with songs of life and hidden treasures, but to Elves and Men, it was a place to be suffered, albeit briefly, for nightmares could not long be held back in a land where no lights ever shone. Nevertheless, they now possessed a light of purpose all their own. It was a binding cord between them, giving them the courage to stand, to walk, to go on.

Kalor stopped their descent to investigate several mining shafts intersecting their own, but he found them all empty save for one, which bore several carts filled with ore-bearing rock, rotten and abandoned. He wondered what had caused the miners to abandon such wealth.

"Mithril," Kur said, examining some of it. "It's only found in schist deposits like these. Do you see these distinctive crystalline layers? It is the character of the stone."

"I wonder why they'd leave this behind."

"Either they left it in a hurry, or they intended to come back for it and never made it. It is enough for a king's ransom."

"Use the scepter, Kalor," Carmen urged. "Show us the way." Its light was bright and blinding, but ever its pull was downward, always deeper into Modrul's mountain. "The shaft seems endless. I fear that some terrible doom awaits us!"

"Fear not the pressing earth!" Kur said. "For the Dwarves were born here in ancient times, and although Moradeus forged us and gave us life with his own breath, the bowels of Tempus were our womb, and she holds us no ill will."

"You are like a great rock that a weary traveler might lean upon," Dao said. "Without you, we would all be lost."

"I'm beginning to feel more at home down here, Kur," Kalor said. "I'm told that some Gnomes still live in the deep, dark places of the world."

Despite their assurances, Carmen's breath grew shorter, and the weight of the walls kept pressing ever tighter. It was then that Kur's firm grip shook her free of its fear with a gasp.

"Remember that your sun still shines above us," Kur said, "and look there, the shaft has ended, and another intersecting tunnel lies just beneath us!"

Dropping down into the tunnel, he determined that it ran somewhat north to south. Standing for some moments, he listened for any signs of danger, but he heard nothing but the breathing of his companions above. "Come down quietly," he whispered. "The new tunnel runs for some distance."

They all descended then, Carmen and Tariq, Leander and Dartin, Dao and Karina, and lastly Kalor, who was their lifeline with an extra rope from the tunnel above.

"I think that we should check the map," Carmen said, "and risk a little light."

A few moments later, Dao had a torch burning. Handing it to Dartin, he rummaged through his pack for his scroll case.

"Let me see," Dao said. "Ah, yes, the map shows this southern passage, but not the north tunnel. Perhaps the artist was only concerned with drawing where he'd come from."

"Or maybe it's a new addition," Dartin said.

"Let's try moving north a few paces," Carmen said, "and discover how far it goes." Staying close together, they used the light of Dartin's torch to guide them. They crept ahead for some time, and in the end, they found only a great downward stairwell, completely flooded. Lying near the water's edge, a rotten and crumpled backpack rested, with the initials "LE" burned into its flap. Within it, they found the moldering remains of a long rope and a rusted grappling hook.

"I'll wager," Tariq said, "that this belonged to the Vanir that Modrul killed."

"If he was a god," Carmen said, "then why didn't he just levitate up there or something?"

"Maybe," Dao said, "his divine powers were not available to him."

"It's a mystery," Kalor said, "that only the dead can answer."

"Well, we can't go any farther this way," Karina said. "We'll have to try the southern passageway, or swim."

"Let's move," Carmen said. "There's nothing else here."

As they walked back, Tariq and Carmen talked quietly. "Do you notice it?" he asked.

"What?"

"Our hardships have brought us together. We're moving together, thinking together, and becoming a team."

"Let's hope it's enough."

Traveling south, they eventually came to a westward and southeasterly bending passage.

The west way ended quickly in a collapsed tunnel.

"I don't like it," Kur said. "Dwarven tunnels rarely collapse by themselves."

However, the passages were very old, and the elements, even here, had an effect over time.

"It's no matter," Dao said. "The map indicates that the southeast passage was the one that was used by the Vanir. This torch has almost had it. I'm going to put the map away before the light goes out."

"Let's rest here for a minute," Carmen said, "until everyone's eyes have adjusted."

"Can you hear it?" Leander asked. "It sounds like running water, maybe a waterfall somewhere ahead."

"The map showed some sort of a cave ahead," Dao said, "and beyond it were more tunnels."

"We'll have to be extra careful," Leander said. "Stormbringer says that ahead of us is a mighty torrent. He can't see very far, though, because his senses are dampened by the unending stone."

"Let's move out," Carmen said. "Kalor, you're on point with Tariq."

Descending further, the river's sounds became deafening, and speech was impossible. The passage soon ended in a great open chamber with a high ceiling nearly beyond the reach of their heat-sensitive eyes.

A long narrow ledge wound around the west wall, skirting a deep chasm below. Water rushed through the jagged gorge, as if it were blood pumped from the very heart of the world. Mist and waves sprayed up from below, careening off the cavern walls. Even the black stalactites above them were not immune to their touch. The ledge looked passable yet treacherous. One slip into that tremendous flow would seal their fate.

Tariq signaled for a withdrawal back to a quieter stretch of tunnel.

"Can we make it?" Carmen asked.

"It looks slick, but most of the ledge is at least a foot wide and seems to span the entire length of the gorge. Kur, what would you do?"

"We'll need to rope off, like we did on the mountain, only this time we'll all be tied together."

"And if we fall?"

"Then we fall as one."

"We should vote on it," Carmen suggested. "It's risky."

"No need," Karina said. "You should know by now that we're all in this until the end."

"Until the end," many of them echoed.

"Then rope off!" Kur said. "Keep the rope taut. Step where I step, or where the soldier in front of you steps. Face the wall at all times. We must move together as one."

Leading the way, Kur began the crossing. Within seconds, the lashing spray drenched them. It seemed that the river itself wanted to suck them into its deadly embrace, but Kur's footsteps were sure, and he tested each foothold carefully before committing his weight onto it. If he found loose stones, he would signal to Carmen, who followed him, and she to Dartin, and so on, and in this manner, they finally reached the end of the great ledge.

Victory was within their reach, but fate's fickle hand was present in the form of a circular portal blocking their passage. It was bound in iron, with wooden timbers swollen by moisture; age had rusted its hinges fast. Carmen signaled for him to try the door, and in doing so, Kur somehow stepped upon a shifting stone, and lo! A great gas poured out from the wall, engulfing him and the next three in line behind him.

What a fool am I not to have known it, he thought, but it was too late.

The Dwarves who had built these lonesome mines had done so with great cunning. Secret traps and constricted passageways, easily defensible by only a handful of warriors, guarded each entryway into their kingdom. The ledge and chasm was just such an obstacle. Kur now knew that he should have been looking for a trap. The thought came too late, because he had already inhaled enough of the poisonous vapors to kill most Humans. The only action that he could manage before collapsing was to aim his fall toward the ledge before him and not into the falls below.

Carmen braced herself. Tariq and Dartin crumpled behind her. Her helmet seemed to be protecting her from the dreadful gas, but dashed on the rocks below, such benefits would be of little use. Somehow, miraculously, her feet found a firm hold, and only Tariq and Dartin fell over the edge. They dangled helplessly, limp, tangled, and unconscious. Luckily Leander had followed Dartin, because only his strength was equal to the task of maintaining his footing and catching the falling weight of two men. It was all that he could manage alone. Hand tendons stressed to the limit, he cried out against the pain of the effort. His strength was holding, but he could not lift them even an inch.

Now the rope was both a lifeline and the potential ruin of them all. Carmen fought against it, discovering an inner strength that she never knew that she had. Struggling, she and Leander strained with all their might, but the angle was all wrong, and they could not raise them. She saw Leander's distress, and he hers, and they knew that the next few seconds would decide their fate. Behind Leander, the rest of the party was pulling back against the rope to help anchor them. It was a stalemate with no easy solution. To resign meant death.

Only Kalor, the last in line, was free to act, one small Gnome among so many tall folk. He had watched the scene unfold like a child at play with dominoes. The door was their greatest hope. Here and now, his size was a great boon, for he could pass around the legs of his comrades without falling from the ledge. Courageously, he cut himself free from the safety line and made his way around them. Quick and nimble, he stepped and climbed, swung and hopped, until he stood next to Kur's body. Carmen looked down at him, but her face was invisible behind the shield of her mask. Her limbs trembled uncontrollably. He knew that there was no time. Swinging his pack off his shoulders, he pulled out his own rope, lashed one end to a large iron ring that was set in the wall, and tested its strength. It held!

Turning, he formed a noose and swung it about his head like a plains cattle wrangler. Repeatedly he threw, until a lucky toss settled it over Tariq's head and over and under one of his arms. Pulling carefully, Kalor had Tariq caught; supporting him with two ropes, he took in the slack and tied it off. Signaling to Carmen and Leander, he urged them to shuffle toward him. They soon understood his plan. By moving toward him, they were slowly lowering their comrades, until Kalor's rope was withstanding the worst of the weight, and they could finally rest.

"You've got to get us through that door," Carmen shouted in his ear. "We have to get them off this ledge. Hurry, Kalor, I think that they're going to die!"

After examining the door, he realized that its noxious gas was expended, its trap sprung. Finding no other dangers, he went to work upon the lock. It was rusted and worn, but its inner parts were well oiled. In seconds, he was able to unlock it with a few assorted picks and tools. Grasping the doorknob, he turned it and pushed, but the swollen door would not budge. Its timbers were thick, its iron well forged, and even the strongest lumberjack would require hours to hack through it. "It's swollen shut! I can't push it open!"

If their fate had rested in his hands alone, then his injured friends would surely have perished, but he was not alone. In an instant, Carmen had joined his side. While he had worked the door, she had managed to tie her own rope off to the same ring and join him. With strength born of desperation, she threw herself against the portal body and soul. Left shoulder, hands and arms against it, her feet firmly planted against the cavern floor and wall. She screamed against it, her tendons straining to the breaking point. When it did not immediately budge, she didn't lose hope, but rather strove harder, and it was then that she heard a strange music, perhaps a chant, perhaps a song. It was one of battle, of carnage, of power, and of pride, and it seemed to issue forth from the space all around her. Beneath its rhythm, she could hear a mighty breath, like the wind passing into a dragon's lungs. It fueled her spirit and granted her an unnatural strength that the door could not match. It groaned and slid until the rock that encased it crumbled and gave way. It was open!

Before them loomed a short passageway, and beyond that, a spiral stair descended into the rock. Dragging Kur's body into the alcove, they helped the others reach safety. Through a combined effort, they were then able to pull their comrades out of the chasm. She examined them using the enhanced vision of her helmet. Their faces were pale and swollen, their breath only weak whispers.

The river roared behind them, but they were finally safe for a moment, and Carmen was able to examine her injured friends. Tariq and Dartin seemed far worse than Kur, whose breathing seemed to be improving steadily. It was a great mystery, because he had breathed in the most concentrated gas, being right next to the burst when it exploded. In a few minutes, he suddenly awoke, coughing wretchedly.

"You're alive!"

"Drellin Gas," he rasped, "nothing more."

"Drellin Gas?" Karina asked.

"Yes, it's made of sulfur and secret liquids," he said, wheezing. "Against most animals…it's deadly."

"And for you," Carmen asked.

"It was weak with age. A strong batch would have killed us all."

"What of Tariq and Dartin?"

"If they're not dead yet, they'll not die." Eyeing Carmen, he said, "Your helm is special indeed."

"I never smelled a thing."

"It's a good thing too," Leander said, smiling. "I don't think that I could have kept all four of you from falling." Chuckling, they finally began to relax after facing so much danger.

"I should have expected it," Kur said with a final deep cough. "We use Drellin Gas to protect our lower tunnels. I was so worried about getting across that I never thought of it."

"We'll just have to be more careful next time," Leander said while pouring some water over his patients' swollen eyes. "It's amazing how quickly you've recovered. You are nearly yourself while they remain unconscious."

"My people are resistant to poison. Snakebites that would kill large creatures will only sicken most Dwarves. My family is known to be particularly immune."

"What else can we do for them?"

"I have dried mushrooms in my pack," Kur said. "If we can make a tea from them, it will help their bodies purge the poison."

"But how to make a fire?" Karina said. "We're all drenched."

"We can use my lamp," Kalor said. "There's still oil in it."

"And my trail cooking pot," Kur said.

Going to work, they prepared the tea.

"Now how do we get them to drink it?" Karina said.

"We don't," Kur said. "Dip your fingers in the liquid and wipe it under their tongues. The tea itself is poisonous, but a small amount will heal and not kill. We should notice some improvement within minutes."

They rested and worried. Their patients were irreplaceable, and to lose them now would surely make success impossible. Miraculously their color improved just as Kur had said that it would, and in time, they awoke.

"How do you feel?" Carmen asked.

"Terrible."

"Wretched."

"Kur says that you'll be fine soon. If not for him, you might both be dead."

"Thanks!"

"It was my fault that it happened!"

"We don't blame you, Kur," Carmen said. "Down here in the dark, we trust you with our lives."

"I won't fail you again, I swear it! I just need to remember. It's been so long since I've tunneled." Everyone knew that he meant it beyond all question.

"We'll camp here until everyone's ready," Carmen said. "Kalor, where does the scepter point now?" Its light flared, and the gem continued to point southward in the direction of their descent. "How far down are we now, Kur?"

"We're several hundred feet beneath the base of the mountain."

"Somehow," Karina said, "I think that we're going to travel far deeper before we're through."

Glowing Mushrooms

Once they recovered their strength, Kur led the way. The stairs ahead of them were merely the beginning of an immense spiraling stair descending through the rock. One hundred steps and they had reached its end. An eerie glow spilled through an arch doorway, framing the last few steps and a small landing. The archway opened into the space beyond. Kur signaled for a halt and called Kalor forward with a whisper. They crept forward quietly, unsure what manner of beast might lie beyond that door. Peering within, expecting every imaginable horror, they were witness to a great vaulted garden of color.

Hundreds of mushrooms and molds of various kinds covered the majority of the cavern floor. It was from these fungi that the phosphorescent glow emanated, and it illuminated the cavern surprisingly well. In fact, they could all see with a vivid clarity that they had not enjoyed since they had begun their subterranean adventure. The grand chamber descended gently for some one hundred feet, with a ceiling above them of similar height. The grotto ended with a roughly hewn stone stair rising to meet an open passageway that led off toward the north. Thousands of bats hung tenaciously to the jagged ceiling, and their refuse had formed an enormous pile of black dung surrounding the distant staircase.

When Kur stepped into the cave, the bats flew out in a chaotic rush through a wide chimney in the cavern's roof. Piercing screeches and leathery wing beats filled the air with sound, but when they had finally gone, the empty void seemed deadly quiet. Moving in, Kur examined the myriad forms of mushrooms that he found there. Great toadstools, green and mottled, lay all about the floor, as well as enormous white mushrooms that were taller than he was. Drawing his belt knife, he carved great chunks out of the largest of the mushrooms and placed them in his food sack. "These will keep for many days. We could survive indefinitely on these alone if we had to. Fill your packs, but don't touch the spotted toadstools. They're deadly poison." Despite his warning, and without explanation, he placed three of them into his belt pouch with gloved hands.

"What do you want those for?" Carmen asked.

"They have many uses. Without them, we could never make an antitoxin."

"I trust that their other uses are good ones, Kur, but in the meantime, lead on."

They followed closely behind him, like a group of schoolchildren at an outdoor lesson. He then taught them what he could about mushroom lore. "I know the names and properties of over a thousand varieties of fungi. I can see over a hundred types in this cave alone. This wrinkled green fungus here will keep a wound from festering if it is made into a poultice, and it can cure many diseases if fashioned into a tea."

"Then we should take some with us," Karina said while collecting some. "This stuff could come in handy down here."

"These red mushrooms will cure a headache or other pains, and these black-capped toadstools will keep women barren if made into a tea." Carrying the knowledge of his people, he knew the beasts of the deepen wilds and plants that grew without light like none other. He led them through the cavern, and they collected many useful specimens. Halfway across it, they came upon a great watery mass of bat guano.

"Notice the slope of the cavern floor and the angle of the far stairs. I would estimate that this muck is at least eight feet deep at its center. We will have to work our way around it, along the cave's outer wall. The refuse should be shallower there."

"Let's move out," Carmen said, "but be ready for anything. I've got a bad feeling about this."

Kur took the point position. Halfway through the stinking refuse, it seemed that his guess was right, because the filth was only six inches deep. They were only forty feet from the stone stair when the beast of horror struck.

A Fistful of Dung

Kur had no way of knowing what lurked beneath the enormous pit of refuse. Even though his ancestors possessed tales of such horrible creatures from the past, there had been no encounters with any of the wretched beasts in centuries. Time's passage dimmed the memories of their forefathers. Lost and forgotten in the sand of God's hourglass were the ancient tales of terrible monsters living in garbage piles. They were stories of beasts born in the darkest places of the world, terrors silently waiting like trapdoor spiders, all hunger within, sudden death without. Old wives' tales such as these, so often based upon the truth, may have benefited Kur had he but remembered them.

The creature was not interested in old stories told around Dwarven cook-fires, nor did he care that his quarry had no prior knowledge of his kind. It was, however, patient above all else, and despite its immense body, it was very much at home beneath the dreadful dung. Terrible to behold it was, with a great gaping mouth centered upon its wide bulbous body and four great limbs that could propel it through the muck of its home with enormous speed. Its two arms were long tentacles, with wide heart-shaped pads lined with suction cups that could grasp and tear; within each cup was a horribly hooked claw. Perhaps its most ghastly feature of all was its solitary eye, which rested atop of a long stock protruding from the top of its ooze-covered body. When hunting, it would lie in wait beneath the filth and debris of its home with only its vestigial pseudo-pod showing, its one lonely eye scanning its subterranean home for wandering prey.

If Kur had remembered his grandfather's tales, he might have noticed the strange stalk standing above the mud, but he hadn't remembered, at least not until the animal struck.

It was a cunning hunter, choosing its victims carefully, even methodically. Erupting from the muck with the speed of a charging lion, the beast attacked, its frenzied movements slinging clumps of foul-smelling septic all about its bloated body. Using its whip-like tentacles, it lashed out to grasp the nearest prey.

Catching Dartin and Leander, it hoisted and threw them. Up and up they flew, only to land in the middle of the mire. Thick it was, but not thick enough to stand upon; nor was it thin enough to swim through, and they both sank helplessly into its wretched embrace. They found neither foot nor handhold, for the mud proved too deep. Sinking neck height, they reached some kind of miraculous equilibrium, for they sank no further.

This was the dung beast's strategy; for once they were in its home environment, they would be helpless against it. In seconds, Tariq and Karina had become victims, and only with a frenzy of sword parries were Carmen and Kur able to avoid the lashing tentacles.

"Kalor," Dao said, "fall back! We can use our ropes to pull them free from the solid ground." However, even at that fear-filled moment, their horror was not yet complete, for when the floating adventurers had oriented themselves, they then realized that the beast was not alone.

One-Eyed Jack's

"Never had I imagined that such a creature could exist," Kalor said. "In a few short seconds, it left us divided and terribly vulnerable."

"How could you possibly have escaped from it?"

"The beast was incredibly strong, and its breath reeked of death. Its maw was filled with thousands of shark-like teeth, large enough to swallow a Man whole. On land, we prepared for battle, but those of us floating in the muck were almost helpless, unable to swim through it or walk out of it."

"It must have been quite a shock," Sonya said, "to have faced such a thing so soon after your journey began."

"I'll tell you all about it soon," Kalor said, "but first I have something to show you." Reaching into the pocket of my coat, I withdrew a large dog-eared book bound in red leather. Placing it reverently upon the table, I placed my right hand on it, in honor of the man who wrote it.

"What's that, Kalor?"

"It is a very special diary."

"The edges are burned," Pauli noticed. "Was it in a fire?"

"I found it beneath the charred remains of a Dragonian soldier at the Battle of the Northern Plains in the year 2033."

"He was burned?" Eric said worriedly.

"He was incinerated by the breath of an ancient wyrm."

"How is it that his diary survived?"

"He died fighting the dragon. His body held fast beneath its raptor's claws, repeatedly plunging his sword into its foreleg until its fire took him. His body and clothes were reduced to ashes, as were all his belongings except one—this diary."

"What does this have to do with your story?" Sonya asked.

"It has everything to do with it. His diary tells much of what Vlad and his followers were doing while we fought our way through the Secret Way."

"Who was he?" Eric asked. "This Dragonian soldier."

"His name was Olak Tempestus, and this is his story." I opened the diary's cover reverently. Carefully turning a few pages, I passed Olak's most private and personal secrets until I came to the part that dealt with our tale, and it was there that I began my story anew.

**Author's note:*

There are two ways to read this work, and either way is entirely dependent on the personality of the reader. The first way is to read on, and that is indeed how I designed the story. However, I would humbly urge you to do so only after carefully considering the following:

The next part is entitled "The Chronicles of Olak Tempestus." It describes in detail the actions and plans of Vlad's revolutionaries, from the time when Carmen led her party into the Secret Way until they became prisoners of war. The brave reader will have to endure a departure from the heroic Fermen of over a hundred pages. The reward will come in the form of a much broader picture of the events taking place.

The second way to enjoy this work is to skip ahead to the chapter entitled "A Fistful of Dung," where one can immediately return to the party's terrible struggle against the monster. The actions of their enemies will remain a greater mystery until near the end, and then one might later return to Olak's Chronicles and enjoy his story. I do, however, recommend that one chooses the first path and reads on, but it will take courage—oh so much courage.

CHRISTOFF

Deep in the bowels of Drakon Mur'-Falor, through twisting pitch-dark passageways and crooked caverns, one could arrive at the eerie laboratory of Vlad's first lieutenant, if one knew the way. Within that well-mined room were countless tables, burners, and experimental phylacteries of its most ingenious resident. Strewn randomly throughout the laboratory in a bizarre system of organization known only to their master were strange devices, tools, and magical apparatus. On this day, there was a great bustle of activity.

"The Orcs speak more and more of this Argor-Dok," Darik said. "His battle prowess and supernatural life grows with each telling."

"It's ironic that this mere Dwarf, in doing nothing more than surviving, has become such a superstitious specter of death."

"A spirit of vengeance that many of the Orcs are beginning to fear."

"They are our most powerful allies in this region. We must not let that fear consume them."

"Perhaps we should consider using additional leverage to neutralize him."

Pacing slowly, purposefully, Vlad walked, as if with each step, his mind set another puzzle piece in place on the board of his world. As he clasped his hands behind his back, his cloak concealed them. He bowed his head, shadows obscuring his face. "His father is famous amongst his people, both warrior and wine-maker, I hear. We can use him to our advantage."

"It will take stealth and subtlety to get him out from under his rock."

"We could send a company of commandos to capture him."

"Or we could hire one man to capture him with cunning."

"Christoff?"

"Christoff!"

"But where do we find him? The last I'd heard of him, he was making a killing in south Elenor."

"Summon Olak and Draco and send them to Itzul in disguise," Vlad said. "I believe that that is where his last known operation was conducted."

"It's been many years since Dragonia has made use of that one's skills," Darik mused. "Do you think that he'll still prove to be reliable?"

"He's no mere butcher. Among assassins, he is noblest."

"I hear that greed is what motivates him."

"Not greed, but a grand sense of his own worth. For the right cause, I believe that he would work for free."

"A noble rogue would seem to be rare indeed."

"He is a rare and useful tool that we'll soon make use of. With Moldrin's capture, the Mountain Dwarves will be greatly weakened, and his son will be forced to yield to save his father."

"I'll inform Olak and Draco."

"Pay Christoff whatever he requires. Consult me only if his request is unusual."

"Will there be anything else, Commander?"

"I may be gone for a few days. Monitor the progress of the party and continue to train the legion." A nod from Darik and Vlad was gone, vanished through the mirror's portal.

Olak Tempestus, Darik thought. *He seems a strange choice for this mission. I would have expected Draco, but not Olak. Chosen for his loyalty no doubt and his other qualities as well, I am sure.*

The more that Darik thought about it, the more Olak seemed to be a perfect choice for so hazardous of a mission. In the academy, he was one of the finest young swordsmen ever to graduate. Thin yet muscular, he was slightly tall and physically well balanced. His peers said that he walked like water, as if his body was in perfect harmony, one part to the next. His features were lean but not gaunt, with a friendly face that he tried to conceal beneath a soldier's air. He was so in tune with himself, he assumed that the strengths that he had developed through years of martial training were the norm rather than the exception. He was strangely unaware of the fact of his own deadliness. It was a naive trait that Vlad found amusing. Indeed, he had said so upon several occasions. These traits were among the many that made him an excellent and capable lieutenant. Olak could lead if need be, but he found greater reward in the perfection of his actions. His hair was long, even for the Dockalfar, jet black and worn tightly braided. His hair was itself a weapon, and when in battle, he would tie blades to its end, in order to whip and lacerate his opponents. However, he was, above all things, honorable, and he would never use such techniques against an enemy that he respected. This was why Vlad had chosen the Blade Master Olak.

Vlad's second choice was far less of a surprise, Draco Pertinax, a master of espionage and political intrigue. He knew the Dragonian political system like none other, and he could stand among governors and speak his case dramatically, even eloquently, with the guile of the finest lawyer. Draco was a coin with three faces, his outer edge with no defined beginning and without an end. While Olak's face was easy to trust, Draco's was powerfully handsome, and his powers of seduction often aided him in his political endeavors. His hair was blond, the result of an academy science experiment gone awry. It was a most unusual color for a Dockalfar, and the green eyes of his surface birth made him very strange indeed. Thick of build and of medium height, he could easily pass for human with the application of a simple disguise. This made him the perfect tool for spying among the people of Fermenor. These were some of his finest qualities, but the best of them all was his ability to make fast friends and blend in and penetrate both high and low societies with ease. He was an accomplished linguist, fluent in several different dialects of Fermish, as well as the fourteen languages of the Dragonian Empire. When he had to fight, he did so roguishly, with deception and disguise. He was a master of the knife in the back and poison darts in the night, but Vlad rarely used him for these purposes. He believed that his other gifts were far more useful.

Very well, Darik thought, *Draco and Olak it is.* It was then that he pulled a small spider-legged mirror from his desk drawer. A swift manipulation of its legs revealed Olak. Campaigning to the north, he was commanding the final subjugation of the barbarian tribes. It didn't take him long to realize that he was being watched from within the confines of his winter cloak. "Hello, Darik! It's been quite some time."

"How fares the campaign?"

"Very well," he said. "The tribes are strong, but their resolve is weakening. Two or three more weeks under siege and their final chieftain should yield. They're prideful, but they don't wish to see the ultimate destruction of their people."

"It's a shame that they wouldn't join us from the beginning."

"They are an honorable people. They grant their allegiance to no nation other than the Four Winds. They consider themselves neither Fermen nor members of any other nation than what they call 'the People.'"

"It's such a primitive way of thinking, yet so pure."

"Sometimes I envy them, Darik."

"Blasphemy!"

"Of course, but are we so different? We are Drakkar Noire, men of the Empire, but we are first loyal to Vlad."

"And may no others ever know."

"Grunick," Olak said to his Red Orcin general, "send in the second rank. Lead your goru into the village. Kill only those warriors who resist."

"How fares your Second Battalion?"

"They're finally learning to fight as a team. In a month or two, they'll be ready to meet any Fermish army."

"They will have to finish the campaign without you."

"What do you mean?"

"Vlad has summoned you."

"Who will lead the army? The Orcs are good fighters, but they don't have the skills to negotiate an alliance with such a proud people."

"I'll send Lycurgus to relieve you. Explain the situation to him and return here by midnight two days hence."

"I will do as you command."

"Prepare yourself, Olak. This mission will be unlike any that you have ever embarked on before."

"I will see you in two days, Darik, for now, I have a battle to win!"

"May luck be with you."

"And you also." And with that, Darik once again manipulated the mirror. "I wonder where he could be." Two clicks of a spider's leg revealed Draco's location. He was some distance away from his mirror, and the room was quite dark. "Ah, I see. Our handsome spy seems to have found his way into the palace of Princess De'Michelle."

It was quite some time before Draco awoke and happened to glance Darik's way.

"I'll be back in a moment, my love," Draco said. "I need to take a trip to the bath."

"Hurry back," the woman said. A covering robe, silent footsteps, and Draco had soon swept up his mirror, exited the room, and entered the privacy of the De'Michelle's guest bathroom. "What is it, Darik? I'm in the middle of securing an alliance between the Countess De'Michelle and Vlad's advisor to the Parliament."

"A man's work is never done."

"Oh yes, quite. But please excuse me, Darik, is this important?"

"You are to report here by midnight in two days' time to meet with Commander Vlad for your new assignment."

"I haven't finished this one!"

"I'm sorry, Draco, but this mission will only succeed if it happens swiftly. I'm sure that you can find some way to keep the countess busy while you're gone?"

"Yes, of course I can."

"I'll see you soon."

Draco said goodbye with a nod, but he did not seem at all pleased.

The Secret Meeting

Well before midnight of the appointed day, the chiming sound of tiny silver bells alerted Darik to the coming arrivals of his guests. Draco and Olak stepped through the dimensional portal of his spider mirror mere seconds apart. They were dressed simply for travel, their weapons either hidden or packed away. Their eyes were full of questions.

"Soon," Darik said, "all of your concerns will be answered. Your previous missions, although important, must take a second seat to this one."

"The barbarian horde was mere hours from capitulating," Olak said. "Lycurgus is stealing my victory."

"Don't worry. Vlad knows that the victory was yours."

"The Princess De'Michelle is mine," Draco said, "in both heart and soul. We can count on her influence in the coming elections."

"That's tremendous! What great news!"

Just then, the bells rang again, and their commander stepped through the portal.

"Good to see you all!" Vlad said. "I'm glad that you could come."

"Commander!"

"At ease! Please let us dispense with the formalities while we are here. Our personal alliances are sacred and well known to all of us who are here. The coming mission is invaluable to our rise to power."

"How can we be of service?"

"Your mission will be exceptionally hazardous, and secrecy is of the utmost importance. You will both journey to the Fermish city of Linea. Once there, you will seek out the professional services of the assassin known only as Christoff. Once you recruit him, you will all return to Safehaven, and from there you will continue on to the Kingdom of Lord Min and the Mountain Dwarves. Christoff's challenge will be to capture the patriarch of the Kegporter clan, Moldrin, and deliver him here alive and unharmed."

"We'd need several companies of Drakkar Noire in order to seize him by force," Olak reasoned.

"This mission may seem strange, even foolish for a small team of agents, but let me assure you that Christoff is indeed the man for the job. Execute the mission with maximum stealth and minimum casualties. I don't want the Dwarves to know who is responsible for Moldrin's capture."

"As you wish, Commander."

"I will tell you both this much, that Moldrin will help us to achieve victory over Lord Cherek and the forces of Safehaven. With the Kegporters leaderless, Lord Min's Dwarves will be slow to mobilize against us, and his son neutralized. I could just have him killed, but he must die in a public spectacle so that the Orcs will finally be rid of their ghost."

"I trust your reasoning, Commander," Olak said. "You have always led us well, and always to victory. Even if that were not so, I would still follow you until the end."

"And I as well," Draco agreed.

"I am honored to have such men at my side," Vlad said with a humble bow. "I'm sure that you'll perform your tasks well. Darik has your detailed instructions. Carry on!"

"For the might of Dragonia!" They said.

"For the might of Dragonia," Vlad answered before leaving through the front door.

"I have acquired excellent forgeries that should help to prove your identities," Darik said. "You will be disguised as sons of the Baron Mornbend, the chief nobleman of a small community several hundred miles north of the city."

"These should work," Draco commented, "unless we meet someone from that region."

"I've included a map of the surrounding countryside and a goodly sum of the local currency to aid you in your journey."

"How will we reach the Fermish shores in secrecy?" Olak questioned. "Perhaps we could sail in a disguised merchantman, or dive from a swift dragon ship and swim."

"If there was no other way," Darik said, "then perhaps we'd try such desperate and time-consuming techniques, but thanks to the magic of my spider mirrors, your journey will occur instantaneously."

"I thought that you first had to physically travel to a destination in order to program your device."

"Indeed," Darik said, "Vlad and I traveled vast distances in the adventures of our youth."

"That would explain your strange disappearances in the academy days."

"Ha! And Vlad and I thought that our sojourns went unnoticed."

"It may have gone unobserved by our taskmasters," Draco said, "but not by your friends."

"Let's hope that's true," Darik said. "There are always unknown eyes watching. Lothdea and the Queen would love to see us destroyed."

"Lothdea's ways served our people well in our exile," Olak said, "but her absolute ways can only keep us from regaining our ultimate freedom."

"We have a right to walk where we will," Draco said, "be it in daylight or darkness."

"Free will isn't the way of our ancient deity," Darik said. "Only together can we achieve our ultimate freedom."

"Together as one!" they said as they often did in such moments.

"But for now we've got work to do," Olak said.

"Of course," Darik said. "Where were we?"

"The mirror?"

"Oh yes! I have encoded the mirrors with only one destination in that region. The portal opens into a small chamber at the lowest level of a deep cavern system. The caves connect with tunnels of an abandoned mine. The quarry opens on the surface some fifty miles east of the city."

"How difficult is the climb to the surface from there?"

"The mine was built by the Hill Dwarves of King Rodamon. The journey to the surface should be easy as long as it remains unoccupied."

"Has Andreul attempted to view these caves with her crystal ball?"

"The character of the stone there blurs her magic."

"It could be another vein of dark-force crystal," Draco said. "It often accompanies mithril deposits."

"It's a possibility," Darik said. "We'll have your team take samples."

"Team?"

"Don't worry, I've put together a small but capable group of Drakkar Noire to accompany you as far as the cavern's mouth."

"All fighters?"

"They're a mixed team of recent graduates. They're young but well trained, and there's a capable Warrior Mage and healer among them."

"I hope your map is detailed," Draco said. "I'd hate to rely solely on Christoff for directions."

"I'll see to it that you receive the most detailed maps available. Anything else that you might need should be easy to procure here in the pyramid."

"We'll need a good disguise for Olak."

"I have donated a special device from my own treasures. I found a necklace among the treasure of a basilisk's horde. The device is a very rare amulet. Its magic is capable of altering the wearer's appearance. One can disguise himself or herself as Human, Elven, Dwarven or half Elven."

"I've often said that Olak's physique is unique," Draco said. "Perhaps a Halfar disguise would be best."

"That was my thinking as well," Darik said. "Just remember that the illusion will disappear the moment that the amulet is removed." Placing the device around Olak's neck produced a remarkable transformation—his skin color paled, his ears shortened, and his eyes changed to ocean blue.

"Amazing," Olak said. "But I've got a feeling that this wouldn't be the best thing to wear around the pyramid!"

"On the contrary," Draco chided. "I think that the Orcs would love you!"

Final preparations filled the rest of their evening. They outfitted their travel packs, checked their weapons, and prepared their clothing. Draco was familiar with the styles of Linea's inhabitants, and he quickly adapted a wardrobe for them to fit in. They would appear as two young nobles, perhaps the sons of a baron or princes too far down in the line of inheritance to become kings themselves. A full head of hair that covered his ears, and a puffy round noble's hat to hide them under, completed Draco's disguise.

"Our costumes should pass the closest scrutiny," Draco said. "Now let's go meet the escort party."

They assembled in a carefully chosen meeting hall. It was a great, naturally formed cavern of some fifty feet in diameter and a ceiling half again as high. Only two passageways entered into it. One led to the honeycomb of tunnels directly beneath the pyramid fortress. The second led deep into the Underearth, where the resident Deep Gnomes were currently mining the dark force crystal. The same substance lined all the floors, walls, and ceiling of the cave, providing an eerie lime-green glow and, more importantly, shielding the cave from all forms of magical spying. Four ill-tempered Giants and their abysmal hounds further guarded the chamber. It was therefore the perfect place for beginning a top-secret mission.

"These two men are your charges, Lieutenant Da'Gol," Darik said. "They must reach their destination safely."

"We'll see to it, sir," he answered.

"I've assembled a crack team. Lieutenants Da'Gol and Tulina will provide the leadership necessary for your success. Every member of this team is an elite fighter and an expert in their chosen fields. They complete the full range of skills necessary for a campaign force of Drakkar Noire."

"All that I need to know," Draco said, "is that they graduated from the academy. That's proof enough."

"They all achieved the highest marks, much like you."

"We need not engage every threat," Olak said, "as long as we can pass them safely and without detection."

"Don't worry," Lieutenant Da'Gol said, "we've been in enough fights to know when it's necessary and when it's not."

"You're all valiant," Darik said. "The dangers are unknown because of the terrain, but if we're lucky, you will reach the surface without incident."

"Ready yourselves," Lieutenant Da'Gol said. "After inspection, we're moving out."

"I'll activate the mirror from here, and when you're gone, it will be as if you've never been. I have entrusted Lieutenant Da'Gol with his own mirror for the return trip. Utilize the portal setting for this room if you must abort the mission. Prepare yourselves, for it is for a free Dragonia that you do battle."

Like in any group of specially trained warriors, there came a widespread "hoo-yeah" from deep within.

Olak mingled with the soldiers, informally inspecting each of them in turn. Stopping briefly to speak with them, he soon had a fair understanding of their qualities. "I see that you pack a Lin Rudian spear," Olak said to Sergeant Goldsmith. "An unusual weapon in these times."

Her hair glistened like her name, an unusual but not unheard of color among the Dockalfar. Her eyes were dark like her complexion. Her face was lean and capable like her physique. "I joined up during the Minion Wars, sir. I never liked the idea of closing in on a Caretaker."

"I have never seen one. Are they as horrible as they say?"

"It usually took four of us to bring one down," she said. "They look like squid, but stand eight feet all. They are the most terrifying beings that I have ever seen."

"They cost us many lives in that war. I hope that I never meet one."

"You'll know a Minion if you see one. They walk upright, upon two thick tentacles. Most have eight arms over ten feet long, covered in suction cups and grasping claws, but some have more. They can fight with all of them, and with their poisonous beak.

Their eyes are black and shiny like wet glass, but their minds are their deadliest weapon. They can control untrained minds. Humans are their favorite food. In ancient times, they enslaved thousands. The Sentiens are descendants of their human slaves who learned enough of their masters' ways to escape."

"Your weapon is noble, thought by my master to be the king of weapons."

"Most people seem to assume that the spear is best used by the clumsy or poorly trained."

"On the contrary," Olak said thoughtfully, "my master could use a Lin Rudian spear with such skill that he could remove each of an expert swordsman's hands in an instant. Only an ignorant fighter would have such reservations."

"I'll try not to disappoint you, sir."

"Nor I you, Sergeant."

"Squad," Lieutenant Da'Gol ordered, "assemble for inspection!"

Moments later, the group stood in formation, including Olak and Draco. Despite their superior rank, this was not their squad, and they deferred their position to Lieutenants Da'Gol and Tulina, Da'Gol's second in command. "Are there any last-minute questions or ideas before last inspection?"

"We may need another mountaineering kit to cover the lieutenants, sir," Sergeant Newmason said. "We can probably handle them with our kits, but one more wouldn't hurt."

"Good point, Sergeant, as long as they can handle the extra weight."

"No problem there," Draco said. "Olak and I can split the equipment, and we should still be okay."

"Anything else, Newmason?"

"Nothing, sir."

"Anybody? No, well then, let's empty those packs for inspection." In moments, each professional soldier had his gear emptied and separated. "Shout out if your pack is lacking. This is crunch time!

"Four canteens, full; one week's iron rations, dry; four pair knit socks, preferably clean; two sets undergarments; one pair of pants; one tunic; rations kit; spork and knife; tinder and flint; rope and grapnel; mountaineer's kit complete with boot spikes, crampons, pitons, and harness; herbalist's med kit with bandages, waterproof cloak, and field toilet kit—is everyone's kit complete?"

"Yes, sir!"

"Repack!" Refilling, cinching tight, and tying down their packs with practiced speed required only a bit more time than emptying them.

"Stand to for weapons inspection!"

One by one, the squad leaders examined each soldier's weapons of war, whether sword or rapier, dagger or dart, and each professional's weapons were of course in perfect care and condition.

"Pack and sheathe weapons!"

"Does any soldier here have any second thoughts about this mission?"

"No, sir!"

"And does any soldier here have any misgivings whatsoever about laying their life down for their comrades and country if such a need be?"

"No, sir!"

"Does any soldier here have personal obligations, or ties to family, which are too great to fully commit themselves and their minds to this mission?"

"No, sir!"

"Excellent! Then here is the mission brief: Our job is to get the lieutenants safely to the surface and on their way to Linea. If possible, we'll do so with silence and stealth, to such a degree that no man nor beast should realize that we've passed, or even breathed the air of their surroundings. If we should have to fight our way through, then every blow should count, every sentry silenced, and every beast vanquished without mercy or regret. We will move swiftly yet cautiously, without stopping, save for an encounter, or to take head counts. We make no camp until the lieutenants are safe and we have returned here. Understood?"

"Yes, sir!"

"Then Newmason's on point, Goldsmith and Carnage are the spearhead, Tulina and I will take the third spot in front of the lieutenants, and Braidwick and McHewn will take the rear by twenty paces. Their job is to keep any following enemies off us and to provide backup as needed. We will stop every half of a league for a head count. The pace will be moderate but unhurried. The standard forty-five-minute leagues should suffice. Stay sharp and keep an eye on your buddies above all else. We leave no comrades behind, unless there is nothing left of them to return home. Squad, attention! Let's move out, into the maw of Darik's Purple Worm."

"Hoo-yeah!"

Da'Gol's team was through the portal in seconds, their passing causing instantaneous transportation through Necromantic folding. They emerged in stride as if their first steps began in one location and landed in another countless—indeed, possibly limitless—miles away.

Behind them, Darik was quick to close the portal on his side and erase any signs that the mission had ever gathered there. There was no need to contact Vlad; he already knew that the pieces were in motion. The game had just begun. Their pawns advanced.

They emerged deep within the bowels of King Rodaman's mine, in a small cave chiseled out by the gnarled hands of the Hill Dwarves. Their surroundings were deathly silent. Pausing for several moments, their eyes adjusted to their lightless world. All of them had pigmented eyes, the result of a childhood exposed to the Sun, but they were Dockalfar, and they could still see in the absolute darkness of Underearth, because their eyes were sensitive to the other energies that existed there. In fact, few other beings on Tempus could see as well in the dark, and none could see any better. This was a large contributor to their deadliness and the reason that many of the other inhabitants of Underearth feared them.

Caution was still in order, however, for their powers below were not absolute. Others such as the Minions, Darg, some dragons, and other more ancient powers that lived deeper still vied with them for the supremacy of the dark. The vulnerability of mortality tempered their elfin longevity, and when wounded, their blood flowed as others did.

Diligent training and a desire to attain perfection in themselves and their profession contributed to their martial prowess. These qualities were not true of every Dark Elf, but they were true of every member of the Drakkar Noire, and it was therefore true of Lieutenant Dagol's team. They moved silently and as one, every hand and arm signal relayed and understood.

They accomplished soundlessness through skill and the use of enchanted equipment. Their very boots and cloaks were especially magical, the standard for adventuring parties of Dockalfar; their material was supple, strong, and fire resistant. In darkness, it concealed their body heat, camouflaging them from subterranean eyes and the heat-sensing organs of many monstrous denizens. Furthermore, it was a quiet and actually sound-deadening material. A secret combination of materials and magical incantations known only to a few families of Dockalfar allowed them to accomplish the engineering marvel. They were the perfect outer garments for a group dependent upon stealth for survival. Enchanted gear aside, their training was such that they were capable of nearly silent movement even without such magical accoutrements, but with them, they were almost quieter than silence itself.

Their eyes adjusted, they moved out with a signal from Lieutenant Da'Gol, Newmason leading, with Goldsmith and Carnage close behind them.

King Rodaman's Mine

The Hill Dwarves were miners of the most excellent sort. Carefully engineered, their passageways were well hewn and stoutly shorn. They cautiously worked hazardous substrates, avoided, or circumvented them. They built strong bridges over natural obstacles such as underground rivers or chasms. Working every vein of ore to its fullest, their knowledge of stone and minerals left few precious materials unearthed. These and many other such qualities made their work as safe as such endeavors could be and the results of their tunneling very lasting. Abandoned mines also created new habitats for other creatures to live in. Such simple facts did not escape Lieutenant Da'Gol.

Darik's portal had placed them somewhere within the lowest level of the mine. Their depth below the surface was unknown, but Newmason estimated it to be at least two miles. Depending upon how far away the Dwarves' elevator shaft was, the journey could take hours or even days, to complete. There were signs to help them on their way. The tracks of mining carts were cut more deeply into the stone in certain hallways, and once they reached the main tunnels, there should be a track.

Closing his raised fist, Lieutenant Da'Gol called a halt. Quietly, he tried to use a direction spell. It quickly became clear that such magic was useless here. Dark Force Crystal lined the walls, a powerful source of energy, but a complete inhibitor of divination spells. They would have to find their way by using conventional methods.

'Move out,' he signaled, and Newmason led them forward. Stealthily she considered the next bend in the tunnel, or the correct passage to take at an intersection. In time, her intuition proved itself, and they came upon a great wide tunnel, three rows of iron tracks passing through it. Several carts stood empty and ready for filling upon them. Covered by decades of dust, they stood rusted and abandoned. It was clear that the Dwarves, at least, no longer ventured here. The carts were all oriented in the same direction. It was the final clue that they needed to bring them to the elevator shaft, and from there, to the surface. The tunnel was immense, over thirty feet in height and in width, and side passageways created many dangerous areas for them to cross.

Cunning enemies could easily plan an ambush from such positions, and Lieutenant Da'Gol had to take all these factors into consideration. Pointing quickly, he split the team; Tulina would lead the left flank, and he would lead the right, behind Newmason. In seconds, the team had assumed their new roles, and they began advancing.

Newmason froze. Her sign language indicating at least twelve individuals hidden in the tunnel ahead. Eight more enemies waited hidden against the walls down two east and west passages. Clearly an ambush, there was no audible sound, but was it intended for them? Da'Gol thought that surely, it must be. A foreign voice within the darkness soon answered his question.

"Your team is surrounded, Da'Gol," the stranger said. "Lower your weapons to the floor."

Newmason's hand signals told him that there was no way for their enemies to see them, or accurately affect them with weapons.

"Who so boldly addresses me?"

"That is of no concern to anyone among you who wish to live."

"My army is close behind," Da'Gol said. "It would be wise for you to surrender."

"We know that you are alone."

"Either way, it's a gamble, but you should know well that we surrender to no one." The longer that he talked, the more time his team had to study the terrain and prepare their defense. Tulina had already cast several protective spells, and he could feel their influence upon his body and mind.

"If you refuse surrender, then you will all surely die."

"An honorable opponent would identify himself and his reasons."

"You possess an object that was stolen from us."

Quickly, he considered all his possessions. Perhaps he meant something that one of his team carried. "What object? Surely you are mistaken."

"I am Vremick, son of Illian, and you carry the sword of my father! It was stolen from the battlefield by your father, Durin Da'Gol."

"Then you speak of the bridge over Kal Zakim and the battle that ended the Sentien Wars."

"That battle proved the superiority of my race."

"Your race left the field on litters, or not at all. My father won this sword in mortal combat against General Illian Psi. It is a spoil of war." He looked to Draco and Olak for their support or disagreement, but he received only thumbs-up signals of approval. Draco clearly intended to fight, but the security of the mission was at stake. Maybe there was another way. "Perhaps there is another way, son of Illian."

"I will listen only for a short while longer."

"In order to spare our teams, I suggest a duel. You and I in single combat. The winner takes the sword. The loser abandons their claim to it as a point of honor."

There was a chuckle and then an arrogant laugh. "We will combat without magic, plain sword against sword without armor, Illian's blade on a flat stone between us. Our companies hold their positions until the end. These are my terms."

"I accept." Draco's vigorous signing told him that he was acting foolishly. He clearly wanted an all-out fight.

'Don't worry,' his hands told Draco, 'the mission is too important. You just might get your wish anyway. Keep an eye on these bastards. They only possess honor among themselves.' Stepping out into the open, he cautiously began removing his cloak and armor. He was somewhat relieved to see the form of his opponent doing the same.

Vremick was tall and broad shouldered. His skin was pale, his features gaunt and hairless, without so much as an eyebrow. His smile was wide, bloodless, and thin, infinitely confident and full of contempt. His eyes were large, dark, and piercing. He provided the weapons, two plain straight long swords, tossing one onto the ground between them.

"By the light of the sword then," Da'Gol said. Kneeling by the flat rock, he carefully laid Illian's Sword upon the stone, its unsheathed blade bathing the cave in golden light. Without taking his eyes off his opponent, he retrieved the weapon provided for the duel.

"By the light of the sword, Black Elf."

Lieutenant Tulina heard well the discourse between Vremick and Jason, and she knew that the Sentiens' leader did not intend to honor his own words. In fact, he had lied through his teeth. She could tell by the tone of his voice and the tremor in his words, and she relayed this simple fact to Olak behind her, in the secret sign language of the Dockalfar.

'He lies,' she told him. 'He will betray Jason at the most opportune moment.'

'I thought as much,' Olak replied. 'Don't worry, we're all ready to fight!'

'One more thing,' Tulina said, 'there are at least eight more of them cloaked by invisibility spells.'

'We must beware their mind powers,' Olak said.

'They're in for a big surprise then, for the Dark Force Crystal should absorb most of their powers.'

'I'll relay the word,' Olak said. 'Keep an eye on Lieutenant Da'Gol.'

Behind him, Braidwick read Olak's signal and relayed it to Newmason on the right flank and on down that line to McHewn in the rear. They were little needed words, for they all knew the chaotic ways of their enemy. The Sentiens' treachery toward all other races was legendary, and many among them had already encountered their war parties in the past. The team's weapons had long since been in hand. Bowstrings were loaded and crossbows cocked.

Lieutenant Da'Gol and Vremick paced around the circle of their makeshift ring. "The sword is mine," Vremick said. "I'll grant you one last chance to surrender it."

"My father never wanted the sword. He acted only in defense of his homeland when your people invaded. It was a fair and mortal combat. The sword itself recognizes me as the rightful successor."

"Your necromancy must have perverted its thoughts. When you are dead, it will once again return to my family from whence it came!"

"The sword is a symbol of Dragonia's victory, Vremick. I will never dishonor the sacrifice of my people. En garde!"

Vremick was the pinnacle of what his race could achieve. Physically strong and gifted with special mental abilities, he could wield a blade, cast magical spells, and shatter stone with but a thought.

The Sentiens were once human, but if that were true in some far distant past, then it no longer was. Centuries of Minion enslavement had changed them forever. The ruthless Minions tortured them with their sinister and alien mental powers, and as time passed, the Sentiens gained these same capabilities for themselves. They could read minds, heat, bend, and move materials with but a thought, or crush through their opponents mental barriers only to leave them raving lunatics, or mere vegetables. Da'Gol's team now faced these enemies. The mighty Sentiens, the descendants of Minion slaves that had left the Dark Elven nation of Dragonia ravaged, and the Sentiens themselves beaten and exiled to the astral plane, which they now called home.

The first clash of swords was titanic, the result of each individual's disgust of the other. It was a test of strength of wills, blade against blade, eye-to-eye, and breath against breath, with little thought of technique.

"You will die here, son of Da'Gol!"

Jason was no fool. He would never waste his breath on speech during battle. He stared back defiantly. Such a look might have proved fatal to any man of lesser conviction, for Vremick's powers were such that he could bore into the psyche of any average opponent and cripple him. Insane images might take that poor soul to some remote place within themselves, never to return, or assault his nerves with pain unending.

Vremick did not intend to engage Jason fairly. He wanted the sword no matter what the cost. Indeed, his failure to acquire it would mean the certain death of himself and his company at the hands of their leader, a disembodied brain so powerful that it no longer needed a body to house itself. The Sentiens referred to it only as the Great Mind. If subterfuge was necessary to insure his success on this field, then so much the better. It was then that he brought all his mental might down upon Jason for one psychologically crushing duel. Electromagnetic waves surged through the neural network of his brain, launching themselves into the mind of his enemy. Seconds passed, and yet the son of Da'Gol was unassailed. Did he possess some unseen magic device that protected him?

"Surprised?" Jason asked. "I am yet unscathed."

"But how?" Vremick said, befuddled.

"You chose the wrong field for psychic war. Now we'll have to finish it my way."

"If you insist!" His assault was savage yet professional, each blow of his sword well practiced and expertly guided.

Parrying, countering, Jason studied Vremick. He was larger and heavier than he was, but no stronger, of this he was certain. Vremick was, however, clearly a more experienced swordsman than he was, almost certainly a survivor of many more combats, but maybe he could somehow use that knowledge to his own advantage. Hiding his true ability, he fought back only well enough to defend himself. Waiting for some moment of weakness, he hoped that somehow one would prevent itself.

Vremick was merciless, hoping to end the challenge soon.

The son of Da'Gol was offering him only a dismal resistance. If this was the best that he could do, then the son of Da'Gol was certainly a lesser man than his father was. "Surrender now, while you still live!"

"Never!"

"Then die like a miserable Black Elven dog!"

Jason had been insulted in his life but never in so vulgar of a way, and such bold lip service made him consider doing something foolish. He did not, of course, but he did consider it. Instead, he opted for a compromise. Vremick was focusing his attacks with the sword only. If he possessed other fighting tools, then he had not thought of using them yet. Jason wasted no time. When Vremick next swung at him from a high en-garde position, he went low, driving his fist into Vremick's groin.

Air exploded from his lungs, and his sword flew from his hands.

Jason grasped him, left hand upon Vremick's right wrist, his right clutching Vremick's groin. In one sudden Herculean effort, he lifted Vremick above his head and hurled him down. It looked like the Vremick was beaten. His fellows rose to attack.

Vremick laughed from the ground. "Now you will all die. The sword is mine!" He had landed close to the Golden Sword, a mistake on Jason's part, and Vremick now reached out to take it up. Suddenly it leaped away from him and into the hands of his nemesis.

"It seems that you've forgotten the character of your own father's sword. Unfailingly will it return to its rightful living wielder's hand. The blade at least, has honor."

"It will return to me soon then," Vremick rasped, "for we outnumber you two to one!" It was then that he signaled his knights to attack. Speaking mentally to his fellows, he raged, *"Destroy them with all of your mental might!"*

Advancing for the killing stroke, they unleashed a mental barrage upon the Elves. Attempting to shut down, confuse, and disable them, they hurled powerful waves of energy toward their enemies' brains. They were confident that the Elves would crumple or weaken, making them easy prey, but they did not know the properties of the very stone around them, and their powers were largely absorbed. What power remained caused little more than a headache to their enemies. It was an undesirable effect indeed, for what more fearsome opponents could there be than Dockalfar irritated to the point of deadly action?

Jason's charges were foremost in his mind, and he wanted to turn for a moment to signal them back to a position of safety while his team handled the threat, but at that moment, he realized that such orders would go unheeded. Olak had joined him at his left flank with swords drawn, and beside him was a squad of eight skeletal soldiers conjured by Tulina from the remains of the mine's fallen. While they lumbered on, as the Undead are likely to do, Olak moved fluidly, his eyes riveted on the coming action. Vremick, gaining his feet, had retreated to his cache of armor and weapons while twelve Sentien warriors poured into the cave from their hiding places.

Eight was the number of Sentien knights that first entered the fray that day, eight chaotic warriors hell-bent on destruction. Ornamented suits of mail, coated with precious metals and exquisitely bejeweled, protected their bodies, both tall and strong. Each set was worth a king's ransom, but despite its beauty, it was also protective. Their faces were pale, lean, and hairless, but whether this was the result of grooming or natural conditions, only the Sentiens knew. In stature, they were heads and shoulders above the Elves and often twice their weight. Their weapons were two-handed and heavily weighted, but as expert swordsmen, they could fence quite well with them. Boots as exotic as the armor protected their feet, and if helmed, their caps were equally ornate. Possessed of diabolical countenance, they were necessarily evil, wholly ruthless, and the most terrible of enemies.

The knights advanced, expecting the Black Elves to be writhing in agony upon the floor, but lo! It was not so, for the Elves were advancing to meet them. They must have some strange magic protecting them! It mattered not, for they would still fall before their superior numbers and strength, and they were not without magic themselves! Behind them were four Sentien warlocks, two of them captains, readying their sorcerous might.

Olak advanced to the right flank of the Undead, who had been long buried in a collapsed tunnel. Tulina had called upon their ancient bones to awaken, and they had answered! Clawing and crawling free of the debris and earth that had buried them, they rose up and found the old tools that they had wielded in life, pickax and hammer, hoe and shovel, and they then formed a small company before the Dockalfar priestess. Some of them arrived without arms, ribs, or other appendages, but they had come to her magical call, and they waited for their commands.

"Attack the Sentiens!" Tulina ordered. "Strike them until they are dead and gone. Only then will I release you!"

It was a command that they could not resist.

Tulina's orders contained a promise terrifying to the Undead, for what greater fear could they possess than to awaken and find themselves lifeless and not yet reborn, only to look through spirit-eyes at a fleshless body beyond their free-willed control. They belonged to Tulina until her spell set them free. Shuffling ahead, their bones scratched the stone in an eerie *scritch-scratch, clack, scritch-scratch, click-clack* that sent chills through the bones of the living. They then set themselves upon a rank of Sentiens, hammers and picks against two-handed swords of war. They had little chance of winning but knew no living fear, and their presence gave Olak time to choose his actions.

Four warlocks stood behind the knights, preparing wicked spells. He would concentrate upon them. Hearing an arrow streaking toward him, he twisted to avoid it and batted two others out of the air before him. Rolling sideward, he came up at a run.

The lead knight moved to stop him.

Olak had to be quick. He was more like a beam of light, almost too fast for the naked eye.

Lesser foes would have found no time to react, but the well-trained knight was his own master, and he placed his blade between them, relying more upon his awareness than his own vision. It saved his life, for Olak's cuts merely pushed his sword aside and impacted his armor as he passed by. The knight would have turned to follow if not for the Undead. A shovel struck his helm, driving him back. Something else hammered into his side. Defense was his only option.

The warlocks were a fraction of a second away from unleashing their magic. He could not neutralize them all, but he would do what he could and hope that his comrades would do the rest. The closest mage concentrated upon him, and his gleeful look told Olak that he was certain that his spell would arrive in time to slay him. Olak had no way of knowing the wizard's speed, but the warlock suffered the same handicap. He could not have known that twenty feet was barely two running strides away for the bladesmaster. The warlock's head rolled away from his shoulders before his lips could complete his incantation. The Sentien beside him was forced to leap away in order to avoid the same fate for himself. His spell wasted, he drew forth his own sword without a moment to spare.

Olak attacked him expertly, testing the warlock's mettle. He was far more seasoned than he expected, surely a captain. The Sentien officer turned his attacks aside with surprising efficiency. Olak could feel his enemy's power through the warlock's blade. It was a supernatural strength beyond the norm, and he then knew that it was either magic or the captain's powerful mind that boosted his natural abilities. A lesser fighter would have sought retreat, but Olak merely shouldered the new challenge, summoning his inner strength. Adrenaline surged through his body, and he pressed ever harder. It was then that his senses became aware of a gathering power. The warlocks behind him were centering their evocation upon him. There was no available cover. His opponent was ever ready to execute a killing stroke. Only with a desperate maneuver could he hope to avoid their spell. Fire erupted around him, magical fire as hot as dragon's breath. He tucked and rolled backward, curling his swords beneath his arms and pulling his protective cloak about himself. He lay curled in a ball while the heat raged above him. He was like a ground squirrel in his burrow waiting out a forest fire, confident that his underground home would protect him. He resisted the incinerating waves of heat, gulped the last bit of fresh air beneath his cloak, and rose up as soon as it ended.

The Sentien captain lay against the cavern wall, a smoking ruin. Gasping for breath, his lungs seared by flame, he tried to rise, but soon fell and did not rise again.

Olak spun. The other warlocks had moved toward the center of the battle behind him. They certainly believed him to be dead. He wanted to show them how wrong they were, but Vremick's reserve forces rushed to meet him. Deep within a side passage, fifteen warriors had lain in wait. They surrounded him in seconds. Somehow, he had leaped out of the frying pan and into the fire.

Meanwhile, the survivalist Dawn Newmason was working hard to put a few arrows into the enemy ranks. An overturned mining cart provided her with good cover and a full view of the battlefield. Four knights poured forth from an east passage and split up, two running toward her and two toward Lieutenant Da'Gol. Concentrating upon those closest to herself, she hit the lead knight in the thigh, but he barely slowed.

Bran McHewn joined her. "How's the view from up here?" he asked with a smirk.

"Nice of you to join us, McHewn."

"Oh, you know how busy I can get admiring your form. I almost forgot to help you."

"Funny," she said, drawing her sword and dagger, "but I'm a little busy right now." Rushing out of hiding, she crossed blades with the evil knight a moment later. McHewn fired a bolt at the second knight, and he fell, poisoned. Reloading, he waited for another shot.

"Lovely Dawn," the knight said, "you've spent so much time training that you've had so little opportunity for more ladylike pursuits."

"You attempt to read my mind," she said, "when you should be concentrating upon my sword instead!"

"Ah, but they are indeed the same thing! You will all fall before our might."

"I think not, Sir Knight. Look deeper into my mind. What do you see?"

"I see a Black Elven wench unable to find love amongst her own, one who is doomed to now die alone!"

"That was your mistake," McHewn said from behind him. "She is most certainly not alone."

The knight's grip loosened, and his sword fell. His legs weakened, and he swooned. McHewn drove his knife deeper. Pulling it out with a violent twist, he knocked the knight to the floor. "Remember, Dawn," he said, using her first name, "never alone."

She could not now know what he meant. There was no time for such matters in the heat of battle. She might ponder it later. There were still Sentiens to kill.

"Sergeant Carnage," Draco said, "two sorcerers are making things difficult for Olak."

"I see them. How do you want to play it?"

"Try and work your way around the fighters. Don't engage anyone except the wizards unless you have to. I'll try and sneak in for a killing stroke along the right wall."

"Luck then," Carnage said while speeding off into the midst of the fighting.

"Luck," Draco whispered. Moving like a hunting cat, he slipped through the mine debris. Combatants now filled the entire passage. It was utter chaos. There was no safe position, but his shadowy movement had thus far gone unnoticed. Creeping closer, he knelt by the cavern wall and raised his blowgun to fire. The sorcerers were riveted upon Olak and Jason at the center of battle. He took aim at his closest foe. It was then that he felt a strange contact with his mind. It was an invasion, a powerful will boring in and trying to possess him. Eyes tunneled into his back. Their hatred struck him like a hammer. He turned. A prone knight had fixed his will upon him. Paralyzed with poison, the Sentien's mind was still powerfully aware. Draco's self-control slipped away. He thought that he raised his weapon to fight back, but instead he found himself aiming upon NewMason. He struggled to regain control. Sweat poured from his brow, but still he aimed at his comrade. He drew breath, fired, and reloaded. To her credit, NewMason remained standing. She even advanced to stand beside Jason, but her strength was quickly leaving her.

She knew not who had struck her.

He tried again to resist, but aimed at her again. To his horror, he drew breath.

It was then that McHewn's dagger severed the spine of Draco's controller. "Not this time, Puppeteer," he said. "This time I'll make sure."

NewMason fell to a knee. Seconds remained before the poison would kill her. He turned and fired his dart at a sorcerer, but it hit some invisible barrier and fell uselessly to the floor. NewMason would be dead if she did not receive the antidote immediately. There was only one way to administer it in time. It stung her. She rolled away and tried to stand.

"Stay down!" Draco commanded.

Her anger kept her heart beating. It kept her breathing. There was no need for apologies between them; they were soldiers. He looked for McHewn, but did not see him. Jason needed help. He drew swords. He felt violated and totally used. To say that his ire had risen would have been an understatement.

His blades were of his own design. He did not forge them himself, but the master smith had constructed them using his own design ideas and sketches. Well balanced and perfectly weighted, his swords had slightly tapered ends that gave them extra weight when used for slashing and chopping. Their hilts' design protected the hands, with cutlass-style pommels that could deliver punishing blows. The blade-guards were full but not oversized, with two fork-like protrusions for weapons trapping. The master smith forged them of adamantium with Dark Eldritch magic and honed the blades to razor sharp, nearly indestructible edges. He trained with them endlessly for occasions just like these.

Two knights circled Jason, and Vremick was moving to cut off any escape route. "Your end is near, Da'Gol," Vremick said. "We'll soon see how you fare against three!"

"We shall indeed." He was without armor, but not without weapons, and Illian's Sword was his to command. The Sentiens read his mind, and although he was a tower of iron will, he could not stand alone against three. They anticipated every move that he made. Every attack that they made was perfectly coordinated. Lacking his equipment, he had no components for spells, but the sword itself had other powers. He disappeared and reappeared a short distance away. The knights had to regroup. The teleportation was short range and random. They could tell when he would move but not where he would end up. He knew it was just stalling, and if luck were all that remained to him, then he surely would have lost, but he was the leader of a valiant team. They just needed a little more time.

In the midst of Tulina's skeletal squad, Kala Goldsmith worked hard against three dark knights. A like number of skeletal warriors remained animate, but the Sentiens hewed a great path around themselves, and the dead were falling fast. Hate empowered the knights, and their fallen comrades fueled their spirit of vengeance.

Tulina's magic suddenly stilled one of them. Paralyzed, the Undead struck at him ruthlessly. His comrades shielded him and shattered the busy trio.

Sergeant Goldsmith used the distraction to execute the disarming maneuver taught to her by her master, the venerable Li An'Joo. Stepping inside of her enemy's guard, she drove her long spear's head forward in a lightning-fast figure eight. The knight looked on in disbelief as his two hands and great sword fell to the ground. Trying to tackle her, he charged at her recklessly, knowing that his fight was over. Simultaneously, he spoke to her in her mind. *"Kala, Kala,"* he said, *"your fight against the Minions was noble. Join us, and we shall make you a Queen."*

"The Minions are our common enemy, but that's the only thing that we have in common."

"Lay down your weapons now, Kala, and we shall spare your life."

"I only see the two of you. Maybe you should have brought a few more friends along." Her training in avoiding charging opponents led to his immediate misfortune.

His arms closed over empty air space.

A simple side step and duck and she was then behind him. Her spear thrust out lightning fast, and he fell dead, one small cut just beneath his helm. Her second thrust passed through the frozen knight.

In order to save himself, he retreated to the Astral Plane. The Sentiens had developed an innate ability during their tortuous enslavement beneath the Minions' yoke. His body became noncorporeal first, and then soon disappeared, but whether Tulina's spell would then be broken was a mystery.

Kala was surprised but not baffled, and she recovered quickly. Just in time to receive the third knight's thunderous stroke. Rotating her body, she withstood it, but it was only through years of training that she avoided death. This warlock was now without reason. Completely berserk, he lashed out at her with violence only possible when one no longer has concerns about his own well-being. Every few moments, an invisible hand would strike him, and Kala knew that the priestess must be behind it.

The knight's rage grew and grew. He was beyond speech, in a place where only mad babbling might exist, or perhaps some insane, wretched drooling.

Whatever the case, she had her hands full. Ducking, rolling, she parried and countered, cutting the knight repeatedly.

His mind was past the pain, living on in a deep pit, with only one thought remaining to him—to kill his enemy.

Kala's skill was to her credit, but that alone would not save her. Her own anger grew, for there was no other way that she might match such a foe in mortal combat. Savagely assailed, his pommel stroke broke her nose. Cut, battered, four of her teeth flew from her mouth; her ribs cracked, and several of her fingers broke as she struggled in defense. She watched, waiting for the right moment, dropped, and then pierced the knight through the heart. His sword fell, striking her again, albeit weakly. Twisting her spear, she tore it free.

He fell.

She stood. Stepping over his carcass, she advanced to face another opponent.

Two sorcerers remained in the party of Vremick. Their focus was still upon the Golden Sword of Illian and upon the Dark Elf rushing toward them. They lashed out at him with spells of lightning and flame, but the Elf's resistance had thus far saved him. To counter this, they invoked a spell of summoning, and the young sergeant Feldwin Carnage soon found himself engaged with a horrifying adversary that only he could see.

Grappling with the beast, streaks of red appeared in his flesh where its invisible talons fell. He struck it with dirk and rapier. Raised up and hurled down, he rolled with it and came to his feet. Just in time, his blades licked out, and its claws cut deeper. He would not quit, but it seemed like he was fighting a losing battle. It was then that his mind dwelled upon a savory plate of Derluvian mussels, a Shang Tzun delicacy. His mouth watered and then bled. He smiled and hit the creature ever harder. The beast seemed invincible; it hefted him aloft again, and its slavering maw opened. Its great paw deposited him inside of it, swallowing him down into its abysmal gullet. The youngest son of Baron Carnage tried to chamber his blades for a last desperate stroke. It held his arms fast. Then suddenly, the creature was gone! Something had broken the wizard's spell. Feldwin landed on his feet. Bloody and laughing, he ran to meet the warlocks, hand to hand. Only one remained, the rightmost one was dying in McHewn's clutches. He now knew who his mysterious benefactor had been.

The sorcerer Dravian O'Blesque knew that Carnage was coming for him. His comrade was dying with a knife in the back, and it was clear that they were fighting a losing battle. He had very few battle spells left, and only two of escape. He could not leave the field without Vremick's orders, so he opted instead to teleport himself to the rear of their reserve forces. They surrounded an Elf that would be an easy target for his spells.

Olak Tempestus stood alone, with fifteen fighters bearing down upon him. They converged, and he seemed to grow smaller—one tiny Elf surrounded by beings who had once been Men. He froze. Fear paralyzed him. His face portrayed horror. He held his swords as if he had accepted his fate. Six knights attacked him, and he crouched even lower, six utterly committed blades crashing down to destroy him, their cuts beyond withdrawal.

It was then that he moved, explosively, precisely, eviscerating one knight, crippling another, and finally escaping through a tiny fleeting phantom gap in the enemy's ranks. The other four careened clumsily into one another, completely caught off guard.

Keep moving, he thought. *Surprise will only gain me a moment or two*, and he meant to capitalize upon it. Nine knights remained guarding the perimeter. They struggled to organize an attack against him. Magical bolts thumped into him, but somehow they were absorbed without hurting him.

Dravian grew more frustrated, more enraged. These Black Elves had some resistance to his magical might. Perhaps a bolt of lightning would finally stop this Elf. Anger clouded his judgment, because Olak was an unclear target amid a sea of foes. Lightning scorched forth, burning through three knights before it came near to Olak. Singing his back, his hair stood on end. Ever on the move, he won his way clear. It struck three more Sentiens before expending its energy. Smoldering and badly hurt, they fell gasping to the floor.

His burns brought pain, pain enough to stop lesser men, fuel to a man such as him. Their eyes showed their uncertainty. They feared him now. Surely, they had never encountered an enemy such as him on any prior battlefield.

Attempting to regroup, they tried to organize themselves against him. Rigid discipline and military training was obviously one key to their history of conquest. This was despite the fact that they prayed to a chaotically evil, disembodied brain. Cleary shaken by his skill at arms, they tried valiantly to steel their resolve. They knew that in order to defeat him, many more of them would have to die, but the Great Mind's punishment for their failure would be certain death, and so they pressed on. Vremick's orders screamed in their minds, *Bring him down! Now!* They attacked him then, with the hopeless determination that Fate's resolve brings.

Their enemy seemed to be nowhere and everywhere. His swords cut mercilessly, and his body danced a ballet of Death's design. *How could he move so?* they thought. Confusion reigned as one by one they fell to cuts that they never even saw delivered. Whenever possible, the Elf seemed to cripple rather than to kill, but when his hand was forced, hearts' blood ebbed and heads rolled.

Olak's blades were drenched in blood. Even the hidden razors in his braid were dripping with the liquid of life. Pausing for an instant to survey his work, his eyes looked upon Dravian and turned black.

The sorcerer had had enough. Fading, he fled into the Astral Plane. Fear had overcome even his evil soul, and somehow, death by Vremick's hand seemed a gentler thing. The subordinate knights that still breathed also disappeared. Some would surely die of their wounds, but perhaps one or two would live to fight another day.

Shaking the gore from his swords, Olak wiped them off upon an enemy's cloak. Breathing deep, he calmed himself. Jason was in a bit of a pickle, but help was on the way.

Draco pressed hard his attack upon Vremick. Using all his vast training, he focused only upon the fight. Vremick tried hard to contact his mind, but he would have none of it. Cut, slash, chop, parry, slice, twist, sidestep, and repeat, he allowed rage to shield his mind. *Kill Vremick*, was all that he allowed his mind to say to itself.

Vremick knew that his attempt to recover the sword was failing. Somehow, the Elves were largely immune to their psychic abilities. He could never return to Yir' Psi without the Sword of Illian, but he could stay in the field, retreat and regroup, and perhaps gain reinforcements. They would lose face, but they might live. They must live to exact vengeance against the son of Da' Gol! His knights tried hard to capture Jason in their snare, but the sword's power allowed him to escape easily. The Black Elves were regrouping to overwhelm them. The day was lost, but they were the soldiers most loyal to Vremick, and they would not surrender. Vremick spoke to the last remnants of his force with his mind. "The hour of our defeat has come, but the war isn't over! We will retreat to the Astral Plane, regroup, and return for the sword with a stronger force. Fall back on my command. Now!"

Each of his remaining warriors then retreated, became ethereal, and passed between the planes to their homeland. It was not merely a spiritual journey, for their material forms traveled there as a whole. One moment they existed in one plane, and the next, they were gone—whole for a moment, a ghostly spirit the next, and then vanishing, going from one reality to the next without physical movement. They chose their destinations by focusing on a particular image in their mind, a unique room in their home, a distinctive sandy shore, outcropping of rock, or comrades' face.

They had built their floating citadel Yir' Psi in the years following their escape from the Minions. They could not return there and report to the Great Mind empty handed, but they could rest elsewhere and resume their quest.

"We will meet again, son of Da'Gol!" Vremick raved. "We will meet again!"

The Elves hacked at their fading forms, but only wisps of smoke existed where they had been, and then soon faded. Many Sentiens lay dead upon the floor.

"I have a spell that will allow us to pursue them, Jason," Tulina said.

"Let them go. It will be a long time before he has the strength to challenge us again."

"But we can finish them all now!" Carnage said.

"Their leader might do that for us, but for now, we have a mission to complete. We'll just have to be ready when Vremick tries again."

"Perhaps enough blood has been shed today," Olak suggested.

"I know that I've shed as much as I want to," Kala said, spitting out a loose tooth. "I could use a little patching up, Lieutenant T."

"Of course."

"Tend to the wounded," Jason said, "and search their bodies. We may find something useful."

Vremick, Son of Illian

Their frantic escape had made precise arrival within the astral realm impossible. Luckily, they hadn't appeared within the walls of Yir' Psi, or inside the territorial dominion of their archenemies, the Forsaken. Instead, they had landed in the Astral Wilds, and there they made a hasty camp upon a tall rocky outcropping, surrounded on all sides by dense forest and tangled undergrowth. Vremick surveyed his surroundings from the precipice, the warm Astral Winds animating his clothing as he tried to discern their location.

"I believe that we are just south of the Celestial Ridge, Supreme Leader," the knight Sai Ignatius said. "Beyond it lies the Dark Pools of Discord and then the realm of Limbo."

"How far is it to the nearest settlement?"

"If I am correct, the town of Tu Grin Psi lies three days to the west."

"Ha! The garrison of my nephew Sai Mishka lies there. He commands a thousand soldiers. He will grant us the help that we need. Indeed, he may join us himself! O'Blesque, I would have a word with you now."

"Yes, Supreme Leader!"

"Dravian O'Blesque!" Vremick roared. "By the hand of the Great Mind, I should have you tortured in the festering gullet of a giant worm!"

"I knew that you would regroup here, my lord. It was logical for me to assume that you would have need of your chief sorcerer."

"Oh. And what need could I possibly have for a coward in my elite force?"

"I know why the Elves were immune to our powers. I discovered the secret in the mind of their witch."

"They must have possessed magic items that shielded their minds."

"That is what I thought at first, my lord, but the Black Witch revealed that the secret lay in the walls of that mine. Some property of the stone interferes with magic, and apparently our minds as well."

"So then they'll not fare so well on another field!"

"No, my lord."

"Excellent! Then we still have a chance, more than a chance indeed. Once we have recovered our strength, we will choose our battlefield more carefully. Our tragedy requires punishment. Twenty-eight knights entered into battle today, and only nine remain. Whatever the cost, I must recover the sword of my father! Dravian, tend to the wounded. If any of them die, then you'll die with them."

"Yes, Supreme Leader."

"I must meditate and contact my nephew Mishka. He will send us a new company of men, and we will train them harder than ever! Save my wounded knights, Dravian. We cannot afford any more losses. Mend them, and then we march for Tu Grin Psi. Very soon, the son of Da'Gol will rue the day that he met Vremick, son of Illian!"

The Mine

"You did well, Jason," Draco said. "Nearly thirty Sentiens against our eight, and yet we all still live."

"We got lucky. Without the protection of the mineral deposits, we may all have died."

"It may have been necessary to have surrendered the sword in that case," Olak said. "I fear that we may well have rekindled the war."

"My father taught me much about Sentien ways," Jason said. "Until Vremick has failed, it will be his sole responsibility to reclaim it. The Great Mind will not consider war until he has utterly lost."

"He is certain to make another attempt," Draco said, "and next time he won't underestimate you."

"My destiny and that of the sword will be revealed in time. Until then, I'll follow the first principle of the Drakkar Noire."

"That without great enemies," Olak said, "one can never achieve one's utmost potential."

"And many great enemies died today," Jason said. "Their handicap saved our mission but made it only a half victory."

"Maybe Tulina can cast a blessing upon them, to speed them on their way to wherever it is that Sentien knights go when they die."

"Their spirits are wholly evil," she said. "They'd probably be happier without my blessing."

"Then to Hell with them," Carnage said. "They attacked us without honor. They deserve no pity of ours." Little talk of blessings followed that simply stated fact. There was simply too much to be done and too little time.

"Sergeant Braidwick," Lieutenant Da'Gol said, "report!"

"Nineteen enemies dead, sir, twelve regulars, one upper rank, a captain, I think, three warlocks, three high-ranking knights, and four burnt beyond recognition. Their swords are okay, but their armor and belongings are ruined."

"Did you find anything special?"

"There are fifteen suits of armor so full of gems that we could all retire on them. Their great swords are enchanted and nearly priceless as well. I found ten rings and three wands that I assume are magical. The wizard that McHewn killed had one of our transdimensional bags of holding with at least five thousand coins in it. I also found a map on the dead captain. I'm not sure, but I think that it's a map of their lands in the Astral Plane."

"Give the rings and wands to Tulina for identification. Stuff as much of the rest of it as you can into the bag. Work fast. We leave as soon as Tulina can patch us up."

"Aye, sir!"

"McHewn, you're on watch. NewMason, as soon as you're able to, take point and keep an eye out for trouble." They went to work quickly and quietly. The bodies of the dead were hidden inside of a cross passage and buried with debris. It was an arduous task, but in a brief time, it seemed as if the battle had never been.

Tulina was a talented physician and a gifted priestess. She was able to bandage or magically heal the entire squad within an hour. Powerful spells that she did not possess were required to heal Kala's teeth, but they were all once again ready to march.

The way through the mine proved to be easier from that point on. The tunnels were quiet and empty, except for many years of dust and debris carried in by animals. They hiked for two miles more before they finally came to the elevator shaft. A new dilemma quickly became evident, because the Dwarves' ropes and pulleys had long since fallen into ruin. Far above them, a tiny point of light lanced down, and for any other beings, escape would only be possible after a hopeless climb along sheer-quarried walls. It was not so for the Dockalfar, for in ages past they had grown in tune with the natural energies of the Underearth, and they had learned how to harness its power to accomplish supernatural things. By focusing their wills, they could borrow that power and use it to levitate, rising up on the warm currents of an unseen wind. It was not a fast process, but it was somewhat faster than a walk and somewhat slower than sprinting. It most certainly was faster that climbing, and far more silent. On Jason's signal, they rose up the shaft in their usual formation. In the lightless mine, they were like darkness itself, climbing higher crawling toward the light, challenging its supremacy. They moved like shadows within darkness, and to anyone who might witness it, it would seem that the night itself had eyes. Wraithlike, they floated up, sometimes using their hands and feet to guide themselves across the face of the stone, but usually just ascending vertically as their minds willed them. Near the top, they encountered a colony of bats. Their shrieking cries filling the air as they flew off in a panic.

Soon after, they came to the end of the shaft, the elevator ending in a great gaping cavern. A company of humanoid creatures lay slaughtered upon the ground, their cook fire still smoldering beneath a wild boar carcass, now overdone.

"Goblins," Sergeant NewMason observed. "It must have been Vremick. They all died by the sword, most by one quick thrust as if they were standing still."

"Their psychic powers are extremely effective against primitive minds," Jason said. "They had no chance."

"Be wary," Draco said, "they might have missed a few." However, if they had, they either were in hiding, or far away, for none showed themselves.

"Amazing," Sergeant Carnage said. "The fortifications are still intact. I wonder why the Hill Dwarves abandoned it."

"There were still countless untapped veins of mithril, I'm sure," McHewn said. "A fortune was left behind."

"And easily defended from here. It has well-buttressed walls, siege defenses, weapons, and a good water supply."

"It's a mystery best left for another day," Lieutenant Da'Gol said. "We need to complete our mission and return to the safety of the pyramid. Only a few hundred feet remain between us and daylight."

They stood for a while, surveying the scene.

The mouth of the elevator shaft was located in a vast hall, behind the defensive outer walls of the mine. On the southern wall, several sets of stairs wound up the natural cavern face and entered the mountain at various points. Great stone fortifications defended each natural exit of the immense cave that was the origin of the mine. Before them, a wide ramp began, equipped with carts and rails and leading due north toward the shattered gate and then the world beyond. The gatehouses were still intact, but what may have befallen the original builders remained hidden. Outside, it was twilight, but whether or not it was dawn or dusk would only unfold in time.

"Fan out!" Jason ordered. "Battle formation." Signaling to each soldier in turn, he directed their movement, indicating to them where to focus their attention. Up the ramp they went, cloaked and quiet, ever ready for trouble.

The great ramp had once been the focal point of an immense operation. Several tons of mithril ore would pass through the gates each day, on its way to smelting and the final extraction into its nearly priceless refined state. However, what had been was not what now was, for time and decay had begun their great work of decline. Approaching the innermost gatehouses proved uneventful.

The gates themselves had been smashed inward. Some incredible forces must have been at work to destroy them, but whether or not it was a natural event or the invincible fists of a Titan remained a mystery.

The gatehouses were still much intact, albeit their doors were now gone and their former tenants departed. Animal bones littered the entranceways, and it seemed that the Goblins had enjoyed many years of uninterrupted living. A quick search of the towers revealed offset stairwells and a multilevel engineering that would make it highly defensible by only a few men. The crenellated rooftop overlooked an inner courtyard, bisected by a wide but now dry moat. Tunnels exited the ramparts into the mountain to both the east and west. One set of stairs led up and the other down. All was quiet.

"Halt the search," Jason signaled. "Let's move on."

Moving beneath the arches of the first wall brought them to the courtyard. A massive stone bridge crossed the moat. "McHewn, check it out."

"It's rigged to fall, but the pull pins are rusted in place. There's no way to collapse it now." Fanning out, they crossed the bridge one at a time, each providing protective cover for the others. Fifty feet more, and the second wall and gates rose from the cavern floor, massively built and cunningly incorporated into the sides of the mountain. The remains of its portcullis stood twisted into a gigantic knot. Beyond it, the outer gates rested a slinger's throw from their archway. Sundered from their once mighty hinges and ripped outward, they were now cracked, rotten, and ruined. *What being could have torn it free?* they thought, but what force may have done it seemed too terrible to imagine.

Engineered like the inner gates, the second set of gatehouses were both thicker and mightier still. Searching the towers revealed a similar system of stairs and passages, with hidden arrow slits and murder holes directed both outside and toward the inner court. The uppermost defenses consisted of a great balcony overlooking the road to the front gates. It had once been complete with a catapult and ballistae. Beneath it, five funneling chutes could deliver boiling oil upon the heads of attackers below. Hidden passageways provided an escape route for overrun defenders.

The outer wall was truly a defensive marvel, but like the first, only vermin and ghosts from the past populated it.

They peered outside cautiously, like gophers leaving their burrows, and soon found that they were alone. The time was indeed the gray hour before nightfall, and a lonely road wound away from the mine and off to the northeast. They had reached the beginning of the road that Draco and Olak would have to travel alone. Around and above them, a vast and spiny mountain range loomed. Surrounded by snow-capped peaks, a heavily forested valley lay below them. The remnants of the Dwarves' mining town began at the base of the mountain and extended throughout the valley. The village looked abandoned, but from their vantage point, it remained uncertain. The stars began to twinkle, and for the first time during their long journey, Jason dared speech, "Our journey together has come to an end for now, gentlemen. We will camp here and rest for a while. I believe that we've earned a moment's reprieve before we go our separate ways."

"It has been a long road," Olak said. "A meal and few hours of sleep should put the spring back into our steps."

"As long as we leave well before dawn," Draco said. "I'd like to get past that village before sunrise."

"We'll take watch while you rest," Jason said. "You should have plenty of time."

"Agreed."

"I'll take the first watch. Braidwick, prepare a meal."

"Right away, sir."

"And I've got just the thing," Carnage said, "I brought along a chain of Frenthian sausages. A little rice, some spice, and we're in business!" After a time, they had all eaten their fill, and Feldwin's only regret was that he would run out of food.

"Thank you, Braidwick," Draco said, "for an excellent meal."

"Yes, delicious," Olak agreed, and after a bit of small talk, they all retired to sleep for a while. They were exhausted from battle, travel, and always being on guard. Their bedrolls felt like the softest down. They woke too soon.

"Lieutenant Olak, sir," Newmason said, "it is time. The sun will rise in two hours."

"Thank you, Sergeant, we'd never have made it without your courage."

"It seemed to me, sir, that you didn't need our help at all."

"We all have our limitations. Thankfully I didn't exceed mine."

"It was an honor, sir."

"Please ask Sergeant Goldsmith to see me."

"Yes, sir."

"Sergeant Goldsmith," Olak said, "before we leave, I just thought that you should know that we share the same master."

"Master Li?"

"Yes, and just as he matched your body to the spear, he matched mine to the sword. Train with him as much as you can. It will help you in the days to come."

"I will, sir."

"Carry on."

"Yes, sir!" And it seemed to all of her comrades that there was a new quickness in her steps and pride in her shoulders from that day forward.

The team packed quickly, stowing bedrolls and checking equipment. They were ready to move out. "Will you return through the mine?" Olak asked.

"That way is too dangerous. We'll travel through the spider mirror instead."

"Then farewell, Jason Da'Gol," Draco said. "Your father would have been proud."

"Watch your backs."

"We always do." They then parted with firm handshakes and a better understanding of each other.

Olak and Draco loped down the hillside. They followed the old road, but stayed well off it in order to avoid potential ambushers. Shortly thereafter, their forms disappeared into the landscape.

Jason moved his team back inside. Activating the spider mirror's portal filled the chamber with its eerie bluish glow. Quickly adjusting the third and fifth legs to their forward position, he set the coordinates for the secret meeting place. After signaling to his team, they each stepped through the gateway in turn. He was the last to leave. An instant later, the portal was gone, and the fortress of King Rodaman's mine was once again as silent as the grave.

Olak and Draco moved swiftly, following the course that they had memorized days earlier. The mining town was now a ghost town. The old citizens had long since departed. Most of the wooden structures had rotted away, but a few still stood or leaned with age and decay. Their foundations remained strong, a testimony to the building prowess of the Dwarves. The Goblins had clearly been over it many times, searching for tools or implements of war, for their tracks and scat littered the ground in many places. Olak looked for signs of life as they passed, but only the wind spoke to his ears. The old mining town of Thorn Mountain was dead, and in a few centuries, it would fade into history.

"It's for the best," Draco said. "Now the secret of our arrival is assured." And indeed, it was, for no birds, insects or mammals were out on that cold night to witness their passing. If everything went well, then they would reach Linea in few days' time, and there, they would seek out Christoff, the assassin.

THE JOURNEY TO LINEA

Draco had perfected their disguises long before they would reach the gates of Linea. With the help of his magic necklace, Olak had become the perfect young half Elven nobleman. He would be Berrick Mornbend and Draco his brother Darius. The practiced their roles heartily until their identities were second nature.

Halfway through the hills, they came upon a small group of prospectors. Most of them were Human, but their leader was an old Dwarf, and their prospect was gold. Camping on the inside bend of a swift stream, they had recently discovered a sizeable deposit of placer gold. Most importantly, they had a number of good horses, and Draco purchased two of them. The old Dwarf invited them to supper, and it seemed that there was no polite way to refuse. The Dwarf seemed suspicious, and Draco looked to Olak for guidance. They would have to kill these men if they recognized their identity. It was clear that Olak did not wish it, but Draco knew that if it came to it, then he would do what was necessary.

"Come and sit to supper," the Dwarf said. "My name is Kabe."

"Thanks for the hospitality," Draco said, "but we can't stay too long."

"The passes are treacherous at night. I'd recommend that you camp here for the night and leave in the morning."

"If you insist, Master Kabe," said Olak, "I think we can afford to rest for a while."

"Just *Kabe* will suffice. I am no one's master but my own. We do not see too many travelers around these parts. Especially not refined gentlemen like yourselves."

"We're just passing through on our way to Linea."

"Where do ye hail from?"

"Our father is Baron Mornbend of Three Rivers Ford."

"Yes, I've heard of it. I traveled there when I was very young. I can't seem to remember too much about it, though."

"It's a quiet place, with clear streams and a large town."

"That's sort of how I remember it."

"How did you come to travel there?"

"Well, that's a long story, best told over supper. Help yourselves to the stew. Take a seat on one of those logs by the campfire, and I'll tell it to you. It all happened many years ago when I was just a boy. King Rodaman's mine was working at full capacity. Six thousand Dwarves lived in the village and worked the mine, pulling out over a ton of mithril ore a day. It was a rich place."

"What happened to it?"

"Well, it was a terrible day, and although I was there, I was only a witness to a small part of it. My father told me the sorrowful tale many times through the years, and I'll never forget it."

"Was there an attack?"

"It was more like a slaughter."

"We passed through the old village yesterday," Draco said. "Our map is very old, and so we expected to find a Dwarven City."

"It was a great place once, as fine of a place to live as any Dwarf could ever dream. To tell you about it, I must look back three hundred and forty years to my fourteenth birthday. It started out with a bright dawn, too golden to look upon with Dwarven eyes. The air was crisp with spring dew, and I was very excited, because my father promised to bring me down into the mine, to a magical place where they had uncovered a crystal cavern filled with emeralds. The first lanterns lit up the entire cavern like a green rainbow. So beautiful it was that they never mined a single stone. Instead, they hid and preserved it for all time. Ah, but the mine was a shining wealthy place, a jewel in a dangerous, untamed land. Well-built and fortified it was, with a soldier garrison of two thousand warriors to protect it and a community of some four thousand more miners, workers, tradesmen, farmers and their families. We were strong, but we were also alone, and many miles from any Human or Elven settlements. Word of our riches spread for hundreds of miles. Little did we know that it had spread across the sea to Dragonia as well. The Dark Elves had begun their campaign of conquest at that time, and they needed one thing above all else to fuel their war machine—gold, jewels, and anything to pay for ships, armor, weapons, and men—and we had more wealth than any single kingdom at that time. It was inevitable that one day a power greater than the Hill Dwarves would come. It was Moradeus's Day, and my birthday, when the Dark Commander arrived with his army of ten thousand. They marched straight into the mouth of the valley, the Dark Elves and their Human allies from across the sea. Driving them on was their invincible general, a twenty-five-foot tall Titan named Uzul, and he craved nothing more than conquest and riches. His liege lord used no name other than Aklon, and he ruled with an iron fist. Before the south gates of the valley, he opened the ranks of his army and made camp. 'Send out your king,' he said, 'for discussion of ransom and the terms of surrender.'

"And of course, by then, our people had fled inside the fortifications of the mine, and only a single company of Dwarves remained at the gates to meet the invaders. They were heroic, foolish perhaps, but the walls of the keep were strong and well defended. There was, at least, a chance that the invaders' siege would fail. King Rodaman marched out to meet Aklon with his personal guard soon after, twenty seasoned veterans, fighters of a least a hundred battles. Lord Aklon acted honorably, and he gave his terms without treachery. 'I have been sent as an emissary of the Dragonian Empire, commanded to return with one hundred thousand mithril coins or their equivalent, and ten thousand per year for as long as the mine remains viable. No other agreement is possible without a similar promise of payment.'

"Well, the king was put out, to say the least, for after years of endless toil, this enemy had somehow learned exactly the sum of the mine's great horde. It was far too much for a hardworking people to tolerate. 'Well, sir,' the king said, 'such a sum is too much for us to bear. Perhaps half of that amount would be enough to prevent bloodshed.'

"'I have my commands,' Aklon said. 'There is no other possible agreement.'

"'Then will you allow me the honor of returning to my army so that I might organize a proper defense?'

"'You have twenty-four hours to reconsider,' Aklon said. 'Tomorrow at noon I will march to the gates and once again request payment.' The king then returned to the keep with his guardsmen and the outer company and prepared his defenses.

"We were in chaos and frantically busy. My father kept his promise to me then, bringing me quickly to the Emerald Cave with my sister, brother, and Jonah, the child son of the king. His best friend Ono Greathelm also left his son with us, a young miner with barely a beard grown. They left us picks, shovels, food, water, and other necessities, told us goodbye, and then collapsed the tunnel leading to the cave. In the days to come, we had only two ways out. The first was through an underground river that began above the Emerald Cave, passing by its southern corner and then falling deep into the lower tunnels, and the second was to dig. The river passage was a great distance to have to hold one's breath, and there was probably not enough air within the cave to dig ourselves out. We had to hope that King Rodaman would win the day. Otherwise, we would have to brave the river.

"The next day, at noon, Aklon marched at the head of his host, ten thousand strong. 'What is your answer,' he called out, 'the settlement or battle?'

"'Battle!' was the king's reply.

"The siege raged, but after hours of fighting, Aklon could not breach the first gate. Men and animals lay dead and dying beneath it, some burned in oil, others mangled by artillery. It was then that Aklon sent forth his general. Holding a great shield wall before him of some twenty feet in height, Uzul approached the gate. No arrow, stone, nor fire could reach him, and he soon stood before it. His chosen weapon was a gigantic war hammer the size of a mule, and with it, he battered the door. Slowly, its hinges groaned, its wood splintered, and once he had breached it, he reached in with his tremendous gauntleted hands, braced his feet, and pulled. We built the gates to withstand any normal enemy, but Uzul was the mightiest of Titans, and they burst from the walls like birds before a gale. Aklon's army then rushed into the courtyard.

"King Rodamon led the frantic defense. Every available Dwarf hurled every conceivable weapon, helped with siege engines, or buttressed the inner gates. When the army reached the trapped bridge, two Dwarves risked everything to pull the release pins, but Aklon, a powerful war-wizard, struck the pins with a bolt of lightning and permanently fused them to the rock. The tide turned soon after, as Uzul used his incredible strength to tear the portcullis loose from its mechanism, and shatter the inner gates. Our people fled for their lives. Some entered the mine while others used secret escape passages that cut through the mountain. King Rodaman and his army held their ground, fighting valiantly. Those few who escaped said that Aklon himself led his troops, risking death equally with his men and facing each Dwarf before him singly and with honor. Aklon must have lost five thousand men that day, but King Rodaman lost his kingdom and his life. Aklon then pillaged the mine, taking exactly one hundred thousand mithril coins and not a penny more.

"My father and his friend Ono survived the battle. Returning to the collapsed tunnel, they signaled to us through the stone. 'Take the underground river now! All is lost. We'll meet you below.'

"We did what he said, but not without filling all of our waterskins with air, for we were really but children and could not otherwise have hoped to survive the swim. Once we had gathered our things, we entered the torrent. It sucked us down with the fury of the mountain, sweeping us through the earth and hurling us into a great heaving vortex of utter darkness and crashing waves. An eternity passed before we finally shot out into a waterfall-filled lake a mile beneath the mine. We called it the Great Pool, and we suddenly found ourselves in the middle of it. We had to swim for some distance, and by some miracle, we had each held on to our air bladders. Without them to buoy us, we would never have reached the shore. We were exhausted, wet, and scared. My father reached us an hour later.

"We escaped through a long series of natural caves and tunnels that he knew well. We walked for two days before we again saw the light of day. My mother was there with fifty or so women and children. Arguing long into the night, they finally decided on what to do. It was then that we marched out of the Thorn Mountains toward the Human settlement. We had enough mithril to make a new start. In the coming weeks, we discovered that many of us had survived, but most did not, and that the mine was no more. Days later, an army of Dwarves came from the Middle Kingdoms to aid us, and my father joined with them and marched back to the mine. Aklon and his army were gone, and only the dead remained. It took three days to cremate them all. After completing their sad, grim task, they erected a towering hill of stone above their remains. The high priest blessed them and sent them on their journey back to the Soul Forger. The tower of stones was a monument to King Rodaman and the glory that was. In the years to come, we built new settlements closer to the world of Men. Our strength and numbers have returned, and thankfully, Aklon's raiders never came again. We named that first village New Hope, and now it is a flourishing town just twenty miles south of Linea. My wife, daughter, and her three children still live there. Indeed, even my own father still lives, scaring his grandchildren with stories of Aklon and his horde."

"It's a sad story," Olak said.

"But one with a moral," Kabe said, "that greed, like all things, must be tempered by moderation. These days, I just content myself with a little gold. It still thrills my soul to find it."

"So many lives were lost," Draco said thoughtfully.

"We should have given up the coin. We could always have harvested more mithril. So many lives would have been saved."

"The king had no way of knowing if Aklon would have kept his word once his tribute was received. He did what he had to do."

"Perhaps," Draco said, "the survivors of the siege can pass on their wisdom to new generations and help to avoid such an end in the future."

"Maybe," Kabe said, "but greed and the lust for gold are powerful forces in Dwarven spirits."

"We all have lessons to learn. We all have our shortcomings."

"I think we've talked about the past enough for one night," Kabe said. "Time for more of the cook's excellent stew!"

"What's in it?"

"I never ask, but it's always good," and indeed it was. Passing the time with idle talk of the world, they became more than mere travelers passing by one another. The bonds of friendship whispered in the wind. "Well, I guess ye fellers need to be getting along soon."

"Yes, we still have a long road to travel."

"Well, I'll give you one small piece of advice. Stay south of the central spire. A bandit lord named Louis Pinch controls the main road there. He might ask you to pay a toll, or he might just kill ye, you never know."

"What other road is there then?"

"There is a road less traveled. My friends and I use it to go back and forth to New Hope. Linea is just a day or two's ride south of there."

"How do we find it?"

"I'll have to take ye. It is more of a mountain path than a road. It is big enough for horses, single file. Let me pack my mule, and then we will set out with my man Jacob. He's a real mountain man and good with a long bow."

"We don't want to put you out."

"It's about time that I got home anyway. The boys will take care of the gold until I get back, won't you, boys?" Then there was a fervent agreement throughout the camp. Shortly thereafter, they bid them all farewell.

Kabe and Jacob led them through the mountains by way of a small meandering path. It crossed great valleys, pierced through mountains by secret tunnels, and skirted sheer cliff walls where a sudden misstep would mean certain death. They journeyed thus for two days, until the mountains gave way to foothills, and they in turn to mere hills, beneath which, in a wide lake-riddled valley, lay the Dwarven town of New Hope. Kabe guided them into town, where many of his family and friends warmly welcomed them.

"Would you care to stay for the night?" Kabe asked.

"We'd love to," Olak said, "but we're rather pressed for time. Our friends expect us in Linea very soon."

"Well, have a safe journey then, and give my regards to Aklon."

"How did you know?" Draco said while reaching slowly beneath his cloak.

"You made one mistake," Kabe said.

"Which was?"

"Easy now, lads," Kabe said, while looking meaningfully toward their hidden hands. "Your error was simply this: you sat, ate, and listened to an old Hill Dwarf tell his tales of your own free will. You shared the warmth of his campfire and treated him equally. No respectable Elf in this part of the country would do that unless he had no choice. Half Elves or disguised Elves might, but none ever journey here, at least not until now. I knew that you came here because of the mine, and that made me suspicious."

"You've put us in a dangerous spot," Olak said. "We won't go down easily."

"Easy, boys, there is no need for that! Your secret is safe with me, at least until you get out of here. Besides, there has been enough bloodshed over the king's mine. My father believed that Aklon might one day return, but I thought that his honor would prevent it."

"So you won't try and stop us?" Draco said.

"It's true that I hate your kind for what you did to us, but I understand why you did it. If it comes to war again, I know which side of the field to stand on. My wish, however, is for peace, and that is why I'm letting you go. Most of us do not think that Aklon was an honorable man, but his actions proved him to be. Your commander isn't planning on returning, is he?"

"Lord Aklon is dead," Olak said. "Our liege lord is Vlad, his only son."

"And what of his son," Kabe asked, "what does he desire?"

"Vlad seeks a much higher purpose," Draco said. "Your mine is safe from him."

"Well then, perhaps one day the Hill Dwarves of New Hope will clasp wrists with their old enemies in peace."

"Perhaps they will."

"Farewell then, but please allow me to bring you a few loaves of my wife's fresh bread to ease your journey."

"That would be wonderful," Olak said, although he and Draco were very nervous indeed. They might soon find themselves fighting to escape from Kabe's trap. The Dwarves around them seemed to be going about their daily chores, but they could not know how many armed fighters might lurk behind closed doors.

Kabe went inside of his simple home and quickly returned with two loaves wrapped in grape leaves. "Eat them soon," he said. "They're delicious fresh."

"Thank you," they said.

Kabe offered his right wrist. It was either a brave and innocent act or a setup, the Dragonian spies could not be sure. Draco was the first to clasp arms. For him, it was a leap of faith and quite against his nature. They shook vigorously and then Olak did as well.

"Well, you had best be moving on," Kabe said. "I won't be able to keep this secret for long."

"We won't forget what you did for us," Olak said.

"I hope that we never meet on the field of battle," Kabe said. "It would be sad."

"Very sad indeed," Draco said.

"Until we meet again," Kabe said. Waving goodbye, he watched them as they rode out, but not until they were out of sight. That would be bad luck.

Once the city of New Hope was out of sight, they relaxed a little. "Either these loaves are poisoned," Draco said, "or they're sending out a party to lynch us."

"I don't think so," Olak said. "I believe that Kabe knew just how dangerous we were. I think that they will find the price of bringing us down too high. It is also possible that he did not even consider coming after us at all. The bread may have been offered purely out of friendship."

"That's a little too much for me to stomach," Draco said.

"Well," Olak said, "I'm starved!"

"If you don't die in an hour or two," Draco said, "I'll eat mine."

"It's delicious!"

"Good poison always is!" They laughed aloud, and Linea seemed closer than ever.

Two days later, they left the last of the hills and approached the gates of Linea. Their disguises were well in order, and they had heeded the advice that Kabe had given them. They would have to be more aloof in order to fit the mold of the Elves in this part of the world.

THE HILL DWARVES

Once the riders were out of sight, there was a sudden tumult in the village. “We should have killed them at once!” the town sheriff said.

“Kabe saw through their disguise. Why’d he let them go?”

“Quiet down, everyone!” Kabe’s wife said. “Why don’t you let him speak?”

“Let him speak,” the sheriff said. “We were both on Thorn Mountain when the Dragonians attacked. If not for Kabe’s father, I’d have died there.”

“I let them go for good reason,” Kabe said. “Believe me when I say that I hate the Black Elves for what they did, but those two were young, and they had no part in it.”

“We should hunt them down before they return with another army!” the grocer said.

“And how many men will die before we kill them?”

“We may all die if Aklon returns!”

“The Elves gave me their word,” Kabe said. “Aklon is dead, and they now follow his son, Vlad.”

“What if the son wishes to finish what his father started?”

“They will not. They said that their master seeks something greater than our treasure.”

“We must be prepared for anything,” the sheriff said. “We can send out a scouting party, to make sure that they are going where they said they were going. While they are gone, we shall summon the Council of Seven. After three hundred years, the Hill Dwarves may once again have to prepare for war.”

"I made the right decision in letting them go," Kabe said. "There's no telling how many they would have killed if we tried to detain them."

"You did the right thing, Kabe," his wife said. "Everyone knows that, but many among us still remember that battle and the ruthlessness of their soldiers."

"The council will convene in twelve hours. They will decide what actions we should take."

The scouts departed, and the great meeting hall was prepared. Citizens came from the surrounding farms to witness the emergency summons. The hall soon filled, forcing many Dwarves to wait outside, peering through windows or eavesdropping by the main door. The people were frightened. Warriors cried out "to arms!" while others argued for an escape to the city of Linea, but most proudly refused to become helpless refugees. The shouting grew louder until it was a frenzied tumult, a maelstrom of indecipherable voices. A gavel slammed down. The voices went silent, all except one.

"We have gathered here for one purpose," said a voice laced with gravel and fed by sand. "What will the Hill Dwarves of Thorn Mountain do to prevent the pillaging of Dragonian raiders? And what purpose did their two spies have in coming here?"

"We must speak with Kabe," the chief of the western village said, "the prospector who encountered them."

"Is the man Kabe present?" asked the steward.

"Aye, I'm here!"

"Come forth and stand before the council." He did so and knelt low before them. "Rise, Kabe, and speak the truth. What did the spies tell you?"

"They told me that they are followers of Vlad, son of Aklon, and that they no longer seek Dwarven gold."

"Did you feel that these men spoke with truth and honor?"

"I did, my lords."

"Rubbish!" the chief of the eastern cliffs exclaimed. "The words of a Dark Elf cannot be trusted."

"They are murderers," said the chief of the southern vale. "The Dragonians wish to rule the world. All who stand before them are either killed or enslaved!"

"I was at the mine when Aklon came," said the chief of the northern caves, "and although he killed those who opposed him, none who surrendered were taken prisoner."

"That changes nothing! We have paid a greater price than any other people have in all of Fermenor. Dragonian power rises, and only that is certain. We've long believed that they are preparing for a full-scale invasion, and our kingdoms lie closer to their shores than any other."

"Kabe," said Jonah, son of the king, "we were children when Aklon came, and we hid in the Emerald Cave together. I trust your insight in this matter. If the spies were not interested in our gold, then what were they after?"

"Their true purpose was secret, but I have known men such as these before. They are searching for something. If I were to guess, they have come here looking for someone. They are hunters of men, possibly assassins."

"Assassins would have killed you once you were no longer of use," said Jonah, "but these are strange times. They may not have come looking for treasure, but it seems clear that we have rested too long. Our castles are crumbling, and our defenses weak. We must fortify our lands and train for battle. The spies are no immediate threat, but they may have revealed a greater danger. We shall speak for a time, and then we shall vote. Preparing for war will tire us. Our commitment cannot be halfway."

They began a great debate then, and not once in over three hundred years had the Hill Dwarves discussed such an important topic in such a serious way. One chief would argue that there was not enough evidence of an invasion, and still others argued that the best defense was a good offense. Some complained that their treasuries were already running low and asked for help. There were many arguments, but the son of the king proved the greatest mediator, and his compromise seemed a stroke of genius in its simplicity. "We could divide ourselves and face the enemy as many separate villages, or we could unite and build one mighty fortress, the likes of which the gods themselves have never seen!"

There then came a roar from the crowd and a fierce gleam in the eyes of all the Dwarves that were there.

"But where shall we build this mighty castle?" the chief of the northern caves asked, yet it seemed that he already knew the answer.

"It's time for the Hill Dwarves to reclaim their mountain!" said Jonah. The shouts and cheers grew, as if the vote was already unanimous. "How vote ye?"

"Let it be war!" cried the chief of the eastern cliffs, and then the voices of seven shouted as one, "War!"

They had been living in peace for too long. Their dreams of reclaiming Thorn Mountain had seemed impossible before that day, but their numbers were now many times what they had been in those dawning days. They were stronger as a people than they had ever been in their history. Their ancestors were pilgrims in centuries past, of the same blood as their brothers under the volcano. They had journeyed west as explorers, prospectors, and settlers. Hardships had kept their numbers low, but peace and prosperity had returned their vigor tenfold, and they were strong. The outcome of the council meeting spread like wildfire. Seven separate Dwarven communities were now gathering to fulfill a dream and protect their people, and when Hill Dwarves choose to build something, it gets built.

Linea

It was a great sprawling city, surrounded on all sides by a mighty wall. Outside the gates, the city had outgrown its ancient defenses, and many roads and boroughs had risen up there. Vendors and their carts were scattered along the roads, selling their wares. Salesclerks greeted them without a hint of suspicion.

"Good sirs," they would say, "would you like some fine cheese, or a bottle of wine," or other such things, and to avoid unwanted attention, they would sometimes stop to purchase a little of this or of that. Several miles of vendors, twisting streets, and general traffic passed before they came to the main gates of the city. Tremendously thick and almost impenetrable, they stood wide open with only a few bored soldiers protecting them.

A guard approached them. "What business do you men have in the city?"

"We've come to visit family," Olak said.

"And how long will you gentlemen be staying?"

"Oh, we shouldn't be more than a day or two, sir."

"Your names, my lords," the guard asked.

"Berrick and Darius Mornbend of Three Rivers Ford," Draco answered.

Jotting their names in his logbook, he waved them forward. "Just be sure to check out with us before you leave, good sirs. Enjoy your stay."

"Thank you." They then rode into the main city proper, and it was even more densely populated and chaotic than the village outside of the walls.

"Where do we find the brothel?" Draco asked.

"We'll have to be discreet. We can't afford to attract any attention."

"Our manner of dress seems perfect," Draco noticed. "We should be fine as long as we lay low."

"Let's just ride around for a while and see what the city is like." Ride they did, traveling down as many streets and alleyways as possible without getting lost. Overrun with soldiers and constables, the roads of Linea and its citizens seemed guarded and on edge. The laws here appeared to be quite strict. In the afternoon, three constables arrested a young man for spitting in the street. Shackled and hauled brutally away by them, he begged for mercy but received none. All this happening while a prostitute stood at a nearby street corner, promiscuously flaunting her wares. "Maybe we should be more careful still."

"Agreed, it seems to be a very strange place indeed."

"Let's find an inn with a good stable and find out what we can." Asking around, they soon found a fine place called the Blind Waiter. Leaving their horses with the groom, they paid him a few small coins and entered the tavern. Porters even helped them with their packs. "Are you hungry, my lords?" the hostess asked. "You're just in time for supper."

"Yes, my lady," Olak said, "that would be wonderful."

It was a full house, but she seated them quickly at a small table. Around them, people of all ages, shapes, and sizes supped. Dinner was an excellent meal of roast mutton, corn bread, boiled squash, and a dessert of custard. In no time at all, they were both stuffed and quite content. Their waitress seemed friendly, even bubbly, and seemed likely to be aware of their nobility. "My lady, we're new in town, and we were wondering if you might have some advice for people who need to go out and about?"

"Oh, it's a good city, my lords. You just have to know the rules and stay away from the high priests, if you don't mind my saying so."

"Oh no," Draco said, "not at all! Perhaps when you have time, you wouldn't mind telling us about the rules."

"Well, I just don't think that it's my place, my lords."

"Oh, nonsense," Draco said.

"Well, I do get off in about a half of an hour. I could help you then if you're still here."

"We'll make sure of it!" They waited and overheard a few conversations that were very enlightening. It seemed that the local king was a puppet of the church. They worshipped a sun god named Lugh, ruling everyone, believers or otherwise, with ruthlessness, whips, and cruelty. They tolerated no other religions, enacting a new set of laws to better control the people. The most strictly enforced rule was a mandatory curfew, permitting no travel between midnight and dawn, except under the direst emergency. The second and most dire law was the forbidding of worship of any god save the sun god. Open worship of any other deity was punishable by death, and the priests were quite eager to enact such punishment. The most popular form of execution was decollation in the town square by a professional headsman. Some time later, the young lady returned, dressed for the road.

"My lords, I have a little time if you still would like my help."

"Please do sit down," Olak said.

"Can we order you anything?" Draco asked.

"No, thank you, my lords."

"Well, we must do away with *my lords* at once," Draco said, "and offer you our names."

"I'm Berrick Mornbend, and this is my brother Darius. We've come from Three Rivers Ford."

"Well, sirs, I have heard of that, but it's a long way off, isn't it?"

"Yes, it was quite a journey."

"My name is Adeline, but everyone just calls me Adee."

"Well, Adee, we had just arrived in town yesterday when we noticed a man getting carried off for spitting in the road."

"It seemed a little harsh."

"Yes, you have to be careful these days. It wasn't always that way, though."

"Oh, when did the new laws go into effect?"

"Well, up until a year ago, our good king James VII kept things running smoothly and very justly, but he suddenly became very religious and joined the cult of the sun god. Some say that the high priest cast a spell on him that made him that way."

"That's too bad. What should we look out for?"

"Well, there's the whole spitting thing and no riding horses on Thorsdays, and definitely don't get caught drinking ale on a Freysday after four in the afternoon."

"Can you think of anything else?"

"Oh god yes," she said excitedly. "Definitely don't get caught letting your horses drink from the public fountain, and above all else, don't let anyone see you carrying a sword or dagger inside of the city. Only the constables are allowed to go around armed."

"Well, that is quite a list."

"Oh my, Lord Berrick, I am just getting started! Hmph, let me see…oh, there is no displaying of holy symbols other than the sun god's golden orb. Church service on Sunnandoeg is mandatory for the whole city, and public displays of affection are completely illegal and punishable by public flogging."

"Well, is that it?"

"Yes, I think that that's about it."

"Thank you, Adeline," Olak said. "That was splendid, Could we get you anything?"

"Oh no, my lords, it's been a pleasure. I hope that I've been some help."

"You have no idea!"

"Well then, I'll be taking my leave. I have to go home and take care of my daughter."

"Good night, Adeline."

"Good night."

"Well, I guess we should be turning in before they come out with any more laws."

"Tomorrow is Saturn's day. We need to find Christoff soon!"

"Yes, I'd rather not have to bow down to this sun god and his priests."

Saturn's day dawned bright and crisp. The city was a little bit slower than it had been the previous morning, and the two disguised noblemen rode leisurely through the streets. Luck was with them, for a lady of apparent ill repute was on her way home from somewhere.

"Excuse me, madam," Olak said, "may we have a word with you?"

"Sorry, lads, but I'd best be getting home."

"We'll make it worth your while."

"I can offer a gold coin for some simple information."

"Well, I'll be hearing your question first."

"Of course," and after a brief discourse, they had an address and the lady her gold coin. Three blocks down, they turned right and trotted to the end of the alley. There they found a plain city door with a small sign. It had a crystal slipper attached to it. An iron hitching post in the shape of a horse's head stood a few yards to the left of it. Dismounting, they tethered their horses there and approached the door. They knocked upon it, four times fast and two times slow, as the lady had told them to.

A small window slid open, and a lone bulging eye ogled them. "Who be there, and for what do you come?"

"A young lady told us that this was the place for entertainment if you're gentlemen with money."

"So it is, so it is," the voice croaked. "Place your weapons in the slot to the left of the door, and I'll let you enter."

"We have no weapons."

"Come now, my friends, my spell of detection has revealed many blades well-hidden. If you're after what you claim, then you'll have no need of them." Foul odors seemed to pass through the door or around it, assailing their nostrils. Looking at one another, they shrugged. Removing all their hidden weapons took quite a while, and the bulging eye seemed to widen ever more. "The hair pins too," the eye said. "I see great danger in the two of you."

"I assure you that our need is genuine," Draco said. "We are friends of the madam Mater-Dee."

"Is that so? Then I now know that you are dangerous indeed! I'll allow you to enter into the first chamber only. It will be up to the madam to let you further in."

The door opened, and the butler hovered before them. Huge and round, several eyestalks writhed atop of his head. His enormous central eye never lifted its gaze from them. He spoke through a crooked tooth-filled maw at the base of his body. "Right this way, gentlemen," he said, all the while chewing upon the remains of an amputated arm dangling from his mouth. Still partially covered in flesh, it soon disappeared. "Forgive me, friends, our last customer received services that he couldn't pay for. It cost him an arm and a leg." His laughter then echoed throughout the parlor. "Get it? An arm"—he crunched—"and a leg!"

"Yes, sir," Olak said, "we get it."

He led them through a short narrow hallway, and they came to a waiting room with a front desk and a long burgundy curtain behind it. Well-upholstered chairs lined the wall opposite the main desk. A brass-hinged door stood closed to the right of the desk. "The madam will meet with you shortly. Please make yourselves comfortable."

Shortly thereafter, the door opened.

"Hello, gentlemen, when I heard that friends of mine had come here to visit, I just leaped out of bed. I barely had time to do my hair and makeup."

"Madam Minx," the butler said, "these two young men say that they know you."

"Oh, but I don't believe that we have ever met?" Walking behind the desk, he caressed the curtain. Clearly a man yet disguised cleverly as a woman, he was obviously a queen of another sort. Fine-featured, he was slim yet muscular, wearing a long blue evening dress complete with ruffled sleeves, a padded bra, and a tight corset. A fine black wig adorned his head. A little too much rosy red makeup disguised his face. Somehow, he had learned to walk skillfully in heels.

"We know each other through a mutual friend," Draco said.

"Oh, and is it regarding business or pleasure? Madam Minx has something for everyone's tastes—that is, if you have the gold. Alas, for our last customer did not."

"We've come to see you about business of a more serious nature."

Madam Minx then moved nonchalantly to face them, his hands hidden beneath the counter. "This wouldn't be pertaining to the sheriff's taxes, because I just paid him in full yesterday?"

"No, madam, this pertains to private business of a more global nature, and I can assure you that we mean you no harm."

"Perhaps if we could speak more privately," Draco said, "then we could better explain ourselves."

"My butler and I are well-acquainted and keep no secrets. Whatever you might say will not surprise him."

"Well then," Olak said, "we've come to hire Christoff the Assassin."

"If only he were here," Madam Minx said. "He left town just yesterday. He said that he was retiring."

"I doubt that one such as Christoff would ever retire."

"Well, I'm sorry, but he isn't here."

"Would he be here for the promise of great riches?"

"He said that he doesn't work for mere money anymore. He's got that aplenty."

"What if the job was the most dangerous and challenging that he'd ever faced?"

"It would have to be very challenging indeed."

"Our mutual friend requests the capture of one of the kings of the Mountain Dwarves."

"They are a noble race," Madam Minx said. "Why would he want to capture him?"

"He needs him as hostage to ensure payment from his son."

"Such a capture would be both perilous and challenging, but I cannot see a just cause in it. I will require further payment."

"Such as?"

"The two of you must help me to finish a job here first."

They then spoke long into the afternoon, and by evening, they had reached a fair compromise and agreed upon it. They would exchange one noble cause for one perilous challenge.

That night, the high priests of the sun god died in their sleep, and the king escaped from their evil sorcery. The next day, the people of Linea returned to their old temples and begged their true gods for forgiveness. Their good king James VII soon repealed all his recent decrees and returned the laws to normal—that is, except for the drinking of ale after four o'clock in the evening on Fridays. The reason for this, he said, was that he received too many complaints from wives whose husbands never made it home on time. That night, the king ordered a grand celebration, decreeing that every year from that day forth, the city would celebrate Freedom Day. There was much rejoicing.

Olak and Draco then began their journey toward the far-eastern shores of Fermenor to a small kingdom called Safehaven ruled by a noble king named Lord Cherek. Traveling in the guise of wine merchants, they practiced their new roles until they were second nature. Christoff purchased a large wagon to house their wares, and its covered interior concealed his faithful butler. It was a front that they practiced in every city and village along their way, and they had soon collected many exotic brews and fine wines. They lacked only one major brew, the champion Kegporter Ale of the Dwarves. Their fabled wine was legendary as well, never served unless it had aged at least a hundred years.

Their road would take them across hundreds of miles of roads, fields, and lonely campsites, and finally a ride through the mountains into the heart of the volcano, and then their collection would be complete.

How Christoff Captured Moldrin, Chief of the Kegporter Clan

They supped in the quiet town of Waysborough. Merchants were commonplace here, and they blended in like trees in the forest. The bartender was happy to give them directions to the Kingdom of the Mountain Dwarves. "Follow the Northwest Road," he said. "Cross the great fields, and it will lead you into the Darkcraggen. Stay on the trail and you will find their kingdom."

Journeying into the evening, they came to a great lake with waters as black as coal.

"Let's camp here," Christoff said. "It seems to be as safe of a place as any."

"Lord Cherek seems to keep his kingdom both peaceful and lively," Draco said. "It seems a shame that we must bring the war here."

"They control valuable seaports, and their land is fertile, but most of all, I think that our Queen fears that we will someday want such things for ourselves as individuals."

"Don't we?"

"Of course, and that is why we follow Vlad, in the hopes that we may bring about a new Dragonian order. The Fermen who have interfered with Vlad's plans come from this region."

"But why this Dwarven chief?"

"He is the father of the Dwarf the Orcs call Argor Dok, a revenant spirit they fear above all other things. Therefore, Vlad needs to neutralize him," Draco said.

"Why not just confront this Dwarf ourselves?" Christoff said.

"It may come to that, but Vlad has a plan, and he values the lives under his command."

"Then we must succeed for him," Draco said.

"Oh, we will," Christoff said. "They haven't encountered enemies like us in a thousand years. They survive by mining and trade. They will allow us into their kingdom with open arms."

"Is there no risk then?"

"On the contrary, we'll have to find a way to see the Father of the Dwarves personally, and that will require the greatest tact. The slightest insult could get us expelled at the least."

"He's sure to have a retinue with him."

"No doubt he'll come with an escort. I expect two-to-one odds at least, but I have a plan—several, actually."

"Such as?"

"Once we set up our first business meeting, we must wait for the opportune moment." They made camp then, and it was peaceful and refreshing, yet for these men, accustomed to constant danger, it was almost too quiet.

"How'd you sleep?" Draco asked.

"Almost not at all," Olak said.

"It's just too quiet," Christoff agreed. "We'll sleep better once we enter the mountains. There's lots more danger there."

Breaking camp, they left quietly and leisurely in case any watching eyes might grow suspicious. Their wagon rolled along the well-grooved road smoothly, its merchant driver whistling a happy tune. The two nobles riding alongside of him were obviously at ease in the saddle, cavalier and confident. They rode as if they passed through their own land, a place where danger never dared to tread. Two days' ride and they would arrive at the home of the Mountain Dwarves, the direct descendants of Baldric, First King of Dwarvencrest and Father of all the Dwarves.

****The diary of Olak Tempestus describes their uneventful journey but is not chronicled here. His detailed description of Christoff's plans portrayed his growing respect for the assassin, and his hopes for the future.*

Lord Min's Fortress under the Volcano

News traveled quickly through the honeycomb of tunnels that made up the halls of the Mountain Dwarves. A wealthy merchant from the far reaches of the continent had arrived requesting a challenge of brews between the brewmaster of Kegporter Ale and the most traveled wine merchant in the world, Master Johan Christy of Linea. No one had dared to do such a thing in centuries, and to say that it caused a stir beneath the mountain would be like calling a volcanic eruption a mere disturbance.

"Impossible!" Lord Min raved. "No brew in the world can match that of Moldrin, nor of any Kegporter for that matter. There's no way that we can accept such a ridiculous challenge."

"But, my lord," said his advisor, "such a refusal might be seen as a weakness among the other races of the world. They don't understand the importance of our craft or the honor and respect that we place in it."

"Hmmph," the king muttered to himself, "that does complicate things. Summon Moldrin and all the chiefs at once. We'll let the council decide."

"What should we do with the visitors, my lord?"

"Just how many merchants have come here? It's not even the peak season."

"There are three of them, my lord, but I believe that only this Christy is the leader."

"Sit them down to supper with the outer wall company," the king said. "They'll teach them the hospitality of the Dwarves." Laughing with his advisor, he soon turned serious once again. "Summon the other chiefs. Bring me Kegporter, Anvilhead, O'Baldric, and Hammerhewn. We will decide together if this Christy gets a challenge."

It took the rest of the evening to bring all the nearby chiefs together. They were the leaders of all the major clans living in and around the kingdom, but there were a great many more clans hidden in remote, far-distant places all over the globe. Nevertheless, here along the eastern shores of Fermenor, there was only one known settlement, the Kingdom of Lord Min under the volcano. Their ancient legends tell of their origins and of their first great realm, which they called Dwarvencrest. Sadly, in ages past, there was a great upheaval, and so over time, even the Dwarves forgot where they had originally migrated from, or why, and the grand citadel that once was, was now only a nearly forgotten dream. Nevertheless, they were still a proud, talented people, peerless in the crafts, although from time to time, someone might have the audacity to challenge them.

"Moldrin," the king said, "what say you to this challenge?"

"What claims does this challenger make?"

"Mr. Christy claims that among his many brews from across the globe, at least one will rival the mushroom ale of the Mountain Dwarves."

"Ha! Presposterous! Unforgivable! Such a thing is insane beyond knowing, and yet I will accept any such challenge. If only to prove once again that Kegporter Ale is the smoothest, least bitter, most refreshing, and incredibly gratifying drink in the entire world."

"But this Human cannot be serious," the Great Anvilhead said. "Either he's a lunatic or his mind has been filled with nonsense. He must be a fool."

"Then perhaps," Lord Min said, "we should prove his foolishness once and for all."

"I have another fear," O'Baldric, the most suspicious of the chiefs, said, "that these men have some hidden agenda and that this challenge is something sinister. Perhaps they wish to see our inner halls and in so doing, find some weakness for an attack of some kind."

"Yes," the king said, "there have been many strange happenings in the last few months, including the loss of my son to the Orcs. Maybe this Christy is a Dragonian spy?"

"It is wise to be careful," Moldrin said, "but I think that this matter is just what it seems, a challenge of brews. We have had them before, although only twice before in my lifetime."

"Then do we vote to allow this challenge," the king said, "and under what conditions?"

"We shall have the contest in the great council hall," Chief Anvilhead suggested.

"And under the watch of a thousand armored Dwarves," Chief O'Baldric added.

"I also suggest that we invite neutral parties from amongst our most trusted friends in Safehaven," said Chief Hammerhewn.

The king drummed his fingers and pondered, "The Sons of Lord Cherek then?"

"And his second daughter, Molly," the chief added. "It is said that of all the fair women in the kingdom, she is the fairest in judging a contest."

"Then she shall make the final ruling, so that no one can doubt that we brew the finest ale," Lord Min said. "Let us be careful and let us be true. The hearts of the Dwarves are strong. Let us finally settle the mystery of whose brew is finest. We are all in agreement then?"

"Aye," they all said.

"Then let each clan send two-hundred strong and let the horn sound out that all who wish to witness the challenge shall be allowed into the hall as long as there is room enough."

"When shall the challenge be?"

"Three days hence," Lord Min decreed, "when the sun sits highest in the sky and everyone is seated and comfortable. Let the royal chefs prepare a feast. Let us show our three guests the hospitality of the Dwarves these next few nights. I have a feeling that this will become the event of the century."

Dwarven Hospitality

Two nights of hearty food and great quantities of ale had left the wine merchants light-headed at best. Their plans had spun wildly out of their control, and they were now at the mercy of fate and of their hosts. The Dwarves had made certain that their reputation as powerful drinkers was unquestionable, and Olak and his companions had no choice but to try to stand with the best of them. In the end, their Dwarven friends carried them back to their quarters.

Carved from solid rock, their rooms were well furnished and comfortable. Untold hours passed before they were again conscious enough to speak about their predicament.

"Well, Christy," Draco said, "what plans do you have for us now?"

"We must go through with the contest," he said. "We can't avoid it."

"We'll lose, and then they'll throw us out."

"Of course we'll lose! But the brews that I have collected will challenge them, and the spirit of the contest will win their trust. We just have to take our time."

"What then?" Olak said. "We'll be surrounded by an army of Dwarves."

"Apex will be our secret weapon," Christoff said. "Listen closely, and I'll tell you all about my plan."

The Great Council Hall

High noon and the heart of the volcano was a beehive of activity. The council hall was full to capacity, and not just with Dwarves, for the princes of Khan had arrived with a great contingent of nobles, merchantmen, and other curious witnesses.

Lord Min sat upon the high seat, his great red beard braided tight and tucked into his belt. His piercing brown eyes were on guard, worried that everything would be safe and in order. The other great chiefs sat to his right and left. Princes Gareth and Connor, the eldest sons of Lord Cherek, sat across from them near the center stage.

Below them all, standing before over five thousand spectators stood the merchant Christy and his two noble assistants. Ten barrels of wine and ale with stacks of mugs had been placed on tables before them, and beside their table was a huge barrel of Kegporter Ale, fresh with the season's finest.

Prior to the contest, the Lady Molly suggested the appointment of neutral judges, and on her recommendation, they selected one member of each of the goodly races.

They came from far and wide on swift horses, and some by magic or upon the backs of fierce Griffons. Seated at a long table beside the central stage, they assembled. Serving them was the honorable household staff of the Lady Molly.

When all was ready, and the audience fully enthralled, the great Lord Min, king under the volcano spoke, "Greetings, guests! It has been many years since a brewmaster's challenge has taken place in these ancient halls. The last such challenge left the title of brewmaster firmly in the hands of the Kegporter clan, and now it seems that the noble Mr. Christy has the courage to challenge us again. Let us welcome the challengers!"

There was a smattering of applause.

"And let us not forget our esteemed judges. Will you introduce them, Molly?"

"Of course, my lord," she said while executing a perfect court bow. She was raven-haired, and her eyes mirrored the blue of the sky. Her dress was simple and red, yet none who saw her would ever doubt her royalty. "We have been greatly honored this day to have received such respected judges from every corner of the region. First, please allow me to introduce the esteemed wizard Tom Zu of the High Elves, who I affectionately call Tomzu. His brave acts in defense of his home and country has brought him both fame and wisdom."

Standing briefly, he graciously bowed. Dressed in his finest tunic, his colors represented the noble Wizards of the Blue Cloth.

"Seated next in the panel is Sir Tiernan Frostbrand, noble paladin of Rieuwood Forest. His selfless acts have proven again and again that his word is his bond, and if any speak the truth in all of this world, then it is he."

Tiernan stood and bent low, and with a wave, he greeted the crowd. He seemed very young, surely only a young man by the standards of other Gray Elves, but his bearing was powerful and confident. It then seemed to the crowd that this young Elf might be a noble paladin indeed.

"Thirdly, please allow me to introduce the brewer Brim Stonewarden of the Hill Dwarves, whose blackberry wine is relished throughout Safehaven. His taste buds are said to have no equal."

Brim then stood and offered a stout salute to his Dwarven brothers before again taking his seat.

"Fourthly, I am proud beyond words to introduce one of the realm's greatest knights, Sir John Anderson of Monson. His valor and personal sacrifices have made his renown known from the hearths of our homes to far distant lands. Beyond this, I must mention that all who have visited his beautiful estate talk about his hospitality. If any man in Safehaven can judge faithfully, it is he."

Sir John himself seemed surprised by Molly's kind words, and he proved too humble to take a bow, so instead, he stood and raised both hands in a double-handed wave that hushed the crowd before again taking his seat.

"Our fifth esteemed judge represents the hardworking Gnomes of the Western Hills. Mister Chiselnook is himself renowned for his distinctive burgundy. His family has guarded its recipe and created Chiselnook Wine for over three thousand years. Mister Tisno Chiselnook everybody!"

Tisno had a grand hawkish nose and a red handlebar mustache that dominated his face. His green eyes sparkled as he stood and greeted the crowd.

"Our final judge," Molly said, "is Mister Duncan Kenworthy of Ibbington, representing the Halflings of the realm. Mister Kenworthy brews his own fine brandy, and he has the utmost respect for other works. We must look to him for his most expert opinion."

Standing briefly, Mister Kenworthy bent low and issued a quick salute to the crowd. His clothes were simple but well cut. His face was fair, like his hair, and gentle in appearance.

"Judges," Molly greeted, "it is an honor to be enjoying this day with you." With a nod, she then turned her head leftward, toward the three brave merchants who brought the challenge. "Now please allow me to introduce our esteemed challengers, who have come here from the far ends of Fermenor to bring their wares to this contest. First, I must bring your attention to the lead merchant, Master Johan Christy of Linea. He has journeyed all across the continent in search of the finest drink in the land, and in his quest, he has chosen ten of those that were the most exquisite. Master Christy believes that at least one of them will rival Kegporter Ale."

What followed within the audience was chaos, laughter, booing, and even cries of outrage, but the open hand of Lord Min quickly silenced them. The king then stood and spoke.

"This is a most serious challenge," he said, "brought here with commitment and honor. Indeed, the pride of everyone concerned is at stake. Therefore, I must ask you to please enjoy the game, but do not do so unjustly." He then sat, nodding to the Lady Molly to continue.

"Master Christy, everyone," Molly said.

The crowd then offered him a proper welcome, clapping and cheering as the tension in the room continued to build. "He is accompanied by his two noble assistants, the sons of Baron Mornbend of Three Rivers Ford, Sir Darius and Sir Berrick, who have guarded and supported their master on his long and arduous journey to our fair homeland." Standing, they bowed humbly in the style of young princes of the realm before again taking their seats.

"Ladies and gentlemen, the introductions are now completed. May I now have a round of applause for all our esteemed comrades and to all who have journeyed so far to witness this contest." The crowd roared and the chamber trembled with the sound of it. When it died down, she asked, "My Lord Min, may we now review the rules of the contest?"

"Proceed."

"I have discussed these rules with the Brewmaster Kegporter, all the judges, and Master Christy, and they have all agreed that the following rules will apply to the contest. This will ensure that we maintain maximum fairness.

"First, we will sip no brews without properly cleansing our palates with pure spring water and pausing until one complete turning of the moment glass has transpired.

"Second, since we are comparing each brew to Kegporter Ale, we will taste each brew separately and sip Master Kegporter's between each sampling.

"Thirdly, following rules 1 and 2, you may test each brew as many times as necessary in order to come to the fairest conclusion.

"Lastly, the contest will continue until the entire panel of judges has had the necessary time to conduct their tests to their complete satisfaction. The panel chronicler will then record a critique of each brew so that the challenge will stand for posterity. When the good and honest critiques are complete, then the panel will vote, first by ballot and then by voice, so that there can be no claims of dishonesty in the ballot box.

"Ladies and gentlemen, during the contest, the charming bard Sir William of Laughlin will play for your enjoyment, and samples of the world's finest brews will be passed among the crowd so that you all may come to your own conclusions. However, let me be very clear, it shall be the words of the judging panel alone deciding this great contest. My lord Min, may we begin?"

"Begin!"

"Then let each judge prepare to taste the first brew of the challenge. Master Christy, what drink will you offer us as your first challenge?"

Standing with the style and flourish of a great entertainer, he said, "Thank you, Molly the Fair. I shall be honored to offer the finely aged wine of the sun god Lugh from the temple friary in Linea. The wine is handcrafted from their own orchard's grapes, passion fruit, and another secret fruit, which only grows in the desert region south of the city. The sun god's wine has an invigorating flavor and is stimulating to the mind. Drink up!"

"Excellent," Molly said, "but let us first allow the great wizard Tomzu to test all the brews for any magic that might in some way alter the honest and fair tasting of the brews."

"Of course," Tomzu replied, casting his spells in moments. He tested each liquid in turn. "I can find no trace of hidden magic. They contain only natural ingredients." His detection spell had revealed many other secrets, however, for the two noble comrades of Master Christy carried many magical items indeed. He could determine little else without addition divination, however, and so he remained silent, pondering carefully what he had learned.

"Then let each cup be poured and served."

The judges then swished and sloshed with pure spring water and tested each sample according to their own distinct method. Tomzu examined the wine like an alchemist, first examining its clarity, fluidity, and color. He then wafted a tiny puff of its bouquet into his nostrils before tenderly testing it with his tongue. He did all these things before actually sipping it, and even then, his examination had only just begun. Closing his eyes, he let its flavor and aroma create images in his mind, and soon the wine of the sun god Lugh took him to the desert oasis of Linea, and through the fountain-filled gardens of the friary. It was an impressive drink, but he thought that his own mother's wine was better still, and he had yet to taste Kegporter Ale. He tested the wine as fully and as fairly as he was able. Its flavor actually seemed to improve with each sip. He would give it a high grade. When he was done, he rinsed his pallet with spring water and turned the moment glass. Jotting a few notes upon his parchment, his study was complete. "Hostess, please bring me a cup of Kegporter Ale."

He truly had no idea of what to expect. Not much of a drinker, he had never had the opportunity to taste any Dwarven fermentations. "Sir William," he said before he began, "do you know the ballad of ancient King Brian of Beal Baru?"

"Of course," Sir William replied, and soon he filled the hall with the richness of the ancient legend. The crowd was jubilant, excited to say the least, for the recent golden years had begun to darken, and this was the most joyous gathering in recent memory. In addition to the music, there was also plenty of good food to feast upon and the wine of the sun god Lugh.

Tomzu then began testing the ale exactly as he had studied the wine, and as he had no preconceptions, the energy of the crowd was first in his mind. His concentration had for a moment wandered, but when he finally tasted Kegporter Ale, he was completely stilled, dumbfounded, and unable to speak. He did not know if he should laugh or cry, run a marathon, or build a set of wings to fly to the moon. He could neither scribe a mark on paper, nor keep his hands from trembling. If only he had a servant to help him. It took all that remained of his considerable will to calm himself. He then realized that he would have to pace himself. When he could breathe freely again, he scribbled one word upon his parchment and emptied his mug.

The contest wore on in a similar fashion, and the responses of the judges were often noted by the crowd, and the gamblers among them had begun to place side bets. Between each course, servers provided the panel with cheese and various breads and crackers so that their heads would remain clear and their taste buds acute. Throughout it all, Molly lived up to her reputation. "We shall now begin our second course," she said. "Master Christy, what do you have in store for us?"

"My lady, I have an incredible brew from the southern shores of the continent, created by the seafaring peoples of Dracmar. There is a fruit-bearing plant that grows only there by the sea. It has a magical flavor unlike any other. I believe that you will find it even more enjoyable than my first entry. Enjoy!"

Rinsing their palates, they turned their moment glasses. The Dracmar wine was truly unique, and it seemed the most appealing to the Hill Dwarf Brim Stonewarden. Brim was considered to be a very stalwart Dwarf, both quiet and kind to people and animals alike. His farm's fields were always fertile, and the animals in his care remained healthy and fat even in winter. It was because of these qualities that he was in many ways a simple man. However, this description did not portend that he was low on wits, but rather that he was a Dwarf in love with the simple things that only nature can provide. It was for this reason that the wine struck him such a hearty blow. His first sip brought him to the crashing shores of the sea, and the soft, dry cushion of the sands above the tide line. The second taste warmed his cheeks like the summer sun at dawn. His third drink was more of a swig, and at first, it filled him with an unquenchable thirst as if he had just eaten an entire salted cod. To counter this effect, he felt compelled to finish his glass in one flame-dousing drink. When he looked about, he could see that the other judges had similar experiences, because all their glasses were empty as well. He just had to try a second glass in order to see if the same effects would be felt, and indeed, it was almost the same, except for the fact that the terrible thirst did not return. He actually felt quite satisfied to say the least. His third cup resulted in a similar outcome as the second, and then, contentedly, he rinsed with spring water and turned the moment glass. It was time for another round of Kegporter Ale. He wasn't a bit thirsty, and this was a strange thing for a Dwarf who'd found himself in the midst of an unlimited supply of drink, but judge he must, and judge he would, so he took a tender sip of Moldrin's prized brew.

In an instant, his love of drink had returned. He was simply astounded. Visions of his orchards in bloom filled his thoughts, and the sweet sight of his children playing by the brook filled his heart with laughter. Each gulp of the ale brought with it a new flavor, a new memory or vision, but never a bad one or a sad dream, and that was its magic. Kegporter Ale had won again.

The crowd had come to its feet several times as the Dracmar Wine was passed about. New bets were placed, and the entire hall was filled with the buzz of life.

"Gentlemen," Molly said, "are you ready for the third round, or do you need more time to deliberate?" She stood, graceful and tall, with hair all black and satin. Her eyes were so innocent and blue that one could not look into them for long without melting.

"We are ready," Sir John Anderson replied. "What wizardry does Master Christy have for us now?"

"I have brought an aged whiskey from Elsborough, a city many hundred miles to the west. It is crafted there by a family of brewers who have created this same blend for twelve generations. It is flavored with the cider from apples that grow naturally there and a secret blend of other fruits and spices. The whiskey itself is made from a tuber that grows underground. It is unlike any other that I have ever tasted. Drink up!"

"Gentlemen," Molly said, "you may begin."

The crowd grew quiet at the introduction of such a potent drink as whiskey so early on in the contest, so naturally they turned most of their attention to the Halfling brewmaster Mister Kenworthy of Ibbington. Mister Kenworthy was an unusual Halfling, in that he was quite lean and a bit taller than average. This was due, it was said, to his constant stirring of his own fermented creations and his ever-present need to stand tiptoe in order to reach into the hickory barrels of stock that he kept in constant motion. Taking the first glass of Elsborough Whiskey, he smelled its bouquet and was quite impressed. The crowd was again hushed in response to his reaction, and thereafter, he was careful to keep a straight face during his examination. Its odor indicated that it was aged well in barrels of hickory wood, and he could make out many of the distinctive spices that they used, including cinnamon and mint, but several more were enticingly intertwined, and he could only guess at their origins. His examination was interrupted by Tomzu of Northwell. "Sir William," he said, "do you know the ballad of Sir Aidan and the terrible Grooz? I think that it would be most appropriate."

"Of course," Sir William replied, and he immediately struck up the tune. It seemed amazing to all who witnessed it, but it appeared that Sir William's knowledge of music and legend lore was nearly limitless, every note and word replayed exactly as if by magic. A new round of betting immediately ensued, for surely, one of the judges would request a song unknown to Sir William. It was a bet that many among them were willing to take, if only to further build the excitement of the day.

Mister Kenworthy was quite caught up in the ballad when he returned to his testing. His first sip was scientific; he sloshed it about, rested it upon his tongue, and rubbed it against his pallet. Its flavor was exemplary, and it was obviously well-aged. It had a bit of a bite and an aftertaste of honey on rye toast, pleasing to say the least and smooth after the first swallow. Closing his eyes, he let its blend of smells and flavors carry his mind where it would. It reminded him of a wonderful summer's day that he'd spent with his great aunt. He was only a boy of twelve at the time, and she was getting on in years, but not yet old. Riding all morning by horse and buggy, they came to the wonderful estate of one Thornton W. Burgess, who was well known to her. They were invited to spend the day walking the grounds and following the course of the twisting babbling brook that has made his lands so famous. His memory of sitting by the streamside paddling his feet in the cool rushing water came vividly to him. His aunt's gentle words that day had lingered in his mind throughout his life, even when he'd forgotten what had actually been said. That is what Elsborough whiskey reminded him of most—a beautiful day, his loving aunt, and the sweet taste of honey on rye. Exemplary! Jotting down a few notes, he rested for a few minutes, taking in the excitement of the day. When his head was again clear and his tears had gone, he swished with spring water and turned the moment glass. It was time for Kegporter Ale, and he was curious what he'd encounter this time. The Ballad of Grooz was coming to a close, and its final stanza was brought to a crashing end by the bard.

"And with one great stroke, Sir Aidan and his men blasted Grooz back to his prison, a crystal cave a hundred miles down below!"

Sir Tiernan was the first to request the next song, and everyone was anxious to hear what the noble paladin would ask for. "Sir William, I've come from the far-distant Rieuwood Hollow, and in days long past, my father, the Emerald Knight of Frostbrand led the charge during the Battle of Moromar Plains against a Goblin Horde four-thousand strong. Many heroes died that day, and a ballad was created to honor them called 'The Charge of the Midday Sun.' I have only heard it recited once, and that was by a minstrel now twenty years in the grave. Have you by any chance ever heard of it?"

"My Lord Tiernan, what kind of a bard would I be if I did not?" He did, of course, know it word for word, and within minutes, he composed a score of music to match it upon his lute.

In the stands, there was again much money lost.

Mister Kenworthy was soon ready to try the Kegporter Ale for the third time. He'd calmed himself, and for the moment, managed to separate himself from the historic contest around him. Pretending that he was home at a merry party, he raised his new cup. This time the ale seemed somehow different. Its odor was like a cool breeze on a hot summer day, and it bubbled and fizzed in a way that seemed to match his merry mood. He hesitated for an instant, wondering if he should again sip it or just drink some of it down, but it was just too exciting to sip. He couldn't help laughing, for the Elsborough whiskey had brought with it a memory of love, and it had also brought with it a tear, but not so this ale. He was happy again, as merry of a Halfling as ever there was. When he was through, he scribbled one simple word upon his notepad.

"Judges," the Lady Molly said before the excitement could in any way diminish, "are you ready for the fourth challenge?"

"We are, my lady," Sir John replied.

"Then, Master Christy, what drink do you offer next?"

"My lady, my next challenge is a honey mead crafted by the barbarian tribes of the far north. It is a most unique fermentation with an exquisite flavor. Every sip of it is as gratifying as the first. Drink up!"

It was again Sir Tiernan whom the audience looked to for this fourth test, for of all the judges, he lived closest to the Northern Tribes. Despite this, he seemed no less interested in the mead than in any of the others that he tried before; indeed, he seemed just as surprised as the rest of them.

Delicious! he first thought. *Very smooth, yet bold like the Northmen themselves.*

Even though it wasn't chilled, it still seemed cold, as if it was still cooled by the mountain glaciers that must have given birth to it. It would be quite a brew for a hot day, and yet it was not so cold that it chilled him. Warmth filled his heart, and he knew that it would be an excellent elixir against the frigid north winds. It was sweet, but not too sweet like some meads, and overall, a wonderful creation. He would certainly try to add it to his own private stock in the future. He gave the mead his fullest attention, and when he was satisfied that he'd unlocked what mysteries that it had for him, he made ample notes upon his tablet. He then rested for a time, listening to the last few lines of Sir William's song, 'The Charge of the Midday Sun,' before rinsing with spring water and turning the moment glass. It was once again time for Kegporter Ale.

The ale tricked his lips in a unique fashion. Whereas the mead was somewhat sweet, the ale complemented it, bringing him back to a comfortable place, like his father's den back at Frostbrand. The mead had cooled him, but the ale brought him back to the warmth of an easy chair and a warm fire. His own family was unusually human for Gray Elves, and although nature's voice still sung to them, they had learned to appreciate such Human things as bread and cheese, meat, and potatoes, and a comfortable chair after a hard day's work. Make no mistake, however, for he was indeed Elven, but he'd learned better than most how to walk and live in the world of Men. The ale brought him back to that comfortable feeling of home, so different from his last sampling of it. When he was through, he swished with spring water, turned the moment glass, and jotted down a few notes. Molly's voice soon prepared them for the next event.

"Ladies and gentlemen, are you ready for the fifth sampling of the contest?"

"We are, my lady," Tisno said. "And I must say that this is the finest gathering of people in centuries!" Standing up and leaning over the table, he offered Master Christy his cup with his right hand, while simultaneously adjusting the curl of his mustache with his left.

"And what brew do you have for us this time, Master Christy?"

"This ale is special indeed," he said, "because it came to our shores aboard a pirate ship, from across the sea. Alas, for the barrels that bore it were anonymous. I have therefore chosen to call it Arendish Ale. Its taste and body is without equal. Drink up!"

Tisno wasted no time. His pallet cleansed and rested, he brought his cup to his lips with all the excitement that filled the hall. Cold, wet, and refreshing, it was indeed quite good. Its flavor was bold and adventurous, with just a hint of blueberry. It had a fine clarity and a lively fizz that clung to his mustache. Thoughts of his youth came to him unbidden. He suddenly found himself dreaming of his past and the town cobbler. Three centuries had come and gone since then, but the Arendish Ale brought his memory back with a clarity he could never have imagined. He and his friends had been doing their required charity work late at night for Handover's elderly cobbler. While they worked, they would whistle and sing merry tunes, dance a jig, and finish the old man's shoes while he slept. Gnomish magic kept their labors silent and secret. The work was hard and went on nightly for several years. Toiling with a love of work that only Gnomes possess, they formed friendships that had stayed with him to this very day. When the cobbler awoke to find all his work done, the gratitude and relief that showed in his face was reward enough for them. Arendish Ale really took him back, awakening threads of memories he thought that he had forgotten. The ale lingered in the past, and try as he might, he could not easily bring it into the future. Swishing with spring water, he turned the moment glass.

When he was again ready for Kegporter Ale, he was still a little sad for times gone by, but one sip of Moldrin's brew straightened his mustache and nearly turned his eyes from green to blue! *Excellent, delicious*, and *in the present* were but a few of the thoughts that came to his mind.

"Judges," the Lady Molly asked, "are you ready for the next sampling?"

"We are indeed ready," Sir Tiernan said, with nods from the other judges, and so it went through the sixth, seventh, eighth, and ninth entries to the challenge. The last entry was a barley-malt brew from Itzul that had nearly tipped the scale away from Kegporter Ale, but Moldrin's Ale had won the judges' hearts over for the ninth time. The tension in the hall had risen to a tumult, and few in the audience could sit through it. This was partly due to the fact that they had consumed enormous amounts of various intoxicating beverages and partly due to the intensity of the contest. No challenger had ever come so far in the history of the Mountain Dwarves, and the tenth brew seemed to be Master Christy's wildcard.

"Ladies and gentlemen," Molly said, "judges and all, I thank you. It has truly been a day to remember. Master Christy, one brew remains. What drink will you now enter into the challenge?"

"I have traveled far across our fair lands, and I have even journeyed once into the Fairy court. It was an accident, of course, for how was I to know that the lovely bed of moss that I'd chosen for a bed one night was at the heart of a Fairy ring? While I slept, I was carried off by a host of the Little People to a banquet hall in a land within the land. Once there, I discovered that my diminutive captives were as large as I, or rather I was as small as they, the truth of which I'll never know. They invited me to their party, and we danced and drank for the night. I must have drunk too much, for when I again awoke, three months and a day had passed, and I was left atop of the Fairy mound just as if I'd lain there the night before. In my pocket was a bottle, and whether I or the Fairies had put it there, I could not remember, but that bottle was as magical as the Fairies themselves. The bottle can pour forth the Fairies' drink without limit. The liquid is indescribable and enchanting, but as far as I know, the drink itself is natural. Perhaps Master Tomzu could test it?"

"Of course." Doing as requested, he cast his spell of detection upon it, and indeed it was of a natural origin and only its container held magical energy. "It is as Master Christy says."

"Then let me pour everyone's glass," Christy said, "and may the best brewer win!"

Soon, the judges had begun tasting and testing, perhaps even harder than on the first or second challenges, because they knew just how much was now at stake.

One judge had remained quiet, contemplative, and most noble throughout the evening, Sir John Anderson of Monson. He would often answer a question with a nod or a wink if either would suffice. But he was also capable of deep introspection and long and detailed explanation, and for this, the audience grew suddenly silent, and hardly a breath did they take, for they were striving too hard to focus. This was because his words came carefully measured, powerful and weighty, and they dared not miss the slightest detail of the moment.

Sir John sat tall in his high-backed chair, and yet he was relaxed and composed, with his left leg outstretched to relieve the pains of an old injury that he'd suffered during the Fermish invasion of North Sissily so many years before. His creased forehead, receding hairline, and bright eyes portrayed his true wisdom. He graciously accepted Master Christy's cup. Smelling its aroma, he gently wetted his lips and was himself amazed! The Fairie Wine was totally unique, and his heart was filled with the desire to dance. Indeed, many in the stands of the hall had begun to do so, and even Tomzu, the wise and venerable wizard, had left his seat to spin about with one of the waitresses. Sir John allowed himself a moment of merriment, tapping his feet and moving to the rhythm of Sir William's music. The wine filled his heart with the wild abandon of youth and the unbridled nature that was the Fairies themselves. The effects grew stronger with each sip, becoming quite intoxicating. Sir John then found himself taken aback. This was truly a drink too potent for mortals, be they Elf, Dwarf, Halfling, or Gnome, and he politely refused a second cup. His notes were brief and to the point. Swishing with spring water, he turned the moment glass and requested another cup of Kegporter Ale.

The Dwarven drink soon brought with it a memory from the past, from the wars, but it was not an unpleasant one. He'd been sitting at a long table of soldiers eating dinner when his red-haired friend at the table's end asked for the salt. The mead hall was full of hungry soldiers talking of home and other matters, and no one heard his friend's request. "Salt please!" the soldier finally shouted, and in that instant, the salt shaker suddenly rose up and floated through the air, across the busy table, and into the waiting hand of his friend. His fellow soldiers sat quietly awestruck while his friend casually finished his dinner. It was a magical moment unanswered, because his friend soon died in battle before he could explain his strange ability. Nevertheless, the ale carried the memory with honor and without sadness, and so Sir John came to a swift conclusion.

The Lady Molly quietly waited until all the judges were ready and then spoke. "Gentlemen, are you ready to deliberate?"

"We are, my lady."

"Then please exit to the outer hall and return once you've reached your verdict."

"Yes, my lady."

"Well, my noble audience, it has been an exciting day to say the least! While they are deliberating, let us all enjoy the remaining food and drink. Sir William, can you play us a merry tune?"

"How about the Ballad of Daldry Moore?"

"That would be wonderful!" Molly said joyfully, and then there was more rejoicing, and a final round of betting among the gamblers before the judges returned.

The crowd grew eerily silent as the Lady Molly asked, "Judges, have you reached a verdict?"

"We have, my lady."

"Then, Sir John, will you please read your decision aloud for the entire crowd to hear?"

"Yes, my lady," he said, lifting himself up to his full and proud height. "Master Christy and Chief Kegporter, noble citizens and friends, we have deliberated and we have arrived at a unanimous decision. Despite the many and unique beverages provided to us from around the nation, none are as satisfying and complete as

Kegporter Ale. We have compiled the notes of each of the judges into one document, and we have each signed it with our noble seals. We can conclude only this: that Kegporter Ale is still the smoothest, least bitter, most refreshing, and incredibly gratifying brew in the entire world."

Master Christy and his men looked crestfallen, for indeed they must have been deeply affected by the verdict.

The crowd was in an uproar, and no single voice could be heard.

The Lady Molly then held up her right hand, and there it remained for some moments before the roar of the audience settled. "Do the judges have any words for the challenger?"

"I do," said Sir Tiernan. "Master Christy, in our reckoning, no brewer has ever come closer to matching Kegporter Ale in all of history, and for that you should be honored. Perhaps in your future journeys you will find even better drinks and return."

"I think that brewmaster Kegporter's Ale will reign supreme well beyond my lifetime."

"Do you have any requests of the panel?"

"I would indeed like to clasp wrists with Chief Kegporter and tell him that it was indeed an honor."

"Chief Kegporter," Lady Molly said, looking to the front row, "do you accept?"

"I do," Moldrin said. Rising to his feet, the senior-most Kegporter was a massively built Dwarf, both broad and taller than average, like his firstborn son. Brushing his beard aside, he walked down to the stage. The audience cheered and laughed. His victory was epic.

The crowd hailed him, laughed for him, and chanted his name. It was then that the ruckus was suddenly broken by the dire words of Chief O'Baldric, the most suspicious of the mountain chiefs. "Hold all! I recognize him now. He is not Master Christy, but Christoff, the Master Assassin! Seize them! Protect the Kegporter!"

The fog of excess drink and the sheer surprise of O'Baldric's revelation stunned everyone in attendance. Only Sir John acted instantly. Rising up, he hurled his seat away from himself and drew his belted sword. Rushing forward to pull the Kegporter away from the assassin, he was then struck in the chest by the first of Apex's eye rays. The Floating Lord had suddenly appeared behind Christoff and his men, and all concerned drew back in shock and horror.

Sir John was suddenly slowed as if he moved in a dream.

Sir Berrick produced a strange device and opened a doorway to somewhere. His brother moved like a leopard and heaved the suddenly sleeping Moldrin through the portal. Berrick followed them while Christoff casually reclaimed his ever-full Fairie mug, bowed to the crowd, and then leaped after them. Apex remained only long enough to unleash all ten of his eyes' horrible powers. Brim Stonewarden was charmed into defending the beast, and it took three Dwarves to bring him down alive. Mr. Kenworthy was hurled fifty feet and injured almost unto death. Sir Tiernan was turned to stone while calling for his sword. The hero of the day proved to be Tisno Chiselnook. If not for his selfless tackling of the Lady Molly, then surely she would have been disintegrated.

Many in the audience fled in terror, injuring many in their panicked attempt to escape, but perhaps worst of all, Lord O'Baldric suffered a terrible flesh-searing injury and fell into a magical swoon from which he couldn't be awakened. Master Tomzu went to him. "I believe that he can still be saved," he said, "but I must return to my mother's alchemical lab in Northwell. Bring your clerics, swiftly now!"

All was chaos, all was suddenly woe.

Shock and silence ruled the hall the moment after the assassins' escape. They were completely and utterly gone.

"What in the Nine Hells just happened?" Lord Min rasped. "And how did a Floating Lord get in here!"

"I believe," Master Tomzu said, "that Christoff had him magically hidden. He must have disguised the invisibility spell by keeping him near his Fairie mug. My detection spell was tragically fooled."

"It's not your fault, Master Zu," the king said. "It is mine."

"Should we search the fortress, my lord," said the captain of the guard.

"Conduct your search, but we can be sure that they are no longer anywhere near the volcano. Search their wagon and their horses. Maybe we can find something useful."

"Yes, sir!"

"Summon my advisor!" Lord Min raged. "And bring the healers. Chief O'Baldric might not last much longer." There was then a flurry of activity. Runners were sent, and the word was passed. "I fear that we have lost Sir Tiernan."

"Nay, my lord," said Tomzu, "I will go home at once and return with a cure. Sir Tiernan was magically turned, and he can be restored by a powerful transfiguration spell."

"And what of O'Baldric?" the king asked. "I fear that my healers will not be able to restore him."

"The Floating Lords possess a dark power that causes instant death to most beings. I believe that the chief's amazing fortitude is all that has saved him thus far. I will return with my mother Jackie Zu. She is the greatest healer in Northwell, and if anyone can save him, she can."

"I would be in your debt."

"Nothing of the sort, my lord!" Tomzu said. "This is a terrible tragedy, and I cannot help feeling responsible. In the meantime, we must save who we can and find answers. I'll return within the hour!" Stepping safely away from the king, he then cast a complex spell and disappeared.

"Wizards," Lord Min mused. "What of Sir John?"

"I seem to have recovered, Your Eminence, at least from the beast's spell. I'm afraid that I cannot say the same for the drink."

"Truly that is a blessing. Your efforts to save Moldrin were commendable."

"It was strange, from the moment the creature's ray struck me I could barely move. Christoff and his men easily outpaced me."

"They will pay for this outrage!"

"The men of Monson will join you when you raise the call, but first we must know where they've taken him."

"The Dwarves of the Volcano have lost a leader this day," the king said, "but perhaps we have gained many new friends and allies that we never knew that we had. You are a credit to your people, Sir John."

"I will take my squire and my other good men and scour the hills nearby. Perhaps we can discover something."

"I shall send a company of Dwarves to aid you. There's no telling what trouble is afoot. I fear that the problems of the West Coast have finally found their way here."

"Dragonia?"

"None other."

"I shall await your company in the stables," Sir John said. "My young squire, Erik, will prepare my horse and assemble my men."

"My raiders will be ready to move out within the hour. Look to the South Road, Sir John. To the north, the mountains soon become impassable without climbing equipment."

"Very well, my lord, I shall return as soon as we've finished our search."

The two warriors bent in farewell.

"What a disaster," grumbled the king. "Bring me the Master of Spies! I must know who has seized the Kegporter."

If the Master of Spies was in the citadel, then they would meet within the hour. It would take a miracle.

Kegporter's Prison

Moldrin awoke disoriented and completely unaware of what had most recently transpired. It wasn't his bed, of that he was sure, because it was very comfortable, with the softest, smoothest sheets that he'd ever felt. He must have passed out from too much drink, but what bedroom in the volcano had such plush accommodations? Beside him, a goblet filled with some orange-colored juice stood beside a plate of biscuits and other snacks. Amazingly hungry, he tore into a small loaf of bread and downed half of the juice. Delicious! Never before had he tasted such a fruity beverage. He'd have to think about adding some of it to his summer brew, but something was definitely wrong. He was dressed only in a nightshirt and loincloth. His clothing, armor, and weapons were gone!

Across from the bed, his room only had one small window. Parting the curtains, he looked down upon a vast plain, and beyond that, a forest stretching to far-distant mountains. Beneath him, rising up from somewhere far below stood the point of an enormous monolith, a great pyramid.

My God! he thought. *The Orcs have taken me prisoner, but how?*

His room was furnished with but a single door, iron-bound, thick, and strong. He tried the handle, and as he had suspected, it was locked. He searched through his thick beard for the thieving tools that he'd kept there ever since his adventuring days, but these too were gone. Orcs weren't smart enough to have discovered them; nor was it likely that they could have built such a high tower as this one. Looking out of his window again, he seemed within arm's reach of the clouds. He was high up indeed! On one end of the room, a strange device stood within a small alcove. Short and squat, it looked like a birdbath filled with water. A round container rested behind and above it, with a brass handle attached to a dangling chain. Beside it was a small open chest with some rolled parchment and a folded letter.

> Moldrin,
>
> Please make yourself at home, as you are now a guest of the Dragonian Empire. The device before you is an ingenious mechanism called a toilet. When you must relieve yourself, please sit and do so here. When you are through, a quick pull of the handle will remove your waste. Give it a try. It's quite remarkable! Don't worry, clothing will be brought to you within the hour, as well as food and books to pass the time. My lieutenants will visit you soon and explain your captivity. I hope that your stay here will be a pleasant one.
>
> Sincerely,
>
> Captain Vlad Leu Sherroan

Dragonians, he pondered, *here?*

Out of curiosity, he pulled the handle, and water was suddenly sucked out of the bowl and replaced with new water from above. *Crafty. But why would they capture me?*

He had only one guess—his firstborn son was up to some mischief again.

One-Eyed Jack's

"Mischief indeed," I said to the boys," but little did Moldrin know that at that precise moment, we were battling for our lives in the vast labyrinth of tunnels beneath Moldrul's mountain.

"What happened to him?" Pauli asked. "Did the Dwarves rescue him?"

"Lord Min would have tried, but even the entire Dwarven army couldn't have defeated the Orcs in their pyramid fortress at that time."

"But the king had no way of knowing where Moldrin was being held, so he couldn't have rescued him."

"Lord Min is a wise king, and he knew that above all else, he needed information, and so he sent out spies far and wide and waited. As for us, we battled the dung beast in his putrid home. And to this day, I wish that that battle had never been."

A Fistful of Dung: A Continuation

"Tariq," Dartin said, "it's not alone!" Struggling to gain some kind of control, he soon found himself helplessly trapped up to his neck in the mud. To his horror, a second beast approached him beneath the pool's black surface, displacing the muck of its home as it wound its way toward him with savage speed. Frantically groping through the mire for his sword's hilt, he found that his fall had lifted the scabbard away from his body, and he couldn't draw it forth against the weight of his surroundings. He tried to prepare his dagger, but it was too late. *Surely this is no way for a warrior of Odin to die!* he thought.

Groping for his knife, the beast's malevolent eyestalk appeared above the surface. Fear gripped his heart, for he was defenseless before a starving deadly creature. Terrible tentacles buffeted his head, grasped his body, and pulled him irresistibly toward its slavering maw. Despite the weight of his body and the mass of the mud around him, the creature pulled him in with the ease of a hunting cat toying with its prey. Struggling against its tentacles with all his might was not enough. It was clear to him then that this was his last battle.

Leander was more fortunate because he'd landed behind Dartin, and he was being ignored by both creatures. When he searched for his sword's hilt, he soon found it, and he was able to draw it forth. Where his blade met the fecal quagmire, steam erupted, because Atran-Doru was a legendary blade, and its very nature repelled the malignant filth around itself. Up and up he raised his sword, and a tremendous thunderclap was heard by all, for here was Storm-bringer, and above them all, billowing clouds began to form, summoning forth the Tempest and all its rage.

Unfortunately for Carmen's party, the horrible beasts cared little for the clap of thunder or the forming clouds. Their craving was for the salty taste of living flesh and the satisfying crunch of marrow-filled bones. It was a motivation that no storm could assuage, and their stomachs had been empty for far too long. Dreadful they were, with monstrous, salivating mouths filled with flesh-rending teeth, and their very breaths reeked of refuse and gore.

The largest and mightiest of the beasts saw its two closest victims. Rushing in, it attacked with a frenzy brought on by its irresistible hunger. Out and out its tentacles flailed, and although both of its arms felt the sting of its preys' weapons, they could withstand much more, and each entwined another victim. Taking a firm hold of them, it brought the first one down toward its gaping, festering maw. Its hunger would soon be appeased.

Carmen and Kur fought valiantly to defend themselves, but without entering the deep mud, they couldn't damage the beast's body. They'd cut the tentacles in many places while dodging this way and that to avoid being grasped, but the attack was too sudden, too unpredictable. They were entwined, squeezed, and hoisted aloft. Its arms were immensely powerful and suction-cupped, like the terrible whips of a giant squid. They quickly discovered that mortal strength alone was not enough to escape.

Kur's right hand still held Korun-Koth. His anger growing with his frustration, but the tentacle clung to him like the unyielding arms of an Ogre, and his left arm was hopelessly pinned beneath its grasp. Before he was aware of what near fate awaited him, he was suddenly before the creature's mouth, and only his iron-shod boots prevented him from being immediately drawn in and devoured. He knew from the teachings of his youth that these monsters were cunning, and it proved to be woefully true because each time that he swung his ax, the beast twisted his body about, thus preventing him from landing any solid blows. Searching through the maelstrom for Carmen, he was terrified. Both of her arms were pinned, and more horribly, she was being bashed against the cavern wall in its attempts to subdue her. She was holding on, trying to brace against each impact, but she was tiring. He prayed for a weakening of the beast's irresistible grasp, or at least some stroke of luck. He struggled on.

Dartin barely felt it as the beast began tearing through his body armor like a seagull feasting upon a defenseless crab. His hazy thoughts were strangely detached, for he could take no defensive action. The creature had his arms and head firmly entwined, and only Odin's mercy saved him from feeling its probing teeth and crushing jaws. He knew that he was dying.

Atran-Doru hummed with gathering power. It was a blade forged with the elemental power of the storm, a self-aware magical creation that could call down bolts of lightning from the unnatural storms it created. "Leander," it said, "the power of the Heavens is now yours to command!"

"But it might kill him!"

"He is surely dead if we don't strike now!"

Leander was trapped by the mud as certainly as any of them. If he sent a bolt of lightning towards the monster, he might kill himself and Dartin as well. He looked on with revulsion as the creature methodically pried away his friend's armor in its unrelenting feeding frenzy. He had only moments to act, but there was no clear answer, no way of knowing if his magic could save or doom them.

If the smaller beast had continued to feed upon him, then Dartin would surely have died, but Odin's most faithful follower was not alone. Dao stood upon the rocky shore surrounding the pool of guano with an arrow fitted to his bow, waiting for an opportunity to fire. The positions of his friends had prevented a safe shot, but Dartin was beyond the need for such consideration. Dao sent his vengeful shafts there. In seconds, his bow sang twice, and the beast was hit high in its body and again in its rightmost tentacle. The sudden pain angered the creature so that it launched Dartin high over its head and onto the steps leading up and out of the cavern. He fell hard upon the stairs, his limp body never moving during its flight, nor upon its landing. It appeared that Dartin, Warrior Priest of Odin, was dead.

The injured monster sank beneath the muddy surface of its home. With only its single eye showing above the dark pool, it advanced toward its shore-bound antagonists. Its writhing eyestalk was a difficult target, and beneath the muck of its home, its food's barbs could not reach it.

The largest beast was enjoying its game with its small morsel. Its prey was growing weaker beneath its toothed assault, and its crushing grip was slowly driving the air from its lungs. It would only be a few moments before it would feast.

While the battle ensued, Kalor had wasted no time in acting. Opening Modrul's book, he opened it to a page that he knew, and lo! The book did rise before him, and with the dragon's magic coursing through him, he channeled it toward the mighty beast. The book held its power within the very runes that had been laid upon it, and when Kalor read and empowered those runes, a great bolt of energy lanced out and impacted the body of the creature. It howled in pain. Kalor didn't know if it had been seriously hurt, but it continued to let out a hideous roar. Its single eye rolled about in a maddened frenzy of animal rage. When Kalor again looked upon the page from which he had read, all the runes of power were gone.

Caught in the beast's numbing grasp, Kur was growing weaker with loss of breath, but when Kalor's bolt struck it, the monster's grip loosened for a brief instant while Kur was being held right before its mouth. With a mighty battle cry, Korun-Koth lashed out, smashing through the body and upper jaw of the beast.

But the monster was far from finished, and with a great pull, it plunged Kur waist deep inside of its terrible mouth. When it then tried to bite down upon its spiteful meal, its wounded maw could no longer close properly, and Kur's hard Dwarven body proved the stronger. Had it feasted upon Dwarves before, it may have chosen more tender fare, but it didn't realize its grievous mistake until Korun-Koth struck once more.

In a stream of blackish blood and gore, Kur struck again and again, with all the might in his single right arm.

Kur-Rogoth bit deeply, and the beast reared up in agony. It hurled the prey in its left tentacle against the stone wall behind itself. Now instead of trying to devour the Dwarf, it tried to extract him, and Kur found himself being spit out and pushed away. Dwarfs were too troublesome to eat. With a shake and a shudder, the monster submerged itself and advanced grimly toward the other two victims still floating in the pool.

Tariq and Karina helplessly watched the battle unfold around themselves. Floating between Leander and the largest creature, they could manage nothing other than drawing closer to one another. Back-to-back, they each drew their blades. Karina held her longsword above the mud, and Tariq his two long ranger's knives. If they were to be eaten, they'd not go without a fight.

Seeing that his arrows could do little more good. Dao prepared his rope and grappling hook. Tying one end off to a large protruding stone, he then swung the grapnel end over end, aiming for a point within arm's reach of them. His actions were frantic, because upon his right, he could see the largest monster rushing toward them, yet before him came the second beast within a great wave of dung, like a large fish slicing through the surface of a still pond. He had only seconds to act. Hurling his grapnel and line as safely near to them as he could, he shouted, "Grab hold!" Bracing himself, he prepared to pull them in, but it was too late. The creature was upon him.

Carmen was sorely stunned by the devastating impact. The cavern's wall proved to be quite unyielding, and her breath was blasted from her lungs. The fall to the ground was only slightly less jarring, and she lay there for a moment wondering if her death was near. Looking toward the battle. Kur floated just beyond her reach. His face color was an odd mixture of red, black, and blue. She couldn't tell if it was the result of pain or anger, or both, but he was barely moving and seemed to be gasping for air. She wanted to help him; she wanted to help the others. Rolling over, she tried to rise, like an underdog fighter with a champion's heart. Using the wall, she clawed her way back up. To her left, she spotted her bow as yet unbroken. With her sword and shield, she was a great fighter, but with Cloud-Seeker in her hands, she was a deadly archer as well. Step-by-step, she waded for it, soon these beasts would pay.

Tariq and Karina were embattled. Side by side now, they tried to hack at the monster, but most of its body was submerged and difficult to strike. Its savage tentacles flailed and tore at them while what was left of its mouth attacked their legs. Slowly, they were being beaten into submission, but suddenly, the beast went into a terrible frenzy. Great bolts of light were smashing into it from the shore. Ordinary arrows were useless in the mud, but Cloud-Seeker's arrows were partly material, partly energy, and they burned through the mud with contempt. The roar of the submerged creature was dreadful. In mindless agony, it lashed out at its two closest antagonists.

It was then that Atran-Doru struck, beginning with a maelstrom of wind and rain, blinding and cold. And then, its lightning arched down, striking the sword-bearer's chosen foe. The electrical charge erupted through the monster's body, and its very eyestalk was blown from its body. In a final frenzy of involuntary motion, it shuddered and finally lay still. The mud absorbed much of the killing energy, but Tariq and Karina were still too close; they were burned and shocked and hurtfully stunned.

Grievously hurt, Karina could do little more than cling to Tariq as if he was an island in a shark-infested sea. His muscles rebelled against his will, but he was strong, especially so for an Elf, and he strove mightily to pull them to safety. His side burned, a searing pain like salt in a wound, only worse. The pain might have stopped a lesser man, but it only fueled his resolve. Screaming, mostly on the inside, he pulled, hand over hand, fearing for a moment that she might let go, but her grip was iron desperate. Slowly, he drew them both to shore.

"Come on then!" Dao taunted. "Come here, you miserable wretch. My sword awaits!" Fighting valiantly, he scored many hits on the beast and its tentacles, but his sword was only one, and the creatures arms two. Finally subdued, his sword arm pinned, he was then lifted up and drawn toward the creature's black foaming mouth. Struggling to break free, he knew that he was losing; the tentacles' grip was crushing, relentless. In an instant, he would be devoured. The beast's bloated eye floated before him, clearly eager for the taste of fresh meat. Anticipating the pain of the first killing bite, he screamed.

If Dao had seen past his all-consuming fear, he would have known that his friends, even then, were striving to save him. In a burst of white-hot energy, Kalor hurled his own spell at the creature. Leander called another bolt of lightning, and Cloud Seeker's streaking missiles slammed into it.

The dung beast was wholly consumed.

Dao was lucky. The monster dropped him in its agony, and he felt none of the titanic energies that had been unleashed. Knee deep in the mud, he shielded his eyes from the white-hot fires and leaped away. When he looked back, all that was left was a blackened smoking carcass, pouring forth the smells of rot and corruption. "Carmen, do you see any more of them?"

"No, but get everyone out of there fast!" Holding Cloud Seeker at full draw, she scanned the cave for signs of life. Above her, windblown storm clouds continued to rain, energy crackling within them. The monsters were clearly dead, their bodies consumed by bolt and flame. Besides her comrades, nothing stirred within the pool. "Kalor, help them. Let's get everyone together. I'm going to check on Dartin."

"Hold on, Tariq," Dao said. "Don't let her go."

"Don't worry about that," Tariq gasped. "She's got quite a grip!"

Kalor could feel Dao's body tremble as they pulled in the rope. "Are you okay?"

"I'm a little shaken up, Kalor. It's not every day that you almost get eaten."

"Give me your hand, Tariq," Kalor said. "I've got you." Dragging them to the safety of solid rock, the four of them just lay there for a moment, catching their breaths and appreciating the cooling rain.

"Are you all right, Mon-sheer?" Dao asked his wife.

"I don't think so. I hurt all over."

"Just rest for a minute. I've got to get Keg and Leander in to shore."

The battle over, Leander still floated in the refuse, his sword glowing like a miniature sun. "Incredible."

"Thank you," it replied.

"You didn't tell me that you could do that."

"I have many secrets and many things to teach you. Once you learn the secrets of the Druids, you will no longer need me to use the power." It was then that Dao's rope landed in front of him.

"We'll have to talk later. I've got to put you away for now."

"Very well, acolyte." Once sheathed, the storm quickly diminished and then it was gone. "Dartin!" Leander called. "Where are you?"

"He's down," Dao said, "lying upon the far stairs. Carmen's going to him. Let's get you and Keg out, and then we'll go check on them."

"How bad is he? Dao!"

"It looks bad, Ash, but we don't know anything for sure yet." Working together, Dao and Kalor pulled him out.

"Thanks."

"Are you hurt?"

"I feel wretched and smell worse, but nothing seems broken."

"When you lads get tired of chewing the fat," Kur said, "maybe you could get me the hell out of here!"

"Right away, Corporal," Kalor said by way of an old habit.

"Hurry up, Private. I've had enough of this floating around. Dartin needs our help." Tossing a rope to him, they had him out in short order.

"You're bleeding."

"A few of his teeth got through, but I'll live, as long as the wasting sickness doesn't take me."

"Wasting sickness?"

"These creatures," Kur said, "carry a disease. If you're bitten, chances are that you'll die within a few days."

"You mean there's no cure?"

"Oh, there are cures. One of them is lying on those stairs, and the other grows in certain places in the Underearth. I found some in this very cave, but we had better pray that there is more in here. Once we have cared for Dartin, we'll need to look for a wrinkled green fungus, like this, and a blue-green mold. If we can't find any, then we had better hope that the priest is alive, or most of us will soon join him."

"Come quickly!" Carmen shouted. "Quickly!" Her last call was abrupt. Her hands had flown to her mouth in fear and horror.

Dartin lay before her, his body unmoving as his life's blood flowed freely down the stairs and into the corruption. Those of them that were able slogged through the last expanse of dung to help. They gently rolled him over. His body was ruined, a horror that none of them would ever forget. His armor was torn from the front of his body, and his stomach and entrails had fallen out of him, torn, ragged, destroyed.

"My god!" she cried. Leaning over him, she heard his dying breath. "Dao, give me the last Orc healing draft. Now!"

"It might just prolong his suffering!"

"He'll die for sure without it. If we can get him awake, maybe he can heal himself." Tilting his head forward, she carefully poured the liquid down his throat. His body convulsed, rebelling against the foreign liquid. They tried to hold him still against the agonizing waves of pain. The Orcs' herbs were potent, and the magic in their drink was strong. Dartin's eyes slowly opened, a dull gleam of life still lingering. He tried to speak, but only shuddered. His pain was beyond his own comprehension. The potion was just not enough; his wounds were far beyond its power to heal.

"Dartin," he thought that he heard, "you've got to hang on. Pray, damn you! Don't give up now. You've got to try!" Squeezing him tightly to her breast, as if will alone could save him, Carmen wept while the last of Dartin's life ran out.

Death's mercy had brought him past the pain, his body now a useless broken vessel. He knew where he was, standing at the top of a rocky precipice at the foot of the greatest rainbow of all, the Rainbow Bridge. Leaving his land and his friends saddened him, but he knew that his mortal fight must be over. He was ready to meet his father.

"Heimdall!" he called, "Heimdall!"

The mist of clouds swirled about him, cooling his skin. The Bridge to Valhalla was bright and colorful, both soft and hard, on the one hand narrow and on the other infinitely wide. Standing before it, he was small indeed.

Suddenly, the earth shook and the bridge quaked, and lo! Striding down from the heavens was a Giant or a Titan. No, it was the god Heimdall himself, with corded arms and grim visage.

"I heard your call, priest, but it is not yet your time. Even now, Odin himself resurrects you, and then he must sleep for a year and a day. Until he awakens, the power of the runes will not avail you. We all must pay that price. Do not dishonor his gift. Now go back! The woman warrior is calling you!

He awoke in Carmen's arms, her tears falling warm upon his face. He prayed then, but his prayers went unanswered.

One-Eyed Jack's

"Dartin had returned to us," I said, "miraculously healed before our very eyes. We all wept because we believed that death had finally come to our fellowship."

"That was a terrible battle," Pauli said. "Luck was with you."

"Little did we know that our hardships had only just begun. We would soon return to our journey, but while we traveled, our enemies were preparing."

"They had Moldrin," Eric said. "How many more hostages did they need?"

"Vlad never left anything to chance unless he had no choice. Olak's diary relates another small part of his plans and the intentions of their deadly Queen. There are also a few small chapters pertaining to Ariana's courtship of Vlad. I have no idea how Olak came to witness the things that he wrote, but I think that you will find it very interesting."

Olak, Draco, and Christoff

"Your work was bold," Darik said with a hearty laugh, "and commendable, a brewmaster's challenge of all things! After a short break, you must depart for Arendal. The three of you must locate and capture a princess of the Druids."

"I have never been to the new continent," Christoff said, "but I need to know for what cause do we do this?"

"The princess is not to be harmed I assure you. She is the Halfar love of the acolyte named Leander. He wields an ancient sword of power that we require to ensure the success of our coming campaign."

"Hostage taking is more along the lines of a common burglar," Christoff said. "I really don't have the taste for it. I can recommend several thieves who do proficient work."

"That, I am afraid, is impossible. Vlad insisted that it be your team. No other souls can know of these events."

"I see, so there is in fact, no other option than for me to comply."

"You will, of course, be rewarded with whatever reasonable demands that you may have."

"My only demand is this: when the time comes, you allow me into your group. I tire of having to walk the realm in disguise. I am wanted in every major city, with a bounty on my head in the thousands."

"You are already in, Christoff," Darik said, "but until we are certain that our secrets will remain between us, then we must keep some things on a need-to-know basis."

"Well, since Apex and I have no choice, and seeing as how we would both like to keep our heads, when, where, and how do we get there?"

"You may rest the night and prepare. At dawn, you and Apex will meet Olak and Draco in the secret chamber. We will discuss the mission there. In the meantime, Ariana will show you to your quarters."

The Dark Priestess had been reading in a small study at the rear of Darik's laboratory. When she appeared, Christoff was stunned. She was everything that he thought that he had ever wanted in a woman. She was exquisitely fit, hauntingly beautiful, tall and obviously evil. To say that he was completely smitten would have been the understatement of the century. "My lady," was all that he managed to say before executing a perfect court bow.

"Christoff," she purred, "I have heard a lot about you. "You have had a great many exploits for a short-lived Human."

"I have only just begun."

"We'll see, Madam Minx," she jested, "but I must admit that you are far more handsome without the dress."

"You wound me, my lady."

"Oh hush, tonight you shall rest in luxury. If you desire a woman, or a man, one will be provided for you."

Christoff knelt before her in a knight's fashion. "Only if there is another lady in the fortress who compares to you."

"That," Ariana hissed, "is impossible! But," she said, softening, "some of the concubines are attractive after a fashion."

"Well then, my lady, I would only be content with your company."

"Fool! You would die before your hands ever touched my flesh."

"Forgive me," he said. "I meant no harm, perhaps only the pleasure of your company over dinner."

"You walk a dangerous path, Christoff, but I accept, if only to see whether or not you survive the encounter."

In the Spider's Web

Christoff's room was luxurious. The finest furnishings, tapestries, and hand-woven rugs were all well coordinated in a relaxing and casually pleasing fashion. A well-supplied bathing room was located across from his apartment in the nearby hall, complete with hot water, a steam room, and numerous slaves to bring fresh water, towels, and a myriad of other pleasures. Laid out on the bed for him were an exquisite tunic of the finest silk, complete with new pants and undergarments. Tall boots made of some serpent's skin stood on the floor beside it as if their owner was soon to return. Much to his surprise, everything fit perfectly! How they had managed to guess his measurements so exactly was a mystery, but like most things with these Dark Elves, it was a secret best left for another day.

"Quite a welcome," Apex said from the hall. "We rarely sleep in such luxury."

"Your room," Ariana said, "is at the end of the hall. You will find it to your liking. I shall return for dinner at seven, Christoff. See to it that you don't smell quite so badly when I return."

Her insult smote him speechless. In his younger years, he might have killed because of such disrespect, but it only made her more attractive than ever.

"I'll see you soon. One of my servants shall bring you the chef's menu. You may choose my dinner as well, but choose carefully." With a casual about-face, she turned and departed, leaving them alone in the hall.

"Well," Apex said, "I guess that you will be off to the bath then!"

"Quite."

"Then I shall see you at dawn. If your room is so plush, I can't wait to see what awaits me in mine!"

"Good night, Apex."

"Good night." Flying down the hall like some demonic balloon, he arrived at his door. "Hello, it is Apex. If anyone lies within, I could use some help with the door." Sounds of light footsteps on tile drifted up from under the door and then a tiny dog-like creature opened it and greeted him.

"Welcome, Master Apex! I trust that we have provided well for you." Beyond him, a fiendish harem of floating females lounged above a giant lily pad filled pool fed by waterfalls. A table was well prepared with freshly butchered meat and other revolting delicacies.

"Amazing," Apex drooled, "just like home," and if tears of joy could have come to a Floating Lord's eyes, then most surely they would have. "Dim the lights, little dog, dim the lights. There is only room enough on this lily pad for one bullfrog."

Christoff's room was everything that a king could have dreamed. Several decanters of liquor were set upon a fine crystal table. When he moved to pour himself a glass, a beautiful maid appeared as if from nowhere and asked, "What's your pleasure, my lord?"

"Whiskey," he said, "the strongest one that you have. I'll most likely be dead by morning." Before his cup had reached his lips, three more servants approached from a small antechamber.

"We have prepared a bath for you," the lead servant said.

"Forgive my foulness," he said, "but it has been a long road."

"Nonsense, my lord," she replied, "we are here to serve. We have been commanded to treat you like a king."

"Well then," he replied, raising one eyebrow, "who am I to argue?" Emptying his glass, he surrendered to their whims. He was stripped and robed in moments. They then led him to the exotic bath. Their attentiveness made him feel awkward and vulnerable like never before. He was fully expecting that at any time, they would loop a garrote around his neck. Try as he might, he could not shake the thought because he had known too many operatives who would consider such assassinations to be the perfect death. Here, in this place, for the first time in his life, he was no longer in control of his destiny. When he finally gave up and accepted his demise, the experience was not altogether bad. Surprisingly, his death never came, and neither was his drink poisoned. Things here were very strange indeed.

Seven o'clock and he was dressed in his finery and ready in his room. Sitting at a finely prepared table, a new set of servants had arrived to wait upon him. The chef's menu was extensive, and he had taken the liberty of ordering the baked cod with crème sauce for himself and the fillet of mammoth for his quest. He had no way of knowing if his choices were right or wrong, and the servants were reluctant to guide him.

"My lady," he said, rising as Ariana entered, "you look lovely this evening."

"Of course I do, you fool," she said. "At least I see that you know how to prepare a table."

"Please do sit down," he said while pulling her chair out for her.

"I do believe that I will. Ah, fillet of mammoth, I see. Perhaps you think that I am a pig with a gluttonous appetite?"

"Certainly not!" Christoff said, a bit flustered. "If it pleases you, you may have my cod, or we can place another order."

"On the contrary, you silly man, you have somehow passed the first test. Fillet of mammoth is one of my favorites."

His face went from confused and nervous to a bit more relaxed. This woman was complicated.

"Tell me, Christoff, how many men have you killed?"

"Well," he said, quite taken aback at such a question over dinner, "I never kept track."

"You cannot lie to me. I assure you that Lothdea makes every deceit known to me."

"Very well," he said, "I have killed seven hundred and thirty-seven assorted souls."

"That is quite an accomplishment for such a young man. I see now why Vlad has chosen you."

"I am no mere murderer. Most of the men that I killed were bad enough to deserve it."

"A noble assassin?" she said. "I have never heard of one before."

"What game are you really playing, my lady?"

"In time, Christoff. For now, let us just enjoy dinner. Ala, play us some music."

The servant, proved to be a talented harpist, and her seductive melodies continued throughout their date.

"Where do you hail from?"

"Well, my lady—"

"You may call me Ariana in private."

"If you insist."

"I do."

"Well then, I most recently arrived here from Linea."

"No, no, you silly little man, what I wish to know is where you were born. What place do you call home?"

"I see. Well, Ariana, I don't think that you would find that at all interesting."

"On the contrary, I think that I will find it very interesting."

"Well then, if you must know, I was the son of a harlot, born in a cheap brothel in the port city of Linea."

"And your mother, what became of her?"

"She was murdered by a drunken pirate named Thrace Gilgilhad, 'the Wooden Shoe.' He is known as the Plague of the South Sea."

"Why do they call him 'the Wooden Shoe'?"

"He lost all the toes on his right foot in the jaws of a giant clam while diving for pearls."

"So you must wish him dead then."

"One day, he will die by my hand, but he is a difficult man to catch. Last that I heard of him, he was hiding out on the island of Sissily."

"Was the death of your mother the reason that you became a hired killer?"

"Not at all, the ladies of the brothel sheltered me from the truth of her death until I was ten, and by then, I had learned to love them all as my mother."

"Why then would you choose such a profession?"

"One day, when I was a young man, I watched as an innocent man was publicly tortured and hung by a corrupt governor. I realized then that I had found my calling."

"So you see your work as a public service?"

"Of course," Christoff said, "which is why I always wish to know what causes I work for. Money is only the smallest motivation, and that is why these latest missions pain me so. The true purpose is hidden from me, and I wonder if the cause is a just one."

"Interesting," Ariana said, "because the Queen would also very much like to know the answer to that very question."

"We'll have to wait and see." Her words spoke volumes. Now he knew that she was plotting to use him as a pawn. Ariana just kept getting more beautiful.

"I am glad that we had this little chat. Now let us just enjoy the music and this excellent meal."

"Quite, my lady."

"Ariana."

"Of course," Christoff answered, "and shall I tell you how I came to be friends with Apex, the Floating Lord?"

"Oh, please do."

"Well, I had just finished a job in the slums of Dracmar when I came to be detained by the local constabulary. Apex, the poor soul, was being mercilessly tortured in a tiny cell, within which he couldn't even hover."

"That's terrible!"

"And how he suffered! You can then imagine how once I had incapacitated my captors, I just had to set him free."

"Your mercy knows no bounds."

"Oh, and that's not even the half of it."

"I am completely riveted. Please do continue."

Their meals and the night were pleasant. Ala's music and Christoff's story did indeed get even better.

Secret Chambers, Secret Plans

Dawn arrived far too soon, and Christoff awoke from bed with no memory of when he had actually retired. It was a mystery that he was quite uncertain about, even nervous, and these were feelings usually foreign to him. Sliding his feet over the edge of the bed, he sat up. He rubbed the sleep from his eyes and reached for his pants.

"How was your night, master?" Apex asked.

He nearly died from fright. "How long have you been here?"

The beast floated above the foot of his bed, drooling. "A few hours," Apex said with a toothy grin. "I didn't want to wake you. So how was your night?"

"Mysterious, wonderful!"

"Mine was quite mundane," Apex said while his master dressed, "but relaxing to be sure." There was no bashfulness between them, for after all, they shared no common anatomy. "It made me rather homesick. The ladies in my room had no knowledge of Tyrannia, as they were all born from eggs sold on the black market. Alas, their mother must have been killed in their collection."

"How horrible!"

"Such atrocities are rare, but they are the makings of our nightmares."

"Let us hope that someday they may return home."

"It is a long journey," Apex said, "one that I know I would never survive alone."

"I will help you if I can, whenever you wish to leave."

"My debt to you in not yet repaid, master."

"On the contrary," Christoff said as he pulled on his boots, "you were free from the moment we first met. I keep no slaves."

"That is why I remain. You are my friend, and one day soon, you will truly need me." At that moment, there was a crisp knock on the door. Apex opened it with his telekinetic eye.

"Masters," the little dog Goblin said, "the Necromancer says that it's time."

"Ready," Christoff said while buckling his sword belt and shouldering his rucksack. "We were expecting you."

"Right this way, masters."

Apex floated close behind the slave, bouncing in a blissful, bubbly fashion that Christoff found both amusing and annoying simultaneously. Pacing a step or two behind them, a thousand fears consumed his thoughts as he tried to piece together what he had learned.

LOTHDEA

Ariana knelt beneath the altar of her beloved goddess. She had lived most of her life beneath the watchful eyes of the coven. They controlled everything—religion, politics, and other darker things. Nevertheless, the Coven and their leader, the Queen, were worried. Their conquest of the surface world had exposed their people to many new thoughts and dangerous ideals, and some Dockalfar, were even rumored to worship other gods! Death or worse awaited such blasphemers, but the trend seemed to be spreading. Perhaps the sun, for eons lost to the Dockalfar, was now somehow poisoning the hearts of their people. There were other rumors even more troubling, stories of secret societies and covert agendas. Lothdea believed that it was just such a plot that Vlad and his accomplices were perpetrating.

It was Ariana's goddess-given duty to uncover their secrets and expose them as traitors. She had already learned enough to condemn them, and yet she hesitated, her heart filled with turmoil. Living among them, she had come to respect them, and an unfamiliar feeling had entered her heart.

She prayed but spoke not a word.

Parliament

Parliament had convened. Military leaders and civilian consuls had all gathered for their annual meeting to discuss the laws and enact new policies. They convened in the grand meeting hall, the centermost room, in the mightiest fortress in Dragonia called the Castle of Lords. Located on an expansive cliff-faced hilltop, it overlooked the Great Lake Farad and protected Farad Hoth, the capital city. Farad Hoth was home to countless wonders, including Hoth, Lothdea's grand cathedral, and the Colosseum.

The Castle of Lords housed a large garrison of troops and provided a safe meeting place for Dragonia's leaders. It also housed a small arena. Sometimes, entertainers performed before the governors, and at other times, they held high-profile trials of law. Occasionally, it was also a place of public execution. This meeting was special because the High Priestess of Lothdea, Queen Aphra, was presiding.

"My people," she said, "I thank you all for coming here this day. Your patriotism and loyalty do you great credit." Her voice was raspy with age but powerful, and none in the crowd dared to give her less than their complete attention.

"Long did we languish in Underearth, banished from our rightful lands by the Liosalfar. They said that our goddess is evil and theirs good, but how can anyone judge the beliefs of another? Without Lothdea, how could we have survived for three thousand years without the sun? Of course, we could not, for without her light to warm and protect us from the beasts of the underworld, we would surely have perished. I then ask you, how could such a nurturing god be evil? At times our survival required sacrifice and tough decisions. Sometimes that meant war, and in these wars, we were always alone, until now. Now Dragonia is a mighty empire, and where once we found enemies, now we stand together as allies! Nevertheless, we cannot rest, for there are still many forces that plot against us. There are rumors that there are those among us who have come to seek out their own private agendas, and some have even sought other gods! How is this possible? Is not the love of Lothdea enough to guide their spirits and fill their hearts? Is not Dragonia cause enough to fight for? I say that these perpetrators are greater enemies than our foes across the sea. Their treason seeks to undo the structure and beliefs of the empire. We will apprehend them and try them as criminals! There is no terrorism greater than that which comes from within. I ask you all to join me in this fight! We must come together and win this holy war!

"My people, fellow Dragonians, we have fought together. We have made peace together. Now our nation extends to two continents and beyond. Let us rise together once again and stretch our swords across the sea. Let us smite the ones that oppose us for the last time!"

"All hail the Queen!" one member of the Parliament cried out.

Ardor filled their hearts. "All hail the Queen!" They cheered, although there was one among them who did not mean it.

One member of the audience, Anselm Der'Marshance, smiled a particular kind of smile. He saw the effect her speech had on his opponent, and he was happy indeed. With a few strategic actions of his own, he would witness the end of his bitter rival. His own campaign on the Shattered Continent was far from over, but island by island, he was stretching the arms of Dragonia's military might with an iron fist. It had earned him the name "the Silent Sword" among his enemies. Nevertheless, he had not forgotten his grudge against the academy's first chosen.

There was then some commotion to the right of the central stage. Guards dragged two men out of the lower dungeons in chains. Bloodied by the bite of many lashes, they limped and hobbled in obvious agony.

"Kneel before your Queen!" their guard ordered.

"Never!" one of them shouted, but a sudden swift blow across his shins brought him to his knees.

"Ranvarwen J'Throi!" the Queen said. "You and your accomplice have been charged with high treason! You have admitted to the worship of other gods."

"All hail the rise of Correleus!"

The guard struck him a hard blow across his face with cat-o'-nine-tails, shattering his right eye and cleaving his nose in two.

"Blasphemer!" she screeched. "From this day forward, no Dragonian will utter his name! The penalty is Soul Death!"

The Parliament was hushed, shocked into silence by the name of Lothdea's most hated adversary since the dawn of time. He ruled the day and she the night. He banished them into Underearth for three thousand years.

"Kill him!" urged a southern consul.

"Death, death, death!" chanted the assembly.

"We will give them to Arachnidon!" the Queen commanded. "He shall decide their fate." Standing before them, she raised her hand and muttered a few words. A portal opened in the floor of the arena. In size, it was over fifty feet across, filled with dark swirling mists and foul bubbling vapors. Where the floor had been was now a portal to another realm, and what came forth filled every heart in that chamber with dread. The beast was huge, bloated, and black. Its eyes alone were over ten feet across, and only its head and forelegs could fit through the portal. Ranvarwen's guard retreated in horror, his prisoners too badly beaten to go anywhere.

"Arachnidon," the Queen said, "you have heard the charges. You must decide the penalty."

In an instant, it held the two screaming traitors beneath its gigantic fangs and then slid back from whence it came. The portal closed, and only silence and the arena floor remained where terror incarnate had just been.

"God shall punish the unfaithful!" shouted a true follower in the crowd.

"God shall punish the unfaithful!" shouted the assembly.

"Remain true to your faith," the Queen said, "and the Goddess will reward us with victory upon victory until all of Tempus is one mighty Dragonia, and only then will our people be free!"

"All hail the Queen!"

"Now go forth, my children. Spread the word and faith in your country and your god, for only two continents remain unconquered. Very soon, we shall renew our war upon them."

"For the might of Dragonia!" her great general Yu-wen Kwan said.

"For the might of Dragonia!" The hall was on its feet, both Dark Elf and Human allies alike. Queen Aphra had once again proven her conviction, and they were all warriors born. A world without battle and the sacrifices of war was unknown to them, and the Queen and the Goddess wanted to keep it that way.

The Tower of Lycurgus

"I need a special creature," Vlad said, "one far more terrible than any that you have thus far conceived of."

"What must this creature be able to do?"

"The time will soon arrive when we must begin our assault on Safehaven. The west passage through the Gnoll Hills is guarded by a mighty high-walled fortress at Harg Pass."

"I have seen it."

"These creatures must have the strength of an elephant, with size to match, and most importantly, they must be terrible to behold. They should inspire fear, be capable of carnage, and be quick thinking in the midst of battle."

"What of the mammoths of the Northern Reaches? Your Orcs have learned to tame them."

"They are prone to turn upon their masters when injured. No, I seek a new monster, completely reliable, without any motivation beyond the service to its masters. We need something new to lead our armies to victory."

"I will do as you command."

"Work swiftly, Lycurgus, and in secret. We haven't much time."

"I will contact you when I have created my models."

"Good luck, Lycurgus, and good day."

"Good day, Commander," he said, but Vlad had already disappeared.

"Very disconcerting that. Now where do I begin?" Looking out of his tower window, he spied a small spider on the window ledge. It was black and fuzzy, compact, and ready to spring. "Yes, yes, my friend, you might be just the thing that I need." Reaching for his glass, he emptied it. His laughter echoed from his high tower and out across the barren forest around him.

Ariana and the Queen

Queen Aphra had come for a visit. Meditating in the Temple of Drakon Mur'-Falor, they prayed, and they talked.

"What have you learned about our ambitious male and his friends?"

"He seeks a magic weapon that he believes will bring Dragonia ultimate victory."

"His heart is no longer with Lothdea," the Queen said. "He pursues his own private agenda."

"He has never said as much."

"You must seduce him and bring him into your confidence. Only then will we know if his secrets are acts of heroism or treason."

"It will be difficult," Ariana said. "His heart is only for an Elf slave named Efmiel."

"Then I will arrange for her swift demise."

"That would only reveal our suspicions to him, and then our hand would be forced to act against him."

"We should plan an accident to remove her then, something unforeseeable and tragic," the Queen mused, "or an illness, regrettably untreatable, to remove his love from him forever."

"He would still know. He has many spies collecting information for him."

"Then what would you suggest?"

"A love potion."

"Yes, yes! Do it at once, and when we are sure that Aklon's son is a traitor, we will place him on trial before the nation and execute him."

"Yes, my Queen," she said with a bow, but even she, evil as most women could never even aspire to be, had mixed feelings. Her face revealed nothing, however. Years of captivity at the hands of the Coven had taught her to carry an unreadable face. It was simply a matter of survival.

"Do not fail us, my daughter."

"I will not fail, Revered Mother."

Within her quarters, she possessed each of the natural and mystical ingredients that she would need to construct a love potion that no mortal could resist. She would combine the essence of a virgin's sigh, the captured wink of a Siren, a cat's purr, and a drop of dragon's lust with honey, red wine, and spices to create the ultimate love potion. A single drop of her own blood, mixed with its magic, would force the drinker to fall in love with her and her alone, forever. She was fast beginning to like the idea, and once Vlad was a slave to his love, Efmiel would become hers to enslave. Things were beginning to look up.

LOTHDEA AND THE QUEEN

Queen Aphra returned to Hoth swiftly. Arriving in the grand cathedral by way of divine magic, servants of the Coven rushed to fulfill her every whim.

"Be gone," she commanded, "empty the hall!"

Wasting no time, she communed with the Goddess. Kneeling before a perfectly carved idol, both dark and beautiful, she prayed.

"We must be very careful of the son of Aklon," the Goddess said. "He has become powerful and ambitious beyond his years."

"It is in the blood of their family. Their clan has always been a challenge to me. Physical gifts and strong minds have always led them away from the true path."

"We should just kill him and be done with his bloodline forever."

"No," the Goddess said, "he still has a role to play in the prophecy. Without his actions, our ultimate power will never come to be. Watch him and learn, my child, so that when the time is right, we can cast him down and take back what is rightfully mine!"

"It shall be as you desire," the Queen said.

"My blessings upon you," Lothdea said. "Continue to teach our children my ways and our future will be assured. Summon me when you must." The idol fell silent, once again only a statue.

She did her penance, recited the Tenets of Lothdea, made her offering of blood, and left. She could feel the ever-present power of divine magic within her. The Goddess was with her still, and she was perhaps the most powerful priestess that had ever lived. She would ensure that the Warrior Mage son of Aklon would never challenge her supremacy.

Vlad and His Court

"Commander Vlad, Commander Vlad!" an annoying little wretch of a Goblin badgered him. "The priestess has invited you to dinner!"

"That is interesting news. I doubt that I'll have time this evening."

"The priestess said that you would refuse, but she insists and requires your attendance."

"Perhaps someone should remind her that I am in command of this garrison, not her."

"She also said to give you this," the Goblin said, holding out a lock of satin-black hair.

He accepted the gift with barely disguised astonishment. He was shocked, dumbfounded; for Ariana to offer so dangerous of a part of herself was unbelievable. The lock of hair left her vulnerable to magical attacks, spells of control, love, even curses. Perhaps it was not her hair, but somehow, he knew that it was. At the least, it was an invitation to her bedchamber, even an admission of love, but that seemed impossible for a woman in her position. All these thoughts both intrigued him and made him as suspicious as hell. "Very well, little butler, what time will dinner be served?"

"Seven o'clock, master," he answered, "in the priestess's chambers."

"Tell her that I will be honored to attend."

"Right away, master!"

A Dinner Wish

Her servants had done an excellent job at preparing her table. They always did, especially considering that the least of her punishments usually involved cleaning toilets used by the Orcs, or endless duty in the oppressively hot fortress kitchen. The worst of her vengeances were truly unmentionable and sometimes ended in someone's death. Nevertheless, she was generally fair, even if only in an evil and especially ruthless way.

This night was going to be special. If possible, she was going to tell Vlad of her intentions, but that was all up to him. Her previous dinner with Christoff had gone quite well, but if she gave herself to him, it would only be to cement his use to her as a tool and nothing more. She found him interesting, but he lacked the layers of their commander, and he was, of course, only Human. She hoped that Vlad would not turn out to be a traitor. He was very powerful, capable of attaining the rank of general, at the least, and maybe even more. His power was what the Queen feared the most. Coupled with his obvious ambition and the unswerving loyalty of his followers, he was a threat indeed. If he were not careful, he would find himself imprisoned, tortured, and finally sacrificed to the Great Spider. Even worse, she would likely be the one asked to apprehend him.

Vlad was the first male that she ever truly wanted, and the thought of it unbalanced her. She was used to taking a mate whenever the urge occurred to her and then discarding them as soon as they were no longer useful. She really had no idea of how to handle him.

"Anna Su," she said to her lead servant, "I do not wish for my guest to want for anything. Wait on him in the most attentive way."

"Yes, my lady," she said, "the chef has prepared you a fine meal."

Footsteps, fast and nervous, echoed in the hall outside. "Knock, knock."

"See who it is, Flavius," Anna Su said. "The lady does not wish to make Master Vlad wait."

"Yes, Miss Anna Su," the guard said. Dressed in light armor and armed with a spear and short sword, he moved like a man who knew how to wield them. "It is the butler, miss."

"Send him in."

"Miss Anna Su," the well-dressed little Goblin said, "Master Vlad said that he will be here precisely at seven."

"Thank you, Miko," Anna Su said. "We will call you if we need you. You are dismissed."

"Oh, thank you, Miss Anna Su," the little runt said, entirely unsure of what to do with himself next.

"Why don't you go down to the mess hall and get some dinner?"

"Yes, yes, Miss Anna Su, that sounds good, yes, yes," and off he went, much to the relief of all concerned.

Confident footsteps and a second knock came soon after, as sharp and crisp as it was solitary and alone.

"See who it is, Master Guardsman."

"It is the commander, my lady."

"Welcome him in at once." The door opened, and there he stood. He was not dressed in the hide and adamant of a Warrior Mage, but rather more simply, in comfortable dinner clothes. He wore black loose-fitting pants and a fine midnight blue silk shirt cut square and sharp without excess. His boots were all-black dragon hide and polished to a high degree. His face and hair were well groomed and clean.

"Right this way, Commander," Anna Su said. "We have prepared a fine dinner for you."

"I am sure that everything will be excellent," Vlad said. "I'm starved."

"The priestess Ariana, sir," she introduced, directing him to the table with a gentle wave.

"Thank you, Anna Su," he said, but the maid had no idea why or how the captain even knew her name. She blushed readily at his acknowledgment and then tried quickly to recover. She was certain that the lady would punish her mercilessly for it.

"Slave," Ariana said with a tone full of horrid implications, "serve Master Vlad some wine."

"We have bottles of all of the house wines, sir, including Hoth Vineyards 1997. The chef recommended it with the fillet of wild boar."

"That will be fine, thank you."

Pouring his glass, she took care to cast her eyes downward, for she desperately feared the wrath of her mistress.

"Have the waiter bring us the first course, slave, and be quick about it!"

"Yes, my lady."

"Oh," Vlad said, "don't blame her, Ariana. I made a point long ago to know the names of every subject within the fortress, be they lord or slave. Each member of our nation has value."

"Nonsense," she said, "she is my slave and nothing more. Her feelings are meaningless."

Meeting her comments with a raised eyebrow, he sipped his wine. "An excellent year. It is neither bitter nor dry!"

"It is adequate," Ariana said, "but I have my doubts that it is authentic Hoth 1997."

"It doesn't matter. It is a blessing from God."

"You mean the Goddess."

"Of course," Vlad said, swirling his glass, "my lady," but she clearly had her doubts. He felt no need to read her thoughts. Her intentions were obvious.

"You must know why I invited you here."

"I think that you have many reasons, Ariana, but first, I must return your gift. Just know that I am honored."

"You would refuse my gift?" she said, not knowing whether she should feel relieved or insulted.

"Your gift is the most selfless thing that I have ever seen you offer. It gives me hope that we may one day be united. I want you to know that I will only have you by your free will alone and not because I have ensorcelled you."

"You know that I have always desired our union. Together, we can rise to new heights in the empire."

"How can you be sure that that is enough? A wave of vertigo suddenly overcame him; he was dazed for a moment, confused. When he recovered, Ariana was even more beautiful than before, if that was even possible. She was desperately beautiful, gorgeous, and alluring beyond measure. He tried to resist his welling passion, but it was impossible.

"Bring dinner to my private chambers in one hour, Anna Su," she said. "Vlad and I want to be alone for a while."

"As you wish," Anna Su said with a formal bow, "my lady."

"Knock three times when the hour has passed," Ariana said. "If we are ready, I shall call for dinner."

"Of course, my lady."

"Come with me, my dear," she said. "I shall show you love as no other women ever could."

His barriers were broken. His passion was part real and part potion. He was a slave to his heart's desire. Perhaps he had wanted this all along.

Their passion was the wild union of young lovers, both equally willing and mutually committed.

Ariana knew that her spell had taken hold, but the power of it surprised her. It could only be due to his real desires for her, a passion that had not resisted her magic but welcomed it. She would attempt to uncover his secrets only when she was certain that he was hers and hers alone. In time, he would tell her of his own accord. She prayed that he would say the right words, but for the moment, his love was enough. Her spell would appease the Queen and increase her favor with the Goddess.

Anna Su knocked thrice.

"We'll take dinner now, Anna Su," Ariana said. "I am very pleased with your service this evening. Leave the trays and then you may retire for the evening."

"Thank you, my lady," she answered, hoping that somehow she had avoided punishment. Leaving her chambers, she banished such hopes. She knew the priestess all too well. Commander Vlad had merely granted her a brief reprieve. She would almost certainly be cleaning the Orcs' latrine at dawn. Trying not to think about it, she returned to her small room next to the kitchens and prayed to the Goddess for mercy.

Anna Su's Punishment

Dawn arrived unceremoniously. The castle's head chef, Thrace Thialfad, was knocking hard upon her bedroom door. "Lady Anna Su," he said, "I have been informed that you are to replace the four dishwashers this day. Your duties shall begin immediately and end at midnight."

"Please allow me a few minutes to dress, sir."

"Fear not, my lady," he said. "I shall see to it that your duties appear far more dismal than they shall actually be."

Smiling, she put on her tattered work dress and pulled on her tall riding boots. Tying her hair back in a tight braid, she was soon ready for the muck-encrusted floor of the castle kitchen. She had received the same punishment at least a hundred times before. Lifting the latch, she opened her door and stepped out into the short hallway between her room and the kitchen store rooms. Closing her door, she turned and walked past an assortment of hanging beasts and the infant white dragon that kept the room eternally cold. Stopping to pet him briefly atop of his four-foot skull, she said, "Good work, Frosty! I think that it's even colder in here than usual."

Perking up for a minute, he smiled as only dragons can, before promptly falling back to sleep, which is what baby dragons do most of the time.

Opening up the swinging doors to the kitchen was a steamy affair, from the freezer into the heat of the castle ovens. Mr. Thialfad was there, directing his team of ten chefs, fourteen assistants, and four Goblin dishwashers newly appointed to prep cooks. He cast a knowing glance at her before directing his gaze to the dish room, a convoluted maze of pots, pans, basins, and racks crammed into a red-tiled room in the back. Making her way there resolutely, she discovered that the sinks were nearly empty, the pots hanging clean, and the dishes shelved. Thialfad risked a great deal in helping her, but rather than bring unnecessary attention to it, she began to work, knowing that she and Thialfad had come to an understanding. He was nearly untouchable as the castle chef, for even the most evil of the pyramid's inhabitants had to eat, and an angry chef was dangerous indeed. Lucky for her, she had found friends in strange places.

She was herself Dockalfar, but her parents were commoners, poor and without influence. Hoping to avoid the curse of poverty and constant hunger, they sold her into slavery at the age of ten. Heartbroken and abandoned, she went to work for the priestess. She was kind to her at first, but as the years wore on, Ariana's evil ambitions grew, and with it, her power. Despite the fact, that Anna Su had passed the age of her contract of slavery, the priestess refused to free her. She said that her service was too important. Instead, she now received a paltry salary, and room and board as per Dragonian National Law. Freedom, it seemed, would be forever beyond her grasp. If only a mighty warrior would someday free her from bondage, or perhaps purchase her from her mistress, if only, but for now, there was a new pile of breakfast dishes to wash.

THE LOVE POTION

The next morning Vlad walked through the halls of the fortress with the same giddy emotions as a child with a new toy. He could not remember the last time that his spirits had soared so high from love; nor could he remember any of his former loves. It seemed strange to him, but only for a moment. He was too happy in love, too filled with lustful longing for the priestess of his desires,

"Ariana," his mind chimed, so sensuous, inviting, and wonderful. Her devious side and evil machinations were merely a facade, protecting her gentle spirit from those around her. It was just her means to an end and nothing more.

His slave, Efmiel, had acted strangely in his chambers. Why she had expected him to bed her eluded him. She said that she was his personal assistant, but he could not seem to remember anything about her before that day. No woman besides Ariana mattered to him. There never was another woman. Surely, he was a little tired this morning; nevertheless, work beckoned. Ariana had informed him that his latest orders had arrived from the Queen. He was anxious to see how her plans would fit into his own.

The letter awaited him atop of the desk of his first lieutenant. When he arrived in the Necromancer's laboratory, he was surprised to find it unoccupied; the letter, however, was there. It was stamped "Top Secret." His name and garrison appeared in the destination space, and the melted wax seal of the Queen's signet ring protected its contents. Opening the envelope with Darik's skull-handled letter opener, he dared not imagine where the bone-knife attached to it had come from. He removed the parchment.

To: Commander Vlad Leu Sherroan
From: The Queen and Parliament

Today marks a new road to victory for the Empire. I addressed the people and sent criers out far and wide with the news of war. The time has come to defeat the infidels of Fermenor, to drive them to surrender and subjugate them. With the new harbor that you pioneered at the Bay of Cod, we have a new and secure landing from which to wage our wars in the North. The war lords of Fermenor no longer have a monopoly on safe harbors. We now have a port from which we will land our armies. The bay is only open during the heat of summer, but through it, we will march with our allies and crush the forces of Lord Cherek. Once we destroy his petty kingdom, we will take the Harbor of Khan for ourselves, and from there we will invade and conquer all of Fermenor.

Your commendable actions have brought honor and glory to the Empire, and because of this, Parliament and I have decided to place you in command of the armies of the North. Organize them as quickly as possible, for it is your appointed task to conquer Safehaven and defeat their king. The following letter of promotion is your official copy of advancement. I shall contact you soon to review your progress. War shall commence once the ocean lanes are again clear. In July, we shall unveil our ultimate might!

Farewell, Commander!

Queen Aphra Der' Lachalet
High Priestess of Dragonia

Tucked behind the letter was a second document. It was affixed with the Parliamentary seal, the official stamped image of a standing dragon clutching a sword between its hind legs. He read it immediately.

> To all who bear witness to this document
> The Parliament of Dragonia presents:
>
> It is with great honor that we, the combined Leaders of Parliament, for recognition of his exceptional service, do hereby promote Captain and Commander Vlad Leu Sherroan, to the rank of general of the armies of the North and supreme commander of Dragonian forces in the Northern Reaches Campaign. All commensurate rights and responsibilities are hereby granted to him. This promotion is henceforth proper and valid by Parliamentary Decree, revocable only by a lawful hearing and majority vote by Parliament. The promoted hereby agrees to uphold the tenets of the Dragonian Constitution, respect its laws and its people, and act in defense of the Dragonian Empire.
>
> Signed, (By Parliament: a hundred signatures do hereafter follow.)

Interesting, Vlad thought to himself, for he was neither surprised, nor overwhelmed by the news. He had considered the eventuality, even expected it, but he knew that the order had arrived too soon. They had secured many allies and defeated many enemies in the region, but there were still years of preparation needed before a full-scale invasion could possibly succeed. Surely, the Queen and the

Goddess were aware of that. There was only one possible reason for the suddenness of it all. They knew his secret. These new orders were a test, a handicap, the many-faceted gem that his father had prepared him for. It was possible that they knew of the relic. He knew that the Duaredheim Staff was beyond even the gods; it was Universal Law, the fabric of existence in material form. Its power was too great for any single being to wield, but he only wanted a fraction of it. A tiny portion would be enough to free his people from slavery. His father's dream was his dream, and the ultimate goal of his Drakkar Noire.

The Queen hoped that this new task would thwart his own personal ambitions and reveal him as a traitor to the Empire. It would take a Master of Plans within Plans to achieve success. Failure meant death. He would not fail himself, his father, or his men.

EFMIEL

She spent the morning cleaning the room of her master. For the first time in over a year, he did not greet her with a gentle touch upon her shoulder; nor had he been interested in making love. It seemed like he barely even knew her, as if she was merely a slave. If she could not bring him back to his senses, then she would soon be in grave danger. Despised for her light skin, only Vlad's commanding presence had kept her from rape, torture, or worse since her capture. What had happened to him? She wondered, and then it hit her. He was under a witch's spell, and it was easy for her to guess which one.

She had vowed to see him dead, but in time, she had come to know a side of Vlad that few people had ever seen. He was an idealist, a revolutionary, influenced by his past but poised to make a new future for his people. Somehow, despite her hatred, she had come to love him.

General Vlad Leu Sherroan

His mind spun with a million thoughts. There were so many new factors affecting his plans that it was difficult even for him to sort through them all. He considered many new courses of action, weighing the probabilities of success of each of them. He even considered revealing his secret plans to Ariana. In so doing, the information was certain to reach the Queen and the Goddess and would soon force their hand. Most likely, they would attempt to assassinate him in secrecy, probably blaming the act on agents of Fermenor or the like. He quickly decided on another more subtle approach to the problem.

It was time to call a meeting of the Nine. It would have to include Ariana, his future bride. The more that he thought about it, the more certain he was that he had to put her loyalties to the test. If she loved the Queen and Goddess more than she loved him, then she would quickly betray him. It would be a test then, a test of their love, or death. He was ruthless, but he was no murderer. His love was far too great to consider it. His will was as strong as any potion. He would find a way for them all to survive, and to win.

Entering the fortress from the lower passages, he stopped to inspect this soldier or that, often asking simple questions such as, "How fares your family, Sergeant?" or commenting upon the care of their uniform. Most often, the answers that he would get were, "Yes, sir, right away sir! Thank you, sir," and the like, and twice, lesser-ranking soldiers called him general, although he still wore captain's bars upon his epaulette. He wondered how the fortress knew of his promotion before he did. He could only guess who had spread the word. Apparently, *top secret* no longer meant what it used to. He found Darik assisting Monica with a company of Orcs.

The Orcs were adapting to military tactics even better than he had expected. Their natural instincts for war and human intelligence made them excellent candidates for training.

"Good day, Monica, Darik," he greeted.

"Good morning, General!"

"I see that your work is paying off handsomely, Lieutenant."

"Thank you, sir," Monica said, "this is the best company in the battalion."

"We must accelerate their training. The Queen has ordered our full-scale assault to begin after the spring thaw. Perhaps we can adapt this company for training, Lieutenant, and spread their new skills throughout the division."

"It seems a little premature, General."

"It is a test," Vlad said, "of our loyalty and our ability. I am calling for a meeting of the Nine this very night."

"Shall I send out word?" Darik asked.

"No, I shall inform everyone myself. We shall meet in the secret chamber. The dress will be full-combat attire. We must be ready for anything."

"Yes, General!" they answered.

"Midnight," he answered, "we meet at the highest hour. Beneath the stars our footsteps shall either step forward or turn back. Be prepared, my officers!"

Saluting, they parted company.

Darik and Monika exchanged troubled looks. In the meantime, there was training to do. The Orcs were growing impatient.

"Pair off!" Monica ordered. "We shall review the unarmed combat drills that we learned last week. If your techniques are satisfactory, I will show you more. Lieutenant Darik, will you assist me?"

"Of course!" he answered. And they filled the afternoon with sweat and the determination of a hundred Orcs.

The Highest Hour

The witching hour came, and the Nine assembled. Hunters of the night in full battle dress, warriors so well trained that no hundred men could stand against them upon a field of their choosing. Nevertheless, as great as they were, and as resourceful, they were not invincible. They were, however, soldiers and countrymen joined in purpose.

Within the secret hall, they were safe from spying eyes, perhaps not from those of the gods but certainly from those born of magic and the material. It was here, in the bowels of the fortress, that Vlad chose to play his hand, in effect, to call the bluff of his true love, the Queen, and the Goddess.

"The Queen has once again called for war," Vlad began. "Spring is close at hand, and our newest legions are not yet fully trained. Every one of us knows of the ancient relic that we search for. It is the most powerful device ever conceived of by the gods. With it, we can achieve victory over any enemy, but therein lies its peril, for what does the Queen want above all?"

"For Lothdea to achieve her rightful dominion," Ariana said, "as Goddess of the Elven race."

"Perhaps that is her most righteous goal," Vlad said, "but here on Tempus, she wishes most to rule over all."

"She wishes for the best for all of the Dockalfar!"

"Does she offer freedom?" Vlad asked. "The right to live and walk and breathe wherever we desire, to walk in the light or in the dark?"

"Those freedoms will come with her victory."

"Is such a victory even possible?" Vlad said. "Our nation is vast, and we are a race that is slow to breed. We overextend ourselves with dubious political interests. Many of our allies would jump at the chance to usurp our rule, especially if they felt that our might was occupied by war in a foreign land."

"So you doubt that the Goddess will bring us victory?"

"In time, it is possible, but only once we have secured our position here and elsewhere across the continent."

"Your words border on blasphemy!" Ariana said, her eyes flashing. She looked around the room. Danger surrounded her, from one pair of eyes to another. "But I cannot deny your logic. Perhaps the Queen is moving too hastily."

She was many things, but she was no fool. The hour of her destiny was at hand. To label them as rebels would surely result in her immediate death, but what of her love potion? It seemed as if he was still under its influence, but something was wrong. Her hold was not irresistible. Perhaps he did not intend to kill her. Perhaps this was only a test of her loyalty. Oppose them, and she might somehow manage a quick escape and return with her Queen and Goddess beside her, but she had other doubts. Her only love was supposed to be for Lothdea, but somehow, she had fallen for Vlad and lost her divine path. She sighed then, removing her enchanted cloak and her chain-mail shirt. "I realize now that this meeting was not about the Goddess or the Queen. It was about the loyalty of this team, and of me."

Dreadful silence dealt her a heavy blow.

"All of the power that I possess is divine. I have loved the Goddess and pledged to protect her people. I swore to destroy all infidels that oppose us. The Queen sent me here to uncover your secret agenda. She believes it to be a threat to our people, and possibly to the Goddess herself. I myself signed your Declaration of Freedom, and though I did not understand the depth of it at the time, I do now. I cannot imagine that any member of the Drakkar Noire could hold any allegiances, save to their leaders, their Goddess, or their country. It is for this reason that I now ask to truly join you, not as a spy for the Queen but as an equal member of this team. When Lothdea discovers my treason, she will feed me to the Great Spider.

He will destroy my body and soul, and so I beg you to cut me down now. Slay me so that some piece of my spirit may live on. Kill me so that some part of my love may linger."

Draco drew his sword and stepped within range. Chambering a killing stroke, he awaited further orders.

"Hold!" Vlad said. "Such drastic measures will not be necessary today."

"General," Darik said, "she will not be able to hide the truth from the Queen. We shall all be lost!"

"If our quest fails," Vlad said, "then we are all doomed anyway. Without Ariana's power, our mission will surely fail. The Queen seeks to rule the world. Lothdea desires the staff above all. If we assemble it, they will try to wrest it from us. Because of this, they will not immediately act against us. Certainly, they will see through Ariana's lies as easily as one sees through an open window. Their egos will lead them to believe that they can still wield her as a pawn. They will believe that they are in control. We must remain vigilant and ever-ready, for when they finally decide to oppose us."

"It is too dangerous," Ariana said. "Better to kill me now."

"Spare me such drama," Vlad said. "You are both wise and cunning. You need not hide your relief by acting the part of the fragile flower now. Every member of this team knows you all too well."

A tiny smile began to grip the corners of her lips. The tension in the room was so overwhelming that laughter was unavoidable, and the cavern walls echoed with them for some time.

"I am glad that that business is over and done with," Draco said. "Forgive me, Priestess."

"It would have been the most merciful gift that you could give me. You may yet have to end me before this is through."

"I pray that such a time never comes, my lady."

"We are a team," Andreul said, "more now than ever. There will be no more secrets between us, and no more need for lies."

"Our survival depends on it," Olak said, "and yours as well, Ariana. We either pull together as loyal comrades, or we fall."

"From now on," Vlad said, "we travel nowhere alone. We shall pair off, so that no one's back is ever left unprotected."

"What pairs? Do we pick or just draw straws?"

"We all know that the pairings have already been chosen," Andreul said, "Olak and Draco, Dorlin and Darik, Vlad and Ariana, Shiran and Monica, and Elrick and I. We have been doing it all along without even realizing it."

"I'll be damned if she's not right," Elrick said, impressed. "We do work well together."

"The pairings are chosen then," Vlad said, "and the nine are now ten. There may be times when we must act together or in different groups, depending upon the mission at hand. We must carefully plan each step that we take in the days ahead. Ariana and I will continue to work primarily in acquisition of the staff. The remaining teams will secure the additional hostages that we need. Fulfill the Queen's orders as needed. Return to your missions and continue to relay news of your progress to Darik. May luck be with us."

"And to you, General," they answered. Continuing to plan for some time, they discussed what the future might bring.

THE DARK DWARVES

In a world where the Mountain Dwarves still prayed to gods of earth and stone and goodness, so too were there Dwarves of the darkest depths who prayed to the lords of evil and of doom. In body, they were still akin to their surface-dwelling brothers, but within, they were completely malign, their actions selfish, craving evil, twisted, ill. To trust them was to call for the Merciless One himself. They called themselves the Darg, and all who knew them felt that they were akin to the Dockalfar in their knowledge of the Underworld, but in truth, their hearts were blacker still, and always they tried to trap and victimize all who entered their domain. Despite their corrupted souls, they were not altogether unwise. They kept many treaties with the races that could do them the most harm, and in so doing their own darkness grew. Their fortresses were many, treacherous, and vile, and to one of these in particular journeyed the Master of Plans within Plans.

Dark Treaties

The world of shadow is a place of the utmost wonder and the swiftest doom. Lying between the worlds of darkness and light, it is akin to the ethers of Limbo yet apart from it. It was now the realm of Vlad Leu Sherroan, part Dockalfar, part demon lord of Shadow, and all the minions of that fell place were his to command. On this particular day, and in that timeless place, he commanded none of them, but instead he chose only to pass through his world, as infinite as the Universe or as small or grand as his will desired it to be. Riding the eerie winds of his world beneath a demon's wings, he traveled with the speed of thought to the lair of the Darg, the Dwarves of Darkness. It was time that they paid for their alliance to the Dockalfar.

GRULTHANK

The Darg ruled from high seats in many Underearth fortresses, but the greatest of them all was Grulthank. Carved from a solid vein of the blackest obsidian, it stood like a jagged pillar, centermost in their great subterranean cave, which they called Noire-Kir, which meant "black sky." The ceiling of their realm rose over five hundred feet above the tallest spires of Grulthank, and the cavern surrounding the citadel stretched some four miles away from its base in every direction. These surrounding lands were a dire mass of secret pitfalls, traps, and natural dangers that only the Darg knew. Enemy forces trying to cross its vast expanse rarely made it past the first few treacherous yards. Grulthank was the pinnacle of Darg achievement, and within its walls, they feared few mortal foes.

In his journey through the Plane of Shadow, Vlad contemplated the vast territory of the Darg, formulating the plans of action that he would need to succeed. His visit would be unannounced, for only through his unexpected arrival could he hope to survive a single-handed encounter with their chieftain. Any formal declaration of his coming would surely have led them to prepare a trap for him. His own powers, though great, were not invincible, especially in the homeland and High Fortress of the Dark Dwarves.

A'Goric

A'Goric, high chieftain of the Darg, ruled from the seat of a black diamond throne. High-backed and shallow-seated, his throne resembled their great fortress with cunning clarity. Its sharp, jagged spines surrounded the king in a chaotic hemisphere of perfection, and from his chair, he could look down upon his great audience hall. He was bald headed, and his eyes peered dark, bloodshot, and diabolical from beneath eyebrows, thick, twisted, and gray. His beard was full and unkempt, his body thick, squat, and still powerful. His armor was that of a king, ensorcelled and perfect. His justice, if one could call it that, was swift and absolute, and most often, it was fatal. His subjects would do anything in their power to avoid his most sinister wrath.

At his sides stood his two chief advisors, both of whom were sorcerers with insidious powers of magic most ill. Darg law linked them in life to their king, for if he were to fall, they would soon join him. In this manner, they were perhaps the only two beings in the realm who would not betray him. Their sorcery protected them and their king with invisible barriers, spells of detection, and terrible curses. Their powers laced the walls of Grulthank, giving it a nearly irresistible strength.

A'Goric's personal guard stood before and behind him, lining the walls of his chamber. They were dressed in plate-mail of adamant, blacker still than their fortress home. Each of them stood ever ready for battle, with short swords, spears, and blowguns with darts dipped in poison most vile. Here, upon his seat of power, he felt invincible.

It was there, at the heart of Darg power, that Vlad made his entrance. In a swirl of shadow, he slowly regained his material form.

To all who witnessed it, his body seemed to stride forth from some ghostly, ephemeral world, only to step forward as solid flesh and bone before the Darg's assembly. Strange shadowy wings like smoke continued to flap around him, as if a strange, illusory wind blew them. Upon his head, he wore the helm of a Dockalfar commander, his hands resting close beside the pommel of his enchanted blade, and his magic wand of fire, Sharakul-Loth. In those first few instants following his surprising arrival, he was ready for anything.

Throughout the chamber, A'Goric's guards rushed to meet their sudden visitor. Drawing black blades from short scabbards and raising blowguns to fire. The instant before their attack was unleashed, A'Goric raised his right hand, his mighty voice thundering across the cathedral. "Hold!" he commanded, and his troops froze, yet never relaxed their guard. "I know not how you breached our wards, but you either have a great purpose or you are a dead fool."

"Slay him," his leftmost advisor said.

"He is but one," said his rightmost.

"Silence!" he said, and because he was king, he somehow sensed the peril in such a rash attempt at destroying this Dockalfar warrior. "Speak, visitor, your time here is measured in heartbeats."

Then in a swirl of shadow, Vlad disappeared, only to step forth as he had done before. This time, he reappeared on the footsteps of the throne, within a sword's length of the king. "Make no mistake," Vlad said, "your weapons cannot harm me."

"Such insolence, my king!" said the leftmost advisor.

"Enough!" A'Goric said. "On your doom, Dark Lord, why have you come before me?"

"A business proposition," Vlad replied carefully.

"The Dockalfar," A'Goric said, "are not known for keeping their side of a bargain."

"And it is also said, that the Darg only bargain with other Darg."

"Then you know the heart of the Darg."

"As strong and black as the mineral adamant."

"Then I proclaim you brother of the Darg, for you know the ancient ways. These words have not been spoken between Dockalfar and Darg for over five hundred years."

"My father, Aklon Leu-Sherroan, taught them to me."

"Aklon?" the king said. "I heard not of a son to Leu Sherroan."

"There is but one, and he is I."

"Then you have come to receive his debt in blood."

"Indeed."

"Speak wisely, son of Aklon."

"Even as we speak, a party of surface dwellers journeys toward your domain. Allow them—nay, guide them safely beyond your realm and into mine, and the debt will be repaid."

"What does the son of Leu-Sherroan care of surface dwellers? We have never allowed any such beings who have seen Grulthank to survive the experience."

"It is a matter which concerns me alone. See to it that they reach the Halls of the Dead unharmed."

"To do as you wish will cost more than the blood debt."

"What price?"

"The Treaty of Leu Sherroan shall be no more, for the Darg no longer need allies among the Dockalfar."

"My father's blood debt seems to have faded from the memory of A'Goric."

"Darg memories are long."

"The treaty shall remain for another fifty years, and the Darg owe Leu Sherroan one debt of honor."

"Forty years," A'Goric grumbled, "one debt of honor and trade rights to the Dark Force Crystal."

"Done!" Vlad answered while executing the Darg hand signs for a promised deal and the honor rite of nontreachery to perfection.

"Ha!" A'Goric laughed. "Vlad is truly brother to the Darg," for it was clear to each of them that Vlad knew well that to shake hands in the fashion of a surface dweller would only lead to certain death for the unwary. In the left hand of every Darg rested a small razor-sharp blade, and any unsuspecting partner would find their throat slit and any deals finished. Aklon had taught his son well, and Vlad knew every Darg custom, even the sinister ways of their honor. He had no misconceptions or illusions; he knew that he had entered a den of evil greater than any that he had ever before known.

"Well then, Vlad," A'Goric said, "who are these surfacers that we are to lead past Grulthank?"

Vlad's father had been a masterful planner, but his son was the Master of Plans within Plans.

Scrying Crystals

A gentle breeze like God's breath washed over Dartin. His lifeless body lay suddenly restored, regenerated, resurrected. When he awoke, it was if his ordeal had never been, but he knew the cost. The power of the runes was now lost for a year and a day, and not even the other gods could wield them. *Odin, what have you done? I am but a man.*

The stairs on which they stood led out of the cavern, into a small antechamber, and beyond it a lightless corridor began that led first north and then bent southward again to a great stair and deepening passage. An aged door still stood well hinged to the stone. "Let's get out of here," Carmen said. "Kur, lead everyone ahead. These beasts are sure to have hidden offspring, and nothing less than fire can cleanse this place."

The guano was reluctant to light, but after much prompting, it burned intensely. The cave soon began to fill with foul smoke, its billowing black mass reaching toward the same shaft that the bats had taken in their escape. It became difficult to breathe, but Carmen lingered. She wanted to be sure that everything burned, that these monsters would be no more.

"Come, Carmen," Tariq called, "the fire will soon grow hotter still."

"May Vanamoinen will it so."

Climbing the stairs, Tariq shut the door and braced it with a large stone. Smoke began to leech through the cracks in the door, and the smell was wretched. The fire in the lair of the dung beast was now an inferno, stealing the vital air from all the spaces around it. Fleeing down the stairs, they encountered a strong draft of fresher air, drawn past them by the fire's great hunger. Luck was with them, for they came upon what must once have been a great audience chamber.

"It seems strange," Dartin said, "that the miners who built these tunnels would work even harder to build such a grand room."

"There are many chambers like this one under the volcano," Kur said. "Down here, there is no sky. High ceilings hold fresh air and room to square your shoulders."

"That does make sense, but the ceiling must be at least forty feet high, and the room is at least twice that in length and width."

"It must have once been a grand meeting place," Karina said, "well-furnished and decorated with tapestries."

"There's nothing left now," Tariq said, "save for ghosts and a thousand years of dust."

"Look there," Kalor said, "centered on the far wall. The door still stands."

"Go and take a look," Carmen told him. "We'll camp here." Damp and cold, it was for the moment refreshing compared to the conditions of their past ordeal. They lent help to each other, cleaning their wounds as best that they could with their limited water and the remainder of Carmen's healing herbs.

"I need fire to make tea," Kur said. "The molds that I harvested will cure us if I have enough. We'll split it between us. A small glass twice a day for a week will work."

"Then we need fire," Dao said, "Perhaps Kalor's lamp will be enough to boil water."

"A most excellent idea, Mr. Greylinx, but it will be a miracle if my lamp isn't long since broken." A quick search of his pack revealed the unbroken lamp. "Ha!" he said while lifting it, "a miracle indeed." Producing their smallest cooking pot, he filled it with water and proceeded to make Kur's herbal tea.

"Boil it well," Kur said. "Tariq, Karina, and I are almost certainly infected. Time will tell us if Dartin still bears the disease. The first symptoms are fever and headache, followed by a rash. Those without treatment usually die. We'll divide the medicine threeways and hope that Dartin doesn't need it."

"I feel fine," Dartin said. "It's as if my wounds had never been."

"You died," Carmen said. "Odin raised you from the dead and healed you. Never have I seen such a miracle. He must have some greatness planned for you."

"The power of the runes is lost through all of the heavens. He should have let me die."

"Time will tell, priest," Kur said. "Don't forget the magic of your will and your wits."

"And if that should fail?"

"Cold steel," Kur said resolutely, "we give them cold steel."

"We have a more immediate concern," Carmen said. "If you are right, then we're all dying. We will rest here. Guard shifts two by two. We move out as soon as we've got some sleep."

"I'll take first watch," Dao said. "I won't be able to sleep anyway."

"Kalor, take the shift with him. I will take the second with Tariq. Stay alert." Dao stood watch by the far door, Kalor by the stairs from which they had come. Everyone else made camp.

Laying on his bedroll, Kur instinctively listened, as all Dwarves are prone to do in such places. With most of his friends asleep and exhausted, the air grew quiet save for dreamers' breath. He concentrated his senses close at first and then deeper into his surroundings until he began hearing tiny sounds from far away. He held his own breath and tried to still his heart to be sure it was not some wistful dream, but after many minutes, he was sure of what he heard. They were the sounds of picks and mining hammers vibrating through the rock from far below. "Can you not hear it?" he said to Dao, who stood guard next to him. "We've got company."

Dao cupped his hands upon the floor and around his ear and listened intently. "All that I can hear is the steady hum of our own breathing and the impenetrable silence of the stone."

"Trust me," Kur said, "there are miners below us, not close but they are there. We must be on our guard."

"You should sleep now," Dao said with a sigh. "There's no telling when you'll get another chance."

When they awoke, Tariq and Karina were showing the first signs of sickness. Indeed, they all were beginning to feel ill, although

Kur seemed the most resistant to it. "Kalor," he said, "brew some more tea. We're going to need it."

"It doesn't seem to be working," Carmen said.

"Without it, we would all be laid out flat, dying of fever. Most of us wouldn't last two days."

"So the tea is keeping it at bay."

"It'll cure us, if we have enough."

"Then we better find more," Kalor said, "because we only have enough for three or four more batches."

"And we have another problem," Dao said. "Kur says that he can hear miners working below us."

"How far below?" Kalor said worriedly.

"They're not close, but we could reach them in a day's march depending on how the tunnels run."

"Do we seek them out or try and avoid them?"

"The scepter got us this far," Tariq said. "We should follow its guidance and worry about the miners only if our paths should cross."

"Just remember," Kur said, "there are some who dwell down here who are friends to the Dwarves, like the Greater Gnomes, but our list of allies is few. Most of Underearth's inhabitants would kill us on sight. We must be very careful."

"We'll move out after breakfast," Carmen said. "Make sure your swords are sharp and oiled and everything's tied down."

They packed, drank their tea, and those that could, ate. They spoke of many things, some of home, others of future dreams. Kur told them how they could overcome some of the dangers that they might face. They talked just to talk, knowing that their next journey would require silence to succeed.

"The far door has no lock," Kalor said, "but its hinges are frozen with rust. We'll have to pry it open."

"Kur, give him a hand. Let's get moving." The door proved difficult, but their strength prevailed. With a raspy squeal, it finally gave way and opened. A small guard room lay beyond it, and then another passageway. "Luck," she told them all.

"Luck," they whispered.

Darg Plots

A'Goric and his advisors planned at length regarding the deal that they had made with the son of Aklon. The eyes of living surface dwellers had never before seen Grulthank, and A'Goric did not intend for such an event to occur now. Countless tunnels and bridges spanning wide expanses of molten lava surrounded the citadel. A maze of lethal traps, deadfalls, and pitfalls warded these ways. There were few safe paths through them, and only the Darg knew those routes. One of them, D'eern Shan'l, led to the cavern system through which Vlad's foreigners were traveling. Indeed, A'Goric's miners had heard many strange vibrations through the stone from that region, and it was within D'eern Shan'l that he intended to ambush these travelers. If any of them strayed from that path, they would find certain doom, for to the east and west of that tunnel-maze lay an endless array of deadly traps that the Darg had labored for centuries to create. If they wandered off the path, there would be no saving these surfacers. A'Goric hoped that they would wander.

"We will have to gain their confidence," said his rightmost advisor.

"They are naive children of the light," said A'Goric.

"Use the cavern creatures to lure them," said his leftmost advisor.

"Disguise the miners," A'Goric said. "Use the creature's scent to lure the beasts. Send the poisoners to help with the capture."

"An excellent plan, my king."

"Carry them beyond our lands. Leave the surfacers at the base of Cleave Maga neither maimed nor pillaged. Do this, and the blood debt to Leu Sherroan will be paid."

"Betray them," said his leftmost. "What need do the Darg have for Leu-Sherroan?"

"Torture them," said his rightmost. "Mutilate them."

"You forget the pact of the blood debt," said A'Goric. "To forget the pact is to lose the favor of Abbathoreus."

"What care does he have for surfacers?"

"For them he cares nothing," said A'Goric, "but for the pact of blood, everything."

"Yes, my king."

"If my instructions are disobeyed," said A'Goric, "every Darg in that company will be tortured. They will be maimed, and they will be mutilated unto death. That is the word and pact of A'Goric."

"It shall be done, my king."

A Daughter to the Queen

Ariana's beauty was supernatural, and within her chambers at the heart of Drakon Mur'-Falor, she was the closest to her power, linked in spirit to Lothdea, Goddess of the Great Spider. Scrimpsh, her pet giant spider, feasted in his own dark and web-surrounded cave at the rear of her quarters. He was the member of a rare phylum of Underearth spiders, a family of both enormous and deadly proportions. The Human male that he was devouring had proven to be a most exciting and virile partner to couple with. In her enchanting and charmed embrace, he had performed admirably, at least until his heart failed. No matter, there were plenty of fine Humans in the slave pits to choose from, and Scrimpsh needed feeding at least once a week anyway.

Lothdea had shared the experience with her, and she was pleased. Lying back upon her soft sheets spun of spider's silk, she traced the firm flesh of her blanket-shrouded body and closed her eyes to commune with her Goddess, an experience of ecstatic bliss greater even than her concubines could provide.

"I am pleased, daughter."

"Vlad will join us soon, Mother."

"He is ambitious and may soon be a danger to us."

"By then he will be in my control."

"I trust in your abilities, Ariana, but the time has come for you to know my wishes."

"Yes, Mother?"

"I've foreseen that he may one day unite the staff. See to it that he brings it to me. If not willingly, then kill him."

"But what of the Parliament?" Ariana asked.

"They are nothing compared to the might of the staff."

"And if Vlad gives it up willingly, then what is to become of him?"

"After that, he is no longer of use to us. He must fall like his father."

"Yes, Mother," she said faithfully.

"Bring me the staff, daughter, and I will make you High Priestess, and all pleasures shall be yours."

"I'll not fail you."

A Trap Is Laid

"How goes the preparations, Darik?"

"Excellent. The First and Second Battalions are on full alert. The Third Battalion will remain ready for the initial assault in the lower levels."

"Remember, Darik, we must take them alive. Andreul has divined that without them, we shall all die on the Ice Moon."

"The Orcs have been fully briefed, Commander. A fine trap has been set, and only rounded clubs and dulled swords shall be used."

"Each company must have magic enough to oppose them."

"Every squad has at least one priest, and each company four war masters."

"Chieftains?"

"The Third Battalion has four chiefs. All of them are handpicked from the Drums of Doom. They are all veterans of war."

"Reinforce them. Even at that strength, it may not be enough to capture them alive."

"Perhaps if the force is great enough, they will surrender."

"That would be against their very nature," Vlad said, pondering, "but it is possible that they might accept defeat once they realize that we possess so many of their loved ones as hostages."

"Let us hope that Olak and Draco succeed in Arendal."

"We must prepare a plan considering their failure. Chief Kegporter may be enough all by himself, but I will soon secure another. My father once knew the Gnome's master. They will not be willing to sacrifice their dearest loved ones."

"Elrick desires to use one of his spell traps to capture them. He claims that he can snare them all without harming them."

"Such an action will rob us of the psychological victory that we need," Vlad said. "It must be a military action. He must act only as a last resort."

"We shall double our preparations, Commander."

"We must also triple the production of the mine. I fear that the recent actions by Jason Da'Gol may soon rekindle to the Sentien Wars."

"The Deep Gnomes have unearthed the largest vein of crystal ever discovered. Our reserves of ore exceed fourteen tons, and the mine continues to produce ever greater concentrations of ore."

"The jewelers must produce amulets enough for the entire garrison. If the Sentiens attack, they will strike here first in search of Illian's Sword."

"That will greatly reduce our supplies of silver and gold."

"Victory must be ours no matter what the cost."

"Then I must tell you of my latest experiments."

"So you have succeeded in empowering the dead with Dark Force Crystal."

"I have achieved results beyond my wildest dreams. Witness the power of my pawn!" It was then that it stepped from the shadows of Darik's laboratory. Once human, life had long since fled the corpse, but some power of animation now inhabited it. Its eye sockets burned with the ill light of undeath, but unlike Zombies created solely through spells, a dark intelligence inhabited this one. Strangely, the stench of death was no longer present. Something was preventing the body's further decay.

"Can it speak?"

"Yes, Commander." He turned to the corpse. "Tell Commander Vlad your name and your purpose."

"I am Pawn. My purpose is to serve my creator."

"You walk a dangerous path, Darik."

"There are few risks, Vlad. The original soul has fled. Pawn is an empty vessel, free of emotion. The power of my spells have animated the corpse. The crystal only preserves its flesh. Amazingly, its reflexes are nearly the same as it possessed in life. It feels no pain, knows no fatigue, and is unrelenting in the pursuit of its commands. Once released, it will never stop unless it is destroyed."

"How long does the crystal's power last?"

"Pawn is the first, and he has remained fully animated for a week thus far."

"What do you intend to do with him?"

"He is the prototype, but I intend to make more as fresh corpses become available. I can imagine scores of uses, from untiring assassins to front rank shock troops. Our enemies will flee in terror!"

"Take care, Darik, Necromancy has always been the most unpredictable form of magic."

"Have no fear. I have begun new experiments combining the magical machines that I recovered from Imperium and the necromantic art. The creation of Pawn was child's play by comparison. An acolyte could have applied the Dark Force Crystal as I have."

"Hardly!" Vlad chuckled. "But we must return to more urgent matters. Step up the patrols of the outer tunnels. We'll need as much advanced notice as possible to tighten the noose properly."

"The slaves should lure them in. They won't be able to resist the opportunity for a heroic rescue!"

"Such a weakness," Vlad mused, "in the Liosalfar and their friends. No Drakkar Noire would ever jeopardize his mission in that way."

"We might."

"Preposterous!"

"Such is the way of the gods of light."

"Perhaps."

"Commander."

"Speak freely, Darik, and may rank never come between us."

"I believe that Ariana's participation in our plans is most treacherous."

"Ariana isn't the problem. Her inner voice is."

"Should we take action?"

"We'll wait for now. The time will come for the right moment to act. Soon our power will threaten to tip the balance away from the Queen's loyal followers. Without a doubt, she will command our immediate sacrifice, but that is not for the good of Dragonia, and it certainly is not good for us. In time, Darik, you and I shall stand behind the Dragonian army in victory, and no gods save the ones of our own choosing will stand with us!"

"The Queen's influence is strong. More than likely we will fail and be sacrificed to the Great Spider."

"Dragonia and the Dockalfar need a new world order, one which can be achieved only through the most daring measures. Our government, our gods, and our laws must change. In order to accomplish this, we must transform the hearts and minds of our entire people. It may be the foolish dream of the few. It may be impossible, but that is why we must unite the Duaredheim Staff!

"The Queen's declaration of war may delay our plans."

"My plan will use the coming war to our advantage. Time is our greatest enemy. We must capture the gem of the staff and the party before the spring thaw."

"So the invasion of Fermenor begins."

"The Queen commands us to invade and occupy Safehaven. The navy will land our legions on the west coast. Shock troops will attack inland from Underearth, and the remaining fleet will create chaos across the seas. Step-by-step, the Queen intends to end the war with this one massive offensive."

"The conquest of Fermenor seems improbable. It is a vast land, as big as Dragonia."

"We have used these tactics in the past," Vlad said. "The last invasion cost my father his life."

"Then how can we win?"

"We have new and greater allies than ever before in our history. The people of Dragonia, who were once our enemies, now battle with us side by side. Even here, in the desolate tundra, we have forged a new partnership with the Orcs. The Giants of the Mountains have sworn fealty, and offered to join in our war so long as they can share in the plunder. With proper leadership, the element of surprise, and a little luck, we can win."

"Then we have much work to do. I say hail to Vlad! Commander and friend of Darik Al Luan," and their firm clasp of forearms held no poisoned daggers.

"We are Drakkar Noire. We have our duty to the Empire. Can we find a way to accomplish our own goals and free our people? Only time will tell, my friend," he said as he stood, "but for now, I must travel to Waysborough. I have important business there."

"Waysborough?"

"Waysborough." Stepping into a shadow, he was gone.

Rock of Granite, Hammers of Steel

They were on the move, cautiously following Kur's lead into the darkest bowels of Underearth. The tunnel leaving the guard room seemed, for the moment, endless. Cool air still flowed past them.

"The draft is a boon," Kur whispered to Tariq. "The wind will carry our scent and the sounds of our passing back to where we've been and away from those below." Fearing that someone may falter from sickness and be lost, Kur often signaled a halt and ordered a head count. Their supply of healing tea was running out, and their fevers would soon end their march.

"I pray that we can find more medicine," Carmen said. "They'll not last much longer."

"We'll not die from fever," Kur said. "We live by the sword."

"Press on."

Perhaps it was the fever, but Kalor's mind had begun to wander. Part of him was still in file, following last in the column behind Karina. The other half of his psyche contemplated Modrul's Book of Shadows. Among the wyrm's spell repertoire were mighty spells of rock and matter manipulation, as well as charming spells and other magic of an unpredictable nature. Sorting through them, he tried to imagine their practical applications, for many of the spells were of untold power, and their uses could not be taken lightly. One day he or Dao would have to use them, of that he was sure. Ahead of him, Karina was beginning to stagger, her breath laboring. Dao would often help her along until she felt strong enough to go on alone, but his strength was in fact little better than hers. Kalor could only imagine how his friends ahead were faring. He knew that it was only a matter of time before the disease would force an end to their march.

It seemed like hours, but time was beyond their fevered grasp. "One hour's rest," Kur called back, and they all slumped gratefully to the floor. "Keep it quiet."

"We'll need real rest soon," Carmen said. "My head aches so badly that I can barely see."

"Our only hope is to find more of the fungus," Kur said. "If we rest too long, we will all sleep the long sleep."

"If I must die this way, then may Odin guide us swiftly," Dartin said. "It's been far too long since I've had a full night of drink and song. My thirst is great."

"Don't you have to die in battle with a sword in your hands?" asked Leander.

"We'll battle this sickness until the end, and we still have our swords."

"We will go on," Kur said, "if I have to carry you all." Testing the edge of his ax with his thumb, he then said, "Korun-Koth is hungry still."

Looking at him fearfully, none of them knew if it was Kur or his ax that had spoken.

Only Kur's great skills at navigating in the Underearth could save them from becoming hopelessly lost, but the ancient magic of the scepter still glowed brightly within its gem, and its insistent pull proved that they still followed the correct path.

"We're still heading south," Kur told them. "It is time. Let's get moving." They journeyed on for several more hours, and in their wretched states, it seemed more like days, each step harder to make than the last. The long passage gradually ended, entering a twisted maze of caverns and precipitous ledge-ways. "Look hard to the walls," Kur said. "The fungus often grows in damp caverns such as these." Stopping suddenly, he raised his hand to silence them. "Listen closely, the sound of hammers upon stone!"

They could all hear it clearly now, wondering with both curiosity and dread.

"Who would mine way down here?" Carmen whispered.

"Only those who dwell here," Kur said. "There are many different races—Gnomes, Dwarves, and Dockalfar. There are others whose names I dare not mention. We must be prepared for battle!"

"Battle?" Dao said. "I can barely stand!"

"If we turn back now, without medicine, we will never make it."

"Courage," Tariq said. "Perhaps these miners will be friendly to us. If we're lucky, they may have medicine."

"You must be sick," Carmen said.

"Just trying to be hopeful," he answered with a smile.

"Lead on, Kur. Kalor, activate the scepter once more."

Ahead and south, it still pointed. They moved more slowly now, as quietly as they could, and soon came upon the mouth of another tremendous shaft; but this was not a passage naturally formed. Attached to the ceiling above were great pulley mechanisms with rotten strands of rope dangling from them. Once, they would have supported immense weight, but their time of glory was long past. The square shaft descended an untold distance. "Even with the helm, I cannot see the bottom." The steady sound of miners' picks and hammers echoed eerily from below.

Peering into the shaft, Kalor was troubled. "Who do you think is down there, Kur?"

"This close to the Orcs' territory, who can guess?" he said. "It could be a Gnomish troop, or even Dwarves, but I have never heard of any of my kind living beneath the Northern Reaches, at least not since ancient times."

Carmen saw the troubled look upon Kur's face, and she knew that his optimistic words were not his full thoughts. "What is it, Kur?"

"Dwarves and Gnomes aren't the only peoples who mine. We must beware. The answers await us at the bottom. Get your ropes out."

Preparing their climbing equipment, they were soon ready to descend.

"We've got eight coils of rope," Kalor said, "over three hundred feet in all. I have tied them all together and anchored it well to a huge docking pin beside the mineshaft. It'll hold two or three men at once, but we have no way of knowing if it will reach the bottom."

"That's great," Dartin said, "nothing like a three-hundred-foot climb down and then up again if we end up dangling."

"Well," Dao said, "who wants to go first?"

"I'll lead," Kur said, "and take Karina with me. If I have to, I should be able to carry her weight and mine."

"I don't know if I can make it," Karina said, shivering.

"You can do it," Kur said. "Think only of the rope and imagine that your body is light, weightless. I'll stay below you. If you fall, we both fall."

"Very well, Mr. Dwarf," she said. "I'll soon be dead of this fever anyway. Why not risk a fall?"

"Why indeed," Kur replied as he slowly lowered himself over the rim and into the pit. Karina followed a short distance behind him, and the others waited for the telltale tug on the rope that would be the ready signal for the next two climbers to descend. Kur examined the complex workings of the mine as he climbed down. Side passageways crisscrossed the shaft in a seemingly random fashion.

They must be mining probes, he thought, *following the veins of ore.*

During its heyday, the mighty lift above them must have hummed with a life all its own, but now it rested, torn, ruined in silent, lonely slumber. Hearing Karina's groan, he paused long enough for her to reach him. Tapping upon her ankles, he placed them, left and right atop of his shoulders. When they were stable, he began to climb again. He was strong, doubly so for a Dwarf, but whether or not his strength would be enough to carry them both to the bottom he could not know, but neither did he tell that to Karina. They had come too far to turn back now; there was no other way. Their rope had to reach bottom. The alternative was unthinkable.

Hand over hand, the rope double-wrapped around his stout legs and braced between his boots, he climbed, with Karina atop of him—fifty feet, a hundred, two hundred, and nearly three hundred feet. They finally reached the bottom, a broad sandy cave with several tunnels leading this way and that. The sounds of mining emanated most strongly from the southmost one. He prayed that the miners' industry of sounds would help to cover the noise of their climbing. Two tugs, followed by three, and the next two climbers began their slide, and so on, until all eight of them had reached the bottom. With an amazing skill, Kalor was somehow able to loosen the topmost knot from the ropes' end, and over three hundred feet of it fell about them in a heap.

"Very stealthy," Kur whispered. 'Pick up your ropes,' he signaled to them all and then toward Kalor and the south passage. 'Scout it quietly,' he indicated.

"I didn't want to have to climb back up anyway," Leander said.

"Don't you know it yet?" Dartin asked.

"What?"

"This is a one-way trip."

"Quiet, men!" Kur ordered. "Speak no more." He waved Kalor on, and the little thief slunk ahead. Following the tunnel for some distance, he found no evidence of nearby enemies or hidden traps. Several empty carts rested on a well-worn set of rails traversing the center of the passage. The tracks were dust free, and the carts' wheels well oiled. He advanced more carefully then, ever closer to the miners, fifty yards, a hundred, one fifty. His footfalls muffled by soft dirt and dust, he moved so closely to the tunnel wall that he was almost a part of it, and then he saw them. In numbers, they were at least twenty, with perhaps ten or more working down side tunnels that he could not see. Several small lanterns bathed the surroundings in a gold glow, and the dull gleam of natural gemstones twinkled here and there throughout the passage.

In stature, they were short, a little taller than he was, and bearded, with hawkish noses and piercing black eyes. Their clothing was simple—baggy pants, waist-length tunics, and soft pointed caps. A few of them wore assorted pieces of armor, a chest-plate here, a coat of mail there, and some of them carried short swords belted at their hips. If he were to guess, he would say that they were Gnomes, but it was difficult to tell at this distance. He dared not go farther ahead and risk discovery. Creeping backward, he moved until he was well beyond any natural sight before turning around and sneaking back to the party. He soon reached them and relayed all that he had seen ahead.

"So you think that they are Gnomes, eh?" Kur said.

"They look like my people, but they seem older somehow."

"It is said that the Deep Gnomes look that way," Kur said. "Life down here is hard, and often short."

"But still you worry?" Carmen asked.

"There are other more dangerous races down here that also could be mistaken for Gnomes," Kur said, "It would be better if we could find some way to go around them."

"We've come so far already, and we've long since passed beyond our map. Kalor, can we risk a little light?"

"They're about two hundred yards ahead. They might see the light, but only if they are looking directly towards us."

"I don't think that we have any other choice," Carmen said. "What do you think, Kur?"

"Try the scepter. If we have to fight in our condition, we're in big trouble anyway." Magical light soon illuminated the maze of mining passages heading off to the four corners all around them. Much as they had feared, the diamond's light pointed south, directly toward the miners. When Kalor commanded the scepter to cease, the dreadful darkness returned.

"I'll scout ahead," Kalor said. "If any of them saw me, they might set an ambush ahead of us."

"We'll give you a short head start," Kur said, "and then we'll set out after you." Turning to each of them, he made sure that they all knew that from there on, it was hand and arm signals only. Moving out, they worked their way quietly along, and as they neared the sounds of mining, a great clamor rung out through the shafts all about them, bringing with it the sounds of horrified screams and a battle joined.

"What's happening?" Carmen whispered.

"It sounds like the miners are being attacked. Many residents of the dark would rather steal gold than work for it."

"Maybe they need help."

"Maybe, but we must be careful. We might end up between two Trolls and their next meal."

Carmen moved ahead purposefully. Her helm-enhanced vision allowing her to see well beyond the range of her companions' eyes. Soon she was winding through the twisting passage directly behind Kalor. The tunnel walls sparkled with gems of every facet and color, perfectly formed and beyond every dream of the kings of the surface. Ahead of them, she could hear the workers hammering, digging, and even singing, although she could not understand the words, and then, a shadow suddenly loomed, lurking just beyond the next bend. She hurriedly pulled Kalor back with her into the nearest alcove. "Something comes, something big!"

"How big?"

"It has to stoop to avoid the ceiling," she whispered, "and it is nearly as wide as the tunnel."

His curiosity was at its height. He could not resist peeking around the corner of their hideaway. She couldn't resist holding him back a little. Whatever is was it had a large heat signature, which he could just begin to see. She pulled him back deeper into the alcove, and her voice was even softer. "I can hear its heavy breathing, and it's dragging something." He felt her tremble then, and her firm clasp upon his shoulder and upon her new spear were only slightly reassuring.

"I'm going to sneak ahead into that next cross-tunnel and hide," Kalor whispered. "When he reaches you, strike him fast if it is some enemy. I'll take him from the back."

Watching his progress, she could hear his quiet footfalls and then the faint sound of his muffled breathing when he stopped. Beyond him, the huge thing approached, dragging something or some part of itself. Behind them, she could make out the almost deafening sounds of her friends' approach, and louder still was the sound of pitched battle.

What could it be? she wondered. In the span of heartbeats, the creature, for a creature it was, had passed by Kalor and entered into the passage between them. Somehow, it had not seen him, and so, with great fear, she stepped into the passageway to meet it head-on. *Vanamoinen protect me,* she prayed, when she finally saw but could not recognize what it was.

* * * * * *

Kur increased their pace, with Tariq following close behind him. Their scouts were no longer visible, and the sounds of battle were intense. The time for silence was at an end.

"Where'd they go?" Dartin said. "I can't make them out anymore."

"I don't like it," Leander said. "They shouldn't have gone ahead alone."

"Push on!" Dao said. "They may be in danger."

"Maybe we should give them a little more time," but their dilemma soon ended when the terrifying sound of Carmen's strangled battle cry gave them no time to spare. The rush of fear's blood drove away their sickness, but their full strength was lost to them. The next precious moments would decide all.

Tariq's new sword was already in his hands, and its blade suddenly rippled with red magical flames. Kur prepared his ax, and his comrades readied their swords. Karina paused to retch, but her stomach was already empty. When it was over, she paused to take a breath and then struggled on.

One-Eyed Jack's

"We didn't have any idea of what we were about to face," Kalor said. "We were expecting Dwarves, or even a mining party of Gnomes, but what we found instead was even more at home in those dark corridors."

"What was it, Kalor?" Pauli asked. "A Troll or an Ettin?"

"Maybe Goblins," Eric said, "or even a Giant?"

"All of those thoughts passed through our minds, and indeed, we would have welcomed such familiar beasts, but none of us had ever seen or heard of such monsters before. Kur knew them by an ancient name, and they had not been seen by any of his kin for centuries. They were an ancient horror, a throwback to another age, a time long before Men or Dwarves were born. Unfortunately for Carmen and me, he was still far behind us in the adjoining tunnel."

"What did you do?" Garad said. "Did Carmen slay the beast with her mighty spear?"

"It is a story that parches my lips with a terrible thirst," I said. "Sonya, would you please refill my flagon." A cool drink, and the chill of my old horror passed just enough for me to begin again.

"It was a time of torment for us all, but I will tell you the tale as fully as I can remember it. Huge they were, over eight feet tall and half as wide. In form, they resembled the mighty ants of the southern jungles, but they stood upright upon four limbs, with their torsos held tall like a man's or a Centaur's. Their upper arms were long and slender, with hairy pincers that could grasp and as we discovered, wield weapons of war. Their heads were large, like a bear's, with bulbous oval eyes, long, sickle-like mandibles, and two antennae that never ceased to writhe, always seeking, sensing, divining. A glistening black rock-hard exoskeleton covered their entire body, from the top of their heads to the tip of their segmented abdomen. Their power and speed was unknown to us, but we would learn it soon enough. Better that we had never met them, better that Carmen had not been the first among us to face them…"

ANTS THAT HUNT MEN

"Vanamoinen!" she cried, hoping that evoking his name would bring her courage and gain the beast's attention. When first she saw it, she wished that she had never seen it. Her imagination could never have conjured such an image; her most terrible nightmare would never even have dreamed it. She gasped, fighting for breath, for strength; her pulse was quick, her palms wet. The Antman, for that is what it seemed, was unsurprised, even, it seemed, expecting her. In its right pincer, one of the small Gnomes struggled. With a casual strength, it smashed him against the tunnel wall until he stopped moving, dropped him to the tunnel floor, and piled a dirty sack on top of him. Looking up in her direction, it stared at her defiantly, and even in the purple-world of her visor's magical vision, the Antman's eyes glowed with an inner savagery. It was then that it uttered a piercing screech, followed by a symphonic alien chatter. Its calls to its brethren echoed through the halls. Grasping at something behind its back, it pulled out a thick-handled spear tipped with stone and charged her.

Despite her fear, Carmen had fought creatures of such size before, and she intended to set her spear for its rush and skewer it. The tunnel floor was smooth, and she doubted that the weight of her boot could hold the butt of her spear firmly enough, but the tunnel way provided few irregularities for her to set her spear against and forced her to set her spear against a thick wooden roof support. In a flash, it was upon her. She raised her spear at the final moment.

Aiming her thrust perfectly, the creature struck it with the full impact of its rush. If she had been familiar with its stone-like shell, she might have tried something else, for her spear point only dug in a little, its handle bowing wide and shattering to splinters in her hands. Unprepared for the utter failure of her weapon, she reached for her sword's handle and was struck a hammering blow to the head. A second hit drove her back into the wall. The Antman's mandibles encircled her helm and lifted her skyward. Another strike blasted the air from her lungs, and she vomited. With a hideous screech, the Antman lifted her skyward and bashed her against the tunnel roof. When she stopped flailing, he brought her back to eye level and examined his prize. Antennae waving victoriously, he was obviously happy with his catch and the promise of a filling meal.

Kalor left his hiding place the moment the Antman charged. If the creature had been as wary as was its norm, it would surely have sensed his approach, for its senses were without equal in Underearth. Nevertheless, Kalor went unnoticed, and his silent approach was unexpected. Quietly drawing his small sword, he padded closer, taking several swift steps and leaping after the last. In a double-handed overhead thrust, he aimed for what he thought might be the creature's spine, but instead, he struck some sort of equipment that formed closely to its body. He struck again and hit its hard shell. The Antman reared back suddenly and threw him. He tumbled backward onto the floor. He landed well, allowing the roll to absorb his momentum, until it came to a quite abrupt and inopportune end against the tunnel wall. He picked himself up, bruised, battered, and stood facing the creature. It had completely abandoned Carmen and was now concentrating solely upon him. It was a feeling that he was quite uncomfortable with. During his fall, he had dropped his sword, and it lay on the floor behind it. He would never be able to reach it safely, so he drew his two gnomish daggers. Reversing his grip for a right-handed throw, he drew back, but a sudden intense light blinded him.

The creature lurched violently, its body wracked as Cloud-seeker's arrows burned into it, penetrating deeply beneath its exoskeleton. It was torn now—kill the meddlesome little pest or return to finish off its new attacker?

Carmen was down but not down for good. She felt wretched. Her own bile clouded her visor, but she could still see. Tariq had taught her how to play possum, and now her helm-guided vision allowed her to send her arrows into the beast.

The Antman was powerful, confident in its resilience, but against this power he was vulnerable. It looked for cover but could find none. It tried to evade and advance, but still barbs of light burned it. Its strength was failing. Without options, it chose to escape over its least-dangerous foe. Batting Kalor aside, it rushed down the hall.

Sighting down the pale glowing light of a mystical arrow, Carmen fired as rapidly as her arms would allow. Some inner sense told her when to release, even how to release, in a combination that targeted the most vulnerable areas of the creature's body. The tunnel flashed brilliantly as each shot streaked into its hulking form.

The Antman struggled to escape. If only it could reach the others, it thought, as a searing pain briefly touched its mind.

Tumbling into a lifeless heap, it twitched for a while and then moved no more.

Moving closer to make sure, Carmen could hear the frantic footsteps of her approaching friends. A small man that looked much like Kalor lay against the left wall, Kalor opposite him. The Gnome, if he was one, was twisted, broken, and quite dead. Kalor was unconscious but alive. Kneeling beside him, she tried to rouse him with the last of her water.

"Where am I?" he muttered.

"That thing gave you quite a slap!"

"Oh," he said, holding his head between his hands, "my head hurts!"

"Carmen!" Tariq said. "Are you all okay?"

"My ribs are cracked, and my head's ringing, but we'll make it. Just a moment," she said. "Muu-Arm." Removing her helm, she emptied its contents onto the floor and proceeded to dry-heave for some time, each convulsion causing an explosion of pain. When her nausea subsided, she wiped off her face and cleaned her helm as best as she could. Donning it, she commanded, "El-Vanira," and she could see. "Dar-croth," and it sealed to her neck, helping her breathe. Standing tall brought more pain, but her inner soldier was in command now; as long as she wasn't dead, she could still fight. "I'm ready, we'd better get moving if we're going to find anyone left alive."

"Who's this guy," Dartin said, pointing his sword toward the corpse beside them. "Looks just like Kalor."

"One of the miners, I guess," Leander said.

"Strange," Kur said, "he carries no weapons, not even a knife sheath."

"Maybe they are near to home?"

"Or else he's a slave," Dao said.

"No mining party that I've ever seen goes so completely unarmed," Kur said. "These miners may not be friends."

"What the hell is that thing?"

"Korg-Troggin," Kur said, "ants that hunt men. If they catch you, they bring you back to their colony to feed to their young. Better to take your own life than to let that happen."

"A tough way to go," Dartin said.

"We better hurry," Kalor said, somewhat recovered as he picked up his sword. "The battle is going on without us, and it is there that we'll find our answers." Staying together, they regrouped as best as they could, Dartin carrying Karina, who was barely conscious and could walk no further. It was only a matter of hours before the rest of them would join her.

The Gnomes were fighting bravely in a great vaulted chamber. Torches burned in many sconces randomly spaced about the area. Many random tunnels entered the cave at all angles, like honeycomb. Several Gnomes lay dead or dying upon the floor, some of them being dragged away by Antmen. The surviving Gnomes were being led by a stout black-bearded captain, wielding two ebon-swords with determined skill. Around him was a tightly formed phalanx of twenty, battling with short swords and mining picks. Their armor was black and well made, although some of them were plain clothed. Several carts filled with ore lay about the room, some of them overturned.

Four of the Antmen lay dead or dying about them, but ten more remained, either fighting the Gnomes or dragging off the fallen.

"Hurry!" Carmen said. "They need our help." Her longsword drawn, she led the way into the war-torn cave. Tariq ran beside her, his blade's edge bathed in mystical red flame. Kur followed closely behind them. Slinging his shield, he drew his off-hand blade. The more that he saw what was around him, the more his suspicions grew. Behind him, Dartin found cover behind an overturned cart. Gently laying Karina inside it, he prepared his bow. Leander ran behind Kur, raising his sword high. A tremendous thunderclap issued forth, and black clouds began to form. Dao ran in last behind them. Surveying the scene, he broke away left with Leander. Kalor paused, calling upon a spell that he knew. Dartin chanted a prayer for battle, "Upon my shield stares Odin's sacrifice. With our hands and hearts, we strike! To fall bravely in a battle well-fought, standing once again beside Odin at Ragnarok!"

The battling Gnomes seemed to fight with renewed vigor when they saw that reinforcements would soon reach them. Lashing out frantically against the Antmen, they seemed to be experts in fighting the huge creatures. Rotating in teams of three, they would harass the Antmen from multiple angles, hoping that one of them would be able to strike some vital area. It was a tactic that seemed to be working, for two more Antmen soon fell, but occasionally one of the Gnomes would go down beneath a mighty blow, and some of them did not rise again.

"To me!" Carmen cried. Tariq ran two swords' lengths to her right, his right hand grasping the hilt of his sword aflame, yet he was unburned. "I'm right behind you," Kur shouted. Dao and Leander took the left flank. Moving quickly, they set upon one of the Antmen.

She was a soldier, past the pain. All was attack; all was fury. Rushing in, she engaged the Antman battling the Gnomes' captain.

The creature slipped left, trying to limit its exposed flank. Driving back the Gnome with a great thrust, it turned to face her. Twisting its head in defiance, its mandibles opened wide. It knew nothing of these new enemies. All that it knew was that the time to flee for its life had come. Stepping onto the bodies of some unfortunate mortally wounded Gnomes, it crouched for a leap.

Carmen's fighting skill was both a combination of training, insight, and a great adaptability. She had learned just how strong these creatures were in her last fight, and she suspected that they were both primitive and savage. With her sword held low, she waited, hoping it would either leap over her or bridge the gap between them in an attempt to crush her beneath the bulk of its body. By some stroke of luck, it tried to leap past her. When it was airborne, she sidestepped. Wielding her sword two-handed, she brought her sword's tip to bear against its lower abdomen. Once it had left the earth, it couldn't change direction. Her blade bit deeply into its vitals. The Antman landed in a devastating tumble, its lifeblood spewing forth thick and green. Running it down, she thrust her sword hard into the base of its head. It shuddered and soon lay still. Turning to view the battle, she again saw the Gnomes' captain. The look that he gave her left her with an uncomfortable chill.

Tariq fought beside two fine Gnomes. Imitating their taunting style of battle, he was able to join them in their fight against two of the Antmen. Between them, they were able to land numerous hits on the creatures. One of the Gnomes bled from several small wounds yet continued to fight vigorously. This close to the Antmen, Tariq's sword blazed a bright crimson, as if the flames hungered for the flesh of his enemies. Both of the Antmen had felt the bite of his enchanted blade and feared it. Soon the monsters began to fight more defensively, searching for an escape from the circle of pain.

All around them, throughout the cave, it began to rain.

In desperation, the Antmen beat down the Gnome on Tariq's left flank, accepting several hits from the others in exchange for a chance to escape. Indeed, Tariq and his allies could do nothing to stop such a concentrated attack, but there was something that a deadly Dwarf could do. Having watched the battle progress, Kur was finally forced to engage, although doubt still lingered within him. With battle-proven logic, he chose to act against their immediate threat, the Korg-Troggin. Stepping in front of the two creatures, he advanced, preferring to fight "on the move. The Antmen screeched in frustration when they saw their new enemy. Seeing no avenue of escape save through this troublesome pest, they attacked. Their combined strength would be more than enough to defeat one small Dwarf.

Needless to say, Kur was considered somewhat large for a Dwarf, certainly taller than was average, and his bones and his body was nearly as tough as the Korg-Troggins'. In fact, he didn't think of himself as being too short or two weak, more like just right for a Mountain Dwarf, and at any rate, his people were known from ages long past for being exceptionally skilled in fighting much larger adversaries. Each time that the Antmen lashed out with their stone-tipped spears, they found only Dwarven steel. Each time they drew too close, their bodies were met by a swinging ax or stabbing blade. Their frustration was complete. They hissed and spit; their mandibles clacked. One of them was struck hard by an arrow. Wheeling away, it charged after its latest attacker.

The second continued to attack, trying to crush him beneath its hulking body and a rain of hard blows. Kur shrugged them off one by one, never standing in one place for more than a second. "Rock of Granite," he sang, "Mountains of Stone, Moradeus' Hammer of Mithril-steel, Korun-Koth is again Kur-Rogoth!" The blood of battle drove hard through his veins. He received its attacks and countered viciously, driving the beast back, hacking off two of its legs. It stumbled. Stepping twice and hacking thrice, he beat back the Antman's spear, chopping off an arm and then its head.

Striding side by side, Dao and Leander moved into the fray. To their left, Kur ran after one of the creatures bearing down on Dartin. To their right, one of the creatures lay dying, and Leander sped it on its way.

Dao went to the aid of three Gnomes who were faring badly. He wished that Karina was by his side, but the sickness was taking her, and she was near unto death. Together, they could fight as one. Two sets of Liosalfar blades joined in a dance of deadly steel, but now he was alone. Leander was near, but he could not join in the dance. He would have to waltz well enough on his own. The Antman was occupied, its back turned to him, but Dao knew that the creature was aware of him. Moving in, Dao readied his first blow, but the creature went into a sudden frenzy. Striking out in all directions with weapons both natural and crafted, it created a killing swath about itself that felled all three of its Gnomish opponents and left Dao with a deep wound to his right thigh.

A terrible thunderclap rang out and then another. Cool rain began to fall. Fear filled the Antmen's hearts, for here in the Underearth, only the splitting of rock by great volcanic forces made such sounds, and to be close enough to hear them meant imminent death—a death their instincts yearned to escape from.

The Antman wheeled about and charged. Bringing the shaft of its spear down, it sought to sweep him away, but Dao rolled under it, spun, and drove his sword hard between the segments of its torso. Reeling in pain, it tried to kick him away, but Leander hit him hard from the left. The creature fell rolling, still in the fight but badly hurt. Abandoning its spear, it grasped Leander and hauled him in, taking him around the chest and arms with its mandibles. Screaming in pain, he tried to resist their crushing grip. Violently shaken, he dropped his sword.

Dao wasted no time. Running along the belly of the beast, his sword lashed out again and again, always striking the softer areas between the segments of his exoskeleton. The Antman tried to bat him away with its legs and pincers, but Dao was always one step ahead. His final step launched him over the creature's head, his final stoke taking it in the neck. Even in death, it continued to squeeze its prey. Leander screamed and went limp. Dao hacked away at its jaws until it released him, but Leander was unconscious and couldn't be roused. Dao looked to Atran-Doru. The storm above was waning. "I shall return you to his hand," Dao said, "unless you burn me," but the sword withheld its sting, and once it touched the young acolyte, the storm returned.

Returning to the battle, Dao discovered that the three fallen Gnomes were not dead, merely stunned, and they looked upon him in a way that seemed to portray respect, but there was more to it; he just couldn't put his finger on it. Raising his sword in salute, he ran to Dartin's aid. Standing with Carmen, they battled hard against the largest of the Antmen. The monster tore about itself with an enormous club of bone, and two Gnomes lay broken at its feet.

Raising his shield, Dartin's sword had long since left its scabbard. His arrows had taken one of the Antmen, but his actions had brought the attention of their apparent leader. The ever-watchful Eye of Odin stared from his shield, but the god still slept, and the runes were lost to him. Carmen worked hard against it, but this Antman was exceptional, its skill with its weapon more precise, more intuitive. Dartin's shield was stuck hard, its frame bent. Carmen's legs were swept out from under her, and she landed hard. The air was blasted from her lungs and her already broken ribs. She tried to rise, but she couldn't breathe. Her armor had absorbed the worst of it, but she was hurt. Still the soldier, she strove to pick herself up, but the creature was on her now, using the weight of its abdomen to pin her down. She struggled to rise, straining every muscle, but while it remained on top of her, she was its prisoner.

Two enemies remained in front of it and one behind. They were small and smelled foreign to its world. It was an odor that brought about a strange fear within him, but the other small things that had attacked him had fallen easily and would feed many of the brood. Screaming in challenge, he raised his club and called its remaining brethren to his side.

Kur was forced to leave Carmen's side by the onrush of another of the beasts. Soon he was in a desperate place, fighting for his life against multiple opponents. He spun and chopped, slicing and hewing, trying to find an opening, but for the moment, they fought at a stalemate.

Dao was driven back by another. Dancing around, the two mortal enemies spun, with neither willing to offer an opening. It would take more than his skill with a blade alone to kill it. Searching his mind, he called upon a Dragon's spell, magical fire, the Will of Bran-Dar, a long-dead sorcerer of old. With his words, he invoked it, and with his hand he channeled it. Power from the earth flowed through him, his mind directing it toward the beast, and from out of his hand sprang fire, a tunnel, a whirlwind, like dragon's breath, and the Antman was consumed. Its savage contortions drove it around the cave until it fell dead, its body aflame. Dao moved back to help his friends, but something stung his neck, and he knew no more.

Dartin struck. Wading in, he accepted another hard blow in order to give one of his own, but he could find no easy mark, for the Antman's speed and power were great. Shifting his weight, he turned his broken shield to meet the club and lashed out with his sword. His forearm was broken, his shield smashed. His blade found a vulnerable notch. He drove it in unto its hilt. The creature struck his sword arm away and took him in its mandibles. Raising him up, it flung him away into the Gnomish host. He landed hard, all wrong, and his world went black. Many bodies were scattered.

Leander was in a far-distant place, a floating place free of pain and awareness, but his sword was well-aware of its surroundings, and as long as its master lived, it could exert its own will. Its lightning would strike down until there was naught left of their enemies but ashes. A terrible bolt burned up through the body of the Ant-leader. It tried to crawl away, but its body was an empty shell. Smoldering, it slumped and died. Carmen was electrocuted; she was burned. She was crushed beneath the body of the beast, and finally, the paladin did sleep.

The remaining Antmen, now leaderless, had lost all resolve. Another lighting strike and Kur faced only a single enemy. His party was faring badly. Several of them were probably dead or near dead, and it was entirely his fault. His father would have found another way for them to go. His brother would never have even risked it. The voices of a thousand Dwarven spirits filled is mind. The skill of a thousand warriors filled his body. He was Death incarnate. The creature was blasted by bolts of light. It reared but drove on. It tried to escape over him, but an ax clove through its breastplate. Its legs continued to push forward, but soon they were severed. Its mandibles still sought freedom. Its head yearning for the security of dismal black caves, but soon it was smashed. Soon it was ended.

Tariq and the Gnomes surrounded their last enemy. The Korg-Troggin was beyond desperate. Seeing its death upon it, it chose not to go alone. Rushing at the nearest Gnome, it dropped its spear and lifted the poor wretch to its mouth. With a sudden snap, the Gnome's head was severed, but its move cost it dearly. Ten Gnomes laid into its legs and its body. Tariq leaped onto its back, driving his sword home in a reverse-handed grip that burned through its heart. Lunging backward, it threw him. Striking the wall of the cave, he fell hard to the floor. The creature tried to run, but the Man-creature's painful claw protruded from its back, stealing its energy. Seven paces were all that it could manage, seven paces and not one more.

The Gnomes immediately went to work, bandaging their fellows and checking the side passageways to make sure that the Antmen were gone. The captain himself led his company in pulling the Ant-leader off Carmen.

Kalor called upon his growing magical repertoire and incanted a spell that he'd learned from Modrul's treasure horde. The spell was a simple one, and above them a miniature sun illuminated the room with the light of day. At first, they all reeled away from the light, for surely such brightness was excruciating to eyes accustomed to the ever-dark.

The storm began to recede, but a few clouds remained, challenging the new light and spilling out a light rain.

"On your feet, Ranger," Kur said, helping Tariq up. Spitting blood, he complied as best that he could, but he could barely stand.

"Thanks."

Moving to the nearest carcass, Kur wiped his blood-wetted blades clean upon it but did not sheathe them. Squinting against the brightness, he strove to see greater detail in their strange allies, and with eyes able to see well in both the light of the outside world and the deepest dark, he looked at each Gnome in turn. Carmen was too close to their captain, too close. His mind screamed out, reliving memories of childhood nightmares, tales of boggle-creatures of the darkest depths. These Gnomes were not Gnomes at all; they were the darkest of evil. They were the Darg!

Tariq, unsuspecting, limped to retrieve his sword; for some reason, it continued to burn, melting through the body of the Antman. Kalor knelt beside Dao, trying to revive him. A small black dart protruded from his neck. *No!* and it was then that he knew. Thinking quickly, he began to chant the words to another spell, but something stung his hand. Looking down, he saw the barb, for one instant, before the walls closed in.

One-Eyed Jack's

"Kur must have rushed in and clove their captain in two!" Pauli said.

"Indeed," I said. "He intended to do that very thing, but the Darg had planned their trap very carefully, and they were wary of Kur most of all."

"But the Darg were having such a hard time against the Antmen," Eric said. "Surely they were no match for Tariq and his enchanted blade."

"Yes, Tariq was a fine warrior, braver and even more capable than even he himself knew, but the Darg had only made it seem like they were fighting a losing battle."

"I see it now," Garad said. "The dead Gnomes must have been real Gnomes that the Darg captured."

"And that was why they were unarmed!" Pauli said.

"Your assumptions are all correct, but back then only Kur knew the truth in time enough to act."

POISON

The Gnomish captain knelt behind Carmen, cradling her head and shoulders in his arms. Several of his kin stood around him, squinting against the conjured light. The captain drew a twisted wand from his coat and touched it to her helm. Miraculously it released its seal upon her neck, and he easily removed it. Her matted hair spilled out, and for a moment, she regained consciousness. Looking into his blackest of eyes, orbs like lumps of lifeless coal, she could see only malice. Looking at his twisted fingers, she could feel only contempt; the eager beat of his heart echoed only evil. Kur was right. She had been a fool to rush them into all of this, and now it was too late.

"Greetings," he said, "I am Sir Gorfar-Norgarkoochinook." It was a good gnomish name, and quite common among them, but he was no Gnome, and to his company, it was only a signal.

In a flash of movement, reaching into the hidden folds of their cloaks, each Darg brought slender blowguns to their lips. In the span of a breath, poisoned darts found unprotected flesh, a part of the face, a bit of neck, or an ungloved hand. In the surprised span of a gasp, Carmen's world vanished, and Tariq fell to the floor but felt none of the pain of it.

"Sever the hand that holds the sword!" their leader ordered, and then the clouds vanished, and with them the rain.

Seven companions were down, seven but not eight, for Kur was born upon a bed of granite near the silent heart of a volcano, and his flesh could withstand more poison than any Human or Alfar. In his hands were the eternal spirits of a thousand ancient Dwarves, and the short sword that had yet to find its name. In his heart burned a seething rage, but his anger was instantly tempered, for poised above Carmen's unprotected throat was the captain's razor-sharp wrist dagger. "Drop your weapons!" he shouted in Kur's own tongue. "Drop them or I will bare her throat to the bone!"

Kur wanted to fight them all. He wanted to crush these abhorrent, twisted likenesses of his kin into the earth. Indeed, with the madness growing within him, he might have been capable of it. Nevertheless, he knew that such an act would mean the certain death of his friends, and he could not live with such a great weight upon his shoulders. Men and women had died under his leadership in the past, but he liked to think that fewer had died than would have had he not led them. His friends were beyond choice, and they had not yet been killed. It was a disturbing fact that told him that they had some other grim purpose for them. All the old tales swore that it was better to be dead than prisoners of the Darg. Their captives lived only long enough to experience suffering so terrible that it was said to cause the death of one's soul. Despite all his terror, something within him told him that while there was life, there was hope, and that is what he had to believe. Lowering his weapons, his heart was filled with grief and impotence. Several more darts struck him, and then some more, and after a while, he knew no more.

"All dying," giggled one of them whose name meant Black Bible. "Them has got the plague, or too many wounds to live."

"Bind their wounds," ordered their captain. "Remember the blood debt."

"After this quest, the debt is paid. We owe the Son of Aklon no more."

"It shall be paid, and no surfacer will yet live who has seen our halls. The plague or their hurts will finish them. It is a long walk to the Great Chasm and Cleave Maga."

One-Eyed Jack's

It was a busy night at the tavern. A band of gypsies had made camp for the night in Waysborough Common and their talented dancers had put on quite a show. Now, well into the evening, the tired performers and their families had filled every vacant seat in the place. Food and ale were almost flying across the bar, and One-Eye's servers were hard-pressed to keep up with it. One of the Gypsy elders named Jan, a man of dark complexion, bright-colored clothes, and long graying hair, had joined us by the fire. Jan was anxious to hear my story because his family had fought valiantly in defense of Safehaven during the Queen's invasion.

A cup full of Kegporter Wine rested in my hand and filled my mind with rising memories as I raised my glass to toast my audience. With the tip of my left forefinger, I swirled Kur's wonderful elixir and then tossed a few drops into the air above the table. Smoke from nearby pipe smokers and steamy air from the kitchen mingled about the ceiling rafters above us, where a solitary mouse scanned the inn beneath him, memorizing the location of the choicest scraps for after the last of the candles went out and his time began. With a word and Kur's wine, my illusion took shape in the vanishing vapors between us, and there, before us all, was the horrifying, sinister, smiling face of Black Bible. Everyone there who saw his face gasped in horror and shuddered. Many said quiet prayers or made signs against the evil eye. I then banished his image with my words and began my tale anew.

"They bound and gagged us all, trussing us up in sacks sewn from the skin of some Underearth beast. They then attached us to long poles like game for the table and in this manner, prepared to carry us through the treacherous ways of their homeland. Their vile poisons were so strong that none of us awoke or had any memories of that journey, save terrible dreams of wicked laughter and sinister voices whispering promises of tortures unimaginable. Our unconsciousness was our blessing, for if any of us had awoken to witness any portion of Grulthank, then that onlooker would have been instantly silenced, condemned to breathe no more.

"Down and down they brought us, carrying us south, across many miles of winding tunnel ways laced with countless traps and deadly pitfalls. If any of us could have seen their labyrinthine killing grounds, we would have observed the bones of their unfortunate enemies resting in their contorted positions of death. Here, so far from the light, the Merciless One had many followers. Their lands were a nightmare to any kind-hearted soul, but it was a heaven under earth to the Darg.

Vulgsharn

The journey required the passage of an entire surface day, but to the Darg, it seemed only the right amount of time. Their bodies' malign strength was commendable, for each pair of Darg carrying a prisoner between them required no rest, and they completed the entire march with no signs of fatigue, need for water, or complaint. Their society accepted no weakness, and such virtues as kindness and consideration were considered among the greatest of frailties. In the same manner, they continued on through their lands without stopping until they reached their southmost gate, which they called Vulgsharn.

Vulgsharn was a succession of gateways ingeniously crafted, with open killing fields between each one. Each gate was designed to easily be collapsed behind the next in titanic avalanches of falling rock. The outermost gate was the most cunning and impervious of them all. Standing in the midst of an incredible fissure, which rose to infinity above and seemingly further down below, its height peaked at more than twenty feet. The enormous vent was called Cleave Maga, which meant "Great Chasm of Lava."

Descending from the mighty door was a long narrow stair that wound its way south between the two gaping outer walls of that abysmal cave. The natural stair had perhaps been formed eons before when the fires of Underearth had once roared with volcanic fury and then slowly receded, leaving only the slender finger of rock behind in the memory of its passing. It was upon this narrow stair at the foot of Vulgsharn that they left their captives, thus fulfilling their debt of blood to the son of Aklon.

"We should take the bounty," Black Bible said.

"The debt of blood forbids it," said the captain.

"Surely the debt of blood was meant for the father and not the son."

"That is not the law. We must leave them unharmed and unrobbed."

"They possess powerful magic," said the one called Fell Sorcerer. "Surely A'Goric will be pleased if we deliver it to him."

The captain well knew that mutiny was soon to befall him. His company was strong, and he could not defeat them all alone. He had to hope that A'Goric would feel as Fell Sorcerer had suggested, or otherwise his days would end here.

"Rob them," the captain ordered, "but hurt them not. Let the plague kill them."

"The Gnome has a powerful magic about his neck," Fell Sorcerer said, "but it won't come off unless I sever it."

"Hold your cleaver!" the captain said. "Leave it. There is plenty more for the taking."

And later it could only be said that if not for the resiliency of the gnomish neck, then the sorcerer would surely have pulled Kalor's poor head off. It is also possible that the sudden discovery of an amazing gem of power that he also carried may have distracted the evil wizard just enough to forget about it. They robbed, and they searched, taking everything that didn't have too great of an aura of goodness about it, until there was no stone left unturned, no trinket untaken.

They had abandoned little, a ranger's sword and a Dwarven ax were all that remained in the cave of the Korg-Troggin, where they had fallen. Their clothing and their armor, the Darg left them, because it had no value to them. The captain himself claimed the Elemental Blade.

"Let us return now to A'Goric," he said, "and may the plague take them." There was much giggling and the ringing of sinister little hands after that. Deep down, in the slumber of Darg poison, they would never notice when their lives finally slipped away from them.

Goddess Fearing

Lothdea has been our Goddess since our creation," Darik said. "Indeed, she is our Mother."

"And our people have lived in fear of her wrath since that dawning day."

"It was Lothdea who led the Queen and our nation out of the darkness and into the light of day."

"And it is she who forbids the uttering of the names of any god save herself, Lue-Raig, and Arachnidon."

"Are there any others?" Darik asked.

"As limitless as the Heavens themselves," Vlad said. "No longer should the Dockalfar be bound by the Deities of the past."

"We are bound," Darik said, "chained body and soul to the Goddess. How can the Dockalfar ever hope to escape their bondage?"

"We must unite and challenge them. We must learn to stand on our own."

"Perhaps we are not ready."

"Those among us with open minds have been ready for centuries, but they are not strong enough. We need a new world order."

"Surely the Goddess would destroy anyone foolish enough to attempt to usurp her rule."

"Then a new leader is needed to take a stand before her."

"How could a mere mortal, even one as long-lived as we, stand and face her?"

"By gaining the strength of a god!"

"The demon binding has given you great powers."

"The Lord of Shadow was one of the Ancients, one of the First Born, ruler of his plane, as now am I. Is it enough to battle Lothdea? Certainly not. For that, we need the Duaredheim Staff."

"I have many fears relating to the artifact, Commander."

"If we are to win, Darik, we must take such risks, but please continue."

"We do not yet know the ultimate power of the staff, nor are we even sure that a mortal can wield it."

"The Dockalfar are nearly immortal," Vlad said, "unless they meet some earlier end."

"And you are even more so now," Darik said, "and rumors of a secret hero of freedom are spreading. More and more Drakkar Noire are flocking to our cause."

"There is great danger in that," Vlad said. "The more soldiers who flock to our banner, the greater the risk of exposure. If the Queen discovers our plans too soon, all is lost."

"Andreul fears that she may already know."

"I have considered that possibility," Vlad said. "If she already knows, and she very well may, then she is waiting to see if we succeed."

"And if we do," Darik said, "then she will choose that moment to act and seize the staff from us!"

"Precisely!"

"Ariana?"

"Certainly Lothdea hopes that she will betray me in the end."

"Or else force her to do so."

"I have come to believe in Ariana's will, but as you fear, the Goddess may take over her psyche and force her hand."

"I shall pray that that doesn't happen," Darik said. "I may even be able to help protect her with spells from the realm of Death."

"She will never agree to it."

"She would never know. The power will only manifest if some outside force tries to possess her."

"Prepare your spells then, Darik," Vlad said, "but do not cast them unless our secret plans are undone."

"Where are you off to now, Commander?" Darik asked.

"Ariana and I have business to attend to. It seems that a company of Darg is certain to betray us."

"Good luck, Commander."

"Continue your work, Darik," Vlad said. "You are in command until my return." Then, uncharacteristically, he left by the laboratory's front door, proceeding to walk through the lower halls of his fortress in a most mundane fashion. The Queen had sent him a new company of Dragonian Marines to reinforce his strength, and no doubt there were spies among them. He made a point to visit their barracks unannounced. Walking casually into the room, he was in uniform yet unarmored. The men were playing cards, lying leisurely upon their bunks, writing letters home, and doing any number of lackadaisical things. He was among them for some time before he was recognized by one of the new lieutenants.

"Company, attention!" In a flash of activity, the rag-tag bunch was on their feet, standing tall, rigidly locked at attention. "Good evening, sir."

"You and your men do realize, Lieutenant," Vlad said, "that we will soon be at war."

"Yes, Commander."

"I trust that the next time that I visit, you will all be more prepared?"

"Yes, sir!"

"Very well, as you were, gentlemen," Vlad commanded, and then the troops, well-trained as they were, returned to their leisure. "Lieutenant Malack, give me the status of your command and their relative training."

"Sir, my company is at full strength, with no men down due to illness or injury."

"And your platoons?"

"Four platoons of twenty-two men, sir. The soldiers are all crack infantry, with extensive training in castle-siege and siege-weaponry."

"And your command?"

"Four platoon leaders, four sergeants, the first sergeant, and I am the lieutenant acting in command."

"What are the qualifications of your first sergeant?"

"Sir, he is a fifty-year veteran. First Sergeant Conrad has fought savages on the Shattered Isles and Fermish Pirates out of Itzul."

"What weapons training does he possess?"

"Sir, he is well-trained in the use of any blade and an expert shot with a crossbow. As an artillerist, he has no equal."

"Lieutenant, I must depart for a short time," Vlad said. "During that time I want you and your men to train the Orcs in the field construction of catapults and siege towers. Your mission is critical if we are to breach the defenses at Harg Pass and beyond."

"We will not fail, sir!"

"See that you don't." He then proceeded to mingle with the men, speaking to each soldier in turn, praising them if their equipment was well cared for, and correcting those whose wasn't. His inspection was casual, quite unmilitary, but if anything, his methods made an even more lasting impression upon them. It seemed that their commander was in some ways like them, a soldier and a man, aloof yet apart. Many of them felt off-balance, even in some ways, giddy. He stayed among them for some time and left after he had memorized each of their names, their rank, and what he could divine about their personalities. He was a good judge of character, even without reading their minds. Within an hour, he knew just who the likely spies were.

"What is the name of your company, Lieutenant?"

"We are the Second Company, Fiftieth Marines."

"Within my command, you will have a different name," Vlad said. "Discuss it with all of your men. When I return, I expect to hear it."

"Yes, Commander!"

The majority of the marines gained a large measure of pride and respect for their general; for him, they would fight to the death.

He had to trust in his men to prepare the fortress in his absence; for now, he had no time to waste. He needed Ariana. They would depart together. His father had warned him about the blood debt of the Darg. His father had known all their ways that a non-Darg could possibly know, and because of this, Vlad knew that they would soon betray him.

He moved through the veins of the fortress swiftly, sometimes like an agile Elf and at other times like a wraith. He was pleased to find his guards alert and his defenses ever ready. When he reached Ariana's chambers, he knocked three times. He was surprised when she answered her door herself, fully armored and equipped with all of the regalia of war. "I am ready, General."

"You must be, or we will both die this day."

"Where will we face them?"

"We will wait for them in Shadow, near the chasm where they are sure to leave Carmen's Rangers."

"Carmen's Rangers?"

"I believe that the name is fitting," Vlad said, "do you not?"

"You give them too much respect."

"They have already done more than most would ever dream possible. You will see that they are worthy, and soon."

"I do agree, Commander."

"To what?"

"That Carmen's rangers is a good name."

"Good, has my armor been prepared?"

"Efmiel has brought it," Ariana said. "But she was willful, so I sent her to the kitchens."

"Yes," Vlad said as he began to change into his armor, "she is difficult, but useful."

"I don't know what you see in her," Ariana said, "or why you insist on protecting her."

"I have a use for her yet," Vlad said. "If she is killed, then my plans will suffer. See to it that she remains unharmed, my Queen."

"Oh, I don't want her dead, Commander. I just want her to suffer a little."

"See to it that she stays alive, Ariana."

"Yes, Commander."

"Then take my hand." With a gentle pull, they drifted into Shadow, Vlad transforming, until they were soon flying above the plane of eternal twilight. His arms wrapped around her, and his wings stretched out to ride the ethereal wind.

"Where are you taking me?"

"We travel through Shadow, my Queen," he said, "my world."

"Your world?"

"My world."

She was stunned. She knew about the demon-binding spell, but not the true scope of his newly acquired power. She thought that it had been her imagination when they had lain together, but now she understood. She had heard two heartbeats, believing the second to be her own, but now she knew the truth. "Why not just use the mirrors?"

"It would have taken too long for Darik to program an exact location. Through shadow, we can arrive anywhere, on almost any plane, in any Universe."

"You speak of the power of the gods!"

"Nay, not of the gods but of myself. Look ahead there, beyond that second black cloud. Can you not see it?"

"I see nothing—no, wait! I see the chasm near the border of Grulthank."

"Indeed."

"But how?"

"That is a secret that I shall keep for now, my love. It is too dangerous to reveal for one so close to the Goddess. I shall build us an island, for us to prepare ourselves on, and to watch."

"Are you certain that they shall come this way?"

"Oh, they will come. It's as certain as Darg treachery," and then, with a flick of his envenomed tail and the invocation of one demonic hand, he soon created a floating black island and set Ariana down upon it. Accustomed as she was to magic, she was nevertheless amazed. "It feels as solid as stone!"

"It is very much so, yet nonpermanent. As soon as my essence leaves, it will begin to fade. Rest for now and prepare your spells. You must armor our bodies against their black magic."

"Then let us begin," she answered, beginning to cast spell after spell upon them, warding them against fire, against ice, against air and earth, shielding their minds against controlling magic, their bodies against pain, against cuts by blade or arrow or hammers of war. Such was her power that her repertoire of spells was barely taxed.

Continuing on, she reinforced them all and extended the duration of their power. She was only halfway through when he called her.

"It is time," he said, and in an instant, they stood upon a wide cavern cliff overlooking the Darg's road home.

"And now it's time for my spells," Vlad said, "for here you must hide, invisible, in the shadows. Act not to save me unless all appears lost. Your most important role will come not in this battle but soon after it."

"You will face them all alone?"

"I owe it to my father. They will pay the price for their dishonor."

"Very well, General," Ariana said, "but you must know that no single Dockalfar has ever faced so many Darg alone and lived."

"One man did, and his name was Aklon. Fear not, my love," he said before kissing her, "if we fail here, then all is lost anyway." Expertly cast, his magic soon took effect, and Ariana disappeared. "Speak not," Vlad said, "and protect your back. Do not believe that the stone protects you. It is like water to them."

If Vlad could have seen her, he would have witnessed her unease; for now, nowhere seemed safe. Needless to say, as Dockalfar Priestesses went, she was one of the most powerful in existence. Indeed, she was to be the next in line for leadership of the coven, but that destiny was no longer her heart's greatest desire. She believed in her divine magic, but most of all, she believed in him.

Dark Betrayal

Shadows cloaked him in their concealing embrace. Waiting patiently for his prey to arrive, he conversed lightly with his dark minions, for he was now not unlike a god, and to the inhabitants of Shadow, he was master. They whispered to him of goings-on in the land of the light and the lands without, telling him what they feared and craving his commands like young men eager to rule but bereft of knowledge. Laughing and crying with them, he both understood and respected their ways, and even their very existence.

"Go and wait," he told them, "it's time for us to hunt!"

Positioning himself carefully, he had chosen the battleground that most befitted him and handicapped his enemies.

Behind a tarantula's eyes lurks madness, behind a tiger's, might; both of which could be found in his eyes, but he was not always thus. The pale blue of his eyes suggested gentleness and a kind upbringing, but his face told another story. His cheekbones were prominent and backswept, his hawk-like nose previously broken. His mane was ebon, and his square well-muscled jaw held none of the softness of youth. In truth, he looked much like his father did—lean, fierce, and powerful.

He was the sole heir to House Leu Sherroan. His father was his primary teacher and principal influence. He remembered his teachings even now, in this dark and desolate place. His memories were gifts to contemplate in idle times, and so he waited, like a trapdoor spider, patient hunter within, invisible death without.

So strange, he thought, *that everything that had happened in the last year had occurred as the result of the actions a few Fermen and one small Gnome's dreams.*

He heard quiet footsteps and a baneful marching song. They were here!

Poison and blood,
Torture and mud,
Take a drink, hammer a link,
Cripple a Gnome just for fun!

A thousand thoughts raced through his mind as he watched them approach. Twenty-one Darg in all, carrying sacks filled with gems and other spoils. Their leader traveled near the middle of their column, with his sorcerer before him. Clearly they had forgotten their debt of blood and the debt of honor. They marched with grim purpose, their formation loose yet methodical. Their clothing was for the most part identical, their cloaks void of insignia to conceal the identity of their leaders, but Vlad knew him. He knew of the one called Silent Scream.

He was strong among the Darg, belonging to an order of evil calling themselves the Hand of Abbathor. That one should have respected the blood debt; indeed, he may have, at least initially. Darg leadership was fragile at best and usually short lived. Perhaps his followers had refused his orders. Exactly why they betrayed him no longer mattered. The deal was done.

Their armor was a mixture of adamant plates and chain mail woven with the darkest enchantments. Their caps were plain and unadorned, their helmets well padded and expertly forged. Their weapons were many: short swords forged of the nearly indestructible adamant, blowguns, and six-foot-long spears with jagged points and wicked barbs. A few of them carried crossbows of unusual design, and many of them carried nets weighted and hooked for capturing, and later torturing, their helpless prey.

There were other wizards hidden among them, including one whose name meant Fell Sorcerer. They possessed terrible powers of rock-shifting, poison, and Necromancy. Even for the greatest of warriors it was both foolish and suicidal to face such a party alone, but he was the son of Aklon, and he had planned this well. Stepping out of the shadows, he confronted them. "Hold! You have stolen that which does not belong to the Darg. Have you forgotten the debt to Aklon?"

"We took it easily," one of them said. "To the strong go the spoils."

"Then the debt of honor is also forgotten?"

"Not forgotten," said Silent Scream, "but perhaps the son of Aklon has grown too weak to protect his family's treasures. We delivered the surfacers past Grulthank unmolested and unkilled."

"That was only half of the bargain."

"The debt of blood is paid. The debt of honor is worthless."

Vlad's eyes grew dark. In the realm of Shadow, his minions trembled. The very air thinned beneath the weight of his angry stare. "Then the Darg have forgotten the honor of Leu-Sherroan, for only fools would doubt the conviction of the son of Aklon."

"The one named Aklon has fallen and will not return," said Black Bible. "His navy was smashed, smashed, in the Harbor of Itzul."

"Stand aside or be cut down," said Fell Sorcerer.

"Return the spoils to me and I will consider the debts paid in full."

"Go back to your fortress, would-be king," said Silent Scream. "You will meet your end here."

Each side watched the other. The air was still, as quiet as death.

Vlad muttered a word, and a wall of energy surrounded him.

The Darg loosed their bolts and poisoned darts, each one a volley of death, but each shaft was vaporized by Dockalfar magic.

Suddenly, the walls began to move, dark ghostly things spilling from every corner, children of Shadow, Vlad's minions. They attacked.

The Darg shrieked, drawing black swords and thrusting adamant spears. Black magic banished his minions and burned away his shield wall. They rushed him, but he was no longer there.

Stepping out of the Shadows behind them, his enchanted wand, Sharakul-Loth, erupted, its flames filling the tunnel, enveloping everything within it. Ariana crouched inside of her protective shell, feeling its heat even there. The magical fire was as hot as dragon's breath, the very stone of the walls melting beneath its onslaught.

Several of the Darg were caught by surprise, and those had no time to raise their evil magic in order to ward off the flames. Their flesh withered, cooking off their bones, their dying screams merely gasps. When the fires ceased, their adamant armor was all that remained of them. The tunnel reeked of burning flesh; for a moment, all things were uncertain because the smoke blinded them all.

The Dark Dwarves had survived for ages through treachery and cunning, and although the fire destroyed the lesser warriors, the greater among them had quickly spoken words of warding or activated the baneful sorcery woven into their armor. To them, Vlad's fire was little more than an inconvenience, and they slogged through the molten rock of the road as if the lava was merely the mud of some dismal quagmire or the sands of some distant shore. On and on they came, Darg, once twenty-one, now fifteen, their faces set with jagged grimace and ill intent. It was then that their sorcerers revealed themselves, and they battered Vlad with all manner of hate-filled spells and vile curses.

He nearly faltered beneath their counterattack, but Ariana's spells held against them all. He was no longer as he once had been. He was now half Demon Lord, half Dockalfar, and he was the ruler of Shadow, the underworld between darkness and light. His body was nearly invulnerable, his flesh and bones as resilient as a demon prince's bones. He had his father's intellect and his family's spirit, as irresistible as a mountain. In this battle versus these foes, he fought like his father would have, like a Dockalfar Lord. Spells and enchantments of war filled his mind, and when he again lashed out, lightning bolts crackled, fire exploded, and the very earth split! In the tumult, many of the Darg were sucked into the gaping maw of the earth, and when the smoke again cleared, the Darg ranks were reduced to ten, but those remaining were far from finished.

His mind calculated every change, flowing with the direction of combat. Raising magical wards to protect himself, his enemies beat at his protective shields with weapons starving for his flesh, parched for his blood. He was powerful, but even his strength had its limits, and Vlad's spells were being consumed one by one as he defended himself.

They circled him now, and it seemed to them that he was weakening. It appeared to them that he was about to fall, and their wicked smiles were terrible to behold! When they returned to A'Goric with his head, they would be the heroes of Grulthank, and all manner of foul pleasures would be theirs. Silent Scream was gleeful; for with this victory, the blood debt to House Leu Sherroan would finally come to an end. Better still, the line of Aklon would die without an heir.

If Vlad had been merely a Dockalfar Lord, then perhaps he would have fallen, but he was his father's Son, trained since childhood to use all the potential of his mind. Knowing the hearts of his foes, he knew that their warlocks often held their most devastating spells in reserve for use when their prey was at its weakest, and so he feigned his own helplessness, allowing fear to show upon his face.

Above him in her hiding place, Ariana trembled, for she had never seen such a display of power. Vlad's act was so perfect that even she was fooled, but she remembered his words, and waited. She had to trust him, but her own worries would soon outgrow her patience.

The warlocks unleashed their fury. Where Vlad stood, the very air boiled, the ground shattered, and spirit itself melted, and lo! They saw him sink before them, his face twisted in a silent agony, his body and armor melted, ruined, and ended. He was utterly consumed. When the smoke cleared, ten Darg stood staring at the pile of ashes, and they all laughed the hearty laugh of thieves who are relieved to have escaped a horrible twist of fate.

"No more will House Leu Sherroan threaten the Darg," Silent Scream said. "No more will the son of Aklon wield his debt of blood."

Black Bible chuckled nervously, and Fell Sorcerer breathed a sigh of relief.

Ariana was beyond reason, her lover murdered and utterly beyond resurrection. She began to chant the first of her killing spells, raising the power of the Goddess.

Ten pairs of black eyes lanced their malice upon her.

It was then the Vlad stepped forth from the shadows. His enemies' hearts were filled with fear, for their sorcerers had no more spells of war, and their armor of adamant was singed, pitted, its magic exhausted. "So easily you seal the fate of a Dockalfar Lord?"

"Our curses are gone, our spells depleted," Fell Sorcerer said, "but our blades still hunger for the blood of Aklon!"

Vlad battled them then in the manner of his father. He was now, indeed, a Dockalfar Lord, like his ancestors before him, and his was a spirit and lineage of honor. No longer would he engage these enemies like a wizard, but rather, like a warrior. This time, he unsheathed Shinpa Grul, which meant "Trusted Friend," his father's own sword; to his father's enemies, it was known only as the Decapitator, and for the rest, he would use his hands and his feet like a dragon. His body moved like boiling liquid, never still, always on the move, at times like a viper, or a hawk, or a tearing tiger. One by one, the Darg warriors fell, until only Vlad, Silent Scream, Fell Sorcerer, and Black Bible remained. Blood dripped from him in at least a dozen places, and their poisons sought his heart, but neither of his hearts were that of just a man, no more! Now he possessed a demon's still-beating heart, and his elfin heart had grown as well. Their dreadful poisons would have slain a hundred warriors, but to him, it was like fuel to the fire, and his body healed itself before their very eyes! Their eyes, which had so recently been filled with the sparkle of victory, were now only mirrors reflecting their own deaths.

"Surrender your plunder to me," Vlad said, "and I'll let you live."

Silent Scream looked to his fellows, and they were all of like mind. "You lie," he said. "You will kill us anyway."

"As you wish," Vlad answered.

Fell Sorcerer produced the Duaredheim's gem, trying to summon power from it, but the flawless crystal refused to awaken, and Shinpa Grul took his head. His second blow removed Silent Scream's sword hand at the wrist, and Atran-Doru fell clattering to the floor. "A hand for a hand, vile paladin," Vlad said.

Black Bible uttered his last curse, but it held no power. Slashing at Vlad, he turned to run, but a column of fire like the hand of god smote him, and he soon fell smoldering, dead. Silent Scream used the distraction to meld with stone and escape. It was one of their most unique powers, and one that the Darg could use after only brief concentration. Somehow, they could manipulate the structure of their bodies in such a way that stone was as pliable as water to them. They could float, walk, and even swim through it, and in some way sense how to get from here to there in it. Vlad considered traveling through Shadow to get him, but it didn't matter, Silent Scream's treachery would get the best of him in the end.

Ariana stood on the edge of the overhang, looking down at the carnage. "Don't do that to me again."

"I had to make it look real."

"Now I know why I hate Illusionists! Are you coming up here, or do I have to come down there and melt off my feet?"

"One moment," he said, taking up Atran-Doru.

"You are no Druid!"

"You will serve me for a time," Vlad said, "and then I will return you to the young acolyte."

"Yes, master."

"Please, a rain to cool the stone." Clouds formed, and soon the rain fell, filling the tunnel with blinding steam, but in time, the stone hardened, encasing some of the bodies, entombing them for eternity. Ariana then leaped down to his side. "Well done, Commander."

"Regretfully, many of the stolen items have now been lost."

"But we have the most important ones—the gem, the Gnome's blades, and the diamond from the divining scepter."

"And Atran-Doru," Vlad said, "but we must hurry. We must recover the Dwarf's weapons, and the ranger's Sword of Flame before Silent Scream returns to alert A'Goric."

"After you," Ariana said, holding out her hand.

The Master Smith

Bellows roared, and the thunder of His hammer shook the foundation of the world. Standing before his gigantic anvil, he was huge beyond imagining, as limitless as the Heavens themselves. Kur knew that he stood watching the Creator. Three strange beings stood around him, appearing as Dwarves yet somehow unfinished. He looked more closely. They seemed to be molded from clay.

"Griznost! Dumalone! Arthorm!" the god said. "Bring me iron and mithril and stone!"

Taking each of the elements from his assistants, he then placed them in his giant crucible and melted them into one upon his forge fire. His work seemed attentive and methodical, as if he was an artist creating a masterpiece. Suddenly, his anvil spouted great gouts of steam, and Kur could see Moradeus no more. The hissing sound continued, and he knew then that he was awakening from some kind of dream.

Lying on cool stone, he first noticed that his right arm was completely asleep, tucked as it was behind his back. Rolling over required real effort, and he groaned against the pain of countless cuts and bruises. It was hot, dreadfully so, like reaching into an oven. He was covered in sweat, sickly yellow-green colored, and he could smell the taint of the Dargs' poison in it.

"Bastards," he muttered. Removing his armor and clothing, he tried to wipe as much of the vileness off himself as he could. Soon after, he was wracked with a coughing fit that seemed to clear still more of it. His head spun, but things were clearing, coming into focus.

He was the first of his companions to awaken. Lying on the ground all around him, they were strewn about on crudely carved stairs bisecting the top of a slender finger of rock. Reaching for his wineskin, he noticed that it was somehow full. He uncorked it. It seemed to be filled with clean water.

Probably a Darg trick, he thought, *laced with poison*. Overcome with thirst, he risked placing some in his mouth and spitting it out. When nothing happened, he tried a little sip and waited. Still alive after some time, he chanced a long drink, saving the last of it for reviving his friends. Some of them awoke with a splash; others needed a slap or two from his callused hands.

It was a miracle all of them were alive and, besides a few sore spots, completely healed.

"Whoa," Dao said, "my head is spinning!"

"That's the poison," Kur said. "The more that you move around, the quicker that your body will shake it."

Kalor groaned. "How is it that we're still here? Everyone was dying."

"I don't know, Kalor," Kur said. "They had us cold."

"And if not the Gnomes," Leander said, "then surely the Antmen could have had their way with us."

"Perhaps we have overstepped ourselves with this quest," Dao said. "Every step of the way is wrought with peril."

"But now we know," Tariq said, "that we are on the course of something immensely important. If it wasn't, then we would all surely be dead."

"We should leave this place," Karina said. "It reeks of evil, and I can feel their filth on my skin. Their voices will haunt my dreams forever. Let us run. I want to run away with all of my heart."

"Easy, Lady Greylinx," Tariq said, "we have no way of knowing if the greatest terror lies behind us, or in front."

"Let's rest for a short time at least," Carmen said. "We need to clear our heads and think about what has happened."

"And Kalor and I should study," Dao said. "A few spells could go a long way towards keeping us alive down here—that is, if we have anything left to contemplate from?"

"It is amazing," Kalor said, "but Modrul's Book was left behind as well. All of the remaining formulae are still intact."

"Most likely the bastards can't read," Kur said. "Leander, how is your hand?"

"What about it? And why are you walking around in your loincloth?"

"The Darg cut it off to steal away your sword, and to answer your second question, I am covered in Darg poison. Would you mind using the flat of your knife to scrape it off of my back?"

"Not at all, but I am a little worried about being poisoned again."

"I'm fairly sure that it only works if it penetrates the skin."

"I'm feeling a bit uncertain about your uncertainty," Leander said, "but here goes. Now that you mention it, my hand is a little sore, and my scar is gone."

"Your scar?"

"A dog bit me when I was five, nearly tore my hand off. If anything, my hand is even better than it used to be."

"By Correlleus, what the hell is going on?" asked Dao. "It seems like we have a guardian angel."

"Maybe we're already dead," Karina said, "and this is the stairway to Hell."

"Not dead," Tariq said, "spared, but why and by whom?"

"Too bad they didn't spare Kalor's neck."

"Someone tried to pry off his necklace."

"If they had pulled any harder," Kalor said, "they would have pulled my head clean off. My neck is so swollen, I can barely breathe."

"My sword is gone," Leander said while checking his belongings, "and all of the gems that I took from Modrul's Lair."

"Mine too," Dartin said.

"Everything valuable is gone," Carmen said. "Kalor, do you still have the gem?"

"I do, it's still in my pack as it always was, and the scepter's gem as well, but no scepter."

"See if it still works."

"Arcanus Verbera Locus," and then its magical rainbow of light burst out, its insistent pull nearly tearing the gem from his hand. "Now I know what the scepter was for!"

"So the magic was in the diamond alone," Dartin said.

"As long as we have it," Kalor said, "we still have a chance to stop them."

"It's strange," Karina said, "but I don't feel sick anymore."

"Nor I."

"Nor anyone, I think," Carmen said. "Someone has helped us beyond measure this day."

"But why?" Dao asked.

"Surely the Darg would have finished the job," Kur said. "I can't believe that they left us alive."

"Someone must have been holding something over them," Tariq said, "something big."

"Probably the same ones who helped us."

"They could have taken it all," Dao said, "the gems, our weapons—everything, and let us die. What possible reason could they have for wanting us alive?"

"There's only one way to find out," Karina said while stretching. "Rangers and Dwarves in the front, little Thieves in the rear."

"Whoever it was that stole Leander's sword," Tariq said, "returned the rest of our weapons to us, even my sword of flame that has no name."

"That's it!" said Karina.

"That's what?"

"Flame!" she said, "the name of the sword that had no name."

"Flame," Tariq said, brandishing it, and by magic, flames caressed its length, and they all agreed that it was indeed a good name.

"Well," said Dao, "I don't like the look of things hereabouts. I'm thinking that a swift departure is in order."

"Get your studying done," Carmen said. "The rest of us will check the gear and pack what we have left. Then we're getting the hell out of here!" They all laughed with her at that, and for a moment, the darkness seemed to fade. "Well, Keg, are you going to come along like that?"

"It is more comfortable in the heat."

"But not so good against a sword," Tariq said. "Clothes and armor would be good."

"Very well," Kur said, grumbling, "but that Darg captain better hope that we never meet again."

Behind them loomed the Darg's impenetrable door, forged of the black alloy adamant. Some twenty feet in height, it stood barred from within, standing like the hideous claw of a devil, shielding Grulthank from the outside world.

"There is another possibility," Tariq said, "that they haven't let us go at all."

"Of course," Leander said, "we can neither travel north, east, or west, and without wings we can't go up or down. Only south remains."

"Then let's hurry along to the next trap then," Kalor said. "I've already gone far too long without being hurled into a wall."

"That hissing," Dartin said, "what is it?"

"Water striking the lava," Kur said, "the blood of the earth to the Dwarves. To fall into it means incineration, but some believe that it is possible to ask the element of fire for help and wade through it without burning."

"Just how hot is it?"

"Hot enough to melt your bones in seconds and your sword in two more."

"Then how could someone wade through it?" Dao asked.

"The Dwarves know that each element has a spirit," Kur said, "a force that can be communicated with. In certain conditions of extreme fear or stress, a Dwarf, or any being, can ask the elements to accept them."

"You told us before," Tariq said, "that the Dwarves were forged with fire. Maybe that's why the lava will accept you."

"Accept you?" Dao said.

"Once accepted, you become one with the fire, and it won't burn you."

"What if you're not accepted?" Karina asked.

"Then you burn."

"Perhaps we can skip the lava," Dartin said painfully. "This winding stair seems perfectly sound."

"I just can't imagine why they let us go?" Karina said.

"I think that our meeting was no accident," Tariq said. "It was a setup."

"Then someone hired them to capture us," Carmen said.

"But who," Dao said, "and why?"

"I think that we're soon to find out," Kalor said, holding the magical diamond aloft once more. "Arcanus Verbera Locus!" Coming to life in a rainbow of light, shining like a lighthouse beacon, it pulled his arm southward until he pointed straight down the length of the slender stair.

"What say thee, Kur?" Carmen said. "Do you think that they have let us go, or left us to die in some foul trap?"

"They never let anyone go," Kur said. "Someone must have made them let us go, or else we would still be their captives, trapped like Tariq said."

"Who are they?" Karina asked.

"The Darg."

"The Darg?"

"Black-hearted Dwarves who thrive on lies and deceit," Kur said in disgust. "They are no kin to other Dwarves, nor were they created by Moradeus."

"It's hard to believe that such an evil could survive without consuming itself," Dartin said. "There are many old tales of evil Dwarves trading powerful magic for souls."

"Yes," Leander said, "I remember the story of Brodir, Chief of the Sea Wolves. He sold his soul for chain mail that no blade could bite and the gift of future sight."

"And it was Brodir who slew the good king Brian, and he who slew Brodir upon the marshy plain of Clontarf in the year 1014."

"And his sons then drove the rest of the rogues into the sea."

"But most of them died as well," Dartin said. "It is a sad tale, but some of King Brian's descendants lived on."

"Let's save the history lesson for later," Tariq said. "Inventory the gear and get packed. We'll stow Kalor's and Dao's for them."

"Get everything ready," Carmen said, "and then get some rest. As soon as the wizards are ready, we're moving out." Much of their gear had been stolen, and so their burden was light. The bountiful treasures that they had taken from Modrul's Lair were largely gone, including all their potions, Kalor's magic scrolls, and all their coins and gems. Most of their armor and arms had been spared. Their rucksacks, although pilfered, still held some useful sundries, and although their food was gone, their waterskins had been filled. Their minds were filled with many questions and few answers, but they were now a party of action. Working together as one, their strength returned anew.

The would-be wizards had learned what they could in those few precious hours, but their position, so precarious, so near to the heart of evil, begged——nay, insisted, upon flight. Fly away, heroes. Run. Run until ragged breath, ruined heart, and useless limbs. Run until pathways end, wall of rock, or endless rift. Flee until witless end.

It was to their credit that they resisted fear's call, for who among them could know what new dangers lurked ahead in the world of eternal dark?

Their first few steps down that long finger-like path of rock were the most harrowing, because the last effects of the Darg's poison still lingered, dizzying, nauseous, and painful. A sea of lava churned far below them, and such was its heat that the very walls of the chasm appeared to their heat-sensitive eyes to be bathed in blood. Looking over the edge was like looking into an abyss, an endless fall into a river of fire. Despite their handicaps, they were whole and well for the first time in days. With each passing step, the Darg's sinister presence began to fade from their memories, but would haunt their dreams for years to come. The Quest had nearly taken all of their lives, and yet they still lived. Perhaps they did have some guardian angel. Hope had been rekindled.

GRULTHANK

"Bring Silent Scream to me!" A'Goric raged.

"Yes, my king," said his captain of the guard, and within minutes, the black-hearted captain stood before his king, chained and shackled, with guards numbering thirty.

"You have failed utterly," A'Goric said. "You have forsaken the debt of blood and brought shame upon the Darg—you, who of all my subjects I had deemed the least likely to betray me. I offer you this final chance to explain yourself."

"We delivered the surfacers as planned," Silent Scream said, "then Fell Sorcerer and Black Bible led a coup against me. It was mutiny!"

"Mutiny? I shall have their corpses resurrected, so that they can be tortured for their treachery! They insult the debt of honor. They insult the law! But what more do you have to say for yourself?"

"If not for the meddlesome witch, the line of Aklon would be dead, dead, and A'Goric would have riches, riches. Let me lead your army against Drakon Mur-Falor. We will crush the Orcs and end Leu Sherroan forever."

"It was mutiny, so my verdict is mercy. Silent Scream, for your betrayal against your king, and against the law, you shall be tortured, you shall be maimed, and you shall be mutilated unto death!"

"Then I curse you and these halls!"

"Cut out his tongue!" And it was done. "You will curse no longer, for it is Silent Scream who is cursed!" Then and there, in the high meeting hall of A'Goric, Silent Scream was tortured, he was maimed, and he was mutilated unto death.

Later, A'Goric's High Priest resurrected him, and what returned was even viler, more wretched, and more sinister than ever before. An evil powerful enough to stand next to the son of Aklon and nearly achieve victory was far too valuable to waste, too full of the favor of Abbathoreus. One day, such a one as he might lead the Darg, but for now, it was A'Goric who sat in the high seat.

Torture, betrayal, mutilation, and mutiny—that's what Darg dreams are made of.

The Hall of Kings

The slender stair upon which they descended was a wonder of natural magic. The great lava flows below them had, in ages past, filled the chamber that they now traveled through. Eons later, its fires diminished, it now flowed far below them. During its descent, it left behind the slender ridge of stone upon which the Darg had carved their stairs. Any travelers stumbling to the left or right would meet their end in a fall of grim finality.

If Kalor had possessed a spell powerful enough to spirit them all away, then he would have done so, but as it was, he and Dao only had time to learn a few simple incantations. Among the magic that they studied were spells that could catch a falling object, slowing its descent in such a manner that it would land unscathed, and an even stronger spell that could levitate an object back to its origin and beyond. Modrul's Book held so much wonder, but its hidden power required time and diligent study to learn. Time, which had once seemed so trivial, was now ever precious and always in short supply. Each time that they stopped to rest, they studied. Pouring their energies into the difficult task, they hoped that they would be better prepared when next danger threatened them.

They traveled for hours and countless miles, the heat and geysers of steam unending. "Perhaps this is no bridge at all," Dartin said, "but the body of Jormungand the World Serpent."

"I hope that he stays asleep," Karina answered. Above them, the cavern walls rose up like endless cliffs, separated, as if they were once part of the whole earth but rent somehow by the blade of an unspeakable god. The steam flowed around them like clouds. "But your Jormungand seems to snore a lot!"

Such were the wonders of nature around them that they began to leave the past behind them, so as to more fully witness the masterful works of the Creator. It was a glory of nature that even Kur, accustomed as he was to the Underearth, found breathtaking. Everything was so much greater than they and yet so much a part of what made them revel in life itself.

"I pity them," Karina said. "Such evil will never experience all of this beauty."

"If you ever meet them again," Kur said, "show them no mercy. They are an abomination."

Despite the awe-inspiring magnitude of the underworld around them, their slender road soon grew more arduous and didn't come to an end until they had traveled for an entire day. The precipitous bridge had begun to rise upward somewhere about midday. The mighty chimney, which had seemed endless, slowly closed in upon them until what they traveled on was no more than a huge tunnel. "We have climbed at least a thousand feet. Notice the surface of the stone. The granite and volcanic rock are being replaced with shale and slate. Many of these rocks were brought here by masons to shore up the walls. Water once flowed through here. It's a good sign."

"Unless it floods while we're in here," Leander said.

The tunnel soon became a twisting maze of branching shafts, some rising and falling, still others intersecting and then falling southward or rising to the north. When the main path wasn't obvious, they called upon the diamond gem to guide them, and its insistent pull seemed irrefutable.

"The gem seems to choose the safest path," Kur said in amazement. "It is as if it has come this way before."

"It's just a magical locator," Kalor assured him, "designed to find the missing pieces of the staff.

"I think that it has a mind of its own," Kur said. "Sometimes it leads us southwest, or north to follow the safest route. It follows the same paths that I would choose, if I was trying to get us out of here."

"Can you hear it?" Karina asked.

"Hear what?"

"The silence. It feels like a living thing. Sometimes it sounds like Tempus is breathing, and other times, all that I can hear are my own heartbeats."

"We are a long way from Father Sun," Leander said, "and Mother Wind. The creak of our boots, the chiming of our armor, and the beating of our own hearts are probably the only sounds that these halls have heard in ages."

"And so close to Darg lands," Tariq said, "there are probably few living things that would brave living here."

"And if they are brave enough, we don't want to meet them."

"Just try and stay ready," Kur said. "Don't let the quiet put you to sleep."

In this manner, they traveled on, each one of them finding their own way to deal with their fears. Tariq found shelter by recalling the forested trails of his homeland, paths full of sunshine and wildlife. Karina and Dao gained strength from each other, and together they believed they were the equal of any encounter. Kalor, so fascinated with magic, puzzled endlessly over the complicated theories of the dragon's spell formulae. He believed that he now knew how to adapt the rest of Modrul's spell formulae for their use. Carmen focused on their mission, trying to piece together all the things that were happening to them. Dartin and Leander both thought of the rocky shores of Sundsvall, its harbors filled with white gossamer sails, its taverns filled with fine ale and bold women. Kur needed no such thoughts to comfort him, for here, beneath billions of tons of pressing stone and earth, he could not have felt more at home. In fact, the knowledge of his forefathers was returning to him from some deeply hidden memory, and the stone around him was coming to life in ways that only a Dwarf could know. He was their strength in these deepen-wilds, and each of them clung to him in some manner of earnestness, as if somehow his very aura could shield them from harm.

Another day's march and their journey again began to ascend, and in places, signs of an ancient civilization were evident. At intervals, strange symbols were carved into the walls of the tunnel, but passing water and time itself had eroded them into ghostly, unreadable images, mere shadows of their former glory.

They rested, now without food or water, and later continued along the Secret Way for yet another day. It was then that a great quantity of luck befell them. The natural tunnels began to give way to mined passages and then to the remnants of an abandoned city.

The diamond's pull led them down a long tunnel, like an avenue that finally ended before a towering doorway fit for a Titan. The door itself had long since crumbled into dust. Its once mighty hinges were now rusted away and gone, leaving only empty holes in the stone where they had once been fastened.

The room beyond was vaulted, with a ceiling of some fifty feet in height, a width of fifty, and a length of a hundred feet or more. Another door, similar in stature to the first, stared at them from the room's opposite end. The room was empty except for ages of dust, and Kur discovered a tall but narrow stair descending from the room in which they stood. Like a blessing from the gods, a small spring of water trickled from a crack in the rock at the top of the stairs. After a quick test, he discovered that it was fit enough to drink.

"Let's camp here," Kur said, "and get some sleep." They drank what they could on empty stomachs, filled their waterskins, and sank exhausted to the floor. Kur told them tales of his ancestors, stories of the adventures, and exploits of heroes long since passed from the world. They assigned guard shifts, and Kur's voice continued throughout them all. It seemed to them then that he was becoming something more than himself, as if his voice was filled with the knowledge of a thousand Dwarves, as if he spoke with the song and soul of Underearth. Only when they had all slept did he then sleep himself. When he awoke, they were ready. "Moradeus has blessed us with safety these few days."

"Now if only he'll bless us with some food," Dartin said. "I have prayed to Odin, but he still sleeps, and the runes sleep with him."

"Is not Fate the way of the Northmen?"

"Aye," said Dartin, "the events of our lives are skeins woven by the Fates. We cannot escape our destinies."

"Then your death and Odin's sleep were also woven in time," Dao said. "Perhaps this is a test to see if you are worthy."

"Let us hope that I pass."

"I think that we are all being tested," Tariq said, "but by someone, not some god."

"Either way," Karina said, "I hope that the Fates have woven in some food. I am starving!"

"The quicker that we move out," Carmen said, "the sooner that we will eat." Having slept beside their packs, they were ready to move out in short order. Descending the stairs, they began their exploration of the ancient ruins anew, waiting and hoping that its mysteries would soon reveal themselves.

The Third Battalion

In the arena of Drakon Mur'-Falor, the Third Red Orcin Battalion was training with deafening intensity. War masters assisted their squad leaders in training the elite soldiers under their command while Dockalfar instructors looked on and assisted when necessary. The Orcs were excellent troops, self-motivated and passionate in the pursuit of the art of war. Their commander and his second were perched above them all, sitting in the shadows of the leaders' booth.

"They are nearly ready, Vlad," Darik said with a confident smile.

"They are too few, too few to face Lord Cherek's Fermish knights."

"There will soon be many more," Darik said. "The new marines are doing a fine job of training the First and Second Battalions. The Giants of the Mountain are also eager to join in the war."

"Shiran and Monica do seem to be doing a fine job with these Orcs."

"Even Ariana has begun to lend a hand. The troops are learning quickly from them, perhaps even faster than Orcs are supposed to."

"Ariana is a ruthless taskmaster," Vlad said. "The slow ones felt the sting of her whip, I am sure!"

"They are valuable allies. Their size and strength combined with our battle tactics will make them elite fighters."

"And the tension between the Orc Tribes and settlements of Safehaven makes them our natural choice."

"We must ready our defenses as well," Vlad said. "The fortress is now threatened by both the Darg and the Sentiens. With our luck, they will attack us when we are weakest and most divided."

"With any luck, indeed."

"What a challenge that would be, but enough dreaming! I know you well enough to know your small talk. I imagine you wish to hear news of our quarry. Why not ask the seeress herself?"

"That is why we have a chain of command, Darik," Vlad said, "so please tell me, how fare Carmen's Rangers?"

"Yes, Ariana told me that you have named them. It is a fine epithet. They have made it beyond Darg lands and entered the halls of the Lost City."

"We must take steps to ensure that they do not fall into the hands of the Lych King."

"What interest would he have in them?"

"He has many fell purposes," Vlad said. "Foremost among them is the constant acquisition of fresh souls to add to his army."

"Andreul believes that they will pass close by his lair, but her divining cards portend that they will win through."

"Originally, I had intended for Lycurgus to take steps ensuring their safe passage, Darik, but his work is all too important now. I will go in his stead."

"Is there anything that I can do to help you?"

"I will need to borrow the rod for a while."

"As you wish, Vlad," Darik said. "I will bring it to your chambers when you call for it."

"How long does Andreul believe that it will take them to reach his lair?"

"Two days at least. They are very tired and hungry."

"Then bring me the rod at dawn, two days hence."

"Yes, Commander," and together, the two long-time comrades watched the Orcs train below them, and for a while, it seemed like old times between them.

The Forgotten Kings

A full day of rest in that deep and dark place renewed their vigor and hardened their resolve. The fresh water spring went a long way toward their recovery, but they desperately needed food to maintain and rebuild their lost strength. "Make sure that every canteen and waterskin is full," Kur said. "There is no telling how long it will be before we find water again." He didn't tell them that most springs like the one that they had found were usually guarded by whatever creatures might be nearby. "From here on we travel together, but just in case, I'll assign buddy teams, army style. Tariq and Carmen, Dartin and Leander, Dao and Karina, and Kalor and I, each of us is responsible for our partner's well-being. Before we move out, we will inspect each other's gear. Make sure anything loose is tied down tightly and securely. We're tired. That will make us lazy, and it could get us killed. When you are finished, tell me you're good to go."

Working diligently, each of them checked their partner and called out "good to go" when they were through. Once he was confident that they were ready, he led them on beside the light of Kalor's magical diamond.

"I know it sounds strange," Dartin said, "but I feel as if we are being led towards some great purpose."

"I have felt that way since the beginning," Carmen said.

"We are pawns to the gods," Dao said, "and I don't like it."

"Nor I," Karina said.

"Destiny or Fate," Tariq said, "neither path is clear, but what is clear is that someone or something desperately wants the artifact. No doubt, the weapon possesses power beyond the scope of mortals.

Even with the best intentions, such devices can only bring ruin upon us all."

"And we are the only ones capable of stopping them."

"Unless," Dartin said, "the wizard has found us some new allies."

"I wouldn't count on Von Mathers," Leander said. "I've had a bad feeling about him since the beginning."

"Once again," Carmen said, "it seems that we won't solve this mystery unless we follow it through until the end."

"We already know that there is no turning back," Leander said, "but there is a bright side."

"Such as?" Kalor asked.

"Never before have adventurers seen such wonders as we have and survived. Our story will be one that we can tell and retell for the rest of our lives."

"If we live that long," Dao said.

"Either way," Leander said, "I have no regrets. How can any of us know the wishes of gods? Here and now, we have chosen to defend our families and our lands. How many did we save for each of the Orcs that we slew? Every evil that we banish, every brigand that we slay, adds meaning to our humble lives."

"We have doubted ourselves since the beginning," Kalor said, "but we are still here. I say that it is time to take some credit for ourselves."

"We have had some success," Tariq said, "but we need Kur's knowledge now more than ever. Without him, our chances of survival are slim."

"I am done being afraid," Karina said. "I have never experienced such evil before, and I hope that we never have to again. Fear empowers evil, and I am done feeding it. It is time that we start thinking as if victory is ours, not theirs."

"At first," Carmen said, "the pressing walls of this underworld terrified me, but I have come to see it as yet another part of Tempus, and it is a world worth saving."

"In the last few days," Dao said, "Kalor and I have nearly unlocked all of the Modrul's magical formulae. With these new spells, we now have a great arsenal for combat. The teachings of my father are returning to me as well. One day, I may become the mage that he once saw in me."

"No doubt you will," Carmen said, "and I pray that I have become the fighter that my father always wanted."

"Without Atran-Doru," Leander said, "I may never be able to finish my training, but I too have learned some of the lesser powers of the Druids."

"Something tells me," Kur said, "that we will meet that sword again, but not in the way we would like."

"Lead on," Tariq said. "We have already made enough noise to alert every creature that may live within a mile of this tunnel."

They saved their thoughts after that; there would be time enough to talk later. Marching ahead for the better part of a day, they followed an immense tunnel that must have once been a major thoroughfare through Underearth. Many rooms and mining shafts branched off it at times, but all of them were either empty or filled with debris shaken loose by earthquakes. The tunnel seemed endless, but eventually end it did, by a towering archway beyond which the darkness was so deep that only Carmen could see through it.

"I have heard of summoning such darkness," Dao said. "It is said that the Dockalfar can banish all light. I believe that this is the same type of magic."

"If they created it," Carmen said, "they are long since gone. The room beyond it is a vast cathedral. The ceiling is at least a hundred feet high. Mighty arches support the roof, and massive hinge stones lock them together. Along the east and west walls are two rows of statues. They are so lifelike and immense that they resemble the gods themselves. Braziers rest at intervals along each wall, but it has been ages since their coals have been lit. The room is fully the length of a Fermish hurling field, at least a hundred and thirty-seven running paces long."

"Carmen," Kur said, "what more do you see?"

"The statues," Carmen said, "they wear helms and armor just like mine! They are dressed in full battle attire, with weapons both mundane and unusual. The detail is so exquisite that they seem frozen in time. They are beautiful, neither Human nor Elves but something in between. I can feel their power!"

"Is there anything else?"

"Yes, at the center of the room, there is a pedestal, or sarcophagus, about waist high and twice again as long. Something lies on top of it. It looks like a body!" It was then that a song began forming in her mind, very subtly at first, and she knew not where it came from. All that she knew was that it did not come from within her. It was a strange melody, a haunting rhapsody that spoke of war and ancient conquests untold. The sound was so magnificent that it compelled her to step forward into that high-vaulted chamber and join her voice with those of that ghostly choir. Somehow the words found their way to her lips, and her song filled all their hearts with wonder. She strode into the darkness, with her voice cascading, lyrics rousing, echoing, filled with memories. The old braziers once again burst to life with bright golden flames, bathing the entire room in their glow.

It seemed to the party that the statues sang along with Carmen and that they were pleased, although neither sound nor movement ushered forth from their cold and grim facade. It was a magical moment for them all, and in a short time, the entire cathedral was revealed. The soft light stung their eyes, but was a welcome miracle, and after a long painful moment, they were finally able to open their eyes and look upon the ancient hall.

Dao and Karina were deeply affected by the sight. The statues summoned up deep racial memories from out of their ancient past. The presence they felt hit them with gut-wrenching impact, but the events that had so deeply affected their forefathers had faded through time, and neither of them knew if they should feel fear, awe, or anger toward them.

"These carvings are wondrous," Kur said, "the equal any Dwarven artisan."

"Perhaps your people carved them," Karina said, touching and examining the statues as Kur was.

"I feel connected to them," Carmen said. "Surely these statues depict Vanamoinen, Ilmatar, and all of the gods."

"Like gods they seem," Leander said, "but there is no way to know for sure. If they are immortals, then where are they now?"

"I know the face of Odin," Dartin said. "These faces have a similar look to them. They may be the Aesir, or even the Vanir. The Vanir were said to be conquerors of worlds, ruthless and powerful."

"What great magic they must have possessed," Kalor said, "to have crafted such a hall."

"We should fear this place," Tariq said. "It may be cursed."

"Nevertheless, the diamond has led us here," Leander said. "We must leave no stone unturned."

"The sarcophagus then," Dartin said, "may hold some answers."

"Be careful," Tariq urged, "there's no telling what traps have been laid."

Carmen approached the coffin without fear, for she felt somehow that her own gods were guiding her footsteps. Upon the sarcophagus, if indeed it was one, was a suit of armor, and of a craftsmanship comparable to what was worn by the statues around them. Beneath layers of dust, it was fashioned of an untarnished silver metal, of the same miraculous form as that which they'd discovered in Modrul's Lair. The only difference was that this suit was whole and un-rent; in fact, it lay perfect and unblemished, unaffected by moisture or time.

"Look there, Carmen," Tariq said, "a helm like your own, and on the breast plate, the symbol of a dragon flying into the sun."

"Vanir armor," Dao said, "but this set is somewhat smaller than the first."

"I'd say that it is about Dartin's size," Kur said.

"The last set nearly killed me."

"It was badly damaged," Dao said. "This suit seems as whole as the day that it was made. My guess is that this one will not explode."

"Unless this suit is cursed like the last," Dartin said.

"Imagine what magic it might hold," Kalor said. "Think of the power that Carmen's helm alone possesses."

Leander carefully examined the armor, blowing away years of dust and laying his hands upon it. "Once again, it seems that something has been left for us to find. This place must hold some hidden power to have survived the centuries, untouched by time or by grave robbers. Armor such as this is coveted by many, and no doubt it is priceless. My question is this, why has no one claimed it before us?"

"Perhaps," Tariq said, "some great curse protects this place."

"It is only a few days' journey from Darg lands," Kur said. "Surely they would have taken it for themselves."

"Maybe Carmen's helm allowed her to see this place where others could not?"

"Or maybe this armor," Dartin said, "and this place are beyond the reach of such black-hearted people. Some magical ward may prevent evil beings from coming here."

"There is no telling," Carmen said. "I still hear their song in my head, and it isn't evil, merely powerful."

"Although I couldn't understand the words," Karina said, "their meaning was unmistakable. It is a song of war."

"This quest is none other than a quest of war," Kur said. "We have faced our deaths many times already. We have an old saying that the only honor in war is life, to preserve it at any cost."

All of them looked to Dartin then for an answer, because of them all, only he and Leander might possibly fit into it, and such armor was not part of the way of Druids.

"Very well," he said. "If it doesn't kill me, it will be a boon to us." While he removed his armor, they cleaned off the new set for him and helped him to don it. "What better armor than this to stand beside the All Father with in the final battle?"

The new armor had an amazing flexibility to it, and it seemed to conform to his body like old clothing. No normal suit of mail would act thus, and putting it on was a marvel unto itself. Soon, all that remained to complete it was its helm, which incorporated a visor similar to Carmen's own.

"Here goes," he said, "maybe everyone should stand back." Standing alone for a few moments, he held the winged helm before him, breathing deep to gather his courage. The armor was etched with artistic designs depicting dragons, men, women, and war. It was perfect beyond imagining. It was the armor of a conqueror, and fate had brought him to it. The moment of truth had come.

One-Eyed Jack's

"We feared for Dartin and for ourselves," the Old Gnome said, "but a profound sense of destiny filled our hearts, and it seemed that the armor had been hidden in that forgotten hall for him alone."

"Was it cursed?" Pauli asked. "Like Tariq said?"

"In a way it was, Pauli, for we would find out later that it had been left there to fulfill an ancient purpose, one that none of us could have imagined."

"But we know that Dartin didn't die," Eric said, "because we saw him here only a year ago."

"Certainly he didn't die at that time, Eric, but the boundaries between life and death are much closer than any of us realize, closer and more malleable."

"Then you are implying," Garad said before taking a draft from his flagon, "that Dartin has died and come again?"

"It goes against all that we hold sacred and dear, but that is indeed so, at least as far as any of us could know. All that will be revealed in my story to come."

"There is still two hours until midnight," Pauli said. "Surely we can hear much of it in that time."

"A long story can be told in the span of hours," the Old Gnome said, "but in honor of those that fell or were lost to fate, only a portion of it can be told at any one time. For such is our story, a tale of friendship, sorrow, and toil, and on that path, ours was a trail of battles joined."

And so he began his tale anew.

Vanir Armor, Vanir Songs

The very moment that Dartin placed the helm upon his head, a terrible silence filled the cathedral, a quiet so hushed that a sudden fear came upon them. None of them dared to breathe lest they break the profound silence, but from out of the calm there soon issued a faint sound, like whispering just beyond the grasp of listening ears. It seemed at first to emanate from the statues themselves, or was it the very air around them? Possibly the sound was not truly heard at all, but rather, chiming within their minds alone. The sound slowly grew in fortitude until none among them could truly know if it had been heard or thought or both. Dartin was the most profoundly affected, although Carmen heard the voices as well.

"As it was foretold, so shall it be!" Dartin's legs weakened and failed. Dropping to his knees, his vision faded and his world turned black. He was vaguely aware of hitting the floor. And then suddenly, he was flying on the back of a mighty dragon with copper-colored scales and vast leathery wings. His saddle was of the finest leather with gold inlaid, and a longbow with a string of golden fire rested atop of his saddle horn. A sword was strapped to his waist, and black reins were in his hands. Around him flew hundreds of his fellows upon similar steeds, some of gold, some of black, and some of red. They all sang a song of ancient adventure and battles long forgotten. In shock, he gazed at his hands, the unmistakable hands of a woman.

When he awoke to the urgent shaking of his friends, he found himself on his back where he had recently been standing. "How long have I been out?"

"For almost ten minutes," Tariq said. "We were beginning to think that you weren't coming back." Tariq knelt beside him, his hands crossed over his left knee. "How do you feel?"

"I'm not sure, but I think that I feel pretty good."

"See if you can sit up."

Rising cautiously, he tried to remove his helm. "It won't come off!"

Carmen was quick to his aid. "Look at the inside of your visor. Do you see any writings there?"

"Yes, a few words. I seem to know what they mean and how to utter them. It is strange."

"One of them should allow you to remove the helm."

Testing each one of them in turn, they discovered that they were the same commands that applied to Carmen's own, but to his horror, the release command failed to work! "It must be cursed!"

"Perhaps not," Dao said, "it may possess a secret command word that we must find in order to free you."

"The answer must lie here," Kalor said. "I will search the sarcophagus. Everyone else look around the room. Hunt for any runes or writing that may help us." The coffin seemed to be carved from one solid piece of pearl-covered marble. Kalor knew that such appearances were often deceiving. Oftentimes, secret panels and latches or levers might be hidden within them. Tracing the outline of the stone carvings, he searched with the lightest touch for any such secrets, like his Master Uldrick had taught him. Besides the nearly imperceptible seam between the lid and the box of the sarcophagus, he found nothing. Trying again produced the same result. "Tariq, help me slide off the lid."

"Carmen," Tariq said, "ready your sword." Sliding the lid to the side, they peered within, but naught remained but air, ancient, still, and stale.

"I don't understand it," Kalor said. "I thought that we would find something.

"I did find some runes carved into the dais at her feet," she said, pointing to the centermost statue on the east wall. Leading them to it, she brushed away the dust to fully reveal the writings there. Wonderfully crafted, the woman depicted must have been a great warrior. Her features were beautiful, almost Liosalfar but more alien, with high cheekbones and pupil-less eyes. Her build was thick and muscular, more human than Fairy, and her armor was nearly the duplicate of that which Dartin now wore. Her hair was braided and long, her hands resting on the pommel of an immense sword, rising more than waist-high to the statue. At her feet, a eulogy was etched, and only Dartin and Carmen could read it.

"What do the runes say?" Tariq asked, and speak them she did, and this is what she read:

> In the beginning, the Powers wrestled for balance as the Universe expanded. Some believed that the birth worlds should be left to their own destinies. Some brought life to them in their own image while others wished that the darkness would rule again as it did before the dawn of time. Yet the Vanir stood apart from their quarrels, for from our awakening, we knew that we were born to conquer. The Duaredheim wished for destinies untroubled, and they vied against us, and we flew to meet them in war. Victory was nearly ours, but they forged a mighty weapon, trapping my brethren in a dying galaxy for all of time. Let this runepage be our decree, for the Vanir will not be so easily defeated. With the last of our power, I leave behind our final curse and our salvation. When the appointed time comes, I will rise again and free my people, for I am Sheena, life mate of Lucidus Rhys El-Vanir, and my spirit is our curse and our salvation. The Vanir will ride again. The Chaos Lords will reign!

Carmen's words profoundly affected them all, Dartin most of all. "What have we done?" he said hopelessly. "Have I awakened this conqueror from her slumber?"

"If we have," Carmen said, "we will find a way to free you from her curse."

"Perhaps," Kalor said, "this runepage speaks of the very staff that we are looking for."

"Then all hope is not lost," Karina said, "for if we can gain the Duaredheim's creation before our enemies, we may be able to prevent this Vanir prophecy."

Pacing about with his hands clasped behind his back, his head bowed in contemplation, Dao voiced his own thoughts, "we seem once again to be a part of some preordained quest, where even our most detailed plans seem to follow a path long ago chosen for us. Maybe it is the way things are meant to be, or maybe we are just pieces on a Ssech board."

"Pawns we may be," Tariq said, "but I won't accept it, even if it is true. I did not choose to be an orphan, and yet I survived by my own hand. If these Lords of Chaos think that they can come again at our own expense, then they did not consider the likes of me."

"I have been thinking about the quest since the beginning," Leander said, "and what has been troubling me has finally worked itself out."

"What is it?" Kalor urged.

"I believe that we are not part of one prophecy, but of many."

"How could that be?" Dartin asked.

"Isn't it logical that what effects one god affects them all? In the Druidic faith, one pebble dropped into a pond sends its ripples across the world."

"And the Duaredheim Staff is a pebble the size of a mountain!" Carmen said. "It makes sense that our actions could even affect them."

"It could unbalance existence itself," Dao said. "Good and evil, law and chaos, all are held in balance by a constant flux of forces. If that delicate equilibrium is undone, it could mean the end of the world!"

"Now you see how nature is a constant reminder of life and death," Leander said, "darkness and light. Why should it be any different among the gods?"

"The old saying," Dao said, "as it is above, so it is below."

"And so we travel once more into a period of turmoil and changing," Carmen said. "Only this time we are agents of that change. Positions most of us relate to heroes, although none of us feel as such."

"If our enemies claim the staff," Dartin said, "we will face the final battle, when both gods and men will stand together to face Loki and his Giants."

"Perhaps there are many Ragnaroks," Leander said, "an end of the world for every generation, a time to fall or a time to change."

"But what if the dark side finally wins?" Karina said.

"Evil can never win," Carmen said, "as long as there is the tiniest spark of hope and goodness left to oppose it."

"Then there is nothing left to do," Kur said, "but to drive on and meet our troubles head-on."

"Spoken like a true Dwarf," Kalor said with a smile.

"Easy for all of you to say," Dartin said. "None of you are turning into a woman!"

A Master Plan

Wrapped in the shadowy embrace of a demon, the Master of Plans within Plans gazed into his scrying pool. It was an hourglass-shaped basin of gold resting upon the overturned abdomen of a bronze model of one of the deadliest of spiders. Within its dark waters, he viewed Carmen's Rangers within the Vanir Cathedral.

An unforeseen development, he thought. *They have unwittingly awakened one of the Ancient Lords of Chaos.* The stakes were now higher than ever, but there was a brighter side. Lothdea would now have to worry about a power even greater than his. It could work to their advantage, although they would have to work harder than ever to succeed. A shimmering of the ethers before him warned him of Darik's imminent arrival.

The gateway appeared, half enshrouded by the mirror's body—the spider. Sore and bruised, Darik stepped out with as much grace as he could muster. Turning about, he depressed the eighth eye, and the portal closed. The mirror reduced, he then placed it in his pocket.

"You have been training with Varul again I see."

"His ability is second only to the Shantu Masters."

"Did you learn anything?"

"I learned that his body is as hard as an oak tree. He nearly killed me."

"Come and sit. Rest a while." There was a small square dining table with four simple wooden chairs by his chamber's fireplace, and there they sat. "Efmiel," he called, "bring us some tea please."

"You do know that it is only a matter of time before she poisons you."

"Of course, but let us hope not today."

The Elf Maid was soon pouring them tea, aromatic and hot. The cups were simple, without handles, and delicately painted.

"Nice set," Darik said. "Perhaps we can invite Andreul over for a tea party."

"Let's just hope that the local merchants don't revolt again and throw it all into the harbor like they did the last time. What a disaster."

"Indeed, but tell me, Commander, is it time? I have brought the item that you requested." Hidden beneath his training robes, he quickly produced it.

"Yes, it is time. I will return it to you in three days' time."

"Then you know that the party has reached the Great Cathedral."

"Tell Elrick to prepare his spells. There may soon be a Vanir among them."

"The armor?"

"They kept it a secret through all of the ages, a perfect cursed trap."

"Everything could be undone!"

"The priest has a strong will. I believe that it will be some time before the Vanir has control over him."

"Then our victory is still possible."

"Our victory is assured as long as my commands are swiftly and competently executed!"

"Of course, Commander."

"I have calculated the time of their arrival in the pyramid's mines at one week, based upon most of the potential misfortunes that they may face."

"Ariana and I have selected the perfect ambush site. Everything is in place to capture our quarry with minimal losses."

"We can't afford to waste our troops," Vlad said. "We will soon face attacks from many fronts."

"I can still have Elrick set his trap," Darik said, "and avoid death altogether, although I could use a few fresh corpses in the lab."

"Elrick must keep his spells in reserve. If all else fails, we will allow the magician to act. Otherwise, we need a martial victory. They must view us as their most hated enemies."

"Oh, I'm fairly sure that won't be a problem."

"With the capture of our enemies, only one piece of the relic will remain out of our grasp. With careful manipulation, the Fermish heroes will pursue us all the way to Hell."

"And in so doing, they will help us to fulfill our destiny."

"Exactly."

"Any last orders before you depart, Commander?"

"Only this, promote morale within the troops. Double their privileges over the next few days but remain ever vigilant and be ready for battle on the sixth day. You will assume command in my absence. Allow Ariana an equal share if you find it necessary to soothe her."

"Anything else, Commander?"

"Just one more thing, my friend," he said. "Efmiel, please bring us my Ssech board."

The game lasted for hours, ending in a rare stalemate. "It was a fine game, Darik."

"I pray that you didn't let me escape."

"Forgive me for being arrogant in the past. I have not allowed you to win since we left the academy. You have become a great player."

"Then I will bid you adieu," Darik said with a nod. Rising from the table, he shrugged off the stiffness in his body. Reaching into the folds of his robe, he produced a small vial. "Drink this before you enter his domain. It will render you invisible to the Dead." Taking it from him, Vlad studied its ever-smoky contents. "The enchantment will last a fortnight, but only as long as you don't interact with them. Touch them in any way, and they will see you."

"I will use it wisely."

"Good luck, Commander." Pivoting about on the balls of his feet in an about-face maneuver, he pulled out his mirror and once again touched the eighth eye. Following that, he moved the sixth leg two clicks to the rear. The portal formed, and he stepped through. Moments later, the gateway disappeared from Vlad's chamber. At the same instant, he arrived in the central chamber of the pyramid library. He would inform Ariana and his war masters in due time; for now, he was curious about something. Some time ago, he had skimmed through an aged and brittle scroll. He seemed to remember something written there about an ancient Vanir prophecy. Somehow, he knew that they had to find that scroll.

Walking in Shadows

"Efmiel," Vlad said, "bring me my armor."

"Yes, master." Piece by piece she brought it, as she had done for him at least a hundred times. Removing it from the weapons rack, she was proud of the job that she had done. It was clean and free of the Darg's filth. The blacksmith had repaired it well, even improving it in places. Vlad was quite capable of dressing himself, but he preferred it this way. Perhaps some small piece of his humanity remained. She served him without complaint, and he was soon prepared for battle.

"I am starting to remember."

"Remember what, master?"

"Our life before."

"Oh."

"In the times to come, the love that we shared will be impossible."

"Yes, master."

"As long as I live, I will try to keep you safe."

"I shall never be safe here. Your enemies will soon create an accident to be rid of me."

"The time of your escape is coming, Efmiel. In two weeks' time, I shall call for the next gladiatorial event in the arena. It will unify the clans. When the day comes, be ready. You will only get one chance."

"How will I know that it's time?"

"Oh, you will know." Bending forward, he kissed her warmly, and she received it thus.

"Now bring me my sword, slave!"

"Yes, master." She handed him his weapons belt, and he donned it.

"You will serve Dorlin Varul in my absence. He will be training the new marines. Treat any wounds that they incur during practice and follow his commands."

"Yes, master."

"Don't worry, Efmiel. Dorlin will not betray me. You will be safe with him." He left her then. Stepping into a shadowy corner, he smiled, and then he was gone.

She spent a long time contemplating his words. When the time came, she would be ready.

Flying through the ethers of Shadow, he spread his demonic wings wide for the sheer joy of it. His minions would come to him at times, whispering new happenings to him. Inumbro, Queen of the Umbra Draco, the eldest female dragon in Shadowland had just laid a new clutch of eggs. When his mission was complete, he would have to stop by and visit her.

The Umbra Draco were the oldest inhabitants of the plane. Dragons of might and shadow, their scales were as black as night, their talons razor-edged swords, and their teeth even, curved, and wicked. The weaving of shadows was their magic, their life's blood the animating force. Indeed, they were certainly the most powerful beings who dwelled here, and they would bow to no power save his. His rule over them was tenuous, however, for they were a living power as old as demon kind. Nevertheless, they were an honorable race, and respect and wisdom could quiet them and tame the beast.

There was no time now to pay Inumbro a visit. Carmen's Rangers were approaching a danger beyond their most terrifying nightmares. It was up to him to lead them safely beyond it. Preparing Darik's potion, he drank it. When he stepped forth into the southernmost passage of the oldest crypt on Tempus, even he knew fear. He was no longer in his realm. He was in the land of Andomar Tabarun, the Lych King.

LYCH

The Lich, or Lych, is a name derived from the term "Lych Gate," which describes the roofed gate often placed over a coffin or crypt in ancient times to shelter the dead. Frequently, flowering vines would be urged to grow upon it, thus lending a peaceful yet morbid beauty to the site.

However, as time passes, so too does the meaning of words, and in this case, "Lych Gate," was borrowed and adapted over time to describe the Dead's resting place and eventually to describe the Dead themselves. In a similar fashion, the final metamorphosis of the term came to describe a certain kind of evil spirit, not wraiths or shadows of the formerly living, nay, but spirits so despicably evil that their souls refuse to leave their corpses. They are not to be confused with mere Zombies granted unlife through magic, but rather beings finding undeath of their own free will. Driven and motivated by their own hatred of the living, they lament and despise their reviled life now lost. It is anger so ill as to drive them on a quest for immortality using fell magic, secret chemicals, ritual sacrifice, and acts so grave that they are unmentionable. Over time, their infinite hate consumes what is left of their living bodies until naught remains but a frightful husk, a shell of once-life.

The mind of the Creature, if such a term applies, remains locked in the remaining body undying. The evil spirit then hides its disembodied soul in a secret vessel, sealing it with magic so grim that legend requires that even the gods refuse to unlock them.

The bodies of these cursed spirits exist partially in the plane of their former existence, and partly in the land of the Dead. Some might call the realm a place of evil, but it is in fact neither good nor ill. In essence, it is the most terrifying neutrality of death, indiscriminate and irresistible. Nevertheless, it is a place where agents of evil are granted free rein to orchestrate their foul plots. Among these are included all the ranks of the Undead, which some call the Nosferatu. Vampires, ghouls, werewolves, ghosts, and all the conjured ranks of the Undead are among them, but none are more powerful than the Lych. Usually, their insane motivations seek resolution to some grave injustice, wrongs that may have occurred countless centuries in the past.

The transformation from life to unlife has been undertaken with success only a handful of times throughout the ages; most who attempt it fail to apply some minor detail, or meet Death too soon, but some have followed in the steps of the first, pursuing a path so dark and twisted that no goodly beings would dare imagine it. Nevertheless, history chronicles the rise and reign of the first, and among Lych kind, He rules supreme. In life, his name was Andomar Tabarun; in undeath, he is known only by one title, the Lych King.

It is ironic that in life, he was once Liosalfar, but the tragic loss of his life mate turned his heart to grief. It drove him to seek vengeance upon the ones that stole her from him. His hatred was so complete that he invented the foul process required to extend his life, even beyond the near immortality of the Elves. One evil spell after another, chemicals, and sacrificial blood slowly consumed his dying body until he had cheated Death itself through undeath. His madness was so complete that he took all his loyal followers with him, and of them, there were many.

—Antineus Morlinar
Chronicler of History

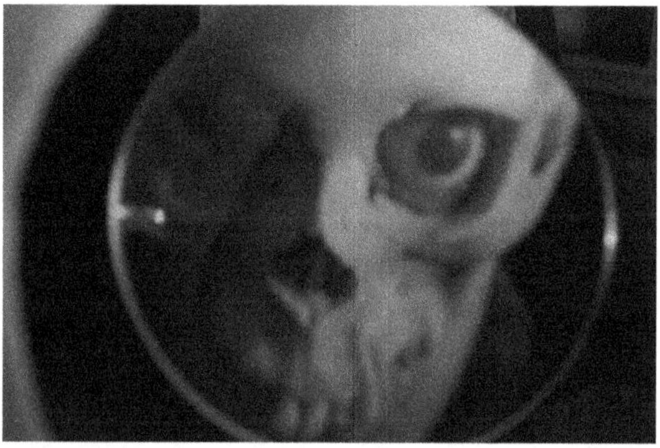

Even the Master of Plans within Plans Knows Fear

He had entered the crypt of his own free will; only now he wished that he had not. Through sorcery, he was invisible to the eyes of the Dead, but that gave him little comfort. He would have to remain here, in the lower halls of the Lych King's Lair, until he had successfully led Carmen's Rangers safely beyond it. If the Lych discovered them too soon, he would be powerless to save them. His ability to travel through Shadow would fail near the center of Tabarun's domain, for there the darkness and the power of evil were absolute.

Four miles below the surface, the crypt was once the lower halls of a glorious citadel. That castle was the center of a once great city and the heart of Liosalfar rule. Flourishing for a thousand years, a vast labyrinth of tunnels ran beneath it, both to extend the fortress, and in search of precious metals and gems. They transformed the lowest of those passageways into vast catacombs, where the dead were laid to rest. It was perhaps the most glorious city that had ever existed on Tempus, but time erodes even the most powerful empires. Slowly, ages passed, and war, disease, and unrest toppled its towers. Andomar Tabarun was its final king, and when his heart turned black, all that was good in the city fled, and what remained was naught but death. Many thousands of years later, the city above had vanished back into the earth, and most of its many tunnels had collapsed or filled with water. All that remained now were the lowest halls, maintained for all time by the magical might of their king and defended by his minions of death.

It was into these catacomb halls that he had willingly come. Was he completely mad? Probably. In his right hand, he grasped Sharakul-Loth, and his left hand rested upon the hilt of Decapitator, the sword of his father. The Duaredheim's rod rested beneath his breastplate, carefully protected near his solar plexus. It was uncomfortable, but he had no intention of misplacing it either. The device would act like a siren's call, luring his quarry toward him, and hopefully away from the Lych King. Always a curious soul, it was likely his greatest weakness, because he was not content to remain in those lower passages unknowing. Step-by-step, he began exploring. He would peer into every unlocked doorway and look within every lonely room.

The crypt itself was a maze of twisting catacombs, worship halls, and burial chambers. He examined the contents of each dusty room and every coffin and cairn. He even journeyed into the many rooms that adjoined those halls, and there he saw treasures beyond imagining, horded eons before in honor of the dead. Powerful guardians had been left to protect those ancient dead and their riches, guardians waiting for some hapless intruder to wake them. All the deathly horrors were there, evil wrapped in ragged rags, the Mummy, the Barrow Wight, Wraiths, and Apparitions, terrors so powerful that he trembled. Once, a hulking form approached him, a Mummy king with rotten orbs and tiny burning points of light for eyes. Shambling toward him, its arms rose, and a moaning wail escaped from its desiccated throat.

Terrified, he stepped back and leveled his wand at the moldering corpse. His fingers nearly unleashing its magical flame, but suddenly, the Mummy grew appeased, as if Vlad had seemed to him merely a phantom memory of its life long past, a window into another time or perhaps a dream lingering only to torture its forgotten soul. When the creature returned to its resting place, he quietly departed.

His searching, although a terrible risk, was not without purpose, for the Fermen would soon reach the catacombs, and he intended to do all that he could to lead them safely past Andomar's realm. He didn't simply need that which they carried; he needed them alive.

It was for this reason that he sought the chambers of the Lych King himself, and much to his horror, he found it.

The crypt, had in levels, three, its tunnels branching from an immense central chamber, like veins from a heart. In Vlad's wanderings, he discovered that except for a few passages, all the roads of the catacombs led there. Silently, he approached, for he could feel the presence of evil thicken, as if he was walking up the face of a sand dune. Each step became a struggle between his will and his subconscious drive for self-preservation, but he possessed a courageous spirit, driving him forward against everything that was natural. What he then came to see was both glorious and sorrowful.

The chamber was ensorcelled by a great glamour. It created an everlasting illusion of what those halls had looked like at the height of their glory. The walls were draped in the most ornate tapestries; the floor and ceiling were a mosaicked masterpiece depicting gods, mystical creatures, and ancient heroes. The east end of the chamber bore the king's ornate throne, behind which was a curtain of eternal flame, burning from floor to ceiling without smoke. Facing the king were his four field commanders, fully armored, and behind them were four ranks of once-elfin soldiers, with golden mail and grim countenance. A casual observer would perceive these illusions of life as real, but to eyes that saw truly, the genuine horrors would be revealed, for here were ranks upon ranks of the Undead, cursed souls who had followed their king on his journey into oblivion. They were lost souls, spirits forever filled with the longing of life's distant memories, eternally cursed to stand in undeath, lingering forever in a skeletal mockery of life.

Standing in the doorway of that great chamber, he saw their true essence. To the skeletal warriors that guarded their king, he seemed to be no more than a passing breeze, and their lifeless stares traveled through him, unknowing. Their sinister gaze chilled him to the bone. His skin crawled with the creeping touch of their presence. His concentration never faltered, although he prayed that his invisibility was complete. He knew that if he had to face the Lych King and his minions alone, he would likely not survive.

Andomar sat upon his throne, but he was not inanimate, as were his soldiers. In life, he was a great leader, wealthy and powerful. In undeath, he was a lifeless husk, his bones and what was left of his flesh had been made nearly indestructible through the processes that had transformed him. His hair was sparse and thin, his face a gruesome mask of mummified flesh and bone. Perhaps the most frightening thing of all were his eyes, eyes that still looked as bright and vibrant as they had in life. His robes, once rich and trimmed in gold, were now rotting and ruined, a mere mockery of what they had once been. Andomar's gaze was fixed upon that which he held in his right skeletal hand—a crystal globe in which several tiny figures danced.

"Come to me, my children!" he said, "and you shall join my ranks forever." He laughed then, a terrible hissing laugh filled with all the glee that a child might feel when they learn a new secret.

So he knows that they come, Vlad thought. He stood there for some time then, listening and studying his new opponent. How then would he lead his pawns past the King of the Dead? Perhaps he would have to leave these halls and intervene before they arrived here, or perhaps he would have to challenge the Lych King at the center of his power. If he chose to act, then there was a danger that such extreme measures might alter the prophecy and change his destiny. Was he underestimating the abilities of Carmen and her rangers, or was he second-guessing himself? He still had time to search these halls. He still had time to contemplate. In the end, the Fates would decide, but there was one thing that could ensure all of their survival. If only he could find it in time.

Stairs and Rooms and Things

The cathedral had but two exits—the great archway that led back the way that they had come and a smaller, man-sized doorway that opened into a guard room and then to a set of wide spiral stairs leading down. Down and down they climbed, perhaps for fifty feet or more, until the stairs ended in yet another room some seventy feet in width, fifty feet across, with a high ceiling of about thirty feet. It was cold, damp, and barren, completely devoid of anything save a fine coating of dust. Strangely, there was no apparent exit.

"Perhaps this was once their arms room," Kalor said, "or even a treasure room."

"Try the gem," Carmen said. "This place worries me." With the words, its light burst forth, pulling Kalor's hand in the direction of the far wall.

"There must be a secret door," Kalor said.

"All right, everyone," Carmen said, "spread out and search." Fanning out, the floor was of well-polished stone and the walls of similar finish. Tariq, walking across the floor, felt a stone suddenly shift and sink beneath his feet. Soon, there erupted a terrible screeching sound, like a rusted mechanism coming suddenly and painfully to life.

"Everyone out!" Tariq said. "It's a trap!"

Running for the stairs proved futile, as a thick stone door fell out of the ceiling and blocked their escape. Noxious gas poured out of holes in the walls. It was then that the ceiling began to descend. There was no way out. They would all be crushed.

"There is no door!" Karina screamed.

"The gem led us here," Kalor said. "There must be a way out. Search the walls for hidden levers or any seams in the stone!"

The gas was increasing. Soon they would all suffocate.

"There!" Carmen said, pointing toward the far wall. "I see the outline of something."

Kalor soon pulled out a hidden lever and depressed it. A small door suddenly slid open before them, revealing a narrow tunnel beyond it.

"Quickly," she ordered. "Everyone out!" Choking, coughing, and feeling wretched, they exited the room mere seconds before the ceiling struck the floor. Gas continued to spill out into the tunnel. "Run!"

"That was too close!" Tariq said as they wound their way along the passage. Thirty paces more, and it abruptly ended. "Where do we go from here? There is no exit!"

"There must be another concealed door," Kalor said. "Why else would anyone dig this tunnel?"

"Maybe it was never finished." Dao said, but Kur soon found a trapdoor buried beneath years of dust beneath their feet.

"Careful," Kur said, "it could be trapped as well."

"I'll search it," Kalor said. "Everyone stand back." Brushing the dust aside, he lightly traced the outline of the door, its frame and hinges. In no time, he found the latch. The door was keyless, simply designed to lift open or push up from below. "If there is a trap, it's rigged on the far side. Here goes!" Pulling slowly, he lifted the door as gently as he could until the lip just passed the frame. With his off-hand, he drew his dagger and propped the door open with it. Crouching down, he peered around the edges of the door, looking for trip wires or other signs of tampering, but he found nothing. Ever so quietly, he eased it open, ready to slam it shut again and leap away, but beneath the trapdoor was just another tunnel, lonely and dark. "Another passage," he whispered, "running opposite and under this one."

"Everyone down," Carmen said. "Tariq, take the lead." Grabbing the frame of the door, he first lowered his feet through the opening, and then his body, until he hung suspended from the ceiling. Looking and listening to his utmost, he dropped the remaining five feet to the floor below. Landing well, he flexed his knees and took the rest of the shock with his hands. Pausing, he listened for signs of alerted enemies. An ironbound door barred the tunnel some thirty feet ahead while behind him the passage seemed to be widening. Nothing stirred. Waving them down, they worked together to make the fall as safe as possible. Searching the passage, Tariq found signs of recent use. "Goblins," he said, "I'd recognize their spore anywhere."

"How many?"

"At least a dozen. They came into the area, milled about by the door, and then traveled back the way they came."

"Kalor," Carmen said, "check the door. Maybe it's locked."

"Not locked," Kalor said, "frozen. No one has opened this door for a hundred years at least."

"Can you open it?"

"Not without a battering ram." Kur readied his ax, but Dartin beat him to it. With a mighty kick, he shattered what was left of the wood around the doorknob and keyhole, fracturing the hinges simultaneously. A slight push was all that it took to collapse the door inward.

"The wood must have been rotten," Kalor said.

"Yeah, rotten," Tariq said, examining the door, but the fibers were as hard as the day the portal was built. It would have taken a woodsman half an hour to cut through it, or a Giant. No Elf or Man could have just kicked it in the way he did. "We should keep moving. That noise traveled a long way."

Kalor called upon the diamond's magic once more. It pulled him urgently west through the broken doorway. Beyond the doorway was a wide intersection between their tunnel, which continued west, and two additional passageways, one bending to the right and northwest, the other left and southwest. A faint cool breeze blew in from the northwest. The west passage reeked of rot and decay, and the southwest passage waited in silence; for the first time, the diamond was indecisive—both west and southwest seemed positive.

"Try southwest first," Carmen said. "We can always backtrack."

The tunnel continued that way for some eighty feet. Its walls were covered with mosaics of once great beauty. Most depicted dragons struggling against humanoid creatures of alien appearance wielding a strange device that seemed to drag lightning from out of the heavens unto itself and then unleash it wherever the aliens willed it. The Aliens, although great in stature, were slight of build, with bulbous eyes the color of starlight, green skin, and slender long-fingered hands. They stood about in a circle of many, facing inward, with their hands interlocked with one another. Few other details could be seen, for time had erased much of the artist's original rendering.

An open-arched doorway, ten feet high and six feet wide, ended the passage. Beyond it was a large room, at least fifty feet wide and over one hundred feet long. "Dao," Carmen whispered, "I think that now would be a good time for a little more light."

"Of course, my lady," he said with a bow and a flourish. Turning about to face them all, he brought his hand up as if to shield his eyes. Receiving his message, they prepared themselves for the blinding light to come. Moving to the front, he stood beneath the archway facing inward. Searching his memory, he soon recalled the words, summoned his inner power, and spoke, "Permitto ibi exsisto lumen!" Pointing toward the ceiling, he snapped his fingers. A brilliant globe bathed the room in light, casting eerie shadows in every direction. When their eyes adjusted, the great room was revealed.

Tall pillars of stone that were evenly spaced four to a side flanked the long walls. Stone Gargoyles sat atop of each one. There was a square opening in the ceiling. It may have once served as a chimney, like those used in the exotic Shamrun far to the east. An ironbound door, like the previous one, stood centered on the distant wall. Two large wooden chests rested on either side of it. The floor was of well-polished stone. The air was dry, still, and forgotten.

"Kalor," Carmen said, "take a look around. There may be more traps."

Cautiously, he stepped into the room. Slipping along the right hand wall, he paused for a moment to peer through his reading crystal. Perhaps his most prized wizardly possession, it allowed him to read magical inscriptions and in some cases, see telltale signs of the presence of enchanted items or dangerous protective wards. "The two chests by the far wall contain some magic, and the far door is magically sealed. I see no protective wards in the room. If there is a trap, it must be mechanical."

"Keep looking," Carmen urged. "Let's not take any chances."

"Everything seems natural, but there is something strange about the Gargoyles."

"They just look like simple statues," Tariq observed.

"There is some magic in them," Kalor said. "It could be another trap."

"Let's just try to get through this one," Carmen said. "Leave the chests alone. Tariq, you take the left wall and, Kalor, the right. Everyone else, follow me."

Moving cautiously, they entered the room, the stone-dead eyes of eight Gargoyles staring down at them from above. Kalor had already reached the far doorway. Kneeling down, he rummaged through his backpack for something.

What none of them could have known was the presence of a pressure-plate activated trap at the center of the room. When Carmen stepped on it, the floor panel beneath her suddenly sank. The eyes of the Gargoyles burst with life, and what once was granite became flesh. A titanic *thoom!* echoed from behind them as a tremendous stone door fell through the entrance archway, sealing them inside.

Shaking off the stiffness of stone, the monsters stretched their bony wings and then swooped down upon them.

"To arms!" Tariq shouted. "The Gargoyles have taken wing!" In a flash, the already tense adventurers readied their shields and drew their swords, too slow perhaps for creatures magically created to guard and to kill.

Attacking from behind, they struck Karina hard and hoisted her aloft, knocking her sword out of her grasp. It fell clattering to the floor. Two Gargoyles carried her, and two more grappled with

Leander nearby, their wings beating hard for the opening in the ceiling. Struggling hard to escape, she twisted and kicked but could not break free because their grip was as strong as iron.

Leander slashed viciously at his rightmost attacker, but the cunning beast caught his sword arm at the wrist with its prehensile feet, and their ascent continued.

Karina struggled wildly, nearly escaping from one of them. They dragged her through the opening, nonetheless. Leander fought them, but paid for it with his blood. The Gargoyles threw them toward the back of what resembled nothing more than a cluttered attic. Boxes, junk, and dusty treasures were haphazardly intermingled with the bones of the Gargoyles' past victims. The four beasts, with flesh as gray and lifeless as death, razor-like talons, and eyes both hungry and sinister, advanced. Crouching low, like birds of prey ready to strike, they blocked their escape.

Karina stood quickly. Looking for some weapon, she got lucky. Lying with the skeletal remains of its previous owner, she found a sword still in its scabbard and wasted no time in freeing it. Kicking nearby debris toward her assailants, she prepared to fight.

Leander was a little slower, a bit more stunned. He rose just as the Gargoyles rushed in.

Beneath them all, the battle raged. The remaining creatures landed, seeming to prefer fighting from the ground.

"Back to back," Carmen ordered, "so the bastards can't take us!"

Tariq was soon behind her, matching her every move. His sword blazed with fire, seeming to crave the blood of their enemies.

The Gargoyles stalked them, six feet tall, hunchbacked, and fearless. Wasting no time, they attacked.

They were a team now, one soldier understanding the other with the near intimacy of lovers, paladin and ranger fighting back to back, one with bow and the other with sword.

"I've got this one," Tariq said, spinning hard to his left. "See what you can do to help Karina!"

Looking toward the opening, Carmen could still see the back of one of them. She drew, aimed, and loosed. The bolt blasted through the monster's chest, and in an instant, it crumpled into dust. Eerily, a new Gargoyle formed atop of the first pillar, all stone and still as it first had been.

"I need some help up here!" Karina shouted. "Our swords don't hurt them. Quickly!"

Tariq held his enemy at bay. The Gargoyle was a savvy fighter and swift to avoid his killing blows, but neither could it bypass Tariq's defenses. Carmen drew, turned, and kneeled. Tariq smiled and sidestepped. "Block this!" The beast tried to leap away, albeit too late, as her arrow blasted it to ashes. "Hurry, Carmen, we've got to help them."

"Beware the center of the room," Carmen yelled after a moment of inspiration. "The trap is there."

"How do we get up there?" Tariq asked.

"I think that I can help," Dao said. "Gentlemen, keep them off of me!"

Dartin defended his right flank, and Kur his left.

"Less talk and more magic, lad," Kur said. "We'll do the rest!"

The Gargoyles worked hard to stop them, but they were either stung by Dwarven steel and hurled back or grappled by a stalwart priest. Neither side gave quarter. The time for talk had ended.

Behind them, near the rear door, Kalor dueled with a third monster. His gnomish blades seemed to hunger for these foes, emitting an excited hum, like the sound of a far-off symphony brought to one's ears by the wind.

Dao raised his right hand, palm toward heaven, and with his left, he coiled the leather tie of his shirt around his index finger. Aiming for the feet of his waiting friends, he spoke these words, "Ex-Surgo sursum ab terra in caelum!"

Carmen immediately began rising up away from the floor. She was off-balance and disoriented for a moment, but she recovered quickly. A few seconds passed, and Dao was able to affect Tariq as well. Soon, they would reach the ceiling.

The Gargoyles around them hissed at the now floating invaders. They battled on, but they were clearly torn between finishing their enemies on the ground or taking wing against those seeking to rescue their helpless captives.

Their combat joined, Dartin began to hear a song, far off at first and then rising in volume until it became clear. It was not so loud that it drowned out all sound, but rather a melody from within, echoing through his mind alone. The tune roused his spirit, and he felt more powerful and vigorous than he had ever felt before. His sword, normally somewhat weighty, seemed somehow lighter, and his armor was now a barely noticeable burden. Ordinarily, facing a horror as unnatural as the Gargoyle would have filled his heart with fear, and with luck, he would have courageously transformed that emotion into action. This time things were strangely different. He was unafraid, all silent calm within, fighting detachedly with a logic and knowledge of swords-craft that he had never before known. The only problem was that his well-forged cold steel blade was without enchantment. When he struck the Gargoyles, his blade would either bounce off their flesh like they were made of stone or pass through them, as if they were merely illusions.

The monsters' blows carried deadly weight, but despite their razor-sharp claws, Dartin's armor proved invincible, and not even a scratch could they leave upon it. Frustrated, they sought to strike at his unprotected throat or to damage his hands.

"Dar-Croth," he commanded, and his helm sealed around his neck. With an instinct that he never knew that he had, he used his well-armored forearms to fend off their rending claws, but without magic, he knew not how he could win.

"Fear not," said Kur, for he had dispatched his enemy with a tremendous blow of his ax and rushed in to fight by his side. "Take my sword," he said, tossing it to Dartin without a thought. "It is made from mithril steel and may well hold Dwarven magic."

The priest was somehow able to sheathe his sword and catch Kur's blade in one fluid motion, and all in the heat of battle.

Undaunted, the Gargoyle attacked. Kur accepted its frenzied painful blows without complaint, patiently chambering his ax and swinging it cross-body, nearly eviscerating the monster. The Gargoyle, gutted, leaped to wing, but Dartin's downward cut finished it the next instant.

Kalor stung his opponent several times, and green blood ebbed from it. Soon, the Gargoyle realized that it would soon face four opponents, and so it then chose to take wing and help its comrades above. Kalor hurled his dagger, striking his opponent in the neck, slowing its escape but not finishing it.

The fourth monster hurtled toward Carmen. Drawing her bow, a mystical arrow formed. Dao's jet of scorching fire took it first, consuming it. He was fully engrossed in his power now, his mind channeling the energies around him, organizing the incantations of his studies, seeking to be ever ready with the most useful spell. Above them, new Gargoyles had formed atop of the pillars, replacing each of those that they destroyed.

"Are you all right, Keg?"

"It's nothing," Kur said. "We had best be after Karina and Ash."

"Beware the pressure plate near the center of the room," Dao said. "I'm certain that these things will reanimate if we set it off again." The muffled sounds of a great skirmish ensued above them.

"Dao," Dartin said, "can you get us up to that attic?"

"Sorry, boys, those were my only spells of levitation, and I can't recast any more until I've had time to rest and study my Book of Shadows."

"I don't think that it is going to matter," Kalor said. "Look there!" It was then that Carmen reached the opening. Floating silently upward, she held her bow at full draw, and Tariq was just beneath her. Her arrow flashed away, revealing the space around her, and she quickly prepared another.

Karina and Leander were fighting like berserks, but their blows were ineffective. Outnumbered and nearly defenseless, they cut and kicked, threw debris, and parried until they could retreat no further. The Gargoyles smiled wickedly at them, their clawed hands open and eager, their mouths wet with the anticipation of a feast. Rushing in, two of them took Leander to the ground, their mouths seeking his throat. Carmen's streaking missile blasted away the third. Karina strove to pull one beast off him, but it shoved her away in contempt. Carmen looked for an opening, but they were now a tangle of wrestling bodies, and she had no clear shot.

Thinking quickly, Tariq threw his sword, hilt first, toward Karina. She wasted no time in catching it up. With the touch of her hand, its blade rippled with flames. Very angry but in complete control, she dispatched the remaining Gargoyles before they could rise to meet her. Leander was hurt but still conscious. Once he knew that his attackers were gone, he lay down and tried to move no more.

"That was a close one," Karina said to him. "You don't look so good."

Punctured and torn by both teeth and claws, his arms screamed with pain when he tried to move them. "I don't feel so good. I'm a mess."

"We'll get you patched up. It doesn't look like they severed anything major."

"Let's get him out of here," Carmen said. "We can bandage him up down below."

"Only one problem," Tariq said, "getting down. We have no rope."

"Maybe there's some up here," Karina said. "There are all kinds of things lying around." Nevertheless, search as they might, they found no rope. They did, however, find four swords of Elven make, an assortment of clothes and armor, three rings, two vials filled with liquid, one white and the other gold, and a large sack filled with gold coins. The skeletal remains of at least four victims lay strewn about the room around them. The equipment had presumably been theirs. They dispersed the gear among themselves and wrapped Leander's arms with pieces of a torn shirt that they found.

"Kalor," Tariq called, "we have no way to get down. Any suggestions?"

"Fear not," Dao replied, "I have just the thing. Once I cast my spell, you may jump down without fear. You will float to the ground as softly as falling leaves." Standing now below them but away from the hazardous pressure plate, he placed his backpack on the floor. "When you jump," he said, "aim your landing here, and my spell will catch you. Wait for my signal." Backing up, he raised his hands once more and channeled his power. "Pluma praecipito!" he chanted. "Quickly now!"

Unsure as they were, they had to trust in Dao's invisible magic.

"I'll go first," Tariq said. "I have the best chance of making this fall."

"Good luck," Carmen said as he took the plunge, but just as Dao had said, some invisible net caught him, and he floated the last ten feet to the ground without harm. One by one they then followed him, and soon they had all reached the ground.

"Amazing!" Tariq said in astonishment. "I was a little bit worried there."

"Sorry," Dao replied, "but I didn't have time to test it before now."

"Didn't have time to test it!"

"Well, it worked."

"'Worked' says he," Kur said, spitting the blood out of his swollen mouth and laughing aloud. "We did well in the fight. Let's get bandaged up and take a look at what we found."

"And the chest too," Carmen said, "but carefully, Kalor."

"Of course, my lady," he said while imitating Dao's previous bow to perfection.

"Very funny. Tariq, go with him."

The chests were small, with silver inlaid walls and frames of gold. Well-made locks dangled from their latches. "What do you think, Kalor?"

"There are no magical runes warding it," Kalor said while looking through his crystal. "The locks look simple enough. I'll just have to watch out for any hidden traps." Removing his tools from his pack, he organized them on the floor before himself and went to work. The locks were a simple and old design, and he easily picked them. Prying up the lid ever so gently, he looked for the telltale signs of tampering. Hidden wires, springs, or levers might indicate that a deadly trap awaited them inside. Searching both chests well, he found none. "Nothing left to do now but open them. Stand back. I'm going to use the point of my sword." Lifting the latches with his weapon, he slowly opened the lids. A king's ransom of coins and jewels filled one, and the other held nothing but a coil of rope and a rolled-up parchment.

Tariq knelt beside the loaded chest. "Unbelievable! I wonder how many years have passed since this was put here?"

"I don't think that anyone's been here for a long time, Tariq. Hold on!" Kalor warned as Tariq was about to dip his hands into the treasure. "There may still be some trap hidden beneath those coins."

"What do you suggest?"

"Put your gloves on and take each coin out one by one. It's what any good thief would have to do. If you see anything strange, stop!"

Tariq did as instructed, slowly and patiently, while Kalor examined the rope. Its strands were black and silver, and it was made of some strange fiber, not hemp to be sure. They resembled nothing more than spiders' silk, tiny, strong, supple, and intricately woven. The whole thing was about fifty feet in length but weighed little more than five pounds. It was truly a treasure to behold. The parchment lay coiled inside of a large ring of white gold, sized for wide fingers, like those of a Dwarf or a large Human. Carefully unrolling it, he found it was old but well preserved. Surprisingly, it was written in common Fermish.

> Greetings,
>
> If you are reading this, then you have succeeded in defeating the Gargoyles and uncovered my treasure. I have enchanted this document so that it will translate my words for whoever should read it in the ages to come. My city is falling, beset upon by a terrible evil, and my remaining days are few. Perhaps the small items that I leave here will be of some help to you. Dockalfar blacksmiths created the rope. A masterwork, it will magically extend to grasp some distant object and release that object upon command. The trigger words are simple: "reach and hold" and "release your grasp." Otherwise, the rope is normal but unusually strong.

> This ring fits Dwarven fingers and offers protection from fire. The last of my wealth rests in the second chest, including a dagger from my adventuring days. If thrown, and it should fail to hit its mark, it will return to the hands of its wielder. I go now to lie down and rest. My liege lord has taken ill, and a terrible madness is upon him. I fear that he will pull the city down upon himself and all of his people. I have tried to reason with him, but he no longer hears my words. I am far too old and feeble to act against him, and so, helpless, I go to my deathbed.
>
> Best wishes,
> Dravian Elurian, Fourth Wizard of the City

"It's a note from the owner of this chest, Tariq," Kalor said. "From what he says, this was once part of a great city."

"If it was, then its days of glory are long past. Perhaps this room was once a hall in a mighty castle sucked into the earth by forces we cannot imagine."

"Or else this city was always Underearth," Kalor surmised, "perhaps one of the earliest Dockalfar settlements."

"Somehow I don't think so," Tariq said, plucking away another layer of coins, "but it's just a feeling."

"According to the wizard, there should be a dagger inside that chest." Working their way through the treasure, they soon uncovered an exquisite gold-handled dagger in a sheath of jade. They drew it out. Its blade was double-edged, with a pyramid-shaped point and deep blood grooves. Completely untarnished, it was sharp enough for shaving.

"It looks like the blade of a Master Thief," Tariq said. "Perhaps you should carry it."

Kalor took the knife from him and examined it.

"There is still some magic left in it," Kalor said. "Let's test it." Wasting no time, he grasped it by the flat of the blade and hurled it into an empty part of the room. It flew farther than any normal dagger, but as there was nothing there to strike, it circled wide like a boomerang and then returned hilt-first into his throwing hand.

"I have never seen such a thing before," Tariq replied in wonder. "Maybe I shouldn't have been so quick to offer it up."

"Not a chance," Kalor said, "unless Carmen orders it."

"Never fear, Kalor, My father's knives are enough for me. Let's help the others with the rest of the things that we found."

Karina had assembled all their newfound gear in a small circle, and Carmen was dressing Leander's arms as best as she could with what they had.

"Atran-Doru was helping me to learn the Druidic way," Leander said while gritting his teeth against the pain. "If I could find some pieces of the earth above, a ray of sunshine, and a maiden's tears, then I could heal myself."

"The earth above is easy, acolyte," Kur said. "I still have some Kegporter wine, only a few precious sips, but much of the soil that we use is carried underground from the valley. The essence of earth is in every drop of my father's wine."

"It just might work," Leander said hopefully.

"The ray of sunshine is also easy," Dao replied. "Just take one look into Karina's eyes. Forever will the sun shine there. Her heart is all fire and sun and love. Her soul is passion and the fury of the storm. You want sunshine, Druid? Just sit in the light and peer into her eyes, but beware, lest your heart be lost like mine!"

"But what about a maiden's tears?"

"Just sit and look, Druid," Dao said. "Wet your lips with Kegporter Wine and start your spell, and I shall produce your tears in short order."

It was then that Dao began to sing, and until that day, none of them had ever heard the young Elf sing thus. His song was a blend of old and new, a tribute to the Heavens and their blessings. He often sang the song when he was tending his crops at Nordtown. His melody would urge the corn to grow tall and strong, the tomatoes thick and fat, and tell the rabbits to eat a bit of this and not that.

Karina knew his song well. She had heard it a hundred times and more. It made her long for the fields of her home, the comfort of her table, and the warmth of her hearth, a place now lost forever in time. All that it was now was a memory, a place of dreams and a family to come, now ruined, smashed, and burned. She started crying tears like rain. Leander held out his hand and caught some.

Looking into her eyes, he sprinted merrily through her fields of gold, stared in wonder at a sky of endless blue, and felt the warmth of rays upon rays of sunshine. With his mind's eye, he caught some of them up. Mixing them with maiden's tears and two sips filled with the essence of earth, his magic was born. No longer was he merely a student among Druids, nay, he now knew the pathway to nature's power. With the ancient words, he spoke to the wind, to the sun, and to the moon. Before their eyes, his wounds began to close, miraculously healing. With a touch, he eased Kur's own pain, healing his torn lip and most of his worst cuts and bruises. He wanted to go on, but there was only so much power left in two sips of Kegporter Wine, and the magic of his healing spell soon faded.

"Well done, lad!" Kur said. "What do you think of that? It is no wonder that your best friend is also a priest."

"And I am no longer an acolyte," Leander proclaimed. "Call me Druid. I have passed the first test."

"Very well, Druid," Kur said. "Just don't you go getting too big for your britches."

"Never."

"Good, and I hope that you'll be able to do that again someday. I think that we're going to need it."

"Are you all right, Karina?" Leander asked. "I couldn't have done it without you."

"It's okay. I am happy and sad all at once. I had almost forgotten why we came down here in the first place and what it is that we are protecting. If ever we return home again, perhaps we can begin again."

"Of course, my love," Dao said, "but for now, Lady Karina, may I have this dance?"

"Why, Mr. Greylinx, I would be delighted." Taking his hand, he hoisted her to her feet, and they began to waltz around the hall as if the battle had never been.

"Mind the pressure plate!" Kalor warned, but Dao's rising voice cut short his words as he filled the chamber with his song of love, his song for her, and each of them could not help but to cry tears of joy themselves.

Leander had heard well Dao's previous words, and his longing for Robbin struck him then like a knife through his heart. In his wisdom, he accepted it, even reveling in it victoriously, for his love was still there, where it had forever been never lost. "Well, Kalor," he said, wiping away his tears, "what have we found?"

"It is an incredible find, Ash!" Kalor said. "Dao, I believe that the inscriptions on the blades and scabbards are in the ancient Elven. Can you read them?"

"Let me see, Kalor," Dao replied thoughtfully, taking one of them up. Carefully examining both sword and scabbard, he was awestruck at what they had found. It was a masterwork, forged of an alloy lighter than steel, with a slender double-edged and slightly upswept blade. Eel skin wrapped the downswept hilt, capped with a round bejeweled counterweight. The handguard was circular, four inches in diameter, and adorned with a casting of a dragon chasing its tail. Runes covered the entire blade and scabbard in mirror image of one another. "The inscription says that this is the Sword of the North Wind, sovereign against the Wyrms of Frost. It is a dragon slayer."

"That explains why it didn't work against the Gargoyles," Karina said.

"Not exactly. The runes etched onto the blade match those on the scabbard. I believe that they are matching sets and that their power will only manifest if the wielder possesses both the sword and its scabbard," Dao explained.

"So that only the rightful owner of the sword could gain its powers on the battlefield."

"Exactly."

"And what about the other three?" Kalor asked.

Dao then studied them all and discovered that they were all of similar design. "The second sword is the Sword of the East Wind, sovereign against Wyrms of Black. The third is the Sword of the South Wind, bane to all Fire Wyrms, and all three are dragon slayers. The fourth blade is special. It is the Sword of the West Wind, and it is a holy blade, blessed against evil. It is the sword of a paladin."

"These three rings hold magic as well," Kalor said, "and each of them bears runes similar to the swords."

Dao then took them up one by one and studied them.

"The rings are matched to the swords," Dao said. "The Ring of the North Wind protects the wearer against the cold, deadly breath of the Frost Dragons. The Ring of East Wind defends its owner against the vile acid spray of a Black Wyrm. The Ring of the South Wind renders its bearer immune to fire, and the Ring of the West shields its possessor like a suit of armor."

"And what of these potions?"

"Potions are difficult to identify," Dao said. "My father recommended carefully testing the odor, in the hopes that some hint as to its function will come to mind. Otherwise, a tiny sample, no more than a wetting of a fingertip, may be applied to the tongue. Barring this, there is no way to tell except through extensive alchemical research."

"Well, here goes," Kalor said while uncorking and testing the odor of the white-colored potion.

"Use your imagination," Dao urged. "Trust in your instincts."

"I somehow feel bigger, as if I am growing."

"I have heard of such potions of expansion," Dao said. "Whoever drinks this mixture will probably double in size."

"For how long?"

"Most potions only last for a few minutes to a few hours at most, but there is no way to be sure."

Kalor then uncorked and smelled the gold potion. "I'm not sure, but it makes me feel more powerful, invincible."

"Probably a warrior's potion. I have heard that such mixtures can temporarily increase the endurance and power of a fighter."

Lastly, they passed the small mace and shield between them. "They are small, sized for a Gnome or a Dwarf."

"And highly enchanted," Kalor said.

"But without runes," Dao considered, "we'll have to wait and see just what properties that they might have."

"Take them, Kalor," Carmen said. "You and Kur are the only ones who might be able to use them."

"I'll take them," Kalor said, "but I'm not sure about using the mace."

"We can't afford to take anything for granted," Carmen replied. "We need to use every advantage that we can find."

"I only wish that we had found some food," Karina said. "I've never been so hungry in my life."

"Well, Kur," Carmen said, "what do Dwarves eat when they are down here?"

"There are many edible creatures down here," Kur answered, "including stone worms and most cave spiders. If you know what to look for, you can eat many of the mushrooms and lichens as well. Unfortunately, there are also vast expanses of the Underearth without life of any kind. All we can do now is to keep hunting and hope."

"That's promising," Karina said flatly.

"We should focus on what we have," Tariq said. "We have already encountered many beasts down here that defy normal steel. Now we should finally be able to outfit everyone with a magical blade."

"But who will wield which sword?" Leander asked.

"Both Kur's ax and sword are fine weapons," Carmen said, "and Kalor's blades have already proven themselves."

"And I have Flame," Tariq said, "and the blades of my father."

"All I know," Karina declared, "is that I don't want to be so helplessly unarmed again."

"Then I say," Kur said, "that Karina should get the first choice."

"Agreed," everyone answered unanimously.

Karina went from one sword to the other, her right hand touching her chin, considering. "Then I claim the Sword of the North Wind," Karina said. "If we make it through this, we're sure to end up in the frigid northland again, and I will be ready." Taking up the weapon, she ran her sword belt through the scabbard loop, set it over her left hip, and tested its weight. Satisfied, she grasped its hilt in her right hand and then drew her sword in a lightning-fast draw. "It's a fine blade!" Sheathing it, she smiled broadly.

"And now you must claim the ring as well," Dao said. You now carry the weapons of the Guardian of the North Wind. Wield them well, my love."

"I shall!"

"And what about you, Dao?" Carmen asked.

"I shall wait until last," he said. "My father's magic will have to stand our tests until then."

"Then Dartin and Leander have the greatest need," Carmen said.

"You first, Dartin," Leander said. "Somehow, I believe that I shall find Atran-Doru again someday."

"In the meantime, we both need to stay alive," Dartin observed. "I choose the Ring and Sword of the South Wind." Placing the ring upon the ring finger of his left hand, he was surprised when it suddenly shrank to fit him, neither too tight nor too loose. He was relieved when he found that he could still remove it. Exchanging his old scabbard for the new one, he too carried his sword over his left hip. "This is a great sword, and I swear by Odin that I will carry it with honor. Only two swords remain, Leander. Which will you choose?"

"There is only once choice, the Sword of the East Wind. The Sword of the West Wind is for Carmen alone." Fastening it over his right hip, he placed the ring upon the index finger of his right hand. He then lashed his old sword to the side of pack. "Our old swords are still good weapons. We must not abandon them."

"Perhaps Dao should take it," Carmen said.

"Nay, my lady," Dao replied, "a paladin should have a holy blade. The Sword of the West Wind must surely be one of the greatest among them."

"I will carry it with honor." Wearing it in like fashion, she placed the ring upon the ring finger of her right hand and belted her old sword across her back. "And what of the other items?"

"The potion of expansion could be used by anyone," Dao said, "in the right circumstances."

"Perhaps you should hold on to it," Kalor said, "until we need it."

"Very well, but the warrior's potion should go to Kur. Once he drinks it, he will become battle's juggernaut."

"Eh? I don't trust it, but if the time comes, I will try it," Kur gumbled.

"And to Kalor a Gnomish shield and mace."

"The shield only," Kalor said. "The mace is too heavy. You hold on to it, Dao."

"Okay, but let me know if you should want it."

"If I carry any more weapons, I won't be able to move properly. A thief needs to be silent."

"All together," Tariq said, "we have almost five thousand gold coins. There is no telling how so much wealth might help us."

"That's about six hundred apiece," Kalor said. "Too much for most of us to carry."

"Then take what you will," Tariq urged, "but I'm taking the six hundred."

"And I can manage a little more," Kur said.

"Me too," Dartin said. "I have never felt so strong."

"There is a change in you," Carmen said. "How do you feel?"

"I feel fine, better than fine even. It's strange, but I haven't felt hungry at all since I put the armor on."

"We've got to find a way to free you of it," Carmen said worriedly.

"There are spells that could help," Dao said, "and maybe even remove the curse upon it."

"If only we had one."

"We'll just have to wait and see."

"Let us rest," Carmen said. "And see if our wizards can open this door for us."

"There is a spell in Modrul's Book that should prove effective."

"Then sleep and study quickly," Carmen said. "We need to keep moving and hope that we find food."

They awoke with uplifted spirits. Better armed than ever before, and for the most part unhurt, they packed with newfound vigor. Before them loomed the portal, magically barred, thick-beamed, and ironbound.

"Well, wizards," Carmen said, "how do you expect to get us through?"

"Modrul has provided us with a possible solution. We used his spell for opening in Modrul's Lair, but his spell for barring a portal remained," Dao explained.

"I don't understand how that can help us."

"Based upon his spell, I designed my own spell of opening, and Kalor and I penned it into his own book. I should be able to memorize and evoke its power at will."

"But will it work?"

"I have no idea."

"We could try and hack the door down."

"That would take hours, and then every creature within a mile will know that we're here."

"Cast your spell, Dao."

"Stand back, everyone. There is no telling what might happen with an untested formula." Standing before the door, he stilled his mind, finding the center of his power. Lifting his hands before himself, he traced the outline of the door and then began his incantation. With his will, he raised his power. In a sense, he battled against the magical energy placed upon the portal by the ancient wizard who long ago sealed the room shut. While the struggle ensued, the ancient runes became visible to all, one by one, as Dao vied against them. In the midst of casting, he had fully entered into the realm of his mind, and his hands would often reach for the phantom symbols, as if to catch one and cast it away. At first, it seemed that the flood of the ancient wizard's enchantments would be too much, but Dao only concentrated all the harder, and soon he turned the tide. "Ostium de lignum de saxum de ferrum, libero tuus, teneo apertus, ille via permitto omnis ad ingredior! Open the way, allow all to enter!"

It was then that the final rune was banished, and for an instant, the seams of the door burst with light. The ancient locking mechanism spun and clicked, tumbled and turned. Rotating slowly, the doorknob released its aged grasp, and the portal swung open just a crack. Dao turned to them all, quite relieved and sweating more than a little. "That old wizard was tough," he declared.

"But you were tougher," Carmen said, quite impressed.

"My father was a good teacher. He would often invent games to develop my concentration. Now I can focus on just one thing at a time, excluding all else. That type of discipline is what is required to win a contest between wizards."

"Well," Karina said, "we should be off to find some food then."

"One more spell." Producing one of his father's daggers, he enchanted its blade with magical light. "Should we need it," Dao said, "we will have the light of a hundred candles to show us the way." Sheathing it, its light was extinguished yet ever ready.

"How long will your light last?" Kur said.

"Unless I end it or another wizard disenchants it. It will still be as bright for hundreds of years after we're all gone."

"That could come in handy."

"Indeed."

"For now," Carmen said, "we go forth in the dark, with what stealth that we can muster. Kalor, lead the way. Tariq, you have rear guard."

Kur grasped the edge of the great door, leaned back, and pulled. It was massive, over a foot thick and ironbound, and its hinges rusty. Nevertheless, it was no match for the determined strength of a grumpy Dwarf, and Kur soon had it open. Kalor slipped through into the deepening darkness.

The next room was an antechamber, some twenty feet square, at the far end of which an open archway stood. The arch framed the entryway of a set of massively constructed stairs heading west, sized for giants it would seem. They would have to climb or jump down each one. Kalor waited for Carmen to catch up. "Maybe we should turn back and try the other way?"

"Let's try it," Carmen whispered, "and see where it leads. Just be careful and keep your eyes open."

Using his training in acrobatics, he worked his way down step-by-step, quickly developing a rhythm that propelled him gracefully to the bottom. He descended some ninety stairs in all, traveling well over three hundred feet in distance and in depth.

There was a small chamber at the bottom, ending with yet another thick door of at least nine feet in height. It was there that he discovered some grisly remains. A skeletal hand with wrist and forearm bones still attached to it grasped the hilt of a rusty dagger embedded into the face of the door at a height of about five feet. There were a few words scratched into the wood just above it, but he would need some light to read them. The doorknob and keyhole were centered upon the left side of it, too high for him to examine properly without jumping up or climbing on something, or some Dwarf. Leaping up and grabbing the knob was too risky. Better to wait for help. Turning about, he looked up the stairs. He could still see Carmen and the others framed with light in the doorway above, but could they see him? He doubted it, but Carmen and Dartin might, if they were using their helms to the fullest. He waved up at them to see if they reacted, and not surprisingly, Carmen waved back. 'Come down,' he signaled, and she gave him the thumbs-up. Returning to the task, he began to search the small room that he was standing in. If there was a trap, he aimed to find it.

When they finally made it down to him, he was sure that the door was not rigged, but he needed to see the keyhole in order to be certain. "Can you give me a lift?" he asked Kur.

"Of course," he whispered. "Ten fingers," lacing his fingers together, Kur created a basket for Kalor to step in and hoisted him up with ease. Peering into the keyhole proved fruitless because the wood was cold and damp, and his night vision could see only a little.

"Dao," Kalor said, "this would be a great time for some of your light." Dao immediately drew out his dagger, and the room was brilliantly illuminated. The disembodied hand then seemed even more sinister, and the words that it had carved were visible to all.

Turn back! Do not pass beyond the door! Death waits…

"Apparently he didn't have time to finish it," Dao observed. "It is written in Elvish, but what Elf would dare tread about down here?"

"We have no way of knowing if it was an Elf," Carmen said, "or even a he or a she, but we may have no choice but to enter."

"We could back track and try the other passage."

"There is no way of knowing if one way is any more dangerous than another," Tariq reasoned. "The two passageways might just connect somewhere farther in."

"What of the door, Kalor?"

"I have found no signs of any trap, and it appears to be unlocked."

"As if," Leander said, "we're being welcomed in."

"More likely," Dartin said, "whoever wrote this was the last person to come through here."

"But what killed him?" Karina asked.

"The bones are sliced cleanly," Tariq said. "My guess would be that he died by the sword."

"More likely whatever killed him is still down here, waiting," Kur said grimly.

"That's comforting," Karina said.

"It just seems right, considering the way that our luck's been going."

"Well, Kalor," Carmen said, "which way does the diamond point now?"

Climbing down from his perch, he pulled the gem out of his pack. Indisputably, it pointed to somewhere beyond the door. "Lead on," she said with a sigh. Grasping the doorknob with two hands, she turned and pulled. The door then opened with ease. Massively constructed, with thick beams and enormous iron hinges, it should have required quite a pull to move it, but rather it swung inward so easily that it seemed to have no weight to it at all. "Have you ever seen anything like it?"

"No," Kalor said matter-of-factly, "it is incredible workmanship."

"Dwarves might have made it," Kur said, caressing the surface, "but I have heard of ancient Elven craftsmen whose magic allowed them to craft doors such as this."

Dao allowed his light to fall inward as they opened the door, and lo! A great hallway running north and south loomed before them. The walls of the passage were easily twenty feet tall and a like distance apart, and row upon row of burial chambers lined them. A thick layer of dust covered everything, including the bones of the thousands who were laid to rest here. Randomly placed jars, ornate figurines, and other decorative pottery lay throughout the hall. Beautiful frescos depicting times of old covered both the exposed walls and the ceiling. Cobwebs hung thickly about the walls but were strangely absent from the center of the passage. The empty eye sockets of the dead stared accusingly at them, as if asking them to quench the light and let them rest in peace.

"Great," Tariq said, "catacombs."

"This must be the lowest level of the ancient city," Dartin surmised. "The great cities of Arendal are said to have miles of catacombs such as this beneath them."

"Which way now, Kalor?" The scepter's gem then pulled irresistibly down the south passage, its light revealing numerous doors and side passageways branching off it. Looking down, Kalor was surprised to see what looked like the impression of footprints left in the dust. "Tariq, look here!"

The ranger inspected the tracks. "You're right, Kalor, someone walked through here very recently. By the tracks, I would say he was about six feet tall and lightly built, more like an Elf's build than a Man's build. He backtracked a bit and then continued south."

"This just keeps getting better," Karina said.

"I've got a bad feeling about this too," Dao agreed. "Perhaps an old prayer will help:

> Dream well, elder spirits of light breezes and gentle seasons. May the livings' footfalls ignite memories of dearest loves and silver beaches. Wake not, ghostly spirits. Be at ease, be soothed, and be still.

Karina clutched his hand with a desperate grip, her left hand holding the hilt of Sword of the North Wind. "Let's get out of here," she begged.

"Kalor," Carmen said, "lead on."

Using Dao's light, they entered the passage. Dao was the last one among them to step through the doorway, and it was then that the portal suddenly slammed shut behind them. Dao rushed for the doorknob, but it would not turn despite his strongest effort. "It's locked!" An eerie supernatural wind began to blow through the tunnel then, kicking up the dust and disturbing the cobwebs. Warm and dry, it reeked of age-old decay.

Carmen's mind suddenly screamed out in warning. A terrible evil was approaching! How she knew it, she could not say, but she understood it as surely as the sun rises. "To arms!" she said, "prepare yourselves. Quickly, Kalor, head to the south!" Holding the magical diamond like a beacon, he moved urgently down the passageway. He felt pursued, but by what he could not know. Perhaps it was simply their own shadows that followed them, but he knew better.

"Odin protects us!" Dartin invoked.

"Pray that he does so," Leander said, "for I feel now that this is the lair of some ancient evil."

The wind blew stronger, and then a terrible voice echoed throughout the halls, "Who dares…disturb me? Rise, my children. Rise and destroy the intruders!"

"What do you suppose he means by 'rise'?" Kalor muttered, trembling a bit in fear.

"Keep moving!" Carmen ordered.

The tunnel was long and except for their magical light, utterly dark. Alcoves were carved into the walls in three high tiers that went on and on. Strange sounds began to rumble from within them, softly at first, like old bones rubbing together.

"What is that?" Karina asked before she saw it, and screamed.

Powers that could cause the dead to rise are perhaps forces best left unknown, but in that place and in that dark hour, they did, indeed, rise. Every skeleton, every slumbering spirit, and every decaying corpse were among the Lych King's legions, and when their master called, they did awaken!

First, he forced their wretched souls back into the vessels that had once held their lives, and such was his force of evil that their bones would organize and reform and, in a sense, reattach themselves. Their jawbones would click and settle, open, and draw un-breath, and in some cases, tiny orbs of red light would appear where their eyes had once been. Their souls, with one foot in Hell and the other attached to their undead corpses could see into both worlds and could feel only one emotion, hate. Only one desire remained in them: destroy the living! Their corpses, now animate, crawled out of their resting places. Slowly at first, as if they were children learning how to walk again, their skeletal feet clicked and scratched along the stone floor, like a dull blade upon a sharpening stone. The old warriors among them armed themselves with what weapons were buried with them while others procured clubs of bone or sought only to grasp a living victim by the throat and strangle them.

It was one of those first awakened that Karina had seen sitting up in his dark alcove and staring, staring.

Flight was their only option, but they had traveled so far already without food or adequate sleep, their canteens, skins, and flasks rarely full. They ran on, their hearts pounding in absolute terror, their lungs burning with swirling dust.

If in that dreadful hour, Kur was their spirit, Carmen was their courage. Leading them on, she sought a place of refuge, escape, or defense. Racing down a side passage, they came upon a door made of stone. It stood ajar, with a symbol of a cross with an orb at its peak carved into its face.

When their light shone within the room, the brilliant gleam of gold and riches beyond imagining tortured their eyes. Whether or not the gold gleamed only in reflection to their light or burned with a luminance all its own was a mystery. Nonetheless, the room was as bright as a clear day in June. Within it were chests of gold and silver coins, trunks with cups and ornate chalices, and carvings of ivory and jewel-hilted daggers. Gems, jewelry, priceless suits of armor, and more were displayed in all their splendor, but there was no time for further inspection, for behind them walked the ranks of the Dead.

"No good!" Carmen yelled. "It's a dead end. Turn back!"

Too late for them, for a legion of skeleton warriors now blocked the passage that they had taken. More terrible still was the sound of thousands of bony feet walking *click-clack* to block their escape and bring about their end.

"Go back!" Dao cried.

Desperate and weary, they fell back into the treasure room. Shutting the door behind them, they were surprised to find that it could be barred from within. They further bolstered it by dragging several heavy chests and setting them against it. Seconds later, the Dead began slamming into it with their bone clubs, hammers of war, and other weapons, but for the moment, it held against them.

"What are we going to do now?" Karina said, tears welling in her eyes.

"Search for a way out," Carmen said. "There may be a secret passage. Why else would the door bar from this side?"

THE TREASURE ROOM

The room itself was multifaceted, consisting of eight distinct walls, seven of which contained deep alcoves that might conceal a doorway or hold the slaves of some long-forgotten king. A massive stone sarcophagus rested in the center of the floor, surrounded on all sides by treasure. Fanning out, they began their search.

Kur fought the urge to drown himself in the riches all around him. He tried to focus on the fact that an army of undead warriors might soon burst through the door, but it was no use. His gold fever had returned twofold, and he could not resist creeping closer to the sarcophagus and the treasure heaped around it. The pile of riches was higher than he was tall. There were platinum goblets, cups of gold, necklaces of pearls, sacks full of gems and more, and toward these, he did tread. The sarcophagus was etched with runes and symbolic portraits of yesteryear, and despite the protests of his peers, he procured one small embroidered sack. Loosening its rose-colored ties, he propped it open and reviewed its contents, and behold! It was filled with rubies, rich and red, clean and well cut. It was enough wealth to build a castle with and more. With hardly a thought, he shoved the bag inside of his tunic so that it slid down inside of it, coming to rest just above his belt. His eyes fell next upon a jewel-hilted sword, short and stout like the blades that his people forged. Grasping it, he pulled the blade free of the mound of gold surrounding it. Its craft was exquisite, its blade wrought of mithril steel, and its handle alone was a master's work of gold. Turning about, he intended to show the glorious blade to his friends and so say, "Look! There is no curse. Let us take what we can and leave," but it was not to be, for as he turned, he saw the eyes of his friends fixed upon Dartin.

Falling to his knees, Dartin cried out in agony. Writhing in unspeakable pain, he fell to the floor. Convulsing, he gasped as he was overcome by a sudden transformation. Where Dartin's face had been, only a beautiful woman's remained. Elfin yet with larger eyes of azure, high cheekbones, perfect teeth, and hair of midnight blue, she drew breath in surprise, as if it was her very first breath. The armor had reformed as well, and where once the breastplate of a man had been, only the cuirass of a woman remained. Perfect of form, she slowly rose to her feet. "At last," she said, "I am alive!"

"Look!" Karina screamed, "Dartin is there," and indeed, he was, standing at the back of the room, stark naked and bewildered, looking at his hands and arms as if wondering how he had come to be there.

"Kneel before your queen!" the Chaos Maiden commanded, and such was her voice that they nearly complied, for here before them was a living god. They did not kneel, however, for they were not the naive children formerly ruled by the Chaos Lords. Nay, they were Fermen, and they knelt only before their own king.

"Perhaps you should kneel before us," Carmen said with her blazing bow drawn. "I have a hunch that this weapon can do you no small harm."

"You dare to wield my own bow against me?"

"I do."

"Infidels!" she cursed. "Without me, none of you will ever leave this place alive."

Carmen could stand no more. The presence of evil was so thick around her that her mind screamed out to act naught, save to destroy it. If there would be any chance for them to defeat this ancient evil, it would be now, before she regained her full strength. Her companions were of like mind, for they stood with her with weapons drawn and determined visage. Loosing her arrow, she struck the Chaos Maiden. Blackened and pitted, the Vanir armor held against it. Kalor hurled his dagger, but she merely raised her hand, blocking it with magic or some force of her will. With a word, she raised a shining barrier around herself and drew the Sword of the Guardian of the South Wind.

"A fine blade, befitting of a queen. Give me the seeker stone and the gem of the staff, or I shall kill you all," she commanded.

"Never!" Carmen said.

Their combat joined, their concentration was locked upon Sheena, a nemesis the likes of which they had never known. It was because of this that they did not readily notice the sinister presences all around them.

The Dead Rise

They had slept for centuries, entombed in their golden beds. Eons ago, they had been members of an elite guard sworn to defend the life of their king, an Elven lord named Andomar Tabarun. Their oaths bade them to follow him when he fell into darkness. In death they waited, guardians through the ages, waiting until the day might come when their tortured souls could move on. In the meantime, all life was a thing they despised. Life, so unnatural to the Dead, required destruction, despoilment. Their kingdom needed warriors, and only the Dead need apply. Their treasure disturbed, their restful sleep was broken.

Sheena moved toward Carmen, clearly intending to cut down all within her path, but something stopped her. Looking to her left, she stared at the sarcophagus. Its lid was sliding open. Inch by inch it slid, stone grinding upon stone; at times, the sliding ceased, only to resume a moment later. When it had opened enough, five bony fingers rose up to grasp the lid more firmly and then hurl it aside, as if it weighed little more than a child's toy! It sailed past Kur, who was nearly decapitated, only to be shattered against the wall behind him. The ragged cloth-wrapped fingers then turned to grasp the lip of the chest, and then a second pair did take hold upon its opposite side. Everyone among them was transfixed with horror!

Up and up it rose, the cloth-wrapped form of some long-dead corpse. It possessed the size and shape of the Men of old, with wide powerful shoulders and a tall stature. No more was this creature one of the living; its once muscular shoulders were now only a memory. Its flesh was dried and sunken, its arms merely bones and desiccated skin beneath rotten ancient trappings. When its eyelids opened, like leather slits left in contact with each other for too long, two burning orbs of rage brought their wrath to bear. Turning its hateful attention first upon the being that had defiled its burial riches, it stood in a jagged fashion, as if its bones had to adjust to the horrific power that moved them. For this monster was not driven by mortal forces, nay, this creature was empowered by the limitless realm of death. Its strength was despair, its body a parody of life. Here were the ancient dead guardians of legend. Here was the terrible Mummy, an unstoppable vehicle of rage, a trapped soul corrupted by evil.

Kur was frozen by a fear greater than any that he had ever known. Never in his wildest nightmares had he imagined that such a thing could exist, for who could be mad enough to create such a being? He couldn't act. Helplessly frozen by its hungry stare, he felt the weight of the sword in his hands and the pressure of the rubies against his stomach.

I'll put it all back the way that it was, he thought, but he knew that it was too late. The Mummy's curse sprung. He was soon to be its next victim. Watching in fascination as the skeletal legs stepped forth from the coffin, he stared on in horror as the seven-foot-tall hulk shambled inexorably toward him. He wanted to run, but he could do nothing. The Mummy's arm rose up above him, and he knew that he was witnessing the moment of his death. Never again would he see his kin. Never again would he taste his father's mushroom wine. Something within him, perhaps some tiny vestige that remained of his own will, caused him to drop the treasure sword and seek out the handle of his ax. In a rush, power flowed back into his limbs. The Mummy's arm descended, and at the final instant, he rolled clear, crashing into a chaotic mass of treasure. The Mummy cried out in rage, and its voice was a hollow moan, an ancient parody of what had once been the voice of a Man. Kur meant to join his companions and escape, but it was not preordained. The very walls were coming alive!

There were seven dark alcoves in that cursed room, and each was issuing forth an undead creature all of its own. In seconds, they suddenly faced eight monsters, each just as terrible as the first.

"Once you are all dead," Sheena said triumphantly, "I will return to claim what is rightfully mine!" She then spoke a single word, too softly for anyone else to hear, and disappeared.

"Fall back to the door!" Carmen commanded. "Dartin, run!"

He was farther from the door than any of them, naked and weaponless. Turning around, he saw the creature stepping out of its dark chamber. Its hands extended, seeking his throat. He tried to summon the rune of banishment and other symbols that all evil beings feared, but his prayers were without power, his god still asleep.

Backing away, he sought some place of refuge, but the monsters were closing their circle around him. They clearly held him in the greatest contempt, perhaps some measure of his runes had been invoked, just not enough to stop them. The most powerful sorcerer that had ever existed, a being that had access to long-forgotten magic and the darkest enchantments, had created the Mummies. Dartin was completely unprepared to meet horrors of such magnitude. Against one such being, he might stand a chance if his powers were available to him, but before eight creatures, his chances were miniscule. They faltered in their initial steps toward him, but their second and third grew ever stronger, and they drew toward his priest-light like moths to a flame. Their eyes had locked all their anger upon him; their steps were heavy with contempt, their moans filled with ancient curses. Carmen's arrows thundered into them. The heroes' swords crashed against their corpses, but it did not matter. The Mummies were among the mightiest of Death's warriors, and they swarmed over Dartin like lions to the kill. Surrounding him, the first Mummy reached for his throat, and Dartin caught its wrists in his hands and struggled with all his might. Staring at the monster in utter defiance, he smiled and began to sing his death song. The Mummy's supernatural strength was almost limitless, and for a few seconds, Dartin held against it. His valiant efforts could not last. Striking him from behind and beside, each blow broke his bones and smashed his organs. His strength failed, and the Mummies' hands found his throat and squeezed the last of the light from his body. His eyes bulged and then grew dark. His body was smashed, torn, and ruined. They defiled him, tearing off his arms, smashing his legs and his skull, and then hurled him to the rear of the chamber, where he would forever rest.

"No!" Leander screamed. The blood rage took hold of him then, and he laid into the Mummies with the Sword of the Guardian of the East Wind. He was berserk, desperate, and fearless. He cared nothing for his own safety, and his enchanted blade proved effective when wielded with such fury, hacking off the left leg of the monster nearest him. The Mummy toppled. Far from finished, it crawled toward him. Reaching for his legs, it sought to bring him down and destroy him.

Carmen's Rangers fought as one now, exhausted, utterly without hope, and filled with sorrow. If they remained in the room, then they would all surely suffer the same fate as Dartin. His remains crushed and strewn around the room, they knew that there was no hope left for him. Never had they left anyone behind, but it was not merely their fate that mattered. The items that they carried could bring about the end of the world, and if they fell, the last hope of all that was good would end. Dartin would want them to save themselves, but there was only one way out—back the way that they had come, back through the Halls of the Dead.

"Fall back!" Carmen ordered. "Leander, fall back!"

"I'll hold them as long as I can!" Kur said. "Get him out of here!"

Leander could hardly see for the tears that bled from his face. All that he could feel was the utter loss of his lifelong friend. Avenge him, was all that he then knew, but something was pulling him back, away from his enemies. "No! Let me go," he pleaded.

"Save your anger for the hall," Tariq said firmly. "Come back to us, Leander. We need you."

The ranger's words crashed into him like a cold plunge into the sea in winter. Once again himself, he nodded to Tariq and joined them in their retreat, fighting as they ran. Forming a defensive circle beside the door that spelled either salvation or doom, they hurled vases and pots, treasure chests, and everything that they could reach into the path of the Mummies. Karina guarded the right flank while

Kalor stood with Dao at the center, the Elf raising his power and Kalor readying the Book of Modrul. Kur drank a hero's potion, and Carmen plied her bow. Tariq wielded Flame like a whirlwind, with Leander beside him.

Karina screamed, "The door is giving way!"

Odin

He awoke screaming. Sweat poured from his brow, and his body would not respond to his will. He felt like he had been sleeping for a hundred years, or at least a hundred Asgard years. Slowly, he rolled onto his side and sat up. Rubbing his eyes, he yawned and stretched. His wife was sitting by the window, knitting.

"You must have had a bad dream, my love," Frigga said.

"It was the most terrible nightmare that I have had in centuries."

"Tell me about it."

"Dartin Odinson, the last priest of our line, is dead."

"Perhaps you should go and get him."

"He has fallen in a place that even I dare not tread. His spirit is trapped by Andomar Tabarun, the Lych King."

"Are there no others?"

"No mortal yet lives," Odin replied, "who knows the power of the runes."

"Then I shall pray for a miracle," Frigga said.

"All is lost. I fear that the time of the gods is coming to an end."

"If anyone can find a way, it is you, my love."

"Summon the Aesir," Odin commanded. "The Council of the Gods convenes in two days' time!"

"As you wish, my love," she answered while her husband sat for some time with his head in his hands.

The Hall

Dao evoked his deadliest magic then, pouring forth a long scorching wave of fire out of his hands. Several of the Mummies were immolated, their rotten trappings burning away, their dried flesh roasting. They were staggered by the fire but not finished, for they were, after all, beyond death, driven by dark powers stoppable only by the holiest relics of goodness.

Ancient swords of power could sting them, but the price of engaging them was too terrible to risk. One blow of their limbs was deadly, their strength invincible.

"Stand clear of the door!" Carmen ordered. "Let them come!"

The portal burst inward. Death's army rushed in, and such was the pressure of the mass that although the corpses in the lead could well see their quarry, they were helpless to stand and fight against the driving tide behind them. The room filled. The Mummies were now embattled by a sea of their brethren. In their rage, they hurled their skeletal brothers aside, striving in their malice to destroy the living. The ensuing chaos created the opening that Carmen had hoped for. "Kalor, if you're going to do something, now would be a good time!"

He could not reply, so deep was he in the casting of Modrul's spell, the dragon's book hovering before him, magic coursing through his body. With his right hand, he reached up, and with dragon's sorcery, he pulled ice, sleet, and snow from the ethers and rained it down upon the Dead. The spell was powerful, dangerously so. It filled the entire room, and he could not prevent the storm from falling upon them as well. "We must flee!" he cried. Closing the book, he tucked it beneath the folds of his cloak and sought refuge. There was no clear line of battle, no obvious avenue of retreat.

Surely, they too would have been overwhelmed, if not for the rallying cry of their leader, "To me, to me!" she called, and to her side the embattled battled, each individual spirit fighting as one to her voice alone. Her sword flashed repeatedly, the Sword of the West Wind, guardian against Evil, and fleshless arms fell, still grasping weapons of war or cracked shields. Spinning a circle of destruction around her, her friends found a new refuge by her side, a place to stand firm and drive on. Her valiant effort won the door and the first few feet of the hall. Her companions were hot on her heels, snow-covered and bruised by hail but alive.

"We must reach the main hall," Kur said, "before they bury us beneath their wretched bones!"

"Press on!" Carmen commanded, holding the rear while her companions forged ahead.

"Together then!" Tariq said, and their blades fought in unison, driving back the tide of the Dead into the room behind them. Kalor's spell continued to rain down on the ghastly mass within, and the deluge of ice and snow soon trapped their old bones.

Odd it was that Dao then took the lead beside the stalwart Dwarf. Fighting on to clear the way for their friends, the battle-lust was upon them. They fought in a style of alliance between Dwarf and Elf that had not been seen since the dawning days of the world! Korun-Koth smote in a wide arc, and when the heavy blade struck bone, the legions of the Lych King were shattered, and where Dao's sword struck, skulls sundered and rib cages smashed. In his fury, Dao remembered powers that had long been dormant within him, secrets that his father had whispered to him while he was still in the womb, forgotten mysteries that his people had been born to wield since the dawn of time. He had ascended in fire as his father had said he would. He was a warrior mage reborn.

Out of fire, we were born, and onto the earth, we rose. Firstborn of God's children, first to discover the magic of earth and fire, air and water! By Tempus, I invoke my power. By Tempus, I ascend!

Dao raised his hand, and a billowing gust of wind rose up before him, sweeping away the skeleton warriors blocking the passage like leaves before the gale.

Wasting neither a precious moment nor a miraculous opportunity, they ran on. Leander and Tariq were the last to leave. Looking into the room, they both hoped that somehow their friend would step out of the storm and shake the snow off his coat, as they had seen him do at least a hundred times before. Tears poured from their eyes as they realized that this time, he would not. Peering through the hail and stinging mist, they saw only the terrifying orbs of the Mummies—delayed, yes, but not beaten. Death's disciples still trudged unrelentingly toward them.

"We must flee!" Tariq said, and when they could safely wait no more, they raced on. Eighty feet and they had reached the main hall. Their friends were embattled from the north, from the west, and from the south, struggling to hold the intersection of three great cryptways and the Mummies to the east; they would soon be surrounded. Tariq and Leander prepared to defend their rear flank. They could see the Mummy King standing defiantly in the doorway, the tempest behind him waning. With one hand upon the door and the other daring them to meet their deaths, he laughed, his gurgling wail echoing down the hall. Forever would it haunt their dreams. It looked for a moment as if he would stoop low and pass through the door with his brethren, but much to their surprise, the Mummy King then slammed the door! Perhaps, they had had enough of the living for one century, or more likely, they could not leave their cursed room.

Behind them, the catacombs were filled with endless ranks of undead warriors, but more so it seemed along the north passage from whence they had come.

"Kur, press on to the south!" Carmen ordered.

But Kur's instincts as a soldier had already anticipated her decision. The well of grief within him had filled once again. This time, Dartin's blood was on his own hands. Fighting like a demon, he wielded his ax two-handed, his every blow crushing bone, blasting his enemies' weapons away or cleaving them in two. Every foot of ground was sorely won, and none of them went uninjured. Dwarf and Elf fought on, now with their leader beside them and their friends holding back the following horde.

Kur and his ax were one. His weapon held many secrets, and at times, the ranks of the dead appeared to him as an ancient army of Elves, and to them, he seemed like Baldric, firstborn of the Dwarves. There were those among them whose spirits could still remember windows of the past, and these would sometimes forget their hatred and return to their catacomb resting places in order to dream of ancient memories of their former lives. The vast majority of the dead, however, were long past remembering. Their contempt was every bit the equal to their distance from life. The Lych King's legions rose and stood against them at every turn.

The southwestern hall was now either their path to escape or the road to their doom. Dwarf, Elf, and Woman fought side-by-side, Druid, Ranger, and Swordmaiden holding back the horde rushing in behind them. Kalor ran between them, struggling to secure Modrul's Book so that he could join in the fight.

They fought, they ran, and they bled. Guardian blades and sword aflame, the columns of the dead began to crumble. Their bones littered the hall, most smashed to pieces, but dismembered limbs still sought to kill them, vacant eye sockets still yearning for their deaths. The bony remains soon became treacherous obstacles, as much a bane to them as it was to the Undead.

Unfortunately, the dead were endless and untiring. They neither gasped for breath nor felt the fatigue of war. Battling without fear or pain, they could only be stopped by their destruction.

Dao and Kalor were beacons of light in the very home of darkness. His diamond glowed brilliantly, urging them ever southward, and the Elf's dagger carried the light of the sun into battle.

Carmen looked ever ahead toward hope, cutting down any creature of evil that drew too close. Her gentle heart attracted their enmity like flies to honey, and they vied to kill her in preference to all others. Her sword was a bane to evil, and such was its power that many of the skeletons that she struck were sent to oblivion or blasted to dust. The passage was a writhing mass of skeleton warriors, so thick that they resembled the scaly skin of a serpent in the moonlight.

It seemed to her that all hope was lost. No matter how many they destroyed, there were a thousand more to replace them. It was then that she saw it; beyond the sea of death, at the furthest reach of her enchanted vision, she spied a door! "There!" she said, pointing, "to the south, a door. Press on. It's our only chance!"

Kur rallied ever harder to her call, as he had once done in service to the king, and as he would gladly do to the end of days. He was Korun-Koth, the embodiment of rage. His arms lashed out to an ancient rhythm bubbling up from deep within his very soul. His grief was a bottomless well. Invoking his god's name, he cried out, "Clangeddeus!" and it seemed that Baldric himself then fought before them, and there was no skeleton warrior that could stand against him. Step-by-step, he took ground and gave none. If there were corpses beneath his feet, he stomped through them; if the dead tried to bring him down, he threw them off. His mind was lost. His inner beast had risen. He was the warrior of countless battles, each one lending to the fire of his soul. Some part of him knew that his friends fought beside him, but it was a small part. Destruction was his path, carnage his very soul.

The distant door grew ever closer. The ranks of dead before them were thinning, but six greater guardians stood barring that portal, six skeleton warriors with golden crowns and rich raiment. Their armor was ornate and silver, their swords long and two-handed.

"None shall pass!" they moaned.

When Kur finally broke through the last column and Carmen shattered the last enemy in her way, these six horrors remained. Clearly they were not as the others were. Some greater evil resided within them, a sinister presence the likes of which none of them had before encountered. Four of them moved to the kill, while the other two stood barring the door. A cackling voice then echoed down the hall. "None of you will ever leave this place. Kill them. Kill them, my brothers!"

The voice in the darkness chilled them to the core, and yet there was one among them to whom those words meant nothing. His mind, at least the part that might have felt doom, was far away. Only the warrior remained. With hardly a thought, Kur produced

Prince Loren's shield and rushed in to meet the nearest threat. The ancient Prince of the Dead actually paused for a moment to salute his valor, raising his sword before him, profering its hilt to Heaven and its blade toward Hell. If Kur had been in his right mind, he would have returned the salute, but his current mental state was a blast furnace of chaos. Its great sword descended upon him with all the might of any knight living. Receiving the blow upon his shield, Kur moved inside, slashing again and again. The skeleton warrior's armor proved resilient, its bones hardened by necromancy. Carmen dueled with two deathly knights beside him, her sword's blade, once the brightest sheen of steel, had somehow turned blue, and in that hopeless hour, Kur thought that he saw a halo of light above her head, but later, he would certainly believe that it was merely a dream brought on by the stress of battle. Moving like a whirlwind, she avoided their deadly blows long enough to decapitate the rightmost knight. Its skull rolled from its neck. Its crown clattered to the floor. Its nightmare hands released their grasp, and its sword fell. With a savage kick, she sent his remains into its brethren behind it, and it fell in a heap of bones and shining metal. Ducking beneath the remaining knight's stroke, she dueled on.

Perhaps it was the light that Dao carried or simply the light of his life that the thing despised; regardless, the fourth knight attacked him with terrible fury. Its sword clove his own in two with its first stroke, and with only a dagger in his hand, he could only retreat, but there was no room for that. Rolling hard to escape the knight's next cut, he came up fast near the tunnel wall. His wizard's intuition goaded him to prepare the small mace that Kalor had given him, but what could a small mallet do against such a thing as this? What indeed! For when he unhooked it from his girdle, it sprang to life, nearly quadrupling in size! Too large to wield one-handed, he left his dagger on the lip of an empty coffin and took up its handle. Just in time, he blocked the knight's next deadly attack. Driven backward into the wall, they wrestled. The knight was strong, far stronger than Dao, and its sword blade pressed closer and closer to his throat. A few more seconds, and it would be over.

The hall beyond them was filling with the wretched Dead. Tariq stood at the center, his sword of flame a burning light blazing against the horde. Leander fought by his side. His sword, enchanted to battle dragons, was nevertheless a masterwork and every bit the equal to destroying these Undead. Karina held the right flank, and her sword sang a symphony of impenetrable death around herself. Her skill would never again be doubted. She knew that this was not the time to protect her husband's ego. A legion of skeleton warriors wielding scimitars and other old weapons with the skill of ancient memories proved no match for her. Her sword was always faster, striking like a viper, slashing like a wildcat, wielding a tapestry of ruin about herself like the Liosalfar swordmaidens of old. A sundered arm grasped Karina's ankle, and she cut it free. A legless torso clawed its way toward her, and she smashed it. Fighting together as one, they actually began to gain a few more feet of hall. Bones and still animate remains piled up all around them. They were holding, but for how long? The dead were without end, and they would eventually tire.

Modrul's Book refused to fit back into the straps of his pack. There was no time for it anyway. Dao was in trouble. Drawing his dagger, Kalor drew back to throw, but there was a sudden upheaval from the floor beneath him. He was hurled backward and thrown down when a massive wall of ice rose up beneath his very feet.

Filling the tunnel from floor to ceiling, it divided their strength in half. Kur, Carmen, and Dao now faced five knights of Death alone, and the rest of them would soon be crushed by the coming tide. "Kalor," Tariq said, "it's up to you to bring it down!"

There was a spell that might work, one of the few of the dragons that remained. Luckily, the book had fallen with him on his side of the wall. In haste, beneath the diamond's light, he turned the pages in search of it.

The horde seemed to sense that their victory was at hand, and they pushed forward en masse.

Cutting them down by the tens was not enough. The pile of corpses and fighting skeletons was being driven hard against them. "Quickly, Kalor, we can't hold them much longer!"

Finding the spell, he struggled to concentrate, his heart pounding beyond his control, his comrades fighting desperately all around him. Reciting Modrul's words, the book rose up before him, and he spoke with the voice of the dragon. Hurling his magical might against the ice wall, he contested the dire power of the knights' necromancy. One tiny Gnome, testing his will against that of evil's princes. There was no doubt in his mind, for if there had been, then he surely would have failed. He believed in the dragon's power, and he had never seen it falter. The spells collided, and the ice wall was banished.

The knight who had summoned the wall was thwarted but not beaten. Raising its jewel encrusted hand, it pointed at Kalor and invoked its most terrible power.

Kalor looked to his friend's plight, but instead, he met only the sinister gaze of the knight who had raised it. Its eyes, nightmare pits, orbs of utter darkness, drove into his very soul, and in the process, the misery of its own existence was revealed. Anger, despair, and sadness so deep and so hopeless that desolation seemed like utopia, pulled his psyche in.

"Lie down and die," it said to him. "Expose your neck. Let the pain end."

His body was no longer his to control. Modrul's Book fell to the floor, its pages still open. Falling to his knees, there was no hope. Sudden pain wracked his body, the dire revenge of the Undead Sorcerer. Writhing in agony, he couldn't act save to scream. He couldn't move save to gasp. Suddenly hoisted, he was draped over something. Somehow he knew that it was Tariq that carried him. Excruciating waves of pain wracked him. He was blind to all save the horrifying images of the Necromancer. His spirit fought to expel the demonic mind that possessed him, but its will was tempered by thousands of years of endless torment. There was no escape from the iron fortress of its mind.

The mound of corpses slid forward, slowed by the heroes who opposed it but yet unstoppable. No longer dueling, their fight had become a wrestling match, three heroes trying to buttress the dam, a wave of corpses propelled by the storm.

What lay behind the door, none of them could know. Their last hope, surely, greater dooms more likely, but to warriors with no other hope, it was the summit.

Kur's mind was flooded with emotions not his own. The Dead knight battled not only with its weapons, but perhaps more terribly still with its mind. All manner of frightful images, feelings, and fear, in its purest and most reasonless form, assailed him. Lesser men would have faltered. Some may have run while others would have been unable to act at all, but Kur was not like other men.

The evil thing croaked with glee, certain of its own victory.

Obviously, it knew nothing of Dwarves, and considerably less about a Kegporter's heart. Fear was soldier's blood, and Kur had known horror on a hundred battlefields. It was one weakness that could not possess him. He should have stood, too paralyzed to move, or run away screaming. The Dead knight prepared to execute its next swing, but its prey kept coming. Korun-Koth removed its left leg at the waist and its right above the knee. It tried to attack but toppled. Kur struck it until the invader's voice was gone. Another knight stood before the door, working its evil upon them. Kur raised his shield and charged.

"Now, Dwarf," it said, "you will die!" With the point of its sword and a simple wave of its hand, it erected yet another wall of ice. Kur was hurled to the floor. Rising to his feet, he gathered himself to charge. Less than twenty feet of tunnel lay between him and the Necromancer, barred in front by a reinforced door and behind by an ice wall two feet thick.

"Don't bother, little one," it taunted, "it will all be over soon." It then evoked its last horrible power against him. Its hand once again reached up, as if to summon power from the floor beneath itself, clenched, and then suddenly opened, bony, clawed, wielding power, and white as death. It was a small space, instantly made into a blast furnace by its evil sorcery. The dead knight needed no air to breathe. Its skeleton no longer had any flesh to consume, and the very nature of its existence made it immune to its own fires. One small Dwarf had no such immunity, but he did possess a magical ring. Without its protection, he would have died on the spot. His lungs would have been scorched and his flesh melted from his bones. Instead, he was hurt, his exposed skin badly burned and his clothing put to flame. The pain of his wounds was so terrible that it drove his mind far beyond reason. His only thought was to end his torment, and he knew from whence it came.

The Necromancer could not believe that he still stood. He would have to end the Dwarf's life by the sword. They dueled, neither having the chance for reinforcement or reprieve—ax and shield against Necromancer's blade. Its ego was such that it had no fear of the Dwarf; nor did it ever consider the possibility of its own destruction. In life, it must never have encountered very many Dwarves and never on the field of battle. If it had, then it would perhaps have given pause before engaging in single combat with a grievously wounded and completely berserk one.

Kur's ax hewed on. If the creature's armor stopped one blow, he hit it over and over again until it shattered or fell apart, and then he hit it some more. The knight struck him on the head with the pommel of its great sword, kicked him in the groin with its steel-toed boot, and struck Prince Loren's shield so stoutly that Kur's forearm was fractured beneath it. If Kur had still been even slightly sane at that moment, then he would surely have accepted his own death, but he wasn't sane at all. The souls of a hundred Dwarves possessed him. Ancient heroes, Dwarven Kings, wielders of the ax who had fallen in battle with it still in their hands filled his body, propping him up, and empowering him with the heart and soul of his people. One mighty blow of Korun-Koth severed its left leg at the knee and sent it toppling. His second cut removed its sword arm at the elbow. The Necromancer tried to overpower him with its dark will but was itself assailed by a hundred heroic minds. Kur hewed on until the Necromancer was a collapsed ruin. When its wretched spirit finally fled its broken shell, its enchanted wall fell, and so too did the yet mortal Dwarf. He tried to rise again in order to help them, but his body would no longer obey him. The last thing that he saw was Carmen's struggle before the darkness claimed him.

Her ancient adversary knew well what she was—a paladin, a holy warrior of God whose highest purpose was to bring about the ultimate end of evil. It knew these things because in life, it too had once been as she now was. Tragedy had caused its spirit to renounce its beliefs in all that was holy and instead sell its soul to all that was ill. Its reward was the curse of eternal unlife, and the never-ending torment of its lost soul. Its pleasure, if indeed it could be said that it could experience any such emotions, was in inflicting pain and ending the lives of all things good. With every cut of its sword, its wretched desire to end Carmen's life grew. Her skill at arms was unquestionable, even before its ancient might, but swordsmanship was the least of its powers. It assailed her then, its voice echoing through her mind.

"Lay down your sword," it said. *"Look at yourself. Your very existence is a lie. Where are your gods now? They have abandoned you."*

"You are the lie!" she said. "Look at what you have become. It is you that should remember the life that you once had!"

"You deny the truth," it said. *"You have sinned. Look within your heart, unworthy daughter. How many gallants have met their end because of you? How many more will die because of your failures?"*

"Any man who stood beside me would do so again," she replied. "They died fighting evil, and I will be honored to join them!" Redoubling her efforts, she drove the fell knight backward into the door. They clashed. Blade against blade, living eyes locked with orbs as black as the abyss. "Your evil makes you nothing. None will remember your death in song."

Throwing her backward, he countered with an unstoppable overhead cut. Full of rage, it searched for a way to spark doubt within her, but her faith seemed unswerving.

"Your soul will drown in Hell for eternity," it told her. *"Your goodness will die this day!"* Confronted by the truth, it was he who doubted.

If she was unworthy, then surely she would not have been such an obedient and attentive daughter. If she had not loved her father, then his teachings would have been wasted on her, and the knight's perfect blow would have cloven her body in two. She was strong, but her skill at arms had shown her in the first few moments of battle that the being that she faced was mightier still. If she had tried to meet its attack with power alone, her strongest arm would surely fail. Her father had taught her a technique unusual to other knights. He had learned it from a blademaster who he had met briefly in the far west. The fastest and most efficient sword parry was none at all, and she used her father's technique now. Sidestepping at the last possible moment, the knight's sword struck so close to her left side that its edge drew sparks from her armor. Raising her own sword high, she struck down with all her strength. Off-balance and committed, the fell knight could not recover in time. Her sword smashed through its crown and skull and did not stop until it struck the hard armor of its breastplate. Its broken vessel could no longer hold its dark spirit, and the empty body toppled.

Dao felt its cold and remorseless blade against his neck. The stench of evil stifled him, and its orbs bore into him searching to destroy his soul. The wave of evil things filled the hall behind him from floor to ceiling, and his comrades were falling one by one. Fighting for every breath, he waited for the sudden stabbing pain that would end his life. The wretched thing that pinned him fought to possess his mind. Its spirit smiled gloatingly. It wanted to savor every moment of pain and every cry of despair, but Dao's mind was the one field where the strength of arms did not matter. Within the oasis of his psyche, he stood defiant and undiminished. Wrapped in the robes of Arch Magi, a ball of flame danced in the palm of his right hand and a staff of power in the other. "Face me here, fallen knight," he taunted.

"You will fall!" it screamed, but at the same moment, the last of its brethren was destroyed. In contempt, it struck Dao hard with the hilt of his sword and then hurled him into the path of the creeping dead.

"Now, would be paladin," it said, "feel my wrath!" Raising its claw-like hand, it summoned its flame. When its hand closed, its magic was ready. When its palm opened, they would all be cleansed by fire.

Down, pummeled, and bruised but not out, Dao was no longer helplessly pinned. Rising to his feet, he saw the knight raising his power. Carmen's back was still turned, and his friends could do nothing. Rushing in, he swung his mace, hammering down on the undead thing. The fell knight was staggered, its hateful spell undone. Dropping to one knee, it again took up its sword. Four feet long and two handed, with a wide straight blade and rounded point, it was designed to be swung from horseback in order to decapitate footmen. It was not primarily a fencing weapon, but it was perfect for cleaving. Spinning about, it swung the flat of its Lewing sword in a great arc around itself, desiring only to clear the space around itself.

Dao swung his mace down to meet it, and the sword's blade was sundered, its shards flying into his body and beyond.

Wrathful, it hurled its useless weapon away from itself, seized the handle of his enemy's mace and clutched the Elf's throat in order to crush the life from him. Lifting him like a rag doll, he wrenched the mace from his hands and prepared to smash him with it. Rearing back to swing, the mace suddenly fell from his hand, and Dao found himself falling. The Sword of the Guardian of the West Wind had taken the fell knight through the waist. Its second cut separated its head from its neck.

"Hurry, Dao," Carmen said, "you must open the door!" Running past him, Carmen hurled herself against the creeping wall of bones. "It's up to you."

Recovering his dagger, he raced to the door. Kicking the broken corpse away from it, he examined it. Surrounded by dark runes, it had neither knob, nor handle, nor keyhole. If one was hidden, they would need a thief to find it, and theirs was unconscious. Magic alone would have to open it. His spell of opening had worked once before, but whether or not it would work again he could not know. He had no time to concentrate. Only ten feet of hall remained to them. If he was weak, they would all die. Closing his eyes, he centered himself. Standing by the shores of a calm lake, he evoked eldritch powers of nature and spoke, "Ostium de lignum de saxum de ferrum libero tuus teneo apertus ille via permitto omnis ad ingredior!" Opening his eyes, he assailed the door with his power, testing each of the runes upon it as he had done before. Never had he encountered so much raw power. The door had been sealed for thousands of years, a barrier made to stand the test of ages. Each rune of power had to be challenged individually. To the living, he stood unmoving with his arms outstretched before it. In the realm of his mind, he stood on the shores of the lake, facing the ancient wizard whose magic had sealed the portal. Tall he was, like the Liosalfar of old, with hair of gray and eyes of blue. His face was pale and lined with age. His robes were red and richly adorned.

Each rune held some small part of their creator, and when Dao faced them, sometimes he would face the wizard himself or some aspect of his spirit. Each one was a test of wills, a duel between samurai. Lions would leap at him, only to be dispelled by his magical spear. The roar of a tiger would raise tempest winds before him, only to be quieted by the sunlight of the love in his heart. On and on they struggled until only one rune remained. The ancient sorcerer ran at him, grasping him in a crushing bear hug and hoisting him off the ground. Their eyes locked. He struggled to free himself. "You are beaten," the sorcerer said, laughing.

"No," Dao answered, "it is you who are beaten. Three thousand years have passed and you are dead."

The sorcerer paled, releasing his grasp. "Then you may pass," he said, "but I would know your name before I release the door."

"I am Dao Greylinx, son of Gwillym and Isidora, descendant of Athenasius High Elven."

"Well met, son of Gwillym," the sorcerer said. "I once was called Andomar Tabarun. Leave this place now, or stay forever." Andomar opened his arms, bowed slightly, and disappeared.

Dao blinked, and the real world returned. Locks and internal tumblers spun and clanked. When the last of the protective wards faded, the door swung open as if pushed by an invisible hand. A massive vaulted chamber lay beyond it. "Hurry, everyone," he said, "the way is open!"

Hope was rekindled as they moved pell-mell for the portal. Dao lifted Kur by the clothing at the nape of his neck and dragged him through. Tariq ran with Kalor across his back, somehow managing to scoop up Modrul's Book in the process. The rest of them were hot on their heels.

"Quickly," Carmen said, "we must bar the door!"

But once they were through, the portal slammed shut behind them and locked itself. The legion of the dead crashed into it. Countless fingers scratched at it. Empty skulls thudded against it, all of them coveting the souls of the living behind it.

The room into which they ran was some sixty feet in length and over a hundred feet wide. An enormous cairn in front of the left wall supported the statue of a god, and its eyes were crafted from emeralds. To the right and left of the statue were two waist-high braziers burning brightly with neither smoke nor fuel. Centered on the floor in front of the statue was a massive pentatram, some twenty feet in diameter. A second door on the same wall as theirs stood closed at the far end of the room; another door faced theirs directly opposite them. Besides the statue, they seemed to be alone.

"Help me with Keg," Carmen said. "He's hurt bad."

PHYLACTERIES

"At last, Marie," the Lych King croaked, "we will soon be together again!"

"My king," said the head of his deathly knights, "they have entered the southern halls. We must awaken the Dead who rest there or they will soon escape."

"They no longer matter, Captain. The son of Odin has joined us in our hallowed halls."

"They have released the souls of my brothers," the knight raged. "I would have my revenge upon them!"

"Save your revenge," the Lych King said, "for the one who betrayed us. Soon my beloved will be returned to me, and then we shall march upon hell itself."

"No mortal has left our city alive in three thousand years," the knight argued.

"They will not get far," Andomar consoled. "The Trolls will soon be grinding their bones. They are insignificant compared to the son of Odin."

"Yes, my king."

"Go forth and bring him to me!"

"Hold!" shouted a voice from the shadows.

"Who dares to question me in my domain?"

"The son of Aklon."

"Aklon? Aklon, yes, yes, he rides the Seven Seas still. Over the gunwale and into the frothy murk he fell, and now he captains a ghost ship in Hell! Yes, yes, that one had power indeed. Gone now, all gone. Kill him!"

Andomar's personal guard drew their swords, hefted pole arms, and prepared their abysmal enchantments.

"Kill me," Vlad said while lifting up an ancient golden urn, "and I will smash this vessel and release your immortal soul!"

"Hold!" the Lych King screeched, his jaw clicking as it once had in life, his hands clenching and unclenching nervously. No being, not even the gods themselves, had ever dared to touch his phylactery. Within its confines was his most despised, most spoiled and wretched soul. It was filled with an anguish and hatred so great that the most powerful entities in existence feared to release it, and yet here was a mere mortal, a lowly Elf holding it above his head boldly as if he feared nothing, nor any end. "You wouldn't dare! Destroy the urn, and you will damn this world and your very soul to Hell for all eternity! Destroy it, and you will never leave these halls alive!"

"Without purpose," Vlad said, "neither of our existences will have any meaning at all! You of all beings should understand that."

"What purpose could be worth more than your soul and the fortune of this world?"

"If I fail, then the Queen of Dragonia will plunge this world into a war the likes of which time has never before seen. Hell will come with or without you."

"So you are an idealist like your father," the Lych King croaked. "It is always difficult to reason with men of your kind. Speak your terms, but know well that you will not leave these halls alive."

"Release the son of Odin, and I shall return your phylactery undamaged and unopened."

"Nay, warrior mage, I shall not release him until he has performed my quests three."

"Those are my terms," Vlad said resolutely.

"And those are mine!" Andomar replied. "Destroy the urn and open the Gates of Hell. Smash it to pieces and your plans will be undone. Open it, and Dartin, son of Odin, will remain in the Halls of the Dead forever."

"Then I shall wait until his quests are done."

"To complete his quests three, he will spend no less than ten years in Hell."

"Ten years in Hell will be but ten minutes to us. Speak then, King of Death, what are your quests three?"

"The son of Odin must overcome the three challenges of Azamod. First, he must swim across the Sea of Endless Torment. Second, he must climb to the tallest peak of the highest mountain in Hell and defeat the Son of Azamod. Lastly, he must find my beloved Marie, release her from her prison, and bring her to me. Only then will he have fulfilled my quests three."

"Then let him be quested."

"If he fails, his soul will be destroyed."

"If he fails," Vlad swore, "I will smash your urn to powder!"

"Very well," Andomar said, "it seems that we both have something to lose."

His knights encircled Vlad to within a sword's length.

"But for now," the Lych King mused, "let us look and listen within my crystal ball, and we shall see what we shall see." Rising crookedly from his throne, he straightened his skeleton and adjusted his rotten robes. Stepping regally toward Vlad, his minions stood aside for him, bowing as he passed. When he was a mere arm's length away, he held up his globe. With a snap of his fingers, it grew ten times in size, and Vlad could clearly make out the priest's naked form.

"How will he know of your quest?"

"My curse will compel him. He may choose not to follow its pull, but the harder he resists, the stronger my magic will become."

"An interesting spell."

"Useful," Andomar agreed, "and now let us watch closely. In ten minutes, Dartin will experience ten years of torment in the kingdom of Azamod, the Archduke of Hell!"

Dartin

He walked in a nightmare world. Where he was, he did not know, but he knew very well that he was dead. His spirit body, if that's what it was, seemed solid. Pinching himself, he felt pain. Even his stomach growled emptily. He was also as naked as when he had been killed. Clearly, this was not Valhalla; nor was Odin's Hall anywhere to be found. His memory of his past life seemed to be slipping away from him, and the more that he tried to concentrate on it, the less that he could recall of the hour of his own death or the names of his friends.

The land before him was twisted, torn, and deformed. Even the meager plant life looked alien and actually quite sad. Mutated insects scuttled around him. Some of them were hairy flying beasts with a hundred eyes.

Walking along a dried up riverbed, he stumbled upon a beetle-winged dog with a dozen legs feasting upon a four-legged chicken with a monkey's head. It was a surreal world filled with horror, and only his iron will kept the madness from claiming him.

Suddenly, he was swept up in a tremendous tentacle. Twisted about and squeezed in its crushing grasp, he tried to orient himself. He had been standing on the back of an enormous creature among other such monsters. He was no more than a flea on its back.

Utterly helpless, his destiny was far beyond his grasp, and only through mercy could he hope to be saved. The Being (and he could comprehend no other name for the Behemoth than *Being*) swept him close to its tentacled face, and with one of its limitless eyes (there were thousands) it peered at him and into him, and he was defiled both body and soul. Strangely, he didn't worry; after all, there was nothing that he could do about it anyway. Turning him in all directions, it studied him.

Galactic and incomprehensible, he began to realize that he had clearly not traveled to any Heaven above, but most likely he had ended up in one of the Abysmal Planes below. He was in Hell. He was oddly comforted by the sheer desperation of his predicament. He should have gone completely insane, but instead, he began to study the beings and the world around him. Feeling detached and quite numb, fear never occurred to him. Looking on, objectively and without judgment, he examined the horrors around him.

He was surrounded by being upon being, gigantic, lumbering, and powerful. Their unending bodies were devoid of human form or any living form that he had known in life, save that they stood upright on a writhing mass of tentacles like octopi. Their bodies were all twisted and terrible to behold, with tentacle-like appendages surrounding the whole and pores oozing vile liquid in river-like creases all about their skin. The creatures' eyes seemed to sprout from anywhere and at random, although there was a concentration of eyes and tentacles about their heads, if such was what they were. Some of the beasts were covered in hair as thick as his own body and many hundreds of feet in length. Others had protruding growths that often extended pseudo pods from where their mouths should have been. Vast clouds of bizarre insects buzzed about them, and many of them were larger than he was. How he got here, he wondered, and who he was, he couldn't remember.

Suddenly, as if he was hearing for the first time, their voices became clear to him, and it sounded just like wind howling through the trees of the deep forest in the dark of night. Their language was at first unrecognizable, but something resonated within his mind, images, meanings, and as if by magic, he understood. "What is it?" they said, "and how did it come to be here?"

"It has no tentacles," one hissed.

"And only two legs," said another.

"I am a Man," he answered, but he was unsure if he had spoken the words aloud or just thought them.

"It speaks!" they shouted, as if they were hearing his thoughts for the first time. Their voices suddenly rushed at him, flooding his mind with a thousand different tongues. He was wracked by pain as the beast that held him squeezed him in its anxiety. Endlessly tormented, they forced him to reveal every memory, every emotion, and these were like food to them. His mind was slowly picked apart, like a freshly roasted chicken before a table surrounded by hungry boys. When they finished feasting, he could once again hear their individual voices. Surprisingly, his mind was clean, open, and he once again remembered who he was and his life that had been. He was dead, but for some reason he had never reached the feasting hall of his father, nor was he anywhere remotely close to Valhalla. This was some other place, a home to Elder Gods, both ancient and evil. He was Dartin, but his name mattered not in this desolate place. His life was gone, and he despaired. The beings came alive around him, rejoicing in his hopelessness, his terror, and his loss. His torment was without end. They probed every recess of his mind until he was completely dissected, naked both in body and soul.

Somehow, deep within himself, his mind still possessed a tiny drop of rationality. He knew then that if he lost the last of his faith, then he would cease to exist. In faith, he found peace, quiet, and the center of his spirit.

Passing him between them like a doll, he crossed vast expanses of space, from one tentacle to another, from clawed hands to scaly fins. Time had no meaning, and he knew no hunger or thirst, only pain and fear. The beings had no concept of his body's limits. He was twisted and pulled, stretched and crushed, his bones broken, his tissues twisted. His body, now spirit, would return to its original form each time. It was indeed Hell, he thought, pain unending, unendurable. Their eerie voices were perhaps the most terrible of all, more abominable than their physical forms, but as if by accident, he learned that he could shut out their thoughts and project his own back upon them. Many times, the creatures would reel away from the pain that his mind seemed to cause them until finally they grew tired of torturing him.

"It is wretched," one whispered.

"Abhorrent," another screamed. "The Man is good! Ugly, ugly, tear him limb from limb!"

"Hold!" commanded a king among them. "The Goodling is cursed. We must cast him into the Sea of Endless Torment. Hurl him into the Halls of Azamod! Let him be twisted, watch him be changed. The Goodling will learn evil, evil. Hurl him, cast him, and drown him in the Sea of Hell!"

He was hurled, he was cast, and down he fell. He spun out of control, at times bouncing off one vast body or smashing through the carapace of a bloated flying centipede. He passed through clouds of vile gasses, green, blue, yellow, and red, some smelling of turned wine, others the decay of death.

Giant stinging insects flew through the ethers. Many of them pursued him, trying to anchor their claws in his flesh. It seemed somehow strange to him, for what juices could he possess for these fiends to feed upon? He fell and fell, beside limitless gargantuan tentacles, constantly beset upon by bugs with a thousand eyes. Time stood upon its head, and he feared that his suffering would never end. Beneath him, the clouds seemed to thin, and hot winds buffeted him.

Punching through the abysmal clouds, he left the Elder Gods behind, only to fall into a wilting, torrid furnace of volcanic fires. A sea of fire flowed beneath him. Beyond it, against a horizon of black clouds and electrical storms was a vast range of jagged mountains. The greatest peak among them seemed to beckon him. Something awaited him there, but he had only a moment to think on it before he plunged into the sea.

He burned. Flesh seared off his bones and reformed, only to melt away the next instant. He was both dead and alive, frying, the stench of his own burning meat turning his stomach, his own screams there and then gone. His existence was pain, his torment unending. A voice inside his head told him to swim, swim, and swim on to the shore! He tried everything to hold on to his sanity for but a few seconds more. Paddling, sometimes with flesh, at other times with bones, he swam through Hellfire for three years, screaming all the while.

The sea ended as abruptly as the shore appeared, as if it was a line drawn by a painter's brush. Crawling out of the fire, he collapsed upon the black sands until his flesh reformed. Crippling agony wracked his body one moment, and the next it was gone. He cried out when the torture ended. Without the pain, he would not have known if he still existed at all. Before him loomed a black desert, and beyond it the rising hills that were the feet of jagged mountains. He felt compelled to hike toward the tallest peak of the highest mountain. Nothing was real except the irresistible pull that he felt. Traveling across the desert, he ran. His lungs, if lungs they were, labored hard, but he reveled in his sudden freedom. Sprinting for all that he was worth, he discovered that the harder he pushed himself, the slower he progressed, as if he ran in a dream. Experimenting, he tried to move with the least possible bodily effort. The purer his thoughts, the faster he traveled, until he had reached the hills themselves. He climbed the mountain in the same manner, until he stood before the massive gates of a tall tower, standing like a lonely spire at the top of the mountain. A knight, armored in black mail, hailed him. "Why do you come here, strange traveler?"

"I am dead," Dartin declared, "and I swam through the Lake of Fire to come here."

"We are all dead here," the knight said. "Why don't you clothe yourself."

"I have no clothes."

"Use your mind, fool," the knight said. "Imagine yourself as you once were."

Dartin did so, and his clothes, armor, and weapons returned to him.

"Where am I?"

"You have reached the Tower of Aneurin, the son of Azamod. This keep guards the nine layers of Hell."

"I must see Aneurin."

"Then you must face me in combat first."

"Agreed."

The knight waved to two dark spirits that served him, and they went to work opening the gates. When Dartin entered the courtyard, the black knight stood alone at its center. They were separated by at least a hundred feet, but in that world it may have been a mile. "What weapons?"

"Any weapon or any power," he said. Opening the right palm of his gauntleted hand, a black sword appeared in his grasp.

"Swords then," and Dartin drew his own sword, and it was the Sword of the Guardian of the South Wind. They stood staring at one another for some time, but the black helm of the knight did not reveal his face or his eyes. The knight saluted him and advanced. They dueled for precisely three years, three months, three days, and three hours. When it was clear that neither man was the stronger, the demonic knight called upon sorcery to defeat him. Flames engulfed him, but Dartin's sword quenched them. A legion of Dead rose from the earth and assailed him, and Dartin called upon the power of the runes, knowing not if the power would exist for him. The rune manifested, and the Dead were smashed to dust. The black knight assailed his mind with images of his past sins and the promise of an eternity in Hell. He was past the pain of his sins, and he knew now that his spirit could indeed survive in this abysmal world, and so the knight's curses were as nothing to him. Calling upon a combination of runes, he wracked the spirit of the vile fiend, and the black knight fell to his knees.

"I am vanquished," the knight yielded. "I am Aneurin, the son of Azamod. Ask of me what you wish and it is yours."

"I seek the Princess Marie Elizabeth," Dartin said, not knowing how it was that he knew what he knew, "imprisoned in your dark tower for three thousand years."

"Much, much longer than that actually," Aneurin replied. "She is my wife and the mother of my seven children. Ask of me something else."

"I desire nothing else of yours."

"Then I have no choice," Aneurin conceded, "but know this, my father will not stop until he destroys you. He will annihilate your very soul."

"So be it," Dartin said. "The princess, if you please."

With a wave of his hand, Aneurin beckoned to his fell spirits, and they soon brought her. She was a supernatural beauty. Dartin recognized her as Grey Elven, diminutive and perfect, though her eyes were haunted, desperate.

"Go with him," he said. "I am defeated. Fly, fly away, for you have little time before an army of devils comes for you."

Taking Dartin's hand, she left the tower with him. She spoke not a word, merely nodding when he led her away. Her eyes were black pools filled with starlight, and her hair was darker still. Her skin was pearl-white and perfect. "You are Marie the Black-haired," Dartin proclaimed. "I shall call you Sky, but first we must escape from here."

Her eyes looked desperate, full of fear. She knew there was really nowhere to run.

"Fear not," Dartin said, "look there to the horizon. See yon ball of light. My father comes, riding Sleipnir!" For it was at that moment that he knew how he had come to possess the power of the runes. He was indeed Odin's son!

Riding the wind upon eight churning legs, with white patches both whimsical and pale, Sleipnir flew through the ethers of Hell with nostrils flaring and gray flanks heaving. Upon his back rode the All Father. Dartin remembered him from his childhood, but never had he seen him in such splendor, and never before as the god that he was. With gleaming mail and horned helm, gauntlets, and a fine gold tunic, he drove his steed to his greatest speed. Drawing closer, his legs were well-covered, and his boots shone dark and polished. Beneath his helm, his eye gleamed glacier-blue, his left vacant and covered by a patch of silver. His hair spilled out from under his helm, dark, curly, and braided, as was his beard. His voice invoked the power of the runes, and the very air of Hell shook in their wake.

Odin rode on and on, drawing ever closer to them. Buzzing things flew too close to him at times, and he smote them down with Gungnir, his enchanted spear. When the span of paces remained between them, they could hear his father's song, calling upon the runes to defend them. Rising up like shining pillars all around them, they best resembled the shields on the hull of a longship, and soon, Sleipnir reigned in before them.

"Hurry, boy!" Odin urged. "Ride at my back and shield the maiden between us." Helping Marie into the saddle, Dartin vaulted behind them. "Hold fast to me," Odin said. "Now on, Sleipnir, ride fast for the gate. Azamod's army of devils will soon be on our heels!" Surprise was their ally, and the legions of Hell were slow to assemble. Riding with the speed of thought, they dodged giant tentacles and twisted flying things. Dartin felt like a child again, supported and protected. He could find no words for his joy or limits to the love of his father.

Using runes that Dartin had never before known, Odin opened a portal through time and the fabric of space, or perhaps it was some mystical power of his steed, but regardless, a doorway was opened, and Sleipnir won through. The Devil's army was thwarted.

"Your destiny is yet to be decided, my son," Odin said. "You must complete your quest. I have returned you from Hell but not from Death. Remember well your father's love. Sleipnir, ride for the Hall of the Lych King!"

Another door opened, and the mighty horse rode through, coming to a halt upon the mosaic floor of Andomar's Hall.

"You do not belong here!" the Lych King rasped.

"Perhaps I should return Marie to her chambers in Hell?"

"Marie?"

"My son has completed his quest. You must release him."

"He is dead, dead! I can do no more for him."

"The king that you once were could have done so."

"Speak not his name! He is gone, gone."

"Andomar," Odin said, "your princess is returned, and your curse need live no more."

"Nay! Nay, nay! Revenge upon the one who took her, I shall not rest until that deed is done. My phylactery, Dark Elf, if you please."

"Release the priest as you agreed, and then I shall return the urn," Vlad said resolutely.

"He is free to go," Andomar said, "but he is dead, dead, a ghost and no more." He spoke truly, for Dartin stood among them in the pale glow of his spirit body.

"Is it true," Vlad asked, "that the man whom you once were could resurrect him?"

"Never! The power is god given! What has he ever done for me? Where was he when my queen was stolen, taken away to Hell? Where was he!"

"You can stop it Andomar!" Marie said. "Look at what you have become."

"I am wretched, wretched, my body long since dead. Do not look upon me!"

In a voice like songbirds on a summer morning, she said, "Let your curse be done, my love."

"How is it that you could still love me? Lies! All lies!"

"Look at me," Marie urged, the only one among them that had no fear of him. "It was my love for you that kept me alive. I love you as much now as I did the day that they took me away."

The Lych King was torn, grumbling, wailing from deep within. His anger and his rage consumed him. His body was a thing of evil magic. His mind was filled with hatred for the one that had taken away his true love, so much so that he had never even considered that she would ever be free, even less so that she would one day stand beside him as vibrant and alive as the day that they had first met. "My phylactery, fallen Elfling!"

Vlad's mind burned with a thousand thoughts. There had to be a way. The Lych had no soul in him—that was the key. It was the very reason that he could deny his true love. Soulless, he could forget the memories of the man that he had once been. The gods feared to release his spirit because greater evils might come of it. He laughed inside at the simplicity of it. Andomar had duped the gods themselves for thousands of years. There was no curse upon the urn; it was merely the vessel that held his immortal soul. The Lych King's evil was the result of despair and a genius mind bereft of love and its spirit! Release his soul and his curse would be broken. What end lay in store for Andomar he could not guess, but it could be no worse than eternity neither alive nor dead. His decision was made. He smashed the urn down upon the floor with all his might, shattering it into a million pieces.

"Nooo!" screamed the Lych King, lunging ahead in a frantic effort to catch the vessel before it fell, but it was too late.

The golden phylactery was obliterated. It was empty save for the remnants of the ancient herbs and minerals that Andomar had used to trap his soul inside it forever. His spirit, now free, rushed back into the remnants of his former body. Andomar paused, raising his skeletal hand. Bowing his skull in contemplation, he squared his shoulders and raised his arms wide. "Perhaps there is still time for a few more spells," he said. With a wave of his hand, he released his followers from their bond.

"Go now to the beyond," he commanded. "I shall join you soon." Their bones crumbled into dust, their arms clattered to the floor, and only their pale spirits remained. With his hands, he drew a great circle from the earth and to the Heavens, and when it was complete, the Lych King was gone and the wizard-king that was had returned. "I saved enough of my life to live again," he explained, "but our time has passed, and I no longer understand this world. I shall journey to Paradise with my love, if she will have me still."

"You know that I will," she said.

"And for your efforts, son of Odin, I shall resurrect you. Lie down and sleep in the ever-burning fire behind my throne, and ye shall be reborn." He held out his hand for Marie, and she took it in her own and walked with him. Tucking her hand into the crook of his elbow like the gentleman king that he once had been, he led her toward a growing ball of light that he had summoned before them.

"Beware the Staff, Dockalfar Lord. It has both the power of life and the power of death, and it is coveted by all of the dark powers. If the Lords of Chaos should wield it, the time of the gods shall come to an end. Find another way, son of Aklon, and farewell. Follow me, my brothers, our revenge upon the Duke of Hell shall be his loss of the purest heart that has ever lived. Let us dance upon the shores of the sea in the Twin Paradises, where our love shall be reborn!"

He waited by the edge of his mystical door as the spirits of his followers began to file past him. No more did they resemble the rotten dead, but rather, the men appeared as they once had in life, with fine raiment and gleaming mail, the women, with jeweled tiaras and flowing gowns. His captain paused for a moment and smiled before leaping through the gateway.

"Not all of my brothers will follow me," Andomar said. "Some of them have chosen to remain here. Soon, there will be a new Lord of Death in these cursed halls. I recommend that you do not tarry long. They will soon sense that my power has gone. Until we meet again, Odin and son. Shall we dance, Marie?"

"I thought that you would never ask!" Hand in hand, they skipped through the portal, no longer hearing any voices save for their own. When the doorway closed, it resembled best the setting sun over the ocean. When its light disappeared completely, the hall was deathly quiet.

"Now, my son," Odin said, "lay down in the ever-burning flame before his magic is gone!"

"You are the one who opposes us," Dartin said to Vlad.

"It is you who have decided to oppose me," Vlad replied, "but you have little time. Do as your father says. We shall meet again soon, I assure you."

"Go now, my son," Odin insisted.

Lying down in the wall of flames, his spirit felt none of its heat. Closing his eyes, he soon fell asleep, wondering if indeed he would ever awaken.

Somewhere deep below, upon his throne of tortured innocents, Azamod, the archduke of Hell roared. The one who had stolen Marie Elizabeth away from him would pay. The man who had defeated his son in ritual combat would suffer a thousand curses. "Summon Raul!" he commanded his fiends. "The son of Odin must fall!"

The Statue

There was little that they could do for the wounded. Exhausted from battle, they lay upon the stone floor gasping for breath as if the floor was a bed of the softest down. "I can't believe that he's gone," Leander grieved, "and he's never coming back."

"He died in battle," Tariq said, "the way that he would have wanted to."

"It was Sheena who killed him," Carmen said, "and her curse."

"If we ever meet again," Leander said. "I swear that I'll see her end."

"Kalor is still out," Carmen said, worried, "but he has only a few minor cuts on him. I don't know what's wrong."

"It was the Undead Knights. They tried to get into our heads and defeat us from within," Dao reasoned.

"Yes," Carmen said, "they blamed me for all of the men who fell beside me in battle. They told me that my life was a lie."

"It was their existence that was a lie," Tariq said. "We stand with you because you are right. If we die for such a cause, then we have died well."

Carmen wept, crying from deep within, crying for Dartin and for all the friends that she had left behind.

"We need to pick ourselves up," Karina said with determination. "Kur needs our help, and Kalor can't help himself right now. We are down but not beaten, and let us not forget our bony friends trying to break down the door!" With her words, they went to work, still exhausted, but soldiers once again. They carefully removed Kur's armor and clothing, at least the parts that were not burned into his flesh. His left forearm was clearly broken and needed to be set and splinted. A great welt was rising from the top of his head, and his arms, hands, and face were badly burned. His beard and most of his hair had been seared off. His other injuries were less severe and didn't threaten his life.

"We need to reset his arm," Carmen said. "I learned bone-setting from the monks at the Abbey, but we need something to splint it with."

"Kur still has some bolts for his crossbow," Tariq noticed. "They should work."

"And we can cut up my old dress to tie it down and bandage him," Karina said.

"Let's do it," Carmen said. Working fast, they broke the arrowheads off several bolts and cut strips of cloth. Soon they had enough materials to get the job done. "We've got to do something for his burns. Leander, do you think that you can heal him?"

"I don't know if I can focus right now," he replied, "but I can try. I will need the same things that I needed before."

"Kur's wineskin is a smoking ruin," Tariq said. "Where else can we find the essence of earth?" They searched the room and their belongings, but besides dust, there was no soil to be found.

"Hold him steady," Carmen said. "Let's get his arm splinted fast. He's bleeding inside. "If he wakes up, you need to hold him down. Ready?"

"Ready." Tariq held him firmly, and thankfully, Kur never awoke. Surrounding his forearm with bolts, they wrapped it well and tied it fast, lashing it across his chest to elevate and steady it.

Eerily, the scratching of bones upon the door came to a sudden stop. Waiting in silence, they dared not to breathe. An instant later, something slammed into the back of the door, and then again, and the walls and ceiling around it began to crack. "They've got a battering ram!" Carmen said in horror. "We've got to move!"

Picking themselves up, they backed away from the crumbling portal. Carmen and Tariq carried Kur between them, and Leander bore his belongings. Karina stood between them and the door, with her sword drawn.

Inlaid into the floor at the statue's feet was a golden pentagram. The moment that they crossed it, the emerald eyes of the statue awoke, bathing the room in green light. "Swords!" Carmen ordered. Preparing to meet the new danger, they moved toward the far wall.

"Dao, get to work on that door," Carmen commanded. "We need to get out now!"

Standing some twenty feet in height, the statue was at least half again as wide at its base. Four steps led up to its giant feet. Carved of granite, the Deity sat upon a high-backed throne. It was squat and bloated, with a great potbelly, four-toed feet, and massive hairy arms. Its head was wide, and bear-like, with two long pointed ears that jutted straight out from the sides of his head.

Its eyes were oval pits filled with massive emerald stones. They seemed alive, its power awake.

The golden pentagram inlaid into the floor before it began to glow as well, yellow and bright, humming with a growing power. Above it at a height of about five feet, a tiny point of light, like a miniature star, appeared from the ether.

"The door is locked," Dao said, "not warded. My spells are exhausted. We need Kalor!"

"I'll try to wake him," Leander said, placing him gently onto the floor. "Kalor! Kalor," he called while jostling him as if he was rousing a sleeping sibling. "Wake up, Kalor!"

He was still lost in the nightmare realm of Death, fleeing dreamlike through a gray world filled with ghosts and evil spirits. That thing was still pursuing him, a force that he could not seem to escape no matter how hard he tried to run. Hearing voices, his terrified mind assumed that the deathly knight had finally caught up to him. He could feel the cold of its killing hands upon him. He awoke with a violent spasm, screaming all the while.

"It's all right, Kalor. It's me, Leander."

"What, who! Oh, thank god! I thought that it finally caught me."

"We need you right now, Kalor! Snap out of it." Kalor rolled onto his side as another titanic blow struck the door. Looking up, the tiny light was rapidly growing. None of them could look away.

Appearing out of the ethers as if a piece of the night sky had been captured, thousands of tiny suns poured into the star from all directions. Brighter and brighter it grew, until every shadow in the room was banished and every mortal eye blinded. With a brilliant flash, the light went out, the statue's eyes slept, and no illumination remained save for the room's two ever-burning braziers. The ram struck again, and the door cracked.

Their eyes slowly adjusted, and when they could finally see, they could not believe what floated in the air before them.

One-Eyed Jack's

"None of us could ever have dreamed what floated in the air before us," Kalor said. "The legions of the Dead were swiftly destroying the door, and amid all the chaos was a miracle."

"What kind of miracle?" Eric asked. "Did the gods send someone to help you?"

"Maybe it was the wizard Von Mathers," Garad said, "teleporting in to help you."

"Yeah, yeah," Pauli agreed, "it must have been him. Nobody else knew that you were all down there, and he could have watched you through his crystal ball."

Sonya considered it. "I don't think so. I doubt that even the wizard could have seen them in that dark place."

"In a way the gods did send someone to help us," Kalor said. "He would one day bear many names, names of honor to men of goodness, and names of fear in the hearts of evil, I remember him on that day as Salvation."

"Please tell us," Sonya said. "We can't wait any longer!"

Borrowing her cup of tea, I swirled the leaves a bit and bid them all to look within. Their eyes widened with their astonishment. In a flash, like drawing back the curtains at dawn, we were there.

Salvation

A naked human form floated above the encircled pentagram. His back was arched, his face pointing toward heaven, his arms and legs dangling as if he was held by the invisible strings of a puppet master. His hair was completely white, both that of his body and of his head. His face seemed somehow older, but it was unmistakable. It was Dartin!

Rushing to his side, they picked him up in their arms, daring not to think how he could possibly be alive again. "He's alive!" Carmen said, bending her ear to his mouth. The ram crashed again, and the door split. "Kalor, you have got to find a way to open that door!"

"I'm on it!" he affirmed. "Dao, can you give me a hand?"

"Of course!" And they went to work.

"Dartin," Carmen said, "wake up!"

With a gasp, his awareness returned. His lips were parched. His body felt strange, as if it had only recently become his own. "Where am I?"

"Alive, it seems," Leander said between tears of joy. "We saw the Mummies tear you limb from limb."

"I don't remember that. In fact, I don't feel hurt at all."

"Strange forces are at work here," Tariq said. "Even the gods seem to be watching our quest."

"But what of your powers?" Karina asked. "Kur is in bad shape, and we are running out of time!"

"It's all coming back to me," Dartin said. "Odin has awakened, and the power of the runes has been restored."

"I set his arm," Carmen explained, "but he is still unconscious. His burns are the worst of it."

Kneeling beside him, Dartin invoked the power of the runes, a combination that he had never before known, and Kur was healed. His skin was restored except for the faintest of scars, and his flesh and his bones mended. When the runes had done all that they could, the resilient Dwarf awakened.

"Praise all of the gods!" Kur said. "I thought that I'd got you killed, boy!" Pulling the priest down to him, he hugged him close in the tightest embrace.

"It's okay, Kur," Dartin replied. "It wasn't your fault."

"Kalor's done it!" Dao said. "Hurry, everyone, beyond the door is a stair, both wide and deep. He's rigged the door to lock itself once we shut it again."

The opposite door shattered, and the ranks of the Dead poured in. Yet another deathly knight led them. It seemed that the Dead had crowned a new king.

"Run!" They slammed the door just as fire erupted where they had stood an instant before. The Dead wasted no time in going to work upon the new barrier between them. "Let us flee this place," Tariq said. "Hopefully they will lose interest in chasing us any further."

"I shall place a rune of warding upon the door," Dartin said. "It should hold them back for some time."

"You can do that?" Karina asked.

"That and much more." Once his rune was traced, shining, and bright upon the door, there came a terrible shriek of rage from behind it.

"They didn't like that," Karina said, laughing. "Let's get out of here!" Down and down they ran, ever southward, their tunnel soon widening until it spilled out along the side of a vast vaulted cavern. The great stair continued along the west wall of the chasm. Above them the cavern rose beyond sight, and where the eastern edge of the stairs ended, a precipice dropped off into oblivion. There was neither rope nor handrail, and even the slightest misstep would end in death. The faintest sounds of rushing water could be heard far below.

"Hug the wall," Kur advised, "and watch your step!"

"Kur," Leander said, "you might want your clothes back?"

"Not much left of them."

"Your armor is fine, and some parts of your clothes survived."

"We'll worry about it later," Kur said. "This is no place to try on clothes! I'll take my ax, though, and carry my gear." With Prince Loren's weapon in hand, he led them carefully down the great stair. Descending some two hundred feet, the stairs ended, and so too did the cavern. A tunnel lay ahead, narrow at first, then widening. Kur crept into the black, and his friends soon followed. Fifty feet of tunnel, and yet another cave appeared. Lengthy stalactites hung down from the ceiling at random. Milling about the cave floor were six enormous albino swine, feeding upon a vast expanse of fungi.

"Tariq," Kur whispered, "our prayers for food have been answered." A single arrow was all that it took to bring one of them down. The remaining animals fled southward into the cave system. "We must beware," Kur said. "Such animals are rarely wild. There is probably some kind of farmer nearby." Spreading out, they searched the cave, but besides the mushrooms and trampled paths of the pigs, they were alone. The tunnel continued on from the south end of the cave, bending east and narrowing to less than five feet in width.

"We'll camp here as long as we can," Carmen suggested. "Let's eat!"

Tariq butchered the pig and divided the meat among them. Drawing his sword, he summoned flame. Cooking the heart, liver and kidneys first, he bade them to eat it. "This meat will strengthen us. Eat it before you eat any other parts." They ate ravenously, their hunger beyond anything that they had ever before known. When they were satisfied, they packed all the meat that they could, and Kur harvested a large quantity of edible mushrooms. They talked and they ate, feeling their strength returning for the first time in many days.

"Dartin," Leander said, "I still can't believe my eyes. I thought that we'd lost you."

"We all did," Carmen agreed.

"You have aged," Dao said. "Do you have any memory of where you have been?"

"I remember some of it," Dartin said, a haunted look in his eyes, "mostly pain and the fires of Hell. I was a prisoner of the Abyss for ten years or more before my father freed me."

"Your father was also in Hell?"

"I know now that my father was not just a Northman. He was Odin himself."

"That must explain your ability to wield the runes," Dao said, "and your name!"

"So we travel with the son of a god," Karina said in feigned disbelief. "This quest just keeps getting better and better."

"What else do you remember?"

"I was resurrected by the Lord of the Dead," Dartin said, "a Lych named Andomar Tabarun, whose wife, Marie Elizabeth, I rescued from Hell. She was the most beautiful woman who ever lived."

"What did she look like?" Tariq asked.

"She was Gray Elven, with hair both long and dark and eyes like the midnight sky. Her skin was all silk and ivory."

"So you are smitten," Leander said.

"No man looking upon her could have felt otherwise," Dartin said knowingly. "It was Andomar's love for her that drove him to madness when she was kidnapped by the archduke of Hell. He struggled to save her and exact his revenge for three thousand years."

"Quite a story."

"Without his magic, I would still be dead," Dartin replied gratefully.

"Then bless this Andomar," Kur said, "for returning you to us."

"There was one more thing," Dartin said, "I met our nemesis face-to-face."

"How is that possible?"

"He is powerful, that much I could tell. He had no fear of Odin or of the Lych King that I could see. He is Dockalfar."

"What did he look like?"

"He was dressed in fine mail, neither shiny nor dull, that flowed with his every movement."

"Adamant," Kur said, "their kind wears it down here. In the sunlight, it quickly rusts, but down here, it is as strong as mithril."

"He was tall and lean, with a proud face and a hawkish nose. His eyes were sky blue."

"Then he is no Dockalfar," Kur said. "Their eyes are built for the darkness."

"I heard a story once," Tariq said knowingly, "that those Dark Elves who are born beneath the sun are born with eyes like us."

"There are legends," Dao mused reverently, "that all Liosalfar were once of one race, separated during a great war between the gods. Those that sought refuge beneath Tempus became the Dockalfar, and as time passed, they were almost forgotten."

"Hogwash," Kur said, grumbling. "Their hearts are as black as their goddess."

"There are good and evil in all peoples," Karina said. "It's up to us to decide which side we're on."

"And what did he say to you?" Carmen asked.

"He said that we shall meet again."

Kur tested the edge of his ax and found its sharpness satisfactory. His look was both cold and grim. "I'll be ready."

They spoke of the Dark Elven commander for some time, each of them asking this or that about him until they all felt that they knew the man as well as Dartin did. They could only imagine what he wanted to do with the Duaredheim Staff when he got it. Conquer the world would be the least of it, they were sure.

They planned and took an inventory of their supplies. Kur salvaged what he could of his gear and discarded the rest. He would be barefoot and pants-less from there on out. Leander offered Dartin his cloak and Carmen her spare sword. Dividing up their gear as best that they could, they tried to supply their companions. Tariq went to work on the pig's hide, scraping off the fat, smoking it, and using the swine's brain to tan it. "I've got enough hide here to make moccasins for your feet," he said, "and put some clothes on you two. If Kalor can break out some of those pots of his, we can boil this fat down. It will help to keep us from starving. We cannot live on lean meat alone."

Kalor rummaged through his pack and soon produced two cooking pots. In the span of a few hours, they produced a good quantity of lard. "Thank the gods for this pig," Karina said. "It was the most delicious thing that I have ever eaten," and there was not a soul among them who did not wholly agree.

"Let's rest now," Carmen said. "We'll stay here and sleep for as long as we can, guard shifts, two-by-two buddy teams." They slept and they ate until they felt their vigor renewed. The tunnels around them remained quiet, and neither the Dead nor the living disturbed them.

They stayed in that place for three days and nights. The pigs returned to feed on the third day, but fled before any more of them could be taken. Tariq used all his skill at leather craft to fashion moccasins for Kur and Dartin. Using the entire hide, he crafted pants for the Dwarf and a kilt for the priest. If only he could have killed another pig, he could have repaired all their clothes, but the animals were wary and fled from the slightest sound or scent.

Kalor and Dao meditated. With the help of Kalor's Book of Shadows and Modrul's Book, they filled their minds with formulae of power—phantasms and bolts of light that struck like arrows, and Dao's spells of levitation, tornado wind, and gentle falling. With diligent study, they were able to add to their repertoire. Modrul had spells to hold and bar a doorway, conceal his presence in a cloudlike mist, and dispel magical effects and enchantments. Dao also learned how to conjure the power of lightning, the might of the Heavens themselves. Kalor was even able to become invisible for a time, one of the most versatile spells of the Illusionist. Their work was tiring, but when they were through, their confidence and their pride as wizards had grown. Together, they were able to accomplish far more than either of them could have managed alone.

Once they had done all that they could to heal and to rest, it was time to travel on.

"Try the scepter's gem once more," Carmen said. "Let us see if we're still on course."

"Antu Dorinumen," Kalor chanted, "atha murak namon!" Bursting to life, the gem pulled him southward still, drawing him forcefully toward the tunnel leading out of the cave.

"Let us move forward in the light for a while," Carmen suggested. "Kalor, you and Kur have the lead. Dao, your dagger if you please." Producing his knife, he held its brilliant light aloft as they began their quest anew.

The passage was narrow and winding. Often they would have to proceed in single file or squeeze between mountains of rock encroaching on the tunnel. Many times the tunnel was partially filled with water, and several times they were forced to explore ahead underwater. During these times, Carmen's helm proved invaluable. Remaining submerged indefinitely, she found the way through again and again. One by one they would follow her, led forward by the rainbow light of Kalor's diamond, or that of Dao's dagger. They traveled on in this manner for many hours, until the passageway finally began to rise and to widen.

As they entered into a series of interlocking caves, their pace quickened. "Something has passed through here recently," Tariq observed.

"Perhaps the pigs know how to swim," Karina guessed. "I saw no sign of where they ran off to."

"They may have had a hidden den," Kur said.

"It's possible, but stay on your guard," Tariq said worriedly, "I sense that something is wrong."

"As do I," Carmen said. "There is something ahead of us, something waiting." She signaled to them all to spread out, and they crept slowly forward until they came to the beginning of an even larger cavern. In size, it was at least two hundred feet in width and twice as long, with a jagged ceiling of some fifty feet in height. A great rift valley crossed through the center of the cave, and water could be heard rushing through it. The river appeared from the west wall and dove into the east. An arched bridge well-fashioned of stone crossed it. When their light entered the room, the entire cavern sparkled. The very walls and floor were permeated with some shining silver metal.

"Mithril!" Kur gasped in wonder. "Never before have I seen so much in one place."

"No doubt it is guarded," Carmen said. "Kalor, check out the bridge."

To Pay a Toll

Kalor approached the structure. Bones littered the ground here and there, some of fish and others larger. Drawing his sword, he felt better and padded closer. The stonework was old but well-wrought and mortared, and he could see no obvious traps. The road across the bridge looked damp, as if something had recently crossed it, but it could just as well have been river spray. Kneeling down, he picked up some loose dirt at the base of the bridge and traced a faint outline that he saw there. It was clearly a footprint, almost Human, but huge and clawed.

Behind him, his companions were fanning out, looking everywhere for signs of danger. Carmen searched with her enhanced vision and soon saw the same damp footprints that Kalor had discovered.

Kur gripped Korun-Koth tightly and readied his shield. His gut feeling was one of dread. "Danger is near, Kalor," Kur warned. "Fall back, laddy."

Carmen could feel the presence of evil. It was different from that which she had felt in the catacombs. A savage presence lurked before them, bestial and hungry. "It hides," she said. "Form a wedge. Carefully now, to the bridge!"

They reached the ledge top, overlooking the river some three feet below its banks. There were fading watermarks along the riverbank as well.

"Whatever is was," Dartin said, "it must have come from the river and then went back in. Maybe it has come and gone."

"Maybe," Tariq agreed, "or it may have a lair of some kind nearby."

"The bridge is the only way across," Carmen said resolutely. "The river is swift."

"Send Kalor across to check it out," Tariq advised. "He should be able to find any traps that the bridge might hold."

"I'll go with him," said Kur, but before they could complete their search, there came a frightful scratching sound from beneath the archway. When they looked up, a ghastly figure had clambered over the bulwark, stooping low at the top of it.

Black it was, with long, drooping arms and a scabrous, dripping appearance that brought forth such thoughts of revulsion that they all had to stifle the urge to retch. Its toes and fingers were both webbed and clawed, and its eyes were glassy, dull orbs with no discernable pupils. Long, gangly body hair clung to it like seaweed. Never before had they seen such a beast. Never before had they felt such remorseless disgust. If their fear had allowed it, they would have immediately known what such an eight-foot tall creature could possibly be, a beast that would call a lonely bridge its home, a monster that would demand payment before allowing any to cross.

And lo! The creature did speak in a bubbling, raspy croak that invoked images of the darkest, deepest depths of lonely passageways where no mortals dare to tread. "I am the Troll King. I smell your blood," it hissed, its gill flaps fluttering with anticipation, "tasty, delicious blood." Rising to its full height, it pointed at them. "None shall pass without first paying a Troll's toll."

The Troll's words ended with an awkward pause, its hands opening and closing in anticipation. The heroes before it were spellbound by its hideous form.

Tariq considered the Troll's words and answered it. "It would seem foolish," he said. "for one as great as you to challenge the might of many."

"Yes, ugly Elf," it hissed, "but a Troll's bridge is treacherous, treacherous, and you are but small, small."

"Our blades are keen and our bodies strong," he said resolutely. "We fear you not!"

"No blood need we shed," it replied, "as long as you pay a Troll's toll."

"What is your price? Do you want gold or jewels?"

"I want," it said with saliva dripping from its jagged-toothed maw, "the Human girl."

"I'm afraid," Tariq said, "that she is not a possible trade."

"Then we shall have to take her!"

Their focus was on the bridge, but instead of an attack from its crest, the battle emerged from the river. Bursting over the banks, the Troll's companions rushed at them from the water's edge, their talons reaching out to engulf Dartin at their left flank and Karina on the right. Before their grasping arms could meet them, their arms were met by Liosalfar barbs.

"Send mine arrows," Dao chanted, "a swordsman's curse, to the heart of my foes, my flying blades doth rush!" Firing swiftly, he struck both of the emerging Trolls before they could take two steps out of the water. To his horror, his arrows barely slowed them, for since time's beginning, the Trolls possessed powerful bodies that could heal any wound save those made with fire. Barely affected, the Trolls attacked.

Kur held back, certain that the monster on the bridge would charge them at any second. When he saw Dao's arrows strike without effect, he was dismayed, but it was at that moment that he knew what the creatures were. "Trolls!" he shouted. "All of their unburned wounds will quickly heal. We must use fire!"

Why the Trolls had chosen an Underearth river to be their home was now made clear; any burning wound that they received could be quickly quenched in its waters.

Karina met the rightmost Troll without hesitation. Fear honed her reaction to a razor's edge, and it was almost a relief when the attack finally began. Her taught muscles sped her out of harm's way. Dodging to the beast's right, her black leather-clad form seemed a shiny and insubstantial thing next to the Troll. It was fast, disturbingly so for so large a being, but she was faster still. Its blows fell upon naught but air, and her dance was fast raining a multitude of cuts upon its hide. Wielding the Sword of the Guardian of the North Wind, her blows punished it, and its rage grew. It turned about quickly to drag her in and tear her limb from limb, but she was always a step ahead, and only the Troll's body knew pain. She cut and she hewed, but the monster's body was fast repairing itself, and it would never slow unless it was crippled. Without fire, she knew that it was a battle that she could not win alone. Fighting on, she tried to conserve her strength, hoping to keep the beast occupied long enough for her friends to find a way to defeat them. In the meantime, fatigue and the Troll were her greatest enemies.

On the left flank, Dartin faced the leftmost Troll near the river's edge. Carmen was close behind him, with her Vanir bow in her hands. He was neither as quick as Karina, nor as enduring as Kur, but he was more than proficient in the use of a sword. The Troll was a mighty foe, over three feet taller than he was, but something within him knew how to face and to kill such a terrible opponent. When the Troll's first paw descended to crush him, he stepped back and called upon Elhaz, the rune of protection. Instantly, his body was protected, as if he wore a suit of the finest mail. The Troll's claws struck him, but his flesh was like tempered steel, and he was barely harmed.

Never before had the Troll encountered a puny Human that could resist its deadly power. It had struck its flesh with all its vast strength and encountered unfaltering resistance. Its doubt was a fleeting thing, for it was not the first time the monster had encountered magic. It was only a matter of time before the protective spell was likely wear off and then it would feast. It attacked more fiercely than ever, and Dartin had to work hard to fend it off. Tariq stood to his right and had called his sword to flame. The Trolls shrank away from his blade, and this brought Kenaz, the rune of the burning torch, to his mind. Wielding his sword in his right, he invoked the rune with his left, and Kenaz manifested. His sword, normal in every way, burst into flame and remained burning like a torch. Backpedaling, the Troll swatted at him in an attempt to disarm him. It hissed and spat. "Your fire will not save you, Manling. We will still eat your flesh."

"Not if I have anything to say about it!" Leander shouted. Side by side with his comrade, they assailed the monster. Carmen stood behind them, sending arrows of light wherever they were most needed. They were fire enough, it seemed, because the wounds that her bow made did not instantly heal. Tariq and Kur climbed the bridge toward the Troll King while Kalor prepared his magic at the foot of it.

Fearing for his wife, Dao sent the last of his arrows into the monster before her. His shots were unerring, and the Troll's body was pierced in many places. In contempt, the Troll plucked each of them from his flesh, and the wounds soon closed. His arrows spent, he slung his bow and began to raise his power.

Karina was too wrapped up in her deadly dance to spare any of her attention. Fighting with precision, she struggled to find a way to bring the beast down. Remembering a technique of pattern-forming that she had learned from a master swordsman over a century before, she began a new strategy. A skilled fighter could control the flow of battle in many ways, and she absolutely had to remain in control. Moving clockwise around her opponent, she lashed out high and low, high and low, in a repeating fashion. Soon the Troll grew to expect it, and he easily parried her blades aside. The trick of the tactic was to change the pattern so suddenly that one's enemy would continue to follow the habitual pattern even after her attack sequence had changed. With a master's skill, she pivoted in a surprise maneuver, reversing her flow and bringing her sword's blade down with all her strength onto the exposed thigh of her enemy. When he attempted his next step, he toppled, for he had no right leg to stand on.

Karina continued her onslaught. Working all about the fallen Troll, she cut it in dozens of places. It roared and lashed at her, and her right calf was badly hurt. Undaunted, she kept moving and slashing, but its restorative powers were great, and without fire, she could not stop it. Its severed leg was somehow inching its way toward its body in an attempt to rejoin with its host. Their bodies could regrow any limb, and if the leg didn't reattach itself soon, the Troll's body would form a new one. More terrible still, the severed leg would not die in the absence of its host body but would instead grow into another Troll, the exact duplicate of its former self! Such was the nature of the creatures they faced, regenerative monsters that would never tire and never stop until their prey was consumed or they themselves were slain.

Unfortunately, these powers were not the only ones the ancient creatures possessed. Since their creation. Every species of Troll held a certain dominion over the elements from which they were born. It was a limited ability, but in the scale of mortal things, it was very great indeed. These Trolls had been formed from the muck and mire of the first swamps of Tempus, and all the beasts of the bog would obey them, as well as spirits of the water element. It was this last talent that the Troll King called upon. Guarding the bridge, the mighty Troll called upon the swiftly flowing river to aid in its struggles. Its summons was soon answered by a being of water and born of water. It was a water spirit as old as the world's beginning. In substance, it was water itself. Its existence was living magic, self-aware and mutable in form. Able to form itself into any shape, it rose like an ocean wave from the river's froth. With eyes like waterfalls, it sprouted arms like whirlpools and splashed with rage at its summoning.

"Why have you awakened me?" It steamed, for to call up such elemental spirits was perilous and unpredictable. The nature of water was to travel with the flow of the world, and to interrupt that flow went against nature itself. Nevertheless, the Trolls were abominations and, since their awakening, cared little for the flow of nature, except when it suited them or when they were hungry.

The Troll King reached out to the water spirit with his power, grappled with it, and won. "Turn your rage against my enemies," he commanded, "for they are the reason that I summoned you."

Rising ever higher, it crested beside the bridge, standing like a living waterfall, its body fed by the river. Its flowing eyes were filled with the anger of the tempest. Its rage at being forced to travel against the flow was limitless. It was a hatred that the Troll King turned against his mortal foes.

The crushing wave that struck them was unlike anything that Tariq and Kur would before have imagined. It was like the surging waves of the southern coasts, only more focused and devastating. Hurled backward by it, they tumbled and crashed all the way to the base of the bridge. When they rose to their feet, the water spirit followed. Towering above them, it raised its watery arms up again to smash them.

Kur was the first to recover. "Tariq, look out!" he screamed, but the ranger was already on the move, rolling backward to avoid the killing stroke. Kur leaped over the left wall, avoiding the first wave, but he could not escape the second. He was hammered into the stone rail of the bridge. The wind was blasted from his lungs and his short sword torn from his hand. Gripping Korun-koth desperately, he gasped for breath. Despite the nature of his opponent, he fully intended to fight! Cursing the conjured beast with every painful gasp, he doggedly waded into the tumult. His ax hewed at it, for surely such a thing would have some kind of heart? Unknowing, he brought battle to the creature, his blade, twice forged, and with magic inlaid. It gurgled in pain, for such was its nature that only magic or the elements could harm it. Indeed, Korun-koth was something of both, forged of the earth elements, formed with fire, and laced with Dwarven magic. These qualities, combined with an unrelenting Dwarf, hurt the Water Spirit gravely, but the Troll's control was strong, and instead of flight, the water being was forced to fight on. Fist after watery fist slammed into Kur, until he was blasted back away from its body. Rolling onto his knees, he emptied his lungs and tried to catch his breath. The water spirit turned his attention toward its then closest foe, a tiny, cowering little Gnome.

Tariq hit the bridge at a run. Knowing well that the water spirit had been summoned by the Troll King, he took advantage of Kur's sacrifice and faced the Troll alone. With a mighty battle cry he rushed in, "For Carmen!" he said without knowing the reason why, for the heat of battle was in his veins. His heart filled with the fires of war, and his sword seemed to gain something from his valiant conviction. Its flames burned hotter and more ferociously than ever, for it had been forged for the sole purpose of slaying creatures such as these. Somehow, he was unaffected by its flame. Perhaps his own spirit was also akin to the element of fire, or perhaps the sword had been his alone since the time of its crafting, and with its blazing fire, he did strike. The Troll engaged him in his duel to the death. Its claws bit his flesh, drawing blood wherever they struck him, but his own blows were deadlier still, and the cuts of his sword did not immediately heal. He thrust through the belly, and the Troll King screamed. Its guttural cry echoed with the rot of the bog, reeking of decay.

The Troll King had not survived for centuries using its powers alone. Cunning by nature, it had faced warriors wielding fire before. All of them had fallen beneath his mighty arms and disappeared between his crushing jaws. Certainly this encounter would be no different. Lunging suddenly, it scooped up its prey between its crushing arms, and the Elf was unable to avoid them. Pulling Tariq in, it opened its jaws wide to engulf his head, and in that attempt, it made one fatal error. Even as his claws encircled the Elf's shoulders and pulled him in, his foe's enchanted blade was driven up to its hilt into his heart. Roaring, it wrestled to free itself of the troublesome pest, for it could feel its life slipping away fast.

He was struck, his flesh torn, but Tariq was in all respects a ranger born, and his tight grip upon his sword would not relent. Even as he was wrenched about and hurt, so too was the Troll killing himself. Tariq pulled and twisted, working his blade throughout its vitals.

Never had the Troll King experienced such pain, an agony from which it felt its life slipping away. Fighting with all its remaining strength, he tried to devour his enemy's head, but it only drove the blade in further. Sinking to his knees, he couldn't hold on. The Elf would have tasted so good, but it was only a minute or two before the burning pain was gone, and so too its body.

Standing over the Troll King's burning corpse, Tariq again cried out, but it was not from the bitter pain of his wounds, nor from his longing to return to his forest home, nay, he cried out only for one thing—victory.

One small success, but three terrors still remained. Dartin and Leander had fought together side by side countless times, and because of this, they had developed a deep understanding of the other's techniques. With careful diligence, they rushed in and retreated, always keeping the Troll off-balance. Both of them were injured, but Dartin's spell had protected him well, and none of the Troll's blows had seriously harmed him. Dartin's burning brand had scarred the Troll, but spray from the water spirit had dampened it, and its fire sputtered. Behind them, Carmen worked her bow furiously, and the Trolls bled from countless wounds that would not heal. Soon the Troll would fall, and then they would need Tariq's enchanted blade to finish it.

Its king had fallen, and though it had retaken control of the Elemental, it knew that their victory was no longer certain. He needed time to heal, and so he formed a plan of escape. The battle had in no way sated its hunger, and so it chose to capture one of its enemies and bring it down to its underwater lair. The Human woman would be the easiest to kill and would most likely be the sweetest. Elves tended to have a displeasing aftertaste, and so its quarry chosen, he chose Carmen to capture and feed upon. With a tremendous effort, it threw the Elves before it aside and closed the gap with the warrior woman in a rush.

Tossing her bow aside, she reached for her sword.

The Troll swept her up in a tremendous hug, turned swiftly, and leaped into the river with her. Its wisdom told him that if he held her under long enough, then she would drown. Once dead, she would be far easier to eat. His mind was filled with scrumptious, desirous thoughts.

Dartin and Leander looked to the river. Carmen and the Troll had disappeared beneath the waves. She would not last long in the grasp of the Troll in its own element. Kur was beset by the raging Elemental, and Kalor was lost within the torrent of its body. Karina battled, but it was clear that she was tiring.

Not sure what to do, Dartin removed his cloak, took a deep breath, and prepared to dive in after her. It was then that a sudden shout rang out from the bridge.

Tariq stood atop the bulwark, soaking wet and bloody, with sword aflame. "Hold, Dartin," Tariq yelled, "stay here and fight!"

Wasting no more time nor words, Tariq breathed deeply and stepped off the bridge and into the torrent.

Seven times Kur had been blasted back by the Elemental's watery fists, and seven times he had risen to attack it again. His body ached everywhere, battered and bruised as he was, but he somehow sensed that the spirit's resolve was weakening, and the one who had summoned it was dead. Feeling that his victory was near, he began a battle chant of his people:

> Rocks of granite,
> Anvils of iron and hammers of steel,
> Korun-Koth is again Kur-Rogoth!

The towering wave descended to smash him, and he raised his ax to cleave it. With each of his blows, the enraged spirit became less and less, and soon he was no longer blasted back by its waves. Soon the living waterfall was only a shallow brook, and then it was banished back to the river from whence it came. In defeat, it gained release from its bondage and rejoined the flow.

Kur spotted a small form lying on the ground at the base of the bridge. Kalor had fallen. Rushing to his side, Kur gently turned him over. He was unconscious and breathless. Listening to his chest, he could still hear his heart beating. Water filled his mouth and his lungs; he was drowning.

"Help me!" he called out. Rolling Kalor onto his stomach, he pushed down on his body in an attempt to clear the water from his lungs. "Come on, Kalor!" he called, but he knew nothing of rescuing a drowning man, and their battle was still joined.

Karina pressed her attack, but the Troll's leg had nearly reformed, and its severed limb was growing another Troll all its own. Dartin and Leander hacked at the regenerating limb. Dartin's sword blade burning brightly again. Dao had summoned his power. Waiting for his wife to stand clear, he arched his bolt of lightning down, and the Troll was struck. His bolt was so powerful that the opposite wall of the cave was singed. The Troll collapsed, its life spent, but still its body strove to heal itself. Working swiftly, Dartin put fire to the carcasses until no part of its bodies remained unburned. Rushing to the river's edge, they prepared a rescue party.

"I'm the best swimmer," Leander said.

"I'll go with you," Dartin replied.

"No," said Karina, "Kalor needs your help now. I'll go with Leander."

"Not without me," Dao vowed.

"The river is swift," Kur said. "You might not be able to make it back."

"We have to try," Leander said. Removing their heavy gear, they prepared for the plunge.

One-Eyed Jack's

"Just a moment, lads," the Old Gnome said. "My story weighs heavily upon my mind, and I need a bit of smoke to calm me."

"But what happened to Carmen?" Pauli asked.

His audience looked at him intently, anxiously awaiting his continued story, for surely he wouldn't stop now and leave them all hanging so desperately.

"Well, my friends," Kalor said, "it is a long tale, and it happened so long ago that I will need another witness to tell it fully and do justice to those who sacrificed so much."

"But how long will that be?" Garad argued. "You have left us waiting in the middle of a fight."

"Oh, it won't be long, because the other witness is already here."

"But where?" Eric asked.

"Here!" a scarred old veteran answered. They turned in surprise.

A stout-framed Mountain Dwarf had somehow come upon them unawares, wearing a short sword at his waist and carrying a shining broad Dwarven ax that was strapped across his back shield-like. With a pained movement, he pulled his wide girth onto the vacant stool next to Garad and helped himself to some of the young man's ale. "It was a black time for us all," he began.

In a Troll's Lair

The current was strangely swift at the surface and calm at the bottom. Tariq's plunge had brought him deep, and his weapons belt helped to keep him there. His sword flamed, the water boiling around it. Its fire was a beacon in the murk, and he used it to light his way. Swimming near the bottom, he could see the stripped carcasses of the Trolls' past meals. Vacant eye sockets stared at him from countless skulls. Animals, Elves, and Men, the Trolls' hunger kept no favorites. If any being was a true monster, it was the terrible Troll. Searching quickly, he scanned the riverbanks. He was strong, but the battle had taken his wind, and he would need air soon. Almost desperate, his mind was tormented by visions of what could be happening to Carmen, but he was, if anything, lucky, and he soon found the black gaping maw of the Troll's lair. Swimming for it, he saw that it first dipped down and then rose again into some underwater cave. He was torn between going back up for fresh air or risking the cave and praying that it wasn't flooded. Carmen's life hung in the balance, and an instant could mean life or death, and so he chose the cave.

Carmen had been taken by surprise. Held fast by arms as strong as a cave bear, she struggled valiantly, but she could not free herself. Kicking and screaming, they went into the river anyway. Cold and dark, the Troll swam deep, its webbed feet propelling them easily. Helpless to act, she was at the mercy of the Fates. Her mind rebelled, for certainly this was her last battle and her last day among the living. She had survived dozens of deadly conflicts, but there had always been fellow soldiers at her side. Now she was alone, her hands on the hilt of her sword and yet unable to unsheathe it, trapped in the hands of a monster beneath the waves of a raging river. She should have quit, allowing terror to take hold, but the calm planning mind of the soldier within her quickly took over. Thinking with amazing clarity, she had taken one last breath before the plunge. With it, she said, "Dar-Croth," and her helm was instantly sealed, filling with precious air to breath, even underwater. The Troll was holding her under, in a branch of the main riverbed, in an obvious attempt to drown her. Playing along, she struggled hard for a while, and then less so, until she finally went limp. In the murky waters, the Troll would never be able to tell that she still breathed. Her hands were trapped on the hilt of her sword, but the way that she was held, she still couldn't free it. She could only hope that it would relax its grip just enough for her to escape before it ate her.

Once its dinner had ceased its struggling, he held it under for a while longer to ensure an easy meal. He was starving, and he wanted to feast. The healing of his many wounds required tremendous energy, and his stomach growled in anticipation. Once he was satisfied that his meal was dead, he swam up to his dismal lair. The Human woman's equipment made her easy to hold, and soon he had her draped over a flat bloodstained stone that served as his dinner table. Admiring her, he gloated at his good fortune. Never again would he have to share his dinner with any of his brothers because now he was the greatest of Trolls. Now he was the Troll king! In time, of course, he would sever one of his fingers or a toe and grow another brother, but for now, he would enjoy being King. "Tasty, so tasty," he said, bubbling spit. "Me thinks her legs will make a nice meat pastry."

THE DRUMS OF DOOM

The Red Orcs' pyramid fortress was the culmination of over a century of slave labor and remarkable Dragonian engineering. Built upon the foundations of an ancient city, it rose to a towering one thousand feet in height and commanded an absolutely dominating presence for miles around itself. A wide river flowed slowly past the northwest side of the fortress, and to the east, it overshadowed the sacred tundra region of the Orcs. The southern side of the pyramid was protected by a vast, impenetrable swamp, beyond which loomed the vast Dragon's Ridge Mountains. The formidable snow-capped peaks of the Northern Reaches began their climb a few miles to the north, and to the west, the Shadow River, whose waters flowed north, emptying into the Bay of Cod. The new village of Bargrum Neck rested at the base of the northern mountains and served as a trade center between the sea, the fortress, and the numerous tribal settlements of the Red Orcs. The pyramid housed many horrors and numerous secrets, and beneath it was a vast honeycomb of mining shafts, hidden chambers, and ancient catacombs. The heart of the fortress, and perhaps the source of its mysterious energies, was an endless vein of dark force crystal, a mineral used by Orc shamans to enhance their magical powers. All in all, the entire realm was considered by the Orcs to be their sacred homeland, a region that they would defend unto death.

The fortress was commanded by an elite group of Dragonian fighters. Vlad's chosen nine were the highest ranking among them, and their day-to-day plans were most often conducted in a well-guarded chamber near the heart of the pyramid. They called it the war room.

The floor of the chamber was over sixty feet square, with a high-arched ceiling that rose to more than forty feet in height. Well-tiled with marble, the artistry of the walls reflected the multiracial nature of the garrison. Battle scenes depicted ancient Orcin heroes, as well as Goblin kings, Giant lords, and Dragonian gods of war. A great round table, hollow at its center, commanded much of the room, and chairs of varying sizes encircled it. The room's two doorways were massively constructed and well hinged, more than tall enough to accommodate the height of a Giant, or even a Titan. Bookcases lined much of the walls, and these were filled with scrolls and historical works from around the world. The war room was often visited by the garrison's leaders, especially with the spring thaw coming and the promise of war, but on this day, there were only two occupants within its confines.

Andreul Do'Nurum leaned over a detailed schematic drawing of the pyramid's lower tunnels. Dressed in her field uniform, her high riding boots, green leggings, and black tunic were immaculate. Her officer's sword hung over her left hip, its gently curved blade well-housed in a scabbard of gold, with a well-guarded hilt cast in silver. Her arms were bare and damp with the sweat of recent exertion. Her face was fair but hardened by military service, and her hair pulled back tightly into a long ponytail. Her dark eyes studied the maps laid out before her with unmatched intensity, and Elrick, her second, assisted her.

Dressed as she was, except for the sword, he carried his wizard's staff instead. Tall and twisted, it had been meticulously carved from briarwood and then ensorcelled. Outwardly, it looked like little more than a well-carved walking stick, but as sorcerer's staves went, it was one of the most powerful in existence.

Tall and lean, with soft cheekbones and a regal jaw, his own hair was short and well-barbered, an unusual style among the Drakkar Noire. His blue eyes were inquisitive and sparkling with intelligence. His comrade's sex appeal did not go unnoticed by him, but his respect for her leadership and capability went far beyond his own personal desires. Their friendship was open, full of care and understanding. Although Andreul had similar feelings for him, they both knew each other too well to risk an affair so close behind the heels of war. If anything, that realization had brought them closer together than ever, and to those around them, they seemed more at ease than a married couple. Their feelings aside, their military bearing was unquestionable, and they never rested until their missions were successful. They had spent countless days planning for the arrival of their long-awaited guests. Their engineers had installed defenses at critical access points and sealed off carefully selected tunnels with walls of stone.

"Everything is now in order," Elrick said, tapping his left index finger excitedly on the map. "We shall soon meet these Fermen!"

"And the field commanders have been drilled to their limits and beyond," Andreul said.

"We are ready," replied Elrick. "When Carmen's Rangers enter the lower levels in search of the staff, they will be systematically led into an inescapable trap."

"The deep mines beneath the fortress can be accessed by numerous tunnels. We have sealed off the most vulnerable among them and protected the remaining ones with heavily armed patrols."

"The main passage will be left unguarded," Elrick continued, "and through it, the Fermen will certainly attempt entry. Neither knowing where they are, nor what they might face, they will undoubtedly send a scout ahead, and he will choose the safest route."

"I have foreseen our success," Andreul said, "but my visions don't reveal everything. It will be interesting to discover just how they will react to the ever-changing dangers that they will soon face. Countless times, they have shown their ingenuity and survived where few other mortals could."

"When their presence is discovered, our scouts will rush to inform us, and then we will slowly tighten the noose until no chance of escape remains."

"And then we shall offer them the terms of surrender. And if they refuse, we shall attack them until they are subdued."

"Within minutes," Elrick described, his hands tracing the outline of their trap on the map, "we shall seal off every adjoining passage and room. No one will escape. It is a trap meticulously laid and perfectly planned."

"Now let's go over it all again one more time."

Steel Cage Match

Fire burned within Tariq's breast, warrior's blood churning in his veins. His anxiety was unbearable. His underwater search had long since used up all the air in his lungs, and his body ached for it, almost as much as his spirit needed to find Carmen alive. He did not know how he could feel so much for a Human woman, but in the very midst of the heat of battle, wrapped in the chilling embrace of the river, it did not matter. Ahead of him, near the end of the underwater tunnel, he could see a faint light, one that he hoped would reveal her. In the span of three desperate strokes, he broke the surface and gasped for breath. His second inhalation ended with his battle cry, and his words did not echo the name of his god, nor some heroic challenge, nay, his only cry was for "Carmen!"

And lo! The Troll did cry out an ugly roar all of its own, and with his enormous bulk, he sought to bear down and crush his new foe. Desiring only to vent its rage, it was suddenly forced to pause, for the disgusting Elf had pulled forth a burning blade from the very waters of its home. Where its flame met the water, steam erupted, and the Troll then knew that any wounds that it received from it would be very slow to heal. Fire was a Troll's death, its greatest nightmare, and there was no escape save past its most hated foe. Hungry Trolls could be counted among those things most terrible in the entire world, but more horrible still was a Troll cornered by Fire. Bellowing in rage, it pulled a large stone from out of the muddy wall of its home and prepared to strike.

One-Eyed Jack's

"You can imagine our frustration," Kur said, "looking down into the waters, looking for any sign of our friends. We were all hurt, exhausted, and desperate. Every second seemed like an eternity. Dartin was working urgently to save Kalor while Leander, Karina, and Dao were removing their heavy gear in preparation for their attempted rescue. With naught but their swords and undergarments, they dove beneath the waves, leaving just the three of us alone on dry land."

Rangers Lead the Way

"You will taste good," the Troll sputtered.

"You will taste nothing," Tariq said, "save for Liosalfar steel." And then the Troll's terrifying scream was such that the very walls of its cave trembled, and the flames of the sword danced.

The Troll was confused. It was experiencing an emotion that it had never before experienced, and in its ignorance, it stepped closer in order crush Tariq with its stone.

The stone descended, and in size, it was over three feet thick and at least two hundred pounds. In the hands of the Troll, it weighed little more than a pebble, and if Tariq had remained in his place, then he would surely have been crushed. The fact that he was still waist deep in the entrance pool to the lair saved his life. Diving ahead face-first, he surfaced next to the rim of the pool and right at the monster's very feet. Such a tactic would have seemed foolish or insane to any warrior save for Tariq himself, but he was well aware of the limits of his own strength, and he knew that he could not defeat the creature with muscle alone.

The effect of his dive was surprising, even to him, for the Troll had so committed himself that his attack propelled him over Tariq and into the water behind him. Scrambling out of the water, turned death trap, he readied himself as the Troll rose up out of the pool angrier than ever before. Its long-fingered hands still grasped the stone, and its enraged eyes blazed with a fire all of their own.

Backpedaling toward Carmen's prone form, the Troll came at him in a rush like an enraged cave bear. If he dove to the side, the monster would slam head-on into Carmen, and although she lay unmoving, it might attack her in its madness. Standing his ground, he raised his sword high to protect her. Ordinary men would have feared for themselves, but he cared nothing for himself and everything for the woman that he protected. Courage and conviction were his gods and fear his demon, but his demon, so often faced, was now a wanton elixir, enhancing his reflexes, delivering his strength with desperation's hand. Knowing full well that the impact of the Troll's charge would most likely kill him, he waited to deal his deadliest blow. The monster closed five paces, then two, then one.

The impact shocked him, for somehow the Troll was not one, but two. Struck from the rear, he found himself thrown into the left wall of the cave. He had hoped to be enough to slay at least one great Troll, even if it should mean his own death, but two monsters were surely more than he could prevail against. Recovering his composure and his wits, he expected to be immediately struck down by the Trolls' hammering fists, but for some reason, the attack never came. Looking up with little hope, he was amazed.

Carmen stood before the Troll wielding the Sword of the Guardian of the West Wind. The monster recoiled from it. "Baneful blade!" it screeched. "Me thinks that I will eat you first." Her cut was her answer, and it countered with a sweeping backhand filled with stone. Ducking backward, it struck her a glancing blow. Tucking into a roll, she tumbled further and quickly regained her feet. "Are you waiting for an invitation?"

Already on the move, he was then beside her, wielding Flame. The Troll was still a terrible enemy, even against two. Its attacks came with an animal's natural speed, and it felt not the wounds of the Woman, only those that were made with flame. The monster knew well its weakness and concentrated all his rage upon his Elven opponent, for it feared his burning blade. He would ignore the Woman and crush the Elf's skull with his rock. Then he would finally be able to finish his meal, only now, he would prefer to eat her slowly and while she was still alive.

The boulder descended. Flame rose to meet it, and the rock sailed harmlessly passed him with its clawed-hand still attached. The Troll's smoldering stump smashed into him, and he was knocked back. Carmen hewed with a professional's skill, and its flesh blistered where her holy blade struck it, but those wounds were fast to heal, for only fire could truly harm it.

Its pain matched its rage. With a sudden slap with its good hand, it hurled Carmen away from itself and stooped down to strangle the life out of the Elf.

The ranger was not yet finished. The Troll's hand met only air as Tariq rolled inside of its defenses, regaining his feet with both hands on the hilt of his sword. Flames erupted from the Troll's skull, and its body twitched and jerked as it fell. Following it down, Tariq did not stop until the beast's entire body was put to flame. The lair soon filled with suffocating smoke, and what air that there was, was quickly being consumed.

"Quickly, Tariq!" she urged, taking his hand. "We must flee!"

"Wait," Tariq said, hesitating. "Under the dais, there is something there." Handing his sword to her, he leaped over the burning corpse. Shielding his face with his sleeve, he stooped low to look into the alcove. Within it, he discovered a small chest with a rusted lock and mineral-encrusted shell. It was heavy but not beyond him. Jumping valiantly over the flames, he took Carmen's arm in his and made for the pool. "Perhaps this fight will not have been without worth!"

Sheathing her own sword, Carmen returned Flame to his scabbard. "Together then!" she said, and they jumped in. Looking back once more, the Troll's body still burned. With deep, smoky breaths, they entered the tunnel and swam. Following the tunnel wall, they passed through the murk and reeled upon seeing three figures moving toward them. A sudden beacon revealed them—their friends, fast swimming to their rescue. Their smiles were broad and bubbling as Dao pointed sharply, "Up!" Kicking hard, they soon met the fast current at the surface. Breaking through, there came a tremendous clamor from the shore.

Kur's loudest battle cry rang out in relief, his tears rolling freely from his eyes, "Hazzaa! Hazzaa!" Beside him, Kalor had readied his magic rope. Pointing his left hand toward Carmen, he commanded, "Reach and hold," and the rope extended swiftly, animate and alive, coiling around Carmen's chest and tying itself fast.

"Ho there now, Kalor," Kur said, taking hold of the rope as well, "the current is strong!" Bracing themselves, they held the rope fast while their friends struggled to grab it. Holding fast to Carmen's waist, Tariq cradled the small chest against his body with his right. The current was unrelenting and so swift that a man swimming hard could do no more than maintain his place against it. Working stubbornly, the others swam across stream to him and used his body to pull themselves ahead toward the lifeline.

Lending his strength to the line, Dartin stood upon the shore, and together they began to haul their friends in. One by one, with the help of Kalor's rope, everyone made it back to dry land. Exhausted, they lay down on the stone and rested for a while as if the mithril ore beneath them was the softest down.

"Kalor," Karina said, "you look none the worse for wear."

"Thanks to Dartin!"

"It's good to have you back, priest. I much prefer the man in you!"

"So do I!"

"We should leave this place," Carmen urged. "I still have a bad feeling about it."

"We have yet to cross the bridge," Dao said, "but perhaps there is time enough to see what's in that chest of yours?"

"Kalor, take a look at it," Carmen urged. "Everyone else, fill your canteens and prepare to move out!"

Tariq drew his blade on a whim, and flames immediately erupted from it. "The sword blazes still, as if danger is near."

"Maybe there is a fourth Troll," Dao reasoned, "one that we missed."

"I sense an evil presence," Carmen warned, "but not as powerful as before."

"Then we had best get going," Kur advised. "There's no sense in staying in harm's way."

"Tariq," Leander said, "your sword earned its name today."

"I have thought of adding to it," Tariq replied. Raising his sword above his head, he declared, "On this day, I rename you Alfar Astru, Elven Star, and to our enemies, Flame!" Blazing hotter still, it seemed as if the sword itself was pleased.

"I have it!" Kalor said excitedly. Prying open the lid with the point of his knife, the Trolls' treasure was revealed—a handful of gems, a scroll, two corked vials of liquid, a wand, and a strange ring.

"Pack it all, Kalor," Carmen ordered. "You can study it when we find a safer place to camp. Let's move out!" Hefting their packs, they quickly crossed the bridge, ever ready for battle, but nothing stirred. The path continued on beyond it, finally narrowing until the cave was behind them, and naught but a narrow twisting tunnel remained.

"Flame still warns us," Tariq said. "We must be on our guard." Walking close beside Carmen, he placed his hand upon her shoulder. "I thought that we had lost you."

"My helm kept me from drowning, but I couldn't free my hands or my sword. Without fire, I knew that I was going to die. It was my faith in you that gave me the courage to play dead." Walking together, no more words passed between them for some time. She was alert, but her mind was fast considering the thousand emotions that were sweeping through her heart like a whirlwind. Her sisters had often spoken of love, a luxury that she believed would never be hers. It was completely impossible, but it had happened just the same; she had a hero.

Down and down, deep beneath the river's edge, in a small smoke-filled cave beneath a boulder that weighed over two hundred pounds, something stirred.

Concealing their light, they traveled on, moving ahead as quietly as possible. With Kur again in the lead, they followed him with no more than five paces between them. Tariq had found more animal signs, and he believed that the pigs had fled down this same passage. The tunnel was tall yet too narrow to travel two abreast. Nearly a half mile from the Troll's lair, they came to an intersection. The main passage continued south, and a cool breeze drifted past them. To the west, the sound of rushing water could be heard, and to the east the tunnel widened. Kur examined the stone lining the walls of the east tunnel, and much of it was cracked, jagged, and unstable.

"Best not to go that way," he said. "It could cave in at any time."

"Kalor," Carmen whispered, "the river sounds close. Check it out, but don't go too far." Stealthily, he padded toward the sound of the falls. Less than eighty feet ahead, the path entered into a small cave and then ended abruptly beside a wide rift in the ground. Creeping to the edge, he peered over it. A torrent of water rushed by at least thirty feet below him, and the chasm itself was over fifteen feet across. The remains of a wooden bridge could be seen dangling from the opposite side. It appeared as if the cliff wall in front of him had eroded and fallen down, taking the footings and the bridge with it. Heading back, he told them what he had seen. "Test the gem again," Carmen said. "Let's make sure that we're still on the right path." When he incanted the words, the gem continued to pull ever southward. "Press on," she said. "Kur, the lead is yours."

The twisting tunnel came to an end at the northern edge of a vast cavern network. The first cave was bean-shaped, over two hundred feet across, and filled with mushrooms over four feet tall, many of them glowing fluorescent shades of green and blue and rose. Wild pigs wallowed here and there, feeding hungrily upon thick clusters of fungi. Tariq's swift arrow took a small boar before the herd fled deeper into the caves. Fanning out, they searched the cave well, and those adjoining it, but besides the pigs, they seemed to be alone.

"Make camp," Carmen commanded. "Let's make the best of it."

Leander helped Tariq butcher the pig, and with the help of Flame, they prepared the older meat first and once again had a great feast.

After they had eaten, Kur and Tariq explored further into the next cave. Tariq worried over a pair of small footprints that he discovered there. "I have never seen such prints before," he said. "They look just like ours do, only they are no bigger than a child's of three seasons."

"Maybe there are Gnomes down here," Kur considered. "Perhaps it is a set of children's feet. Look here, this little stream of water passing through the rock. Its water is saltier than the sea, and minerals have built up all along the banks of it."

"My body has screamed for salt for days," Tariq said. "In the Ogre Fangs, it is worth more than gold or silver."

"Then we are rich," Kur replied, "and if we work hard, we should be able to scrape a few pounds of it off of these rocks."

"No wonder the pigs like it here," Tariq said while laboring with the back of his knife, "They have everything that they need—food, water, and shelter." In no time, they had several pounds of salt collected. "It's excellent!" he exclaimed, licking his fingers clean.

"I have been thinking about those tracks," Kur said. "Gnomes may hunt here, but there are other small races of Underearth. We should beware."

"You mean like the Darg?"

"Only in their evil, my father once told me a tale of tiny murderers that he called the Gree-Neer. They once killed fifty miners beneath the volcano before their lair was found."

"Now I'll never sleep!"

"Come, ranger, let us see if the wizards have identified the treasure!"

By the time they had salted and packed the remaining meat, Kalor had identified the magical contents of the chest. "The vials are indeed potions," Kalor reported. "One will heal, and the other will allow the drinker to climb any wall like a spider."

"The scroll was written by an ancient priest. Its verse will protect the reader from the Dead."

"It's a little late, don't you think, dear?" Karina said, smirking.

"Yes, of course," Dao agreed, smiling back, "but the last two items are even more mysterious. The wand is full of unpredictable magic. The symbols upon it are from every school of magic: Evocation, Summoning, Necromancy, Divination, and more. Uttering its command word might help the magician or harm him. It might summon a tiger to battle or an earthquake. There is no way to know for sure what might happen."

"And what of the ring?" Leander asked.

"None of the items in the chest were fashioned by the Trolls, of that I am sure, but the stone upon this ring is filled with their blood. Whoever wears it should quickly heal any wound that is not caused by acid or fire."

"Oh, do let me borrow it," Kur begged. "I feel as though I have been run over by a herd of stone worms."

"What are these worms that you speak of?" Karina asked.

"They thrive near the planet core," Kur said, "Baldric once tried to journey to the center of Tempus, but he never made it. The heart of the world is a vast sea of molten rock. The stone around that sea is soft with the heat. Baldric endured the heat until he could go no further, and it was there that he saw the Lava Sea through the mouth of a deep chasm. His food and water were gone, and he knew that he would never make it home. So he just sat there at the edge and pondered, waiting for Death to claim him. Before the day had passed, a mysterious creature emerged from the stone. Red-shelled, six feet in length, and six inches thick, it had a hundred little feet like paddles and a wide circular mouth filled with diamonds. Crunching a whole in the stone, it soon disappeared. Baldric believed that he had imagined it, but before long another appeared, and then another. Ravenously hungry, he hewed off the head of the next animal that appeared and cooked its meat in the superheated steam that rose through the vent. When Baldric had eaten enough to recover his strength, he attempted to make the journey home. According to legend, the creatures taste foul, like burned meat. So goes the tale of Baldric and the Stone Worms."

"He obviously made it back," Leander surmised, "or else there would have been no one left to tell the tale."

"It is also said that his ax has been passed down from generation to generation to young Dwarves who still bear his blood."

Was Kur's ax the same? they pondered, but dared not to ask.

"Tariq should bear the ring," Karina declared. "If not for his sword and his courage, we would all be Troll food."

"And Dartin must carry the scroll," Leander said, "although his power has returned."

"He can still keep it safe," Carmen said, nodding, "in case the runes should fail."

"And what of the wand?" Dao said. "I believe that it is too unpredictable to use."

"Sounds just like you, Kalor," Karina noted, laughing. "Random magic for a wild heart!"

"Save it for dark times," Dao said, "when nothing else will avail you."

"The potions then," Kalor said. "Perhaps you should carry the healing draft, Kur."

"I accept."

"And the climbing potion?"

"Give it to Karina," Carmen said. "I don't know why, but I feel that she may need it sometime soon," and it was hers. Dartin healed them while they rested, and Tariq told them of the tracks that he had found.

"We'll set a double watch tonight," Carmen ordered, "just in case."

They slept and they guarded, but no greater dangers did they face than their own haunted dreams.

Despite beds of stone, they awoke refreshed and with merry hearts.

"There is nothing like a full belly," Leander declared smilingly, "to lighten the spirits!"

"Let's just hope," Dartin said, "that the rest of the day is as kind to us."

"Time to get moving," Carmen said. "This place worries me."

Traveling on in a loose formation, the cavern maze led off in many directions, but always the gem led them to the south. Around noon, they entered a cave with a vaulted ceiling and stalactites that dangled from the roof to the floor. The rocky tendrils created a maze that was difficult to navigate, and no clear path could be found through them.

"Stay close," Kur urged, "and don't get lost!" Tariq walked close behind him, and then Carmen and Dao, and at times, the Dwarf would disappear from view around this column or the next and then reappear when the next man in line turned the corner. Somehow, he seemed to hold his direction, a skill that Tariq had learned well in the land above beneath the sun and the stars, but here, so far from the light, he was little more prepared than the rest of them. When they were fully immersed within the maze, disaster struck.

A hole opened up beneath Kur's feet, barely wider than his shoulders, and he fell with a shout.

Tariq stood over it and saw Kur some ten feet below. Several small creatures, like little Goblins, suddenly attacked him from all sides, striking him on the head with heavy little sacks. If he leaped down to help, he wouldn't be able to bend forward or engage them in any way. "Carmen, come quickly, and bring your bow."

"What's going on?" Karina shouted from the rear.

"Hold your position!" Tariq warned. "There are traps in the floor."

Carmen bent over the hole, aimed, and fired, killing one of them. Kur's feet were slowly disappearing as the creatures began dragging him down a side passage.

"Bring Kalor up with his rope!" Tariq said. "I'm going down there."

"It's too narrow," Carmen observed. "You won't be able to fight."

"It's okay," Kalor said, "I'll do it." Preparing his rope, he commanded, "Reach and hold," and it coiled around the nearest pillar. Dropping its end down into the hole, he placed his dagger in his teeth and descended. Fifteen feet down, a series of tunnels branched away from it. A tiny little misshapen man lay dead at his feet. About half his size, naked, and oddly proportioned, it still clutched a small knife in one hand and a little sack filled with rocks in the other. Sensing eyes upon his back, he spun. A little man waited in hiding behind him, charging him with its sack. Kalor took his knife from his teeth and stabbed it through the neck. It dropped dead. Looking quickly down each tunnel, he didn't see any more of them. Their disturbing giggles were growing fainter as they dragged Kur farther into the maze. He could be attacked from any angle at any time. It was their home, and they knew its secrets; all that he knew was that his friend was being dragged away to his death. With a few words, he became invisible. Sheathing his dagger, he crept ahead quietly. Passing by several of the creatures, he stayed with the kidnappers. Soon the giggling levels rose, and the little tunnel ended in a small room no more than ten feet across, with a ceiling of three feet in height.

Kur was sprawled out on his stomach, with a dozen of the little gremlins stripping off his clothing and his armor. Whenever he would begin to wake, they sapped him again, which brought about still more rounds of sinister laughing.

Anger was a rare emotion among Gnomes, but at that moment, he was very angry indeed. He would have to kill them all before the other ones got there, or else he and Kur would be finished. With a word, the giggling stopped, and he appeared. Four bolts of light flashed from his hands and four of the Gree-Neer fell. His hand drew a dagger, coiled, and threw, taking another in the chest, but it lodged too deeply and would not return. Drawing his sword, his surprise was spent, and they rushed him. To the Gree-Neer, he was like an Ogre, an unusual feeling for a Gnome, but he used his advantage, laying all about himself with his blade. He eviscerated the first, taking a cut on the arm. The second latched onto his sword arm, and he punched it in the face with his left. Another one jumped on him, trying to bite down on his neck. Heaving mightily, he rose up hard and smashed it against the ceiling. Cutting right, he killed the one with the bloody nose. Grabbing the one on his back by the neck, he hurled it down and stabbed it through the heart. The other four kept coming, screaming savagely to alert their brethren. Stepping forward, he thrust with the perfect form of a fencing master, and the little murderer was skewered. Its momentum carried it to the hilt, and the other three bore him down. Punching him and stabbing at him, he was pierced in the shoulder, his mouth was torn, and he was kicked in the groin. His sword was trapped inside of a body, and he couldn't free it. Letting go, he punched and he kicked until he was again on his feet, and another one was down. The two remaining Gree-Neer wanted no more of him, and they turned to flee out of one of the side tunnels. Having none of it, he wrenched his sword free and chased after them. The first one lost its legs at the knee and fell screaming. The second one would have escaped if Kur's massive hand had not wrapped around its ankle in a death grip. Falling on its face, it tried to kick free, turned, and swung its knife at him. Kur caught it by the wrist, snapping its arm bones in one violent twist. Rising to his knees, he stretched it out between his arms like a sack of flour. Lifting it up, he then brought it down hard over his knee. Its spine snapped, and it went limp. "I hate these things," he said.

Kalor retrieved his sword and dagger in haste and dispatched one of the Gremlins that still stirred. "Get dressed quickly! The other ones will be on us any second." Guarding the main passage, he hid beside it, waiting for the first of them to come through. Two Gree-Neer ran straight on at Kur, not knowing that Kalor was among them. He killed the first, and Kur ended the second with his ax. A few more were in the passage, but fled when they realized that they faced not one opponent but two.

"Let's get out of here, laddy," Kur urged. "There could be hundreds of them down here." Kalor slunk, but Kur had to crawl. There were tense moments when the Gree-Neer would threaten attack and then retreat, but win their escape they did, Kur climbing out first, and then Kalor, who was showered with rocks by the evil things before he made it. Carmen sent a few arrows down the hole to quiet them, and such was its power that the shaft began to cave in and the Gremlins fled.

"We'll have to prod our way out of here," Kur said. "Don't take a step unless you know that the ground under your feet is solid." It took over an hour to escape the cave, and the Gree-Neers' giggling could often be heard from around one corner or the next.

The exit tunnel was wide, and when they had finally escaped, they could all feel it, as if some evil pall had been lifted. "You have my thanks, Kalor. You did me proud!" Kur praised. "The laddy killed twelve with magic, his fists, and his blade."

"What the hell were those things?" Karina asked.

"They were the Gree-Neer, all right," Kur said, "the blight of Underearth. You would call them Gremlins."

"Let's put some distance between us," Carmen pleaded. "I pray that we never meet again, unless it is to end them."

"That's the problem," Kur said. "You can't get to them, and if you try, sure you might kill a few, but you will never get them all."

The tunnel wound on, at times sloping upward and at others steeply down. A great chasm followed it on the left side for nearly a mile and then ended abruptly. Further on, another sloping passage joined it from the northeast, and then the tunnel widened still more until it ended in a large cave. A stagnant pool filled the east half of the cavern, and at its most extreme southwestern corner, a thick oaken door, bound in iron, blocked their passage. Evidence of a pitched battle lay strewn about the cave. A broken crossbow bolt lay upon the floor, its arrowhead missing. Near the pond, a severed hand rested beside a broken sword, and the walls were scorched black as if fire had swept through it.

"It's a Goblin hand," Tariq said. "I would recognize their green flesh anywhere."

"But where are the bodies?" Kalor questioned. "Many must have died here. Someone must have taken them away."

"Do Goblins lie beyond that door then?" Karina asked. "Perhaps they have the next piece of the staff."

"Somehow I think that we're soon going to find out."

"Try the gem again," Carmen said. "Let's be sure." Kalor's hand was then pulled, irrefutably toward the door and beyond. "Check it out," Carmen directed, "but quietly."

"The door was recently built," Kalor said. "There are piles of stone dust on the floor where the bolt holes were drilled, and the timbers are still wet with sap."

"Goblins could have built it," Kur considered. "Their mining is fair, but this work seems too fine for them."

"It is both locked," Kalor observed, "and magically held. No Goblins did that!"

"Then work your magic, Dao," Carmen said, "and may the gods be with us."

Standing before the door Dao summoned his power and began removing the warding symbols guarding it. The other wizard was skilled and far more experienced than he was, but overall it was a simple spell, and the technique of countering it was always the same. It required all his strength, but when he was finished, the door's magic was broken and its lock tumbled. Covered in sweat, he breathed a sigh of relief. "The wizard who barred this door was strong," Dao stated. "I don't know if I could defeat him."

"That's what friends are for," Kur said. "You are not alone."

"Then dare we enter?" Karina asked.

"The time for stealth has come," Carmen said. "Kalor, you said that you could become invisible?"

"I can only use that spell once more without resting."

"Now is the time, and Tariq will follow you with his chameleon cloak."

"Explore as much as you dare and then return. If you do not return in twenty minutes, then we will come looking for you."

With a word, Kalor was gone, and the heavy door slowly opened. Tariq wrapped himself in his robe and slipped in, quietly closing the door behind him.

Their wait seemed like forever. When Carmen could stand it no more, she reached for the door just as the lever began to turn. Stepping back, she reached for her sword, but it was only an invisible thief. "Tariq waits for us within. It's a huge mine filled with Orcs, and they have many slaves working it. I'll lead you to him. There weren't any Orcs in the tunnels between us. Come!" Tugging on her sleeve, he pulled her along. One by one they entered, with Leander in the rear. When they were all through, he closed the door behind him.

The new passage continued south for about twenty paces and then dropped. Wide stairs were cut into sloping floor and then branched to the southwest and east. Kalor led them southwest. The natural tunnel was soon replaced with well-mined passages supported by thick hardwood beams, evenly spaced. The floor was quite level and free of debris. Kalor led them south and west toward the sounds of heavy mining, crossing several intersections. Mining carts filled with ore stood at random. Kur examined the stone, but he had never before seen the crystal within it. "Some kind of sapphire would be my guess," he whispered.

Approaching a main corridor, they paused for a moment, seeking danger. Well-lit with large oil lamps, the smoke made it hard to breathe. Kalor carefully skirted away from their light, taking them instead along a mine shaft that ran parallel to it. Continuing southwest, the air became stiflingly hot, and their heat-sensitive vision could see as if it was the light of day. Tariq's huddled form crouched low behind a thick beam by an open archway. Kalor urged them to hug the wall, and Carmen quickly communicated this back along their ranks. Soon they had crept close behind Tariq, and they could all see the amazing sight before them.

Beyond the door was a gigantic encircling balcony. Inside of its ring was a vast shaft that dropped beyond sight and rose above them a like distance. Tremendous heat rose up through the vent and spilled out into the adjoining passageways. Five doorways exited the balcony in random places, and an ornate, well-forged iron rail of about four feet in height protected the residents from a long fall. Looking more closely, balconies and windows were built into the walls of the chasm throughout its extent, appearing with no clear pattern of architecture. What most interested Tariq was a large group of prisoners, slowly being led away by Orc slavers.

"They have given the lash to them a dozen times," Tariq said. "I believe that we can take them."

"There is no telling how many more of them there are," Carmen warned. "We must remain focused on the staff."

"This place is huge," he said. "It could be anywhere."

"Let's follow them, and if we can help them, we will." Waiting for the last of the Orcs to disappear through a far doorway, they snuck into the natural cathedral. "Unbelievable!" Carmen gasped, because the magnitude of the place was beyond her wildest dreams. Peering over the edge, she could see the lava pool several miles below. Even here, so far above it, her hair was singed by its heat. Looking up, the shaft towered beyond even the sight of her helm. Pockmarked with parapets, balconies, and windows, it resembled the inside of a vast ant colony. With a gasp, she realized that they had been seen. Far above her, standing over a balcony rail, was a dark figure. Armored in black mail, with a winged-helm and gauntleted hands, he spread his arms out wide as if he could fly and then brought his hands swiftly together. The resounding clap echoed about the Hall. Placing his hands upon the parapet before him, he smiled down at her. It was then that the Orcs began beating their drums.

Thrum-doom, thrum-doom, doom, doom!

"We are undone!" Carmen shouted. "Fall back to the door. They have seen us." The drums continued, growing ever stronger as more and more percussionists joined in. Their noise almost drowned out the titanic sounds made by hundreds of armored soldiers. The clang of armor, swords, and shields echoed from every doorway and every hall. "Tariq, quick, we must retreat!"

The ranger led them on then, back to the northeast from whence they had come. Entering into the mines, it seemed as if they might escape, but the ceiling in front of them was rigged, and some unseen hands collapsed it, completely blocking the tunnel. "They are trying to hem us in!" Leading them back, he tried another passage east, and seconds later, it too was blocked as a portion of the roof caved in. "Go back," he said, "we'll have to try the main passage," but before they made it fifty paces, it too was blocked, and not by cave-in but rather by a legion of Orcs. Stopping, they stared at one another for a few moments, both sides weighing their opponents. One of the Orcs was the first to speak, and his voice was strangely eloquent. "By order of the commanding general, you are hereby urged to lay down your arms and surrender!"

"We will never surrender to the likes of you!" Tariq said.

"The commanding general has included a list of terms and generously outlined the reasons why you should surrender."

"A list?" Carmen asked.

"Maybe we should hear their terms," Kur said, "before we kill them."

"Speak your terms."

Unrolling a small scroll, the Orc emissary read the terms:

> From General Vlad Leu Sherroan Commanding,
>
> It is with great anticipation that I welcome you here as guests of the Dragonian Empire. You are all fighters, and I fully expect you all to fight to the death. I beg of you, do not throw your lives away needlessly. Surrender and you will be treated fairly as prisoners of war. Resist and you abandon all hope. Additionally, I urge you to consider the following reasons for your surrender: first, that

you are completely surrounded by a force that outnumbers you by more than a hundred to one.

"He has got a point," Kur said.

Second, that the Chief of Clan Kegporter is already my honored guest.

"Father!" Kur exclaimed. "I will kill you all!"

"Hold him!" Carmen commanded. "There's no telling what they will do to Moldrin. Save your anger, Kur. We have yet to hear all his terms."

Additionally, the following individuals are already guests of the Dragonian Empire: Robbin the Silver-haired of Arendal, The Lady Lisette Anastasia of Safehaven, the widow Isidora Greylinx, wife of Gwillym and mother of Dao, the princess Mia A'Kiva, sister of Karina, the Lady Gretchen of Iconerthra, mother of the Son of Odin, the master illusionist Uldrick Swifthands of Waysborough, and the baron Duchings of Nordtown.

All the aforementioned guests are being treated with the greatest care and respect. Resist and in addition to the waste of your lives, those of your loved ones shall also be sacrificed. Fight to the death, and you will be considered terrorists, and three generations of your families will also die. Surrender and their lives will be spared. These are the terms. Do not let your great sacrifices end here.

Signed,
Vlad Leu Sherroan
Commanding General

"You have three minutes to consider the terms," the herald declared.

"They have my mother," Dao said.

"And mine as well," Dartin replied worriedly.

"They have someone dear to us all," Carmen said, "save for Tariq."

"Maybe they are bluffing," Kur said. "There is no way they could have taken my father from under the volcano."

"The Dockalfar are known for their treacherous ways," Dao reasoned, "but they are also known for their honor. I don't believe that they would deceive us with lies."

"I will never surrender to their kind," Tariq said. "I would rather die."

"Then you will throw your life and ours away for nothing," Karina scolded. "I see no victory for us here. Let us live so that we may fight another day and in a better field."

"I will have my revenge!"

"But what of the rest of us?" Dartin said, "If we all die this day, our loved ones die with us, and our quest ends in failure."

"So you will not fight?"

"Oh, I will gladly join you in a fight to the death," Dartin replied, "if Carmen orders it."

"But they are just filthy Orcs!"

"Their masters are not Orcs," Carmen said. "We can fight, and we will most likely die, with our families alongside of us. Or we can lay down our arms and pray that the gods give us another chance. Dead, and there is no chance."

"But what of our quest?" Tariq argued. "If we surrender, the quest is a failure."

"We don't know that," Kur said. "Who knows what fate awaits us? My heart begs me to fight, to the death if I must, but I cannot ask my father to join me, especially when he has no ax in his own hands!"

"Very well," Tariq said, "but I will have my revenge before this quest is through. That is my vow."

Their time was up, and the herald stood before the Orc legion awaiting their reply. Carmen looked to her friends, and their torment was as great as their anger. Surrender was their only choice, but their hearts were filled to the brim and begging for a fight.

"I stand with you, Carmen," Tariq said resolutely.

"As do we all."

Her hands dropped first to the hilt of her sword and they to theirs. The Orcs raised their shields and readied their clubs. Then slowly, her hands went to the buckle of her weapon's belt, unfastened it, and then removed it. Holding it out before her defiantly, she paused for a long while contemplating battle or surrender. If they fought now, many would fall with them, but the war would be lost. If they surrendered, they might live to see some future victory. She had pledged to fight evil, but the lives of her friends and family were more precious still. Opening her hands, her weapons fell, and those of her party soon followed.

"We accept the terms," she answered.

Their weapons and belongings were taken. They were blindfolded, their wrists shackled behind them, and they were led away. Their treatment was firm but not abusive. They did not resist. The time for that had passed. They were led on for miles, it seemed, climbing higher and higher into the complex. One by one, they were placed in holding cells and chained wrists and ankles to the walls. Only then were their blindfolds removed. Food was brought to them, and buckets and cloths for their bodily needs. They remained that way for a long time before anyone but Orcs came to them.

When Kalor Was Helplessly Chained in the Dungeon

Kalor's bonds were tight but not overly so. Testing their strength, he tried to free his hands, but it was useless. He would only hurt himself if he tried any harder. His cell was lightless save for that which spilled through his cell door's small window. He studied his prison carefully, but without his equipment, he was helpless.

Suddenly the darkness of his cell deepened, and there before him, no more than three feet away, was the Orc's dark commander. He kicked at him, but his nemesis was just beyond his reach. "You bastard! He's in here! He's here!"

"No one can hear you, Kalor. They are all asleep."

"Impossible!" Hysterical with rage, he struggled to free himself. "Help!"

Vlad sat casually, cross-legged upon the floor. Resting his hands upon his knees, he waited patiently.

"I will kill you!"

"I would feel no different if I was in your shoes, Kalor. Now please, do sit down. You will only hurt yourself."

He struggled stubbornly. Vlad's amusement only increased his ire.

"Sit!" Vlad finally commanded, and although Kalor tried to resist, he found himself sitting nonetheless. "I have many things to tell you, Kalor, so that if I fail, someone will remain who knows my story."

"You are insane!"

"Just look into my eyes, Kalor," Vlad said, "and I will show you everything." He tried to look away, but the Elf's eyes seemed to bore into his skull, shattering his ego's defenses with ease. The untold wonders that filled Vlad's intellect were methodically hidden away in the distant corners of Kalor's psyche. They danced behind his knowledge and played hide-and-seek like children behind the curtain of his own memories. He no longer struggled. The knowledge was intoxicating. His eyes widened; he let it all in. He wanted more, but his mind was only one, and Vlad's was among the most powerful in existence. A brilliant flash of light exploded in his consciousness, and he knew no more.

"When you hear the guard's footsteps, Kalor, you will awaken refreshed. You will feel as if you had the most restful sleep in your entire life. You will remember nothing of our meeting until the appointed time. Sleep now, Kalor, and rest."

In the Dungeons of Drakon Mur'-Falor

Dao found himself inside of an eight-by-ten-foot cell. A single door with a small barred window stood opposite him. His shackles provided just enough slack so that he might lie upon the small cot standing beside the right wall. He still wore his clothes and his boots, but every other item that he had possessed was gone. "Hello!" he called out, "is anybody out there?"

"Dao," another voice said, "is that you?"

"Yes, your voice sounds faint, but I can hear you! Is that you, Carmen?"

"Yes, it's me. Everyone is here. Tariq is in the cell next to mine."

"Quiet!" ordered an unseen voice, "or your cell-block windows will be closed." Testing the strength of his restraints, Dao found them to be formidable, and his powers were gone. Maybe it would have been better if we had fought them, he thought, but he knew better. They had made the right decision, even if it didn't seem that way now. Their minds were their greatest weapons now. Studying his cell, he looked for any weakness but found none. It was then that he heard a loud knocking from somewhere close by. "Who is it?"

"Lieutenant Du'Raneurden," he said. "I have come to interrogate one of the prisoners." The rattling of keys proceeded then, followed by the complaints of rusty hinges.

"Good afternoon, Lieutenant," the guard greeted, "which prisoner?"

"The Elf named Dao."

"I'll take you to him." The guard's footsteps were heavy and ponderous, but the lieutenant's were crisp, and light, striking the stone floor in a steady rhythm. The cell window darkened, and the lock upon his door tumbled. The portal opened. The guard was a massively constructed Orc whose lower canines curved up powerfully almost to his eyes. The other man was no Man at all, but rather Liosalfar like he was—no, Dockalfar! Blue eyes, short, neatly trimmed hair, and an impeccable uniform, he stood before him with unwavering confidence. "Unshackle him," he commanded.

"Shall I remove his wrist irons as well, sir?"

"Yes," he said, "I am certain that there won't be any problems."

"Who are you?" Dao asked.

"I am Lieutenant Elrick Du'Raneurden, fourth in command of the Dragonian soldiers garrisoned here. Follow me. I have much to show you." Turning about, he exited the room and led on. "Guard the prisoners well, Scrimshaw," he said. "The general will be arriving soon."

"Yes, sir!"

Dao quickly surveyed the prison chamber. Five cells faced one another, along the sides of a wide passage some seventy feet in length. The chamber doors were stoutly built and reinforced with iron. Two pony-sized hounds sat patiently beside the hall's entryway, red-furred. Their eyes and fangs were black, and they smelled of soot. Smoke poured from their nostrils as they breathed. The Hounds of Azamod, the Wild Dogs of Hell, servants of evil masters—never had he imagined their real existence, but here they were nonetheless, sitting patiently like faithful hunting dogs! Without weapons, there was no hope of making their escape from here.

"Mind the dogs," Elrick warned, "they are foul-tempered beasts at best." Despite his warning, they barely stirred as they filed past, pausing for just a moment to blow smoke upon them and check their scent. "Come, Dao," he said with barely contained excitement, as if he was talking to his dearest friend, "I have much to show you!" Walking through the heart of a vast prison complex, they entered into an area of vast halls, with stairs and chambers carved for Giants and Elves alike. Vast numbers of Orcs moved about with purposes known only to them, and smaller, more wretched creatures as well. Lesser Orcs and various other Goblin races seemed to mingle freely here without strife, something that he had never heard of before. In one room, he glimpsed a company of Dockalfar soldiers, and there were many Humans among them as well.

So Dragonia is here after all, he thought, *allying themselves with creatures of evil, and no doubt building their strength for a full-scale invasion.* Following closely behind his guide, he did his best to memorize every stair, chamber, and twisting passage that they passed through. There were thousands of soldiers here, countless slaves, and a fortress complex so vast and powerful that it surpassed imagining.

"This was once a great city," Elrick recalled, "perhaps the greatest ever on Tempus. The Orcs built their pyramid on top of its castle ruins, and our own engineers have overseen the reconstruction of the halls that you see before you now. Farad Moor is now the most powerful fortress in the Northern Reaches."

"The perfect site to launch an invasion."

"Come now, my friend," Elrick said, "our nations have been at war for centuries. Surely we are not so naive as to think that either of us could in any way change the happenings of the world around us alone?"

"One man can do much."

"Of course, and we will, but we are enemies by our allegiances only. In another field, I believe that we could be fast friends."

"That remains to be seen."

Coming to the end of a wide thoroughfare with towering arches supporting a roof painted to resemble the night sky, they turned right, entering into a man-sized hallway with a handful of adjoining rooms. The door at the far end of the passage was closed. Two Dragonian soldiers stood guard outside of it, lightly armored, with belted swords and long spears. "Make way, gentlemen," Elrick ordered.

"Yes, sir!" The rightmost soldier soon produced a set of keys, and with a quick turn, he had the door open.

"After you, Dao," Elrick said.

It was a library filled with row upon row of books, scrolls, parchments, and the furniture necessary to properly study them. The room was brightly lit with magic, and a small inquisitive little Gnome sat at one of the tables, almost completely surrounded with books. Little more than the top of his head could be seen above them. A bright globe stood on the table before him, filled with some kind of insects whose abdomens periodically emitted bright flashes of light. "Giant fireflies, I always enjoyed catching them as a child. Their light is a kind of magic all of its own, don't you think?"

"Why have you brought us here?"

"You and Kalor will be guests here for the next six days and nights. You may study any of the resources that you find here. Through the door at the far end of the room is a bath, where you may relieve yourself and bathe at will. Servants will bring you clean clothing, food, and anything else that you might require. I advise you to learn all that you can because in the morning of the seventh day, you will be forced to fight in the Colosseum. If you fail to use your time here wisely, you will both surely die on the first day."

"This is an outrage!" Dao said. "What if we won't fight?"

"Then you will die, but within the pages of this library, you may find a way to die with honor."

"Why not just kill us?" Dao asked, clenching his fists. "You have everything that we had of value."

"Our destinies are not yet certain," Elrick replied. "Prepare yourselves and expect a visitor. There is more arcane knowledge in this library than most wizards ever see in a lifetime. The right wing is my favorite. It is almost entirely Evocation. If I am not mistaken, I believe that is yours as well. Good day, gentlemen." Turning about, he left them alone, ordering the guards to lock the door behind him. A basket of pastries lay on the table with a pitcher of fresh milk.

"Try the blueberry Danish," Kalor said. "It is delicious!"

Dao looked at him incredulously, but Kalor didn't notice, not one bit.

The General's Questions

Shortly after Dao had left them, a second visitor arrived.

"Good afternoon, Scrimshaw. How are the prisoners?"

"They are well, General. A slave has gone to fetch their supper."

"Open all their cells. I wish to speak with them all personally."

"Yes, General." Scrimshaw performed his duties quickly and then returned to his post.

"Carmen, Carmen, Carmen," he said. "You have become a fine leader. It is a pity that things have to end like this."

"I know you," she spat. "You are the one who planned all of this!"

"And I couldn't have done it without you! You and your sister are so different," he said with his hands clasped behind his back, "but equally beautiful."

"What are you going to do to her?"

"Oh, she's just insurance really. Once you are all safely dead in the arena and Safehaven is sacked, she will be spared. She knows nothing, and for that reason, there is no need to kill her."

"You bastard!"

"Now, now," he soothed, "you should be proud. Without your courage, I might never have acquired the staff. You and your friends have done me a great service, and for that, I will spare your families. For the rest of you, I am afraid that such leniency is impossible because you know too much. My priests will be here soon to heal your remaining wounds. Rest well, for one week from today, you will all die in the Colosseum. Don't worry, it will be an honorable death."

"Son of a bitch!"

"Farewell, Carmen." A few paces down the hall, he entered the cell of a very angry Dwarf.

"Kur, son of Moldrin," he said, "I am Vlad. Well met."

"Well met? You dirty stone-licker!" He strained at his chains. It seemed for a moment that he might actually be capable of breaking them.

"Your father is an interesting man," Vlad said. "I can see where you get your spark from!"

"What have you done with him?"

"Oh, he is someplace safe. He will be among the spectators when you face Gorthog in the arena."

"Gorthog?"

"Yes, Gorthog. He is a dragon, very large and always hungry."

"Dragon?"

"Don't worry, Kur, your death will come swiftly. I just wanted to thank you for all your help."

"A thousand curses on you, Dark Elf! I will have my revenge against you!"

"We shall see, Master Dwarf, but it will be a shame if your father has to pay with his own life as well." Straining with all his might, Kur could find no more words for his nemesis.

"Ah," Vlad said, "the Lady Greylinx, I presume."

"I'll stand for none of your lies," she answered. "Just kill us and be done with it!"

"Execution," Vlad pondered, "an interesting idea, to say the least, but no way for a Liosalfar swordmaiden to die. Instead, I will grant you the opportunity to die with honor in the arena."

"So generous," she purred. "Tell me, Fell Commander, just what do you hope to accomplish with the Duaredheim Staff? Surely no mortal can hope to wield it without disaster."

"The staff is the key to my ultimate victory. With it, I will create a new world order."

"You will bring about the end of the world!"

"Ragnarok!" Dartin cried out from across the hall.

"It will be an end," Vlad said. "Of that you can be sure, but it will also be a new beginning. Dragonia is on the brink of a war to end all wars. The Empire will rain its destruction across the globe unless it too is destroyed. I am a soldier of Dragonia, loyal to its people. Fate makes us her pawns, but I shall not surrender to her!"

"Surely there is another way? The staff was hidden for a reason. Only its Creators were wise enough to wield it."

"I am afraid that there is no other way, Karina, and I have all of you to thank for my coming success!"

"Then face me blade to blade so that I may end your madness!"

"Oh?" Vlad said amusedly. "I would relish the challenge, but alas, it cannot be. Some other day perhaps and on another field, but not now, not when my victory is so close at hand."

"Coward!"

"Oh, I assure you that that is not the case, Elf maid. Perhaps we will meet again in the afterlife. Maybe then we can have our duel."

"I will pray for it."

"Prepare yourself, Karina. Seven days from now, you will fight and you will die."

"Well met, Druid," Vlad said, stepping into his cell.

"Why don't you just get it over with?"

"All in due time."

"I have nothing to say to you."

"As you wish, Leander," Vlad said, clasping his hands behind his back. "You have somehow managed to continue your training without a master, and that is truly exceptional."

"Atran-Doru!"

"Yes, I now wear your blade beside my father's. Both swords are masterworks."

"So it was you who saved us."

"Very perceptive, Leander, but more precisely, it was my priestess who did so."

"Why did you even bother? You could have just taken what you wanted and left us to rot."

"It is complicated. Just suffice it to say that I needed you alive."

"So why kill us now? You have what you want. Surely we are no threat to you now."

"The forces that I command will suffer no weakness in their leaders. Regrettably, you must all die before thousands of witnesses."

"Then you are a bastard!"

"We all must die, Druid. We can either run from Death in terror or face him with pride and honor."

"What have you done with Robbin?"

"She is safe for now, and when you are gone, she will be returned to her home unharmed. You have my word."

His eyes filled with tears and then firmed with anger and resolve. "Atran-Doru will not bear your ownership for long!"

"He and I have already come to a mutually beneficial agreement. I have need of his power in the upcoming campaign."

"He will not stand for it!"

"I assure you, Master Druid, that he has no choice. The secret is in the will, Leander, and mine cannot be swayed!"

"You cannot control the staff. No one can. You will unbalance nature itself."

"The industry of Dragonia has already begun to affect the world. The great forests of my country are being felled to build battleships, our factories burn coal to forge steel, smoke is filling the sky, and Tempus warms all because our leader has a taste for war! Nature will be undone with or without my help, Druid! My wish is for something greater. Fill your heart with that hope, Leander, and I swear that I shall not squander your sacrifice."

"I pray that we meet again," Leander said defiantly, "under different circumstances."

"We all have our own destinies," Vlad replied. "If you believe in the faith of your friend, then you know that our fates are already written. Personally, I believe in writing my own, but is that pen and ink our own? We may never know. Pray thee well, Leander, because in seven days, you go to meet Silvaneus."

"You may leave now," Leander said, his tears still flowing. "I have no more words for you."

Vlad turned then, pausing for a moment in the hall, for he too was deeply affected. Squaring his shoulders, he steeled his resolve. Sacrifices had to be made in war.

"Odin's son, Odin's son," Vlad said, tapping his fingers on his scabbards, "and just like I predicted, we meet again."

"My father should have killed you in the Halls of the Dead!"

"He may have desired to do so," Vlad said, "but there is a grand price to pay when gods meddle in the affairs of men. If he had killed me, then he would have undone his own future and the fate of Valhalla itself. No, no, Dartin, your father has done all that he can for you. Now you are on your own."

"Unchain me and we shall see what I can do," Dartin taunted.

"No doubt you would enjoy unleashing the power of the runes," Vlad said, "but you must think of your mother. My associates are far less merciful than I am."

"I will bring this fortress down upon you!"

"Save your empty threats. You are mine now. There is no possible escape, and you will have no revenge!"

"You will bring about the end of us all. Unite the staff, and you will release Loki from his bonds!"

"We have no way of knowing that for sure," Vlad said. "The Duaredheim used it to create order in the Universe. I shall wield it to create a new one. It is the only way that my people can be free."

"Then you are my enemy."

"I could hope for nothing less! Fare thee well, Odin's son, and save your prayers for the arena."

"And last but not the least," Vlad said, "Tariq Longstride, wandering ranger and long-lost son of a forgotten family."

"Return my sword and face me like a man!"

"Alas, for we are ever at the mercy of our times. We are both men of honor, and in a more perfect world, I would gladly meet your challenge."

"I accept!"

"Then you would gladly throw your life away? You, the last of your family's line?"

"I will meet them again."

"Soon enough," Vlad agreed, "but my purpose is too great to duel with you now. I will, however, grant you your dying wish, ranger. You will face the eldest warriors of the Followers of the Moon in the Colosseum Arena, the very Orcs who slew your family and raped your mother. You will surely die, but if you are strong enough and lucky enough, you may have your revenge."

"I will kill them all!"

"I will be watching," Vlad said. "But know this, Ranger, I hold you and your friends in the highest regard. It is only with the deepest regret that I must see your end."

"Then let us go and end your foolish mission."

"I am afraid that that is impossible," Vlad said. "Soon after your deaths, we march on Safehaven."

"Safehaven?"

"Yes, Master Longstride, my orders are to march on Safehaven as soon as the mountain passes are free of snow. Once Khan is taken, a fleet of dragon ships will land with an invasion force greater than any ever before assembled. Within ten years, the nation of Fermenor will become part of the Dragonian Empire."

"*If* you take Khan."

"When is the only uncertainty," Vlad replied. "Everything will go according to my master plan."

"If a single one of us escapes to warn the king," Tariq said, "your plans will be undone."

"It is too late for the king to muster sufficient resistance, even if he knew today. Focus on your revenge," Vlad instructed. "It is the last thing that you will know before the end."

"We shall see, General, we shall see!"

"Until we meet again, ranger," Vlad said. "Scrimshaw, lock down the cell block!"

"Yes, Commander."

Their doors were swiftly closed and locked, the confident footsteps of their nemesis slowly receding into the distance. They whispered to one another for a long while after that. Somehow, they had to find a way.

THE LIBRARY

One day became two, then three, and more. Sleeping little, they poured their every energy into learning. Just like Elrick had said, they were in a library filled with secrets and knowledge meticulously collected for centuries. Every shelf was packed with spell formulae from every known school of magic and other schools as yet untested.

Time was their enemy, their only limitation. They decided to remain focused. Instead of dabbling in a wide range of magic, they concentrated on their own specialties. Kalor poured through every treatise of Illusion that he could find, and Dao focused upon the disciplines of the warrior mage. He learned spells to call forth fire and lightning, magic that could conceal the approach of an invading army, warn sleeping soldiers of a trespassing thief, or undermine castle walls. He studied all these things and more, committing as many of the formula to memory as he could and scribing them onto the blank scrolls with which they had been provided. They could not know if these would be taken away, but the writing was a necessary part of the learning, and so they did it anyway.

Kalor advanced himself further in six days than he had done in six years under his mentor. This wasn't due to a lack of skill on the part of his master, but rather to a lack of focus on his own. Now the prospect of their unavoidable deaths provided suitable motivation indeed. He was determined to become the illusionist that Uldrick had seen in him. If nothing else, he could find some honor in that before he died. He started out with the simplest spells, and he soon perfected the art of the ventriloquist, refined his knowledge of phantasms, and mastered the art of invisibility. If he had a few more days, he could have learned how to conjure illusions of substance, magical monsters that would fight for him while his magic lasted, but they had but six days and no more. On the eve of that day, they met their nemesis.

The library door opened often. Usually it was one of the servants bringing them food, or an Orc emissary named Cage, who would ask them if any of their needs had not been met. Kalor would often answer with the request of freedom, but Cage would politely say that that was one of the things that he could not grant. When the door opened, it was neither servant nor Orc but the commanding general himself.

"How do you like my library?" he said. "Magnificent, is it not?"

"It is," Dao agreed.

"I trust that you have not squandered your time here."

"Don't worry," Kalor said, "we have plenty of surprises."

"Excellent. At dawn, you will be taken in chains to the arena holding cells, and there you will await your doom."

"And what of our families?" Dao pleaded. "Will you have them killed as well?"

"You have my word that they will not be harmed," Vlad said. "They know nothing that might harm me. They have neither seen the full scale of this fortress, nor learned anything of my plans."

"And once we are dead, what then?"

"Once you are dead, I will make my final preparations for the invasion of Safehaven."

Enraged at the prospect of his country in flames, Dao tried to summon his wizardly might, but for some reason, his magic was lost to him.

"Ah, Dao," Vlad said. "Magic will not work in here. This entire portion of the fortress contains minerals that prevent the use of magic. Save your strength for tomorrow's gladiatorial games."

"And what of my master?" Kalor asked.

"Uldrick will stay with us for a while. He is useful but dangerous, and he could cause considerable mischief if he ever escaped. When my plans are complete, he will be returned to his home."

"Even if you empty these lands," Dao said, "it will not equal the forces of Lord Cherek."

"Oh, there you are wrong, my friend. My scientist has developed creatures that will tip the scales in our favor, and my assault will come on the heels of a much larger invasion. Dragonia will bring her entire strength to bear throughout your realm. Within ten years, this war will finally come to an end."

"And you will use the staff to defeat us," Kalor said.

"Let us sit together and have tea," Vlad urged, "so that the two of you might know that your sacrifices have not been for nothing."

He clapped twice, and the chamber door again opened. Servants quickly brought tea and crumpets upon a platter of silver. "Come and sit with me as equals. Let us forget for the moment that we are at war."

Reluctantly, they sat with him, for what other choice did they have. Pouring the tea, he served them with practiced skill, then sat back and took a muffin for himself. They sipped and dined. And all the while, he asked them many questions about their family and their lands, as if he was a distant uncle come from far away to visit. In return, he told them about himself, from his lineage to his upbringing and how he had come to command so large of a garrison. When they learned what he planned to use the Duaredheim's Staff for, they trembled, for what sane man would dare to challenge the gods themselves? They talked long into the night and learned much of each other's natures, but there were some secrets that he would not reveal. "There is one small loophole in your plan," Kalor said. "You still have not completed the staff."

"Unless you have somehow acquired it," Dao reasoned, "the final piece still remains on the Ice Moon."

"A small hurdle," Vlad said. "I will soon travel there to claim it."

"Travel there? The legends say that the dragons of old could travel through space, but their kind has disappeared from the world."

"I will need no dragon to fly to the moon. In my youth, I discovered a Duaredheim star vessel."

"Star vessel?"

"A flying ship that can travel to the stars."

"Ha!" Kalor said. "No such thing exists."

“It does not matter if you believe me or not,” Vlad replied, “because by tomorrow night you will most likely be dead.” Emptying his cup, he placed it resolutely back upon the tray, slid his chair backwards, and stood. Bending slightly at the waist, he bowed to them. “I must now be on my way, gentlemen. I did so enjoy our conversation. Without your help, none of this would have been possible.”

They stood as well. “Our fight is far from over, Vlad,” Dao said. “If there is a way, we will find it.”

“I can hope for nothing less, my friend. Rest now, the slave masters will come for you at dawn.”

“This isn’t over!” Kalor promised.

Vlad stared intently into their eyes. An irresistible force invaded their minds. They swooned. Their knees buckled, and they knew no more.

“It soon will be,” Vlad replied. “Farewell.”

The Arena

The sun rose on the seventh day, and as was preordained, the slave master came with a large host. Armed with clubs and staves, Carmen and her rangers were shackled together one after another. Tariq could not bear the Orcs' foul touch, and so he struggled, but his efforts were useless, because an Orc shaman had cast a spell of weakness upon them. Once their bonds were secure, they were led past the hounds and out of the prison.

Walking briskly, a second detachment of guards soon joined them, escorting them through the Halls of Farad Moor for over a mile. The last leg of their journey was along a wide thoroughfare, fifty feet wide, with arched ceilings of comparable height. Countless passageways large enough to accommodate giants branched away from it at regular intervals along its entire length. Its walls were painted in varying styles, depicting both the primitive animal images of the Orcs and the sophisticated artistry of the Dockalfar. The floor was well-polished stone, immaculate and perfectly level. They followed this road yet another mile, past incredible vaulted cathedrals, public baths, and even a mess hall filled with thousands of feasting soldiers. Fifty paces beyond the arch of the cafeteria door was a titanic portal. Built with beams carved from massive tree trunks, hinged and riveted with adamant, its double doors stood over forty feet in height and twenty feet in width. A pair of Giants stood guard beside it, armored in mail and holding massive spears.

"Open the gates!" the slave master commanded.

Leaning their weapons against the wall, the giants lifted the beam that barred the door, grasped steel rings large enough to surround two large men, and pulled. The doors were heavy, even for them, but they were equal to the task, and the way was soon open.

The roar of cheers filled the way beyond the portal, the road coming to an abrupt end a hundred yards ahead. Another set of doors like the last ended the passage, and it was clear that they had entered the Colosseum. Spectators mingled in the very hallway with them, climbing stairs into stadium seats or buying food and drink from vendors. The Slave-master then led them down a dark side passage, past more guards and a handful of hounds posted beside closed doors. The crowd's fervent cheers continued, so loudly that the sound passed through the stone walls of the place, vibrating with excitement and echoing through every chamber. They walked down stairs and up again, through long curved passageways and beyond until they came to an expansive holding area contained within walls barred with steel and with windows opening into the gigantic arena. A barred gate served as the cell's arena door along the far wall. Several prisoners had already been left there, and Dao and Kalor were among them. Two guards stood watch by the cell entrance and acted swiftly to open it when the slave master appeared. One by one, their shackles were removed, and they were shoved into the cage.

"Armor and weapons have been provided to you," the slave master told them. "I recommend that you wear them. When your name is called, enter the arena. If you refuse to enter on your own, you will be dragged out by whatever means necessary. Good luck, gladiators!"

The slave master and his entourage soon left, and only the two cell guards remained.

There was a sudden silence outside, then a scream, followed by cheers.

"What's happening?" Carmen asked a young Elven captive.

"Two Highland barbarians were fighting. Now there is only one left standing—their chief, I believe."

"What do they face?"

"Prepare yourself first, Woman. Sometimes they take people before they can arm themselves. The equipment is along the far wall."

Moving quickly, she saw that her friends were already picking through the odd pieces of arms that were available. "It has been an honor, Carmen," Leander said. "I would never have wanted it any other way."

"We are not dead yet," she replied, slipping a rusty suit of mail over her head. "We have been in worse scrapes than this."

"I wish that I was so optimistic," Kalor said. "I have learned many new spells, but I think that the general has no intention of letting us live."

"You are right, Kalor," Dao said. "He just hopes that we might last a little longer."

"For a greater spectacle," Tariq agreed.

"The power of the runes escapes me," Dartin observed while testing the weight of a sword. "There is something strange about this place."

"We can only hope that your magic will work in the arena."

Suddenly, a great roar erupted from the crowd.

"The barbarian chief has fallen," the young Elf said. "Soon they will call out the next combatants."

Dressed and armed, they moved alongside of him and peered into the arena.

"What is your name, Elf?" Kur asked.

"I remember him," Karina said. "He was one of Baron Duching's soldiers."

"I am Brent of the Crumbling Cliffs," he replied. "I was with Baron Duchings when Nordtown fell."

"Who is that one?" Kur said, pointing to the opposite side of the cage, "and why is he naked?"

A lone Elf sat cross-legged there. His body was covered in scars. Even his face, once fair, bore the brunt of many battles. He was wearing only a loincloth. His feet were bare, his hands heavily callused, and his body lean. His head was shaved bare, and torn stumps were all that was left of his ears. His eyebrows, if ever he had any, were now simply a mass of scars. His eyes were ocean-blue, large and piercing.

"He is Kolren, son of Garad, Lord of the Berserks. He will not wear armor against foes that he feels are unequal to his skill, even if it costs him his life."

"My father once told me a story," Tariq said, "of an ancient tribe of Elves who lived like nomads on the Northern Steppes. It was said that their horsemanship was surpassed only by their ferocity. They were so savage that even Death feared to claim their fallen spirits, for even in the afterlife, they fight on. They disappeared over a century ago, and no one knows what happened to them."

"Kolren, son of Garad, comes forth," a commanding voice introduced.

The arena gate opened. Four heavily armed Orcs flanked the passage leading outside. The battered Elf stood, taking up a pair of swords that he had leaned against the wall beside him. More than walk, he flowed, his every movement controlled, balanced, and yet without conscious effort.

"Fight well, Kolren," the largest Orc said.

"I will miss you, Twisted Fang."

"It has been an honor," the Orc answered.

When he entered the arena, the cheers of forty thousand spectators filled the air, but he heard none of it. His heart was filled with the song of his people, the battle song of a lost race. Its rousing rhythm filled him with strength far beyond normal limits, allowing him to block out pain and drive his body to superhuman limits.

Going into battle for perhaps the last time, he promised his father that he would know no fear and his mother that he would see her soon. Standing proudly, he awaited his next opponent. He had long ago forgotten the day of his birth, and he knew not what season it was. He had been a captive and a slave since childhood. His memories still held on to what were important, things like his mother's face and the face of the one who had killed his father.

The great gates of the arena opened then, and the floor of the Colosseum trembled as Kolren's gargantuan adversary entered. When the crowd saw who would face him, their cheering was like the crashing surf of a stormy sea.

Kolren, Son of Garad

"Finally, I come face-to-face with thee, Kolren!" the Titan Uzul exclaimed. "I have waited five hundred years to destroy the House of Garad!"

"I am all that remains, Titan, and by my blood oath, I swear that you shall fall!"

"Your father died easily by my sword. His head adorned my lodge pole for a hundred years."

"My father was exhausted from battle when you stabbed him in the back."

"You lie!"

"Nay, I was but a child of seven seasons, held flat beneath my mother's dying body, helpless but to watch when you then slew my father like a coward!"

"You will pay for your insults, son of Garad. Prepare to die!"

"You cannot kill a soul that has died a thousand times, Titan! You will see." Moving with the speed of a hunting leopard, he sidestepped behind one of the arena's great stone pillars and waited with his blades held low.

With each step of Uzul's feet, the ground shook. He was enraged and perhaps even a little embarrassed, which only made his anger grow with every breath. In size, he was among the largest of his kind, soaring to over twenty-five feet in height. Kolren was little more than a tiny child to him, indeed, little more than an insect. Kolren, an Elf of the Northern Steppes, weighed no more than one hundred and fifty pounds while Uzul weighed easily twenty times that. Juggernauts from ancient times, most of his race were giants of a kind and gentle nature. Greed and desire would sometimes tempt them, but most would never call an Elf their enemy. Uzul was not one of these types of Titans.

Immortal, unless they meet some untimely end, Titans were among the first creations of the gods. Uzul was one of the first of these, but his heart was corrupted by greed and later driven to evil by the words of a cunning Elf of the Underworld. He became a tool, a powerful pawn at the head of Lothdea's ancient army. In time, his soul was bathed in blood, rewarded with gold and jewels until his own people were long forgotten, and only his evil desires remained. It was this kind of Titan that Kolren now faced, one tiny Elf of the North against an adversary proven in battle for ten thousand years.

"Where are your people now?" Uzul provoked. "You are all alone in a city of enemies, and your people are memories and dust. They were too weak to survive, yet Uzul remains!"

"Then your task remains undone, for Kolren, son of Garad, Elf of the Wandering Nation, still remains."

"But very soon, you will join them!" Charging with surprising speed, he slammed into the back of the great pillar protecting Kolren. Ten feet thick and three stories tall, its marble stood polished and glistening, rising from the arena floor with twenty of its brethren spaced throughout. It had withstood centuries of gladiatorial games, but even its massive strength was no match for Uzul; it cracked, shattered, and toppled. Dust filled the air, obscuring vision, and Uzul raised his giant sword for the killing stroke. When the dust had settled, Kolren wasn't there.

"Ha, ha, ha!" Uzul laughed. "It seems that you've been crushed flat. That was too easy."

The crowd greeted his swift victory with loud boos. Their spectacle was stolen. There was no gore and no pain-filled screams to satisfy their lust for blood.

"What an outrage," a wealthy merchant commented. "Twenty-five drachmas and this is the great sport that Vlad has promised? Thank goodness I didn't bet on this match."

"I just lost a hundred on the Elf," his comrade said. "I've never seen him lose before. It was inevitable. The Liosalfar was old."

"No, wait! Look there, at the opposite end of the arena, crouching low. It's him!"

And indeed it was, for there was Kolren, alive and well, completely unscathed.

"By Lothdea's hand, I never would have believed it. Another hundred on the Elf!" he said to the bookkeeper.

If Uzul had known that his victory was not yet assured, then he might not have been so quick to celebrate; as it was, the crowd told him with their hushed silence and then their cheers. He barely had time to turn.

Kolren struck him on the run. In the span of four great strides, his blades lashed out eight times, slashing Uzul's feet and ankles, and his retreat was even swifter, almost faster than the eye could follow.

Uzul roared in pain and disbelief. If his feet had been bare, Kolren's blows could have debilitated him, but his tall boots were fashioned from mammoth hide, thick, protective, and strong, and the Elf's most powerful blows only stung him. His knees were protected by two great shields of adamant, his waist and groin by steel, and his body by a suit of mail adorned with a hundred enemy skulls. His head was unprotected, save for a crop of flame red hair and a tangled beard that had grown so long that he tucked it into his belt to control it. In anger, he swung his sword in a great swath all around himself, and two more pillars were laid low. "I'll destroy you!" he screamed. He lay about himself, right and left, spinning, slashing. His sword was gargantuan, over fifteen feet in length and two feet thick, and there were few mortal beings that could lift it even and inch, but Uzul swung it with ease. "Stand and fight me if you dare, little man!"

"I do not fear you, Titan! Nor did my father! We were three hundred against ten thousand, and if we were three hundred more, the battle horn would have blown the other way."

"You ramble on because you know that death is near! I cannot see you, Kolren, but soon, not a pillar will stand to hide you." Uzul then began to set about himself, laying all the pillars in the arena low. Luckily, they had been raised, only to improve the spectacle of the countless battles that had been fought there since its creation, for if their presence was structural, then Uzul's blows would have brought the mountain down upon them all. One by one they fell or shattered, and with each swing, Uzul's maniacal rage grew. Where was his enemy? There was no doubt that he was hiding like a frightened mouse. Remove the brush or log that hides him, and he runs beneath another. Well, Uzul would see to it that not one log remained.

The betting in the arena stands grew feverish. Kolren had become a huge favorite, an underdog survivor of over a hundred contests. Riddled with scars, his skin reflected a life filled only with strife, and yet, somehow, he lived. Uzul, his giant opponent, was a veteran of countless wars and individual battles against all manner of beings and mythical beasts. They were both undefeated champions. If Kolren lost, he would be no more. Uzul could neither afford to lose his life nor his face before the incredible hosting of his allies.

It truly was the match of a century! Commander Vlad had outdone himself.

"Five hundred Drachmas on the Elf!"

"A thousand upon Uzul!"

And so, on and on it went. For each pillar that fell, a hundred new bets were made, with each roar of titanic rage, the crowd's cheers grew. It was a deafening tumult, an adrenaline-charged spectacle the likes of which no one had ever before seen. Where was the Elf? Pillars were falling everywhere, clouds of dust rising from the floor. Someone would exclaim that they'd seen him, or at least something moving about upon the floor. Was it Kolren or just an eddying swirl of sand?

What no one knew was that Kolren had never been in any of those places. It was not he moving about through the dusty clouds like a jaguar. It was not he tormenting Uzul from behind a pillar. He was no swirl of dust, no warrior phantom. He had, however, quietly, secretly, leaped onto Uzul's great skirt of mail and climbed like lightning, sight unseen onto the Titan's immense shoulders. Whispering in his ears, as if he was a shadowy cat just behind the next obstacle, he fed Uzul's anger, until his rage was itself like unto a real thing.

One might ask how he remained hidden from the eyes of thousands of bloodthirsty fans, and one might answer that perhaps their eyes were all drawn to the spectacle of Uzul's incredible power, or maybe it was the fact that Kolren had crawled beneath the crimson mane of the Giant, and no one save the resident fleas could have seen him. Whatever the case, Kolren continued his taunts, his whisperings, until the pillars were made rubble and no stone big enough to hide a diminutive Elf remained.

He was the last of his people, both tough and cunning, a genius in the art of warcraft, and this was the final enemy whom he wished to face before accepting death. The revenge of his fallen race was finally within his reach. Six feet away, Uzul breathed heavily. His voice was a slavering mess of confusion, his heartbeat pulsing hard through his veins. A short climb, one fatal cut, and Uzul's life's blood would burst unquenchably. It would be over, the Titan's end, but Kolren knew that such a victory would be hollow; it would be brains over brawn, without honor, and he wouldn't do it, not that way.

Resting for a time, he paused to remember his life and his home, and suddenly he longed to wander the steppes of that land again. His people were gone, but he knew where their spirits still lived. They walked the Northern Steppes, dancing beneath the stars, singing songs of love and of war; these were songs that he still knew. His people lived on as long as he remained. He owed it to them to survive. He suddenly understood just how it might be possible; for the first time in four decades as a slave, he thought that he had a chance.

Elrin Von Mathers

"Where could he be?" Dartin asked. "I could've sworn that he was just behind the last pillar to fall."

"He may be beneath it," Leander answered.

"No way," Kur said, "that was too easy."

"I agree," Tariq said. "He moves much too fast for that."

"But he might have been too hurt," Carmen guessed, "and a little too slow."

"Wait!" Kalor said. "Someone comes."

They watched the hall leading to their arena-side cell. Some commotion was occurring among the guards just outside. Maybe the warden was coming to release them into the arena to sweeten the pot. All of them listened with dread, the roar of the crowd seeming somehow distant and muffled.

"Prisoners, stand to the rear to receive your commander!" their guard roared.

Keys rattled, mechanisms cranked, and the door to the holding cells was opened. A tall dark figure entered, silent save for the sound of his well-heeled soles striking the floor in a quiet, purposeful cadence. Carmen looked to her friends for courage and they to her. When they looked toward the hall again, a familiar face greeted them.

It was Vlad. "I couldn't help but wondering what you thought of my little spectacle?"

"You sick bastard!" Carmen said.

"Now, now, I'll have none of that. Guards, leave us at once and secure the door. I'll call you when I'm ready."

"Yes, Commander," the massive Orc replied. The door soon shut with metallic finality, portending some great doom soon to befall them.

"Look closely, my friends," Vlad said, "beneath the veil of the glamour that I have created."

"Elrin!" Kalor exclaimed. "But how?"

"You, of all people, should know, Kalor."

"An illusion."

"Of course, but a very powerful one. The Dockalfar are masters of magic, and many of their wards weaken my spell. I won't be able to keep it up for much longer. That's why I have combined magic with a detailed disguise, should my spells fail."

"Can you get us out of here?"

"I have glimpsed an incident in my crystal ball that should help us all to escape. Be ready, for in a few minutes' time, an unexpected and momentous event will occur outside. Here, Kalor, take this package. Within it you will find a map of the tunnels beneath the arena."

"But how will we get through the cell doors?" Dao asked.

"Inside the package is a small set of picks. Kalor should be able to open the locks with them. The guard will be distracted. Subdue him and make for the tunnels. I have hidden your weapons and armor in a small chamber at the southern end of this hall. You must move through the passages with all due speed, for Vlad will soon discover your escape."

"But what of our families?" Carmen said.

"I have a spy inside the fortress," Elrin explained. "She has drugged the guards assigned to your loved ones' cells and freed them. They should already be waiting for you beneath the arena."

"Where do we go from there?" Tariq asked.

"The tunnels will end in an ancient ruin in the deep mines. I will try to meet you there with my company. If I don't make it, head for the river. It'll be hard going, but at least it's a chance. You have no chance if you stay here."

"Hurry! The lock, Kalor. There is no time. I must go." And with that, the glamour that was Elrin faded, and only Vlad remained.

"Prepare to die, my friends. Uzul will need more blood to satisfy his thirst this night!" His deep laughter was haunting, merciless, just like the man he was supposed to be. "Open, guard! I may call for them when Uzul has finished with the Berserker Lord."

"Yes, Commander." And the door shut with a clank, mechanisms tumbled, and the lock slid shut.

"Hurry, Kalor," Tariq said. "Everyone, ready yourselves. We may never get another chance."

"It feels like a setup," Kur warned. "I don't trust that wizard."

"Setup or no," Dao observed, "it seems like a fighting chance at least."

"What's happening out there?"

"Uzul has crushed every stone big enough to hide the Elf," Carmen said. "His mouth is coated with a white froth from rage. I can't see Kolren anywhere."

"Kalor!" Kur said.

"I've almost got it. There, it's done."

"Can you see the guard?" Tariq said.

"Yes, his back's turned to watch the arena."

"Get ready to head for the door."

"Vanamoinen protect me," Carmen prayed. "The Titan is talking to himself."

"Not himself," Karina said. "To Kolren. I can see his right boot. The crazy wanderer has climbed the Giant and is speaking in his ear!"

"Tariq, it looks like we're about to get that break."

Wanderer's Revenge

"Uzul," Kolren whispered, "I am here."

"Where are you, cursed one?"

"Here, can you not feel my steel against your throat."

"What? I will crush you flat like a fly upon my forehead!"

"Then we will join each other in death!"

"Your tiny swords cannot kill me."

"My sword rests beside your heartbeat. Can you not feel it?"

"I..." Uzul stammered, "I c-can."

"Then by the gods, you are going to take me outside to the light of day, or we both are going to die here and now."

"They'll never let you escape!"

"No, but you'd better see to it that I do." He pressed his point, and Uzul gasped in pain; he knew that he'd finally lost a battle.

"Now, quickly! To the great door!"

It was then that the crowd realized that something was terribly wrong. The great commanders were shouting orders to mobilize their troops and secure doorways and so on. The bookkeepers were holding all bets until one of the combatants was proven defeated. It was too little too late because Uzul was only ten giant strides from the tremendous double doors that exited the arena and led to the great hall.

The doors were built like all those in the Colosseum, of giant cedar trunks bound in adamant and riveted with iron, but even they couldn't withstand the pommel stroke of a Titan. In one incredible blow, the four-foot-thick timber that secured the doors' opposite side was shattered, and the pathway was open.

"Don't let them escape alive!" the crowd heard their commander say. "Bring them down if you must bring the whole mountain down upon them!"

It was the most opportune moment. All the battalions had gathered in the arena to witness the match of the century. They were unarmored and without weapons, drunk and full, their leaders even drunker. By the time specific orders were given, Uzul was a hundred yards closer to the front gates of the pyramid.

The great hall was a straight tunnel of immense size. It was built to allow even the largest of beings to enter the compound, or in the case of a captive dragon or perhaps a Titan, the arena. It was a weakness of sorts, a way for an enemy army to penetrate the defenses, and because of this, all sorts of siege weaponry was set and ready for defense. Yet on this day, there were only a few of the lowest-ranking souls left to man them, and these soldiers were more than a little surprised to see Uzul.

"My Lord Uzul," they asked, "where are you headed in such a hurry?"

"Open the gates!" Uzul commanded, for even he couldn't breach the mighty portal that sealed the pyramid shut. They were accustomed to him giving orders, and so, even though it seemed strange, they did as he commanded, partly because they were of little rank and partly because they were terrified. The great winch began its groan, and the doors slowly opened. Uzul put forth his might to them, and they swung faster.

"Stop them!" their Dark Commander screamed from down the hall. They must not escape. Bring the mangonels to bear!" The terrible defenses were hastily readied, their mechanisms cranked, the devices swung into position.

Uzul was nearly through the gates when destruction was unleashed from behind him. The mangonels were devastating. What they lacked in accuracy, they possessed in firepower, and a thousand barbs were launched from them all at once. The soldiers at the gates were pierced through in a hundred places, the walls barraged, and Uzul was stung countless times. He was a Titan, and the greatest of beings, but even he couldn't have withstood the onslaught without his armor. Fifty bolts struck his boots, but the mammoth hide withstood the brunt of them. His thighs received the worst punishment, and twenty bolts struck him where his mail didn't reach. His back was lashed hundreds of times, and fifty enemy skulls were shattered, his chain mail dented, but somehow, his flesh and his heart below remained unharmed. The Elf at his throat would surely have been slain, if not for Uzul's great mane, for so thick it was, that not one arrow passed through it to harm him. Uzul strode on.

"Faster!" his rider exclaimed, and Uzul began to run. The earth shook beneath his feet, like a herd of charging bison.

The gates of the citadel trembled with the gathering fury of their master. The great weapons required time to reload. The soldiers of the pyramid were slow to muster.

"Run!" the Dark Commander screamed. "Revel in freedom while you can, for Death is on your heels!"

Uzul ran and ran, the miles sweeping beneath them, but his leg wounds bled freely, and his incredible strength began to fade.

"Why do you stumble, Titan?"

"A great weakness has come upon me. My death is near."

"What enfeebles you?"

"Many bolts have pierced the flesh of my legs, and my blood has left me."

"Drop your sword and sit."

"Will you now finish me? I am broken, defeated. My heart is wholly evil, and death will surely propel me into Hell. I can neither remember my mother, nor my father."

"Revenge compels me to kill you."

It was at that moment that Uzul, the mightiest Titan that ever lived, passed out from loss of blood.

"Uzul?" And even though the Berserker Lord tried to rouse him, his enemy was past his ability to respond. Slumping against the rocky outcropping that he'd rested against, Uzul moved no more.

Kolren's ultimate victory was stolen from him, but for the first time in countless years of battle and torture, he was free. In minutes, he was able to build a fire with sparks from his sword's blade and a great clump of flame-red beard.

Quickly, almost mercifully, he drew the arrows from Uzul's body and cauterized the Titan's wounds. He would have many scars. He might live or he might die, but the Titan's death wouldn't dishonor his ancestors or Kolren himself. Somehow, he knew that they would meet again. Perhaps then his family would be avenged, but now all that he wanted to do was run, not in fear that he was being pursued, because he knew no fear, but rather because he was the last of his race, and he wanted the spirits of his people to feel the life in his lungs, the beating of his heart, and the joy of freedom beneath the stars one last time. Kolren ran.

Free for the first time in untold years, he ran until his heart's joy was satisfied, and when he was done, he knew not where he was, for he knew not where he'd left from. The region and mountains around him were unknown to him, and the stories of his father about other lands couldn't grant him clues enough to deduce where he'd ended up. Ravenously hungry, he foraged. With his sword, he fashioned a spear and harpooned three fat trout of a kind unknown to him. They were colorful, with bright-colored speckles and a prominent pink stripe along their midsection. To honor the gods of the sky, he named them rainbow trout, and they've been known by that name ever since. He then built a fire, roasted the trout, and his hunger was at last satisfied. Unsure of what to do next, he meditated. Uzul, if he lived, would soon seek vengeance against him with an army of Orcs. He was a great warrior, and indeed he could be titled the Lord of the Berserks (after the fact that he was the last of his kind left on the planet), but long life had brought with it a kind of wisdom, and he knew that even he would probably die against such odds, so he chose instead to move on. Let Uzul see if he could catch him and then let them rue that day!

Kolren had built his fire next to a vast boggy marshland. Miles and miles of its tangled wetness lay before him. Dangers untold certainly lived within it. Venturing there would be foolhardy at best, insane to anyone with a little common sense. Even a Titan and an army of Orcs would find it to be a deadly quagmire. He smiled.

Tariq's Fall

Here begins the tale of how Tariq Longstride, son of Eonid and Oswin, fell.

Kalor opened the door. Its hinges squawked, but the guards didn't notice. They had left their posts in order to better see the incredible struggle outside. By the time they noticed that their prisoners were escaping, they were pummeled by two Elves and an amazingly powerful Dwarf. Tariq raised his sword to finish them.

"Not that way, laddy," Kur said, catching his forearm on the down stroke. "Don't forget your honor!"

"They are Followers of the Moon, murderers every one," Tariq swore.

"But they are helpless," Brent said.

"So was my mother when they raped her!"

"We are not like them," Kur stated. "If you cut them down, you are no different than they are."

Tariq lowered his sword, no less enraged.

"Not like this, laddy," Kur said. "They are just pups. There is no way that they were among the ones who killed your family. There will be plenty more to kill before we get clear of here."

The ranger's eyes softened slightly. He nodded that he was again in control of himself.

"Lock them in the cell," Carmen ordered.

"If you don't mind," Brent asked, "I'd love to tag along."

"It's going to be a hard fight," Carmen said, "to get out of here."

"I'll take my chances."

"Quickly," Kalor said, "the guards are starting to come to!"

"Kalor," Carmen said, "you and Kur are on point."

Waving them ahead, they fled down the south passage. The tunnel worked its way around the arena, past cages filled with animals and beasts of all kinds and portals in the wall through which the arena could be seen. What guards there might have been had moved higher into the stadium to better view the contest, and no eyes viewed their flight. Halfway around the Colosseum, the passage entered a large storage area.

"Search it," Carmen said, "let us see if the wizard is a man of his word."

Trunks, boxes, and containers of all kinds were stacked about the room, some holding food and wine, others containing costumes and props. Fanning out, they searched every shelf and corner of the room.

"Over here in this back corner!" Kalor exclaimed. "I have found it."

Most of their confiscated gear was there, including all of their swords and Kur's ax and shield.

"Do we get dressed," Leander asked, "or carry it with us?"

"Put it on," Carmen said. "I think that we're going to need it!"

"I'll stand watch," Dartin declared. "Hurry!"

Dumping their gladiators' arms, they suited up with all haste.

"I don't see anything here of yours, Brent," Karina said.

"This old sword will be fine for killing Orcs," he replied. "When they found me on the battlefield, I was almost dead."

"It's a miracle that they didn't kill you."

"They need slaves here. I've been digging in the mine for weeks. When they get low of gladiators, they sacrifice some of us."

"Everything that we had is here," Kalor observed, "except for the pieces of the staff and the food."

"We're being set up," Kur said.

"Unless the wizard is on the level," Carmen said. "And if he isn't?"

"If he isn't," Tariq said interrupting, "at least we've got a fighting chance."

"The map shows this whole section. If we backtrack to the first east passage, we should find a flight of stairs leading to the lower area," Dao directed.

"Let's make for it," Carmen said.

Chaos reigned in the Colosseum. Screams of terror and shouts of outrage were joined by every voice of pandemonium. "Tariq, lead on!" A hundred yards and they turned left, down the first east passage. Two hundred more and they reached an intersection.

"Carmen," Tariq shouted back, "the passage continues on. There are stairs to the north leading down and south leading up. Which way?"

"Take the stairs down!" Dao replied, and no sooner had the last man turned the first bend in the stairwell than a large company of Orcs rushed down the very hall where they had just been. It was then that the Orcs' drums began to beat so violently that the very foundations of the pyramid shook.

Thrum-doom, thrum-doom! Doom-doom!

"They have raised the alarm!" Karina said.

"Quickly!" Dao implored. "At the end of the stairs is a long corridor running east and west. Turn right and east. It will take us to a network of stairs and passageways leading deep beneath the fortress." Tariq led them in full flight. No more were their thoughts on stealth; there was no time for it. If they encountered guards, they would have to cut their way through them. Trusting in luck, they made it to the tunnel's end, honeycombed with passageways leading in six directions; two led down and the others up. "Take the rightmost stairs down. There are several rooms below us and another passageway leading deeper."

Reaching the next level, they entered a labyrinth of rooms. Several were equipped with running water baths and steam rooms; others were filled with cots and the furnishings of soldiers' quarters. Miraculously, they were unoccupied; it seemed that everyone capable of doing so was in the Colosseum above.

"Kur, me boy!" came a cry from the far room.

"Pappy!" Running ahead with barely contained excitement, he embraced his father dressed in nothing more than his nightshirt.

Seeing the room for the first time, Kur realized that they were not alone. His father was the only one that he recognized. Eleven women, one man, and two boys also waited there. Their reunion was filled with emotion and a thousand unanswered questions. Still the drums quaked, urgent and unending.

"Come," an Elven woman urged, "there is no time!"

"Who are you?"

"I am Efmiel," she said, "Elrin's spy. The Orcs will soon discover your escape, and we must be far away from here when they do."

"In the last room there are two flights of stairs. One leads north and the other south," Dao said. "Both of them lead off of this map. I have no way of knowing which passage is the best one."

"The north tunnel leads to the mines," Efmiel advised. "I have never been down the south stairs."

"Wait," Kalor said, "has anyone seen my master, Uldrick?"

"I couldn't find him," Efmiel replied. "He is being held somewhere else in the fortress, someplace secret."

"We've got to find him!"

"There is no time," Carmen said, "you know that. If we can, we'll come back for him another day."

Kalor was shaken. His mentor was being held captive because of him, and he knew that there was nothing that he could do about it.

"I'll become invisible and find him," Kalor said hopefully.

"You saw the hounds," Dao reminded him. "Their noses won't be fooled by your spell. You won't stand a chance."

"And we need you with us," Karina said. "You are a little thief, but one hell of a thief."

"And I'm awful rusty," Moldrin confessed, "and a bit underdressed."

The drums continued, and from somewhere far off, a horn blew.

"Do we go south," Tariq said, "or try some other way?"

"South," Carmen decided, "there is no other way."

"So what she is saying," Kur said to no one in particular, "is that nothing has changed."

"Exactly!" Leander joked with a wink.

"Tariq," Carmen said, "it is your lead, and Kur follows second. Dao and I will take the rear. Everyone else walks between us."

"Do we travel with light or in darkness?"

"Flame must light our way," Carmen said, "and Dao's dagger the rear. There are too many among us who will be blind without it."

Leaving the room, they took the south stairs. The only man among the refugees other than Moldrin was Human. His body was covered in bruises and burns and other obvious signs of torture. Limping along, his eyes were pained yet filled with resolve, his shoulders squared and carried with pride.

"Dartin," Carmen said, "heal this man."

"No," he replied, "there is no time for it now. Let's move on."

"Who are you?"

"I am Baron Duchings, and these are the last survivors of my town."

"Lead on then," Carmen said. "We will be right behind you."

In a romantic tale, it might be said that they descended those stairs with courage and the bravest hearts, but in reality it was full flight, a scrambling, falling, all-out desire to escape from terror that they could no longer control. Having been a hair's breadth from death for so long had numbed them. Until now, they had no chance. Behind them was a fortress filled with every manner of nightmare, torture, and agonizing death. Knowing full well that if they were recaptured, their ends would likely come swiftly and without mercy, their fears could no longer be subdued. Their minds were full of every dreadful imagining, thousands of Orcs and beasts swarming about the pyramid in search of them, driven ever onward by their Dark Commander. Exhausted yet determined to escape, they ran on and on down stairs, along tunnels, past enormous labyrinthine mines and bottomless pits.

The sounds of searching Orcs echoed from every distant hall, their drummers beating the alarm from one end of their kingdom to another, *thrum-doom, thrum-doom,* ever and again, hoping to paralyze their enemies with fear and cover the advancing sounds of their hunters. It was working.

"Where to now, Kur?" Tariq confided. "It seems like we have been running for miles."

"The distances always seem greater down here. Few tunnels run straight and true. Most of these are following veins of precious ore at random. We are perhaps only a mile down, but we have traveled ten to get here."

"I wonder if they have found our trail."

Placing his hands and an ear against the tunnel wall, Kur listened. "The stone trembles beneath thousands of footsteps. Most are still far away, but at least a hundred are close behind us, maybe two miles back."

"We need to lose them," Tariq said. "The baron's people are in rough shape. Most of them are barefoot, hurt, and tired."

"We could make a stand here," Dartin offered. "The passage is narrow. They can only come at us two at a time."

"We have got to keep going," Leander said. "They won't bother taking us prisoner this time. They will keep coming until we are all dead."

"He's right," Dao agreed. "It is time that we need, and I can give us that. I have learned a spell to shape the stone. If you wish, I can seal the tunnel behind us."

"Then there will be no going back," Carmen said.

"There is none anyway," Moldrin admitted. "Our only chance is to run."

"Go on ahead," Dao said. "I'll catch up."

"I'll wait with you," Kalor replied. "Someone should watch your back."

Raising his left hand toward the passage they had passed through, his right hand pointing toward the earth, Dao chanted, "Tenther-rok, mor quenthin ta-un!" His right hand summoned the power of Tempus, and his mind directed it. The walls of granite then became as soft as dough, shaping and forming beneath the invisible force of his hand until a thick wall sealed the tunnel shut.

"Well done," Kalor praised, "that should hold them for a while."

"Unless they have a wizard with them," Dao said, "or a Giant."

"No Giant can pass through these tunnels."

"Come, Kalor, let's hurry!"

"Dao bought us time," Tariq said. "Let's not waste it." Marching on quickly yet more cautiously, they followed Kur's trail-consuming pace. Along the way, they passed by many crossroads, natural tunnels, and bridges over torrential rivers.

The passages were often a marvel of natural engineering. Eons of runoff from above had carved away the softest stone, leaving behind a honeycomb of tunnels and trickling together into streams of irresistible force below. In many places, cunning masonry bridged chasms and traversed cliff walls. The Orcs had tamed their environment in ways that might have been considered a marvel, but when one is being mercilessly pursued by thousands of them through the vast labyrinth of their home, it could only be described as one's worst nightmare. Their family of refugees was beyond terror. If they stopped, it would be unlikely that they could be moved again, and for this reason, Carmen urged them ever onward. "We must not stop," she said, "until we are either free or we cannot crawl another inch."

In that desperate hour, the baron was a pillar of strength. The tortures that had been laid upon him would leave him forever scarred, but rather than let his pain stop him, he used it to fuel his inner fire. To his fellows, he seemed to be a Juggernaut, more god than man, but on the inside, his god was pain. His desire to redeem himself, to rescue some of those that he had so desperately failed, was his rosary.

Kur assumed the lead. His stout body, so often a handicap in the open wilds beneath the sun, was now moving through the terrain that it was born for. Where Men and Orcs had to stoop and crawl, he could still stand erect; where long Elven legs stumbled over loose stones, his legs grabbed and dug in. A two-hundred-pound man of strength could stand fast and hold well once he braced himself, but a two-hundred pound Dwarf was nearly immovable. There were many among them, then, who wished for at least a day to be Dwarven. Luckily for them, Kur was Dwarf enough for them all.

The trail descended ever onward, and it seemed that all hope would soon be lost. The farther down they went, the chances of their ever finding their way home again dwindled. In the end, their bodies were mortal, fragile, and limited. They could travel no farther. Carmen called a halt. Bringing everyone together, they took a head count. So far, they had all made it together. "What do you think, Kur?" Carmen asked him privately. "Is there any hope at all?"

"Of course, the veins of Tempus run where they will and however far. Salvation could lie just around the next bend."

"We will need food and water," Tariq said. "At this pace, they won't last another day."

"Fear not," Carmen consoled. "We'll find food, and we have already passed many rivers. We'll find one soon that's not too far below us."

"There are a few things that he's not telling you," Kalor said.

"Like what?"

"That this tunnel could simply end or drop off into an endless rift."

"No, Kalor!" Kur said, "I believe that his tunnel does not just end."

"How could you possibly know that?" Kalor said, abandoning hope.

"Have you not noticed the breeze? Every step that we have taken for the last mile has led us towards fresh air."

"It cannot be the surface?"

"No, no, Kalor, but I think that it must be either the Underearth Sea or a great cavern."

"Everyone, find a place to rest," Carmen guided.

"Take a seat," the baron said to his townsfolk. "We'll need to regain our strength for the next march. Moving to each of them in turn, he offered what help to them that he could, trying to ease their ever-building dread.

Kur watched him and was reminded of the watchtower at Highcrest Garrison the night that the Jackals came. He was there again with his men, Cloghan and Nenagh, and his other boys that had died, reassuring them that everything would be all right, but it was not all right. Slumping down the side of the tunnel wall, he lowered his head and cried.

Carmen allowed them a little light, urging Dao to unsheath his dagger, but down here, where the denizens of eternal night walked freely, it was as dangerous as it was helpful. "Find a place to sleep as best you can," Carmen said. "When you are settled, the lights must go out."

Their charges were scared, ready to break and run, but they were far too exhausted. Most of them were too tired to sleep.

"There is a rune that may feed us and bring us water," Dartin explained. "I will invoke it now." With his hands, he traced it and with his voice, invoked it, and two goats then appeared before their very eyes. Opening his hands, water spilled from his palms, and he filled their wine skins. "These are Thor's goats," Dartin said. "We may eat their flesh, but do not break their bones. If anyone does, his wrath will befall us."

"Won't he mind that we are eating them?"

"He is welcome to join us," Dartin said, "but I do hope that he dines at my father's table this night!"

Slaughtering the goats, they cooked them with Flame and shared them equally. Full bellies eased their anxiety, but their fear was far from extinguished.

"My pain is endless," the baron moaned, "and soon Death will come for me."

Dartin knelt beside him. "I am a healer," he said. "I should have cared for you when we first met."

"My pain isn't important. I deserve it for my failure."

"No man could have done more," Dartin said. "Now let's have a look at you."

Carefully removing the man's tattered tunic, he was horrified by what he saw. The flesh of the baron's torso was ruined by cat-o'-nine-tails and meticulously burned to control the bleeding so that he might last a little longer. Many of his ribs were cracked or bruised, and some even showed through gaps in his torn skin. It was a wonder that he still lived at all. Dartin again invoked his power, and the baron was healed. When his pain was gone, he gasped in surprise. Feeling his body whole again, he smiled and put his tunic back on.

Moving to each person in turn, Dartin healed their worst hurts and eased their pain. When he was through, he stumbled from exhaustion and lay down upon the cold stone. "I think that I'll just lie here for a bit," he said, but he was soon fast asleep.

"Perhaps," Carmen said to Dao, "you can remember a song that will lighten our hearts, so that some of us might find sleep this night."

"My lady," Dao replied, "I do not know if I can find my voice tonight."

"I remember it," she said. "It is as beautiful as the sound made by the ocean's waves striking the beach. Sing to us the way that you sang in the Gargoyles' lair."

"I shall try," Dao said, "but my voice is not so much lost as it is forgotten. I have had no reason to rejoice since that time, and it is usually out of joy that I sing."

"Think of our life before the war," Karina said, "when our first planted fields were growing tall and Nordtown was filled with hope and love."

"For you," he said, "I will try."

At first, he hummed basic tunes to a myriad of songs; for deep down, he knew many songs of love and merriment and some of lost Elven magic. It was some time before he chose one to sing. Into the darkness he peered, seeking to find some light, some ray of hope within it, or perhaps the restless spirit of his own heart. His voice began at a whisper and then grew in confidence because he had remembered his mother's lullaby and how she had sung it to him and his siblings. Soon her voice rose up to join with his, tears flowing from her eyes, and this is how it went:

The Lullaby

Lie down and dream, my babies,
little boys and little ladies.
Dream of smiles and Love's sweet daisies,
your mommy is here, and we'll shed not a tear.
For when we rise, we shall dance and we shall sing,
through Moonlight and Fairy Wood,
until we come to the Mushroom Ring,
and enter the realm of the Fairy King.
We will dance and we will dream,
with his Host sight unseen,
to our sacred home, the land ever-living.

Sleep well, my babies,
for when you wake,
we will be in the land of love and golden morn,
where the water is always crystal,
where Magic's children, the Tuatha, were born.

Dao sang on, his forgotten voice found, gentle, soft, fair, and so good that if evil was near, it would have been forced to flee or face its own terrible ugliness. His song was a testament to the wise leader that Carmen had become because long before his song was through, most of their charges were fast asleep. They were beyond dreams, blissfully exhausted, sleeping upon stone as soft as down. Only he, Carmen, Tariq, Kur, and the baron had found it possible to resist his lullaby. "Who shall take the first watch?"

"We'll take watch," Carmen said. "Tariq and I won't be able to sleep anyway. Sheathe your dagger. We have risked the light for too long."

"Sleep isn't a bad idea," Dao sighed. "Who knows when we'll have to start running again? Karina has already joined her Sister in dreams. Maybe I'll just sit by my mother for a while. He did, and soon, he too slept.

Kur spoke with the baron about many things until the baron had forgotten his own weaknesses long enough to fall asleep himself. Kur rested his head against the stone, listening to the vibrations from above, at times awake and listening and at other times drifting far away.

Carmen and Tariq sat back to back well past the hours of first watch. She watching where they had come from and he where they were going, but everything was eternal dark and everlasting quiet. They whispered of many things and various topics but soon ran out of words. They had run out of things to say, except those things that people rarely feel free to speak of. Perhaps it was their desperate situation or the danger, but both Carmen and the ranger spoke the same words at precisely the same moment.

"Yes."

"Yes," Tariq said. "If it is not as I have dreamed, then I shall fall upon my sword at this very moment."

"And then I would join you."

"I have never loved any woman, Human or Elf, but I love you as surely as the stars shine in Heaven."

Carmen's next words were then cut short because they had already turned and embraced each other with a passion as unbridled as the hearts of wild horses.

I knew that I wouldn't get any sleep tonight, Kur thought as he quietly assumed guard. *I can never understand why this sort of thing always happens at the worst of times.* Checking on his father, he saw that he was fast asleep and snoring. It made him think of home.

The lovers entered a place where no one else could follow. She removed her helm and her armor. She was completely blind, surrounded by the pressing dark. Tariq was her eyes, and she was his soul. All that she could do was feel and smell and listen to his heart and his breath. He was her first love, and she was his, and there could never be another. It was there, two miles below, that they shared a lifetime of love, surrounded by stone and beset by evil. There were no witnesses to their joining save for a stalwart Dwarf, and he dutifully kept his back turned and his thoughts far away. They loved for a long time, in a joining that had been forced to wait too long, and which could no longer be stopped. When it was over, they collapsed into exhausted sleep, two lonely warriors forever joined.

Kur covered them with their cloaks when he heard the first murmurings of life from the sleepers. Their love, though no longer a secret, was understood by them all.

"Dao," Kur said, "it is time for your light."

"It is a little cold down here," Kalor joked.

"On your feet!" Kur ordered. "Our leaders had a few difficult wounds to bind, and as everyone knows, some bandages are hard to apply alone."

"And as it is quite chilly down here," Leander said. "It only makes sense to share bodily warmth." His own hand was wrapped around Robbin's when he said it.

"Don't get any ideas," Dartin grumbled.

"Strap your armor tight," Kur said, "and empty your boots. There are things that crawl around down here that would just love to dine on your feet."

It was then that the Orcs' drums began again, *thrum-doom, thrum-doom*, from above them.

"They are upon us!" the baron said.

"No," Kur replied, "but they have breached Dao's wall.

"Then they are less than a half day's march behind us!"

"Ruck up. As long as we have the lead, we may yet escape." He led them down again, through twisting passageways and long jagged stairs cut through mined tunnels and natural caverns. Carmen's party spread themselves throughout their charges. Their armed presence helped to calm them, thus preventing the all-out flight that fear's nightmare deigned to bring. Beneath them, a low rumble could be heard, echoing toward them from far below. It was a sound that they were beginning to understand well.

"Another river, Keg," Tariq said.

"Yes, but it is a ways off yet."

"Let's just hope that there is a way across it."

"This trail is well-used," Kur said. "The stairs show signs of centuries of wear. Whether they use the river for a water source or a means of travel remains to be seen." The stairs soon led to a tremendous cave and chasm, over which a stout rope bridge had been built. The river screamed through the gorge far below. "Bring Kalor up. We should check this bridge before we dare cross it."

"What is it?" Kalor asked.

"An old bridge," Kur said, "but who knows what traps may have been set."

"I'll check it out." Moving cautiously, he looked into every dark corner before approaching it. The stone before it looked solid, as did the massive iron pins that held the thick cable supporting it. The cave continued upward beyond his sight, and he could see no dangers lurking there. Creeping closer, his senses were alive, the sound of his own footsteps seeming like hammer falls, although, in truth, he walked as quietly as any mortal could without floating above the ground.

On the bridge, there were signs of recent movement. The dust on its wooden planks had been displaced by Man-sized footprints, and there was little dust upon the trail itself. Reaching the edge of the chasm, he peered over it and under the bridge, but he could see no traps or defects in it of any kind. Setting himself, he placed a little pressure on the top ropes, and they seemed solid. There was nothing left to do but test it, but as a precaution, he tied his own rope to an iron pin and traveled with the rope onto the bridge. His own weight barely shook it. Step-by-step, he searched and moved, until he was across. Securing his line to a stone outcropping, he beckoned for them to cross.

"One by one," Kur commanded, "and don't let go of Kalor's rope."

Tariq led the way and even jumped in the middle to test it. It was hardly affected by his weight. Carmen followed closely behind him.

"Go on ahead with Kur," he said. I'll make sure everyone gets across okay."

The rest of them soon followed, emboldened by the ease and safety of her crossing. It then seemed to all of them, even the young boys, that they could do it. Tariq counted them as they crossed, twenty-three of them in all, eleven women, two boys, Moldrin, and their party with Brent. Relieved that they had left no one behind, he pulled the last boy that came past him aside. The young man had wide shoulders and a thick crop of brown hair; his eyes were wild with a mixture of excitement and fear.

"Kyle, send the word to the front," Kur instructed. "I shall now take the rear guard." Leaving someone behind was now a constant threat. With such a large party, spread out along winding tunnels, it might be a long time before someone's absence was discovered.

"Okay, sir," Kyle said, and he was quick to whisper into his brother's ear ahead of him, and he to the Lady Lisette ahead of him, and so on, until the word finally did reach Carmen in the front.

When the boys were safely ahead of him, Tariq drew Flame and laid into the ropes of the bridge. The hemp cables were massively thick, but he hacked away relentlessly until it fell away into the rift. Dangling from the opposite bank, it would take a long time to repair.

The chasm was wide, too wide for any Orc to jump. Smiling at his handiwork, he turned and ran, hurrying to catch up.

"Very well," she told Leander, "send Dartin back with him. The rear is now the most dangerous position of all."

"At once," he answered, and her orders were quickly followed. "Kur, how does it look?"

"Another river is close by. I believe that the chasm is part of a vast network of streams leading to something much larger. The trail is well-used, so we must be ready for anything."

"Send back the order for quiet march," she said. "No talking unless it is an emergency."

The path led them ever deeper into the earth, twisting this way and that so randomly that no one among them, save perhaps for the Dwarves, had any idea of what direction they were headed in. The darkness ahead was diminishing, and even the Humans among them could begin to make out the shapes and sizes of things.

Are we near the surface? some of them hoped, but it was clear to the levelheaded among them that they were approaching something entirely different.

The Fortress

When the roar of the river peaked (and in volume it was such that one man's voice could not be heard unless his lips were pressed closely against the ear that he wished to hear it), the trail led into a cavern so gigantic that neither its roof nor its end could be seen. The entire chamber was eerily lit by glowing fungi of all kinds in a myriad of phosphorescent colors; the bright mushrooms extended for at least a mile to the east and west and even farther along the road ahead.

A hundred paces or so ahead of them, the foot of a massive bridge rested. Wide at its feet, it grew narrower at the summit and then widened again on the far side. Beneath it raced a gargantuan torrent of water, cresting over mighty falls near the west wall of the cave.

Beyond the bridge was a once mighty fortress, now mostly a crumbling ruin. Its ancient builders must have stood watch against darkness and doom. The path that they followed led over the bridge and into the fortress.

It was then that the Orcs' terrible drums again thundered, and not from several hours behind them but near, oh so very near.

"To the fortress!" Carmen shouted. "Over the bridge as fast as you can."

Their fellows from Nordtown were now scared beyond reason. Their bodies were spent save for the surge of terror's blood. The boys, Zachary and Kiel, showed great courage, helping those too scared even to run.

"Come on!" Zachary shouted. "We've got to go, now," until finally, they were all fleeing for their lives.

Carmen and her party were hard-pressed to keep pace with them, the Dwarves lagging somewhat behind due to the shortness of their legs. Leander stayed back with them. "Not a bad place to make a stand."

"There is at least a battalion of Orcs behind us," Kur said while breathing hard. "Terrible odds, but we may have no choice."

At the crest of the bridge, they could see beyond for some distance. The ruins stood between the chasm below them, and a wide swift river beyond it. The bridge was the only safe way across.

"See there!" Tariq directed, pointing ahead. "Four longboats are moored by the river."

"Let's make for them," she said. "To the boats, everyone, quickly!"

"We can stand here," Kur replied, "and fight!"

"But what of them?" Carmen said. "What happens to them if we die? Let us save the fight for when there is nowhere else to run."

Nodding, Kur consented, and all of them agreed that it was the best thing to do. When they looked back, the enemy had begun swarming out of the tunnel like bees from a hive, and there seemed to be no end to them.

"Run on," Carmen cried. "Everyone to the boats!"

They flew on winged feet down the bridge and through the ancient keep. Its walls were breached and crumbling, its stones moss-encrusted and glowing. In some yesteryear, it must have been a glorious sight, but the blast of siege and the ravages of time had left it a lonely ruin. The path was well-worn, almost a road. Clearly the boats were often used by either the Orcs or some other denizens of Underearth. Reaching the river, they looked back. The Orcs were approaching the foot of the bridge, and it was there that their Dark Commander ordered their formation.

"First battalion!" she commanded in a voice made loud by sorcery, "battle ranks of threes!"

The Orcs immediately tightened their formation, unslung their thick round shields, and readied their spears.

THE LONGBOATS

The boats were both long and wide of beam, having space enough for a crew of forty and ten benches for oarsmen. The craft was steered from the stern by a well-built tiller and rudder assembly. Four in all, they were tied well to moorings, riveted to docks jutting out into the river.

"I can handle it," Leander said. "Dartin and I used to work boats just like these in the port harbors of Arendal."

"The river is swift and deep," Kur cautioned. "It might be hard to pilot."

"I know that *I* can steer it," Leander assured him, "but with so few oarsmen, we won't be able to fight the current."

"There is no time to worry about it now," Carmen said. "Everyone, into the boat."

"Dartin, take Dao and cut the other three loose," she commanded. "We can't have them following us."

"We're on it," Dartin said. Racing against time, they ran from dock to dock, cutting the tether lines and pushing the boats off. The current took them swiftly, and in moments, they floated into the dark tunnel leaving the cavern.

"There will be no turning back once we shove off," Dartin warned.

"There never is," Dao said with a grin.

"Let's get out of here!"

Running back, Dao turned away and looked to the bridge. "I shall leave them with something to remember us by."

"Hurry!" Dartin urged. "They are waiting to shove off."

Dao hardly heard him because he had already begun to raise his power from within and without. Ancient Elven words, the names of things given to them by the gods from the day they were born, poured from his mouth and his memory. He called out to them now, a warrior mage, once dead, now reborn, and his heart was filled with fire. In the palm of his right hand a miniature sun burned, and this he hurled like a meteor at the ranks of the Orcs who had reached the top of the bridge. His ball of fire exploded among them in a tremendous torrent. Most of the Orcs there were burned unto death in an instant, some others throwing themselves over the parapet and into the river below to extinguish themselves, and in so doing, died anyway. Chaos reigned among them for some time until their leaders regained control.

Dao sprinted for the dock and leaped over the gunwale and onto the deck, obviously quite proud of himself.

"Can we go now?" Carmen asked.

"Please proceed," he answered, hardly fazed, with his fists on his hips. Tariq held the ship's line fast from the dock, waiting for the moment to cast them off.

"Is everyone aboard?" Tariq asked.

"All accounted for," Kur said. "Now climb aboard, laddy. The bastards are on the move again!"

The ranger turned back, and a strange countenance came upon him.

"Don't do it, lad," Kur pleaded.

"You'll need time to get them to safety."

"No!" Carmen pleaded. "Get aboard at once."

"I'll catch up," he answered as he released the line, pushing the boat hard and away into the current. "I will love only you forever!"

"No!" she screamed. Moving toward the gunwale, she prepared to swim to shore, but Leander held her fast.

"You will die if you try it," he said. "Even with your helm, you will never beat this current. While you both still live, there will always be a chance."

"Tariq!" she cried, but he was already gone, concealed beneath the folds of his chameleon cloak.

"Foolish boy!" Kur exclaimed. "He swore that he would have his revenge."

Kalor tried his rope, but the current had already carried them well past its magical reach. Passing into the tunnel, they soon entered the dark world of Underearth once again. Dao unsheathed his dagger and stabbed it into the prow to light their way. Borrowing a locket from a young woman named Susanna Merchant, he cast another light spell upon it, and with it, they brought light to the boat. Darkness might have been better, because Tariq had become dear to them all, and each of them was crying. Carmen leaned over the gunwale, sobbing, desiring most of all to cast herself into the water and die. Never before had she known such pain, but she was a soldier still, and they needed her. She picked up the pieces of herself. She would never abandon hope, not as long as she still lived.

He had seen his death in a dream many years before. He knew that this place was to be his end. It was a destiny that was more than destiny—it was his duty. Revenge and its call seethed within him. His people called out to him for it from the grave. Running into the ruins, he paused to fire arrow after arrow into their ranks. Blending in, he was invisible, but his arrows were not. In moments, the Orcs believed that they faced many enemies and not simply one. They formed tight ranks in defense.

His arrows spent, he removed his ring and swallowed it. Taking a vial out of his pouch, he drank it, and soon the strength of a Giant was his. Moving swiftly, he used what cover he could and prayed that his cloak would do the rest. Slipping from rocks to ruin, between pits and crevasses, he worked his way wraithlike toward the Orcs. He knew that he had no chance of surviving against so many, but he would buy his friends time. Very soon, he was among them upon the bridge.

Allowing his mind to relive the horror of his youth, his father's murder, his mother's rape, and her death within his arms, he remembered the wolves and the burning; it was enough, more than enough. He would kill them until his arms could no longer wield a blade. Reaching the bridge, he crept slowly forward, allowing his cloak to work to its fullest potential. Waiting while many of them passed him by, he lurked, huddled and concealed, hoping to strike at their heart.

Near the formation's center strode an aged war master. Eight feet tall and still hugely muscled, he bore many scars and carried many scalps, but it was his eyes that Tariq recognized, for here was the very Orc that had slain his father and defiled his mother. If he killed no other Orcs this day, it would be enough to kill this one alone. Moving desperately quickly, he stood before the shocked war master. Speaking not a word, he hewed at his knee, desiring only to bring him down to eye-level. Tariq had no way of knowing the full effects of the potion that he had drunk before that moment. His blow was so forceful that he severed both of the Orc's legs above the knee. Blood burst from the stumps as the stunned beast tried to step forward upon legs that were no longer connected. Tariq caught him with his left hand as easily as if he was catching a hurling ball.

"This is for my father!" he said in Orcish as he drove his sword into his enemy's heart, "and for my mother." Gutting the beast, he tossed what was left of him off the bridge like a rag doll.

To the army of Orcs, it seemed like the hand of god had torn their leader in half before their very eyes. Nearly invisible, Tariq infiltrated their ranks and then began to slice one throat after another. Camouflaged, it seemed that his blades alone would appear and then disappear, leaving another Orc or two dead, and then two more several columns further in.

Tariq knew that his surprise would not last long. He did not hesitate. Using what luck that the gods had given him, he attacked on the run. How long his enchanted strength would last, he could not know, and he did not intend to waste any of it. With one of his father's knives in his left and Flame in his right, he cut and spun, crashing into their ranks like the waves of a tempest. The Orcs tried to rally, but confusion reigned among them; their enemy was a ghost, a flaming sword now there and then gone.

"You fools!" their commander shouted from the rear. "He is invisible! Form tight ranks, shields and spears!"

Well-trained, they summoned their courage and rallied, closing their gaps tightly in order to either trap or extricate their adversary.

"Surrender!" she shouted.

"Never," Tariq answered flatly.

"Then you will surely die," she said. "Notice now that your invisibility cloak is failing."

She spoke truthfully, for indeed some other magic was canceling out that of his cloak's. He was invisible no more.

"My friends have escaped," he replied. "I have no purpose now but to kill you all!"

"Your friends may have escaped for now," she said, "but if they fail to steer down the right fork, they will be driven over the Falls of the Damned and smashed to pieces three thousand feet below. Die well, ranger!"

His battle cry was a guttural scream, a death knell, a desolate gurgle of despair for his failure, a shout from his very soul that stole away all the other sounds around him and made his enemies pause.

The Orcs surrounding him pressed inward to crush him between their ranks. A hedgerow of spears assailed his front and his back. A stone rampart five feet tall railed the bridge, and onto this, he leaped. They followed, thrusting and hurling spears at him, but war's blood seethed within him now, giant's strength fueling his legs and adding to his every move. With him cleaving Orcs' spears in two and smashing their shields to splinters, few among them avoided the devastation of his blows. Often he leaped like a running deer to avoid a hail of javelins, farther and higher than any normal man ever could have, only to land expertly, still on the run, always hewing and never still. His cloak no longer concealed him, but it now acted to catch dozens of barbs from bows and arrows, Atlatl-hurled spears, and Red Orcin death bows. Its magic foiled, it was pierced, it was torn, but somehow, Tariq was not. Reaching the crest of the bridge, he neared their center. Behind him were two hundred Orcs and scores of dead. To his front were twice that number, and their leaders were among them.

Dockalfar, Fairies of Darkness, dressed in adamant mail, one helmed, the other, a woman with her hands held high. Working feverishly, she began casting spell after spell against him.

Killing Orc after Orc, the narrowing at the bridge-top allowed only a dozen enemies to press him at one time. Fighting expertly, he moved in circle and counter-circle, using his next foe as a shield to protect him from those behind him. The Orcs began piling up beneath his feet, body after body crashing down dead and dying. Caring nothing for his own life, he welcomed the spirit of revenge that had claimed his soul. He was Death incarnate.

"It seems impossible," their leader considered, "but he is actually holding his own."

"He cannot win," she said. "He is but one ranger."

"One ranger indeed."

They watched him then, for here was just the kind of nemesis that they had always dreamed of. This ridiculous Elf could challenge even them! Orcs surrounded him, assailing him from all sides. Wherever his sword struck, he severed limbs or clove bodies in two. In order to reach him, the Orcs now had to climb over a mound of their dead. His defense was pure attack, completely berserk; he was then their master.

The Orcs were now beyond angry themselves. They wanted their own revenge, and they sought it with madness.

Tariq was indeed but one ranger, one Elf after all, and his luck had its limits. The dark witch had called upon the unholy powers of her goddess, and with her magic, she battered Tariq with an invisible hammer. He barely felt the pain, but it was the first major wound that he had suffered, and this from an unseen assailant. He faced either an invisible foe or the fell powers of their evil gods. Laying about himself like a whirlwind, he fought blindly, but his blades met nothing but air. He was struck in the face, his nose smashed and his cheeks torn. He knew now that it was magic alone that had struck him, and atop of his mound of death he was a target too easy. His only chance was to kill the witch and the Orcs' leader.

"For Carmen!" he cried as he charged down the rightmost parapet. Killing any Orc that came too near to him, he rapidly closed the gap, but the witch's hammer struck him again and again. His left arm was hit hard, his wrist broken. Struck again, he lost his father's blade. Knocked off the parapet, he fell into the Orcin host. Decapitating one, he caved in the chest of another, eviscerated a third, and hewed the legs off another.

One ranger, indeed alone, oh so very alone, and inevitably, an Orc's spear did find his flesh. Stabbed through the kidney, Tariq cut off the spear's head and snapped off the shaft behind him. The Orc tried to punch him and paid with his life, but victory was not to be his that day. War clubs crashed into him. A spear pierced his thigh and another his calf. He was overborne. They piled their bodies on top of him to press the rest of the life from his lungs. Gathering the last of his fury, he heaved, standing mightily. Many of the Orcs were hurled off the bridge and into the maelstrom. Ten more were thrown back, and still he held his sword ever burning. "Face me!" he croaked to the Dockalfar commander.

"Hold!" their adamant leader commanded. "Drop your sword and surrender, and you will be treated with a soldier's honor."

"I challenge you to single combat."

"And to the victor?"

"To the victor, life."

"Agreed."

Tariq stood, bleeding, pierced yet resolute, only able to see through one eye, nearly naked, his clothing ruined, ragged, removed. His left arm was useless below the elbow, his forearm smashed, destroyed. His right arm still held Flame with a giant's strength. He could barely stand, let alone fight, but stand he did, nonetheless.

"Surrender," the leader said, "you cannot win. You have done well. There need be no shame, no more waste of life."

"You will not take me alive."

"There is no honor in this duel. You are dying. I will not fight you, but if you allow us to take you prisoner, I swear that I will face you in single combat once you are healed."

"What is your name, Dark One?"

"I am Elrick DuRaneurden, son of Oswald, descended of Marcius, and yours?"

"I am Tariq, son of Eonid and Oswin, who were murdered by the Orcs of this tribe when I was but a child."

"Lay down your sword, Tariq. The battle is over."

Suddenly, his strength faded, and his sword grew heavy, his wounds debilitating. His life's blood nearly spent, he knew that he had no chance. One Orc stood between him and the parapet.

"I'd rather see you in Hell!" he swore. With a sudden thrust, he planted Flame in the Orc's heart, pulled the dying wretch down into the path of the advancing host, then half-jumped, half-crawled over the lip. With one last glance at Elrick and the witch, he smiled and let go. The Orcs tried to catch him but failed. One heartbeat more and then the maelstrom took him.

"Such a waste," Elrick said.

"And at a great cost," the witch answered. "How many of our battalion did he slay, and alone?"

"It would appear," Elrick said, "that one ranger can do much."

"If ever we meet him again, I shall not underestimate him," she praised.

"He has fallen into Chaos," Elrick said, "the mightiest river in Underearth. His body is being dragged down into the bowels of Hell, where it is said only the Ancient Ones dwell. We will only meet this one in the afterlife."

"These Fermen are full of surprises," she mused. "I will never again count one of them dead until I see their corpse cold, and even then, I will remain cautious!"

Tariq fell and fell. His landing was violent, nothing pretty. More of his ribs were crushed, his right arm broken, but he hardly felt any of it. The water was cold, colder than the Arctic Sea, yet unfrozen and salty, like the ocean itself. He inhaled as much of it as he could.

Better to hasten death, he thought.

He drowned forever, and then everything went black.

"Bring me War Master Bruin," Elrick said to his Goblin runner.

"He is dead, master."

"Then bring me War Master Zin!"

"He was hurled into the river."

"Dare I ask, little one," Elrick said, somewhat amused, "do I have any war masters left?"

"War Master O'Urg is alive, but he cannot walk, and War Master Tang is gutted but yet alive. The only war master unhurt is Rend."

"And where, pray tell, is he?"

"Down by the docks."

"Well?"

"Yes, master?"

"Bring him to me at once!"

The little Goblin was foolish and irritating, but swift once he was sufficiently motivated.

"Ariana."

"Yes, Elrick?"

"Could you please tend to the wounded? My war masters are more useful to me alive."

"Oh, but they have failed us so."

"Ariana!"

"Oh, all right." Reluctantly, she tended to their wounds, and for a moment, it almost seemed to him that she was a caring and able nursemaid. Her divine powers were undeniable, however, because in a short time, O'Urg could walk, Tang's bowels made whole, and thirty more of his soldiers saved.

The Ranger had cost them dearly, however. Sixty-three of his Orcs had been killed, and twelve more were missing, presumably in the river.

"Surely some of them can be raised, Ariana?"

"I have power enough to bring three of them back from the dead," she said, "but I will have to rest for a long time after that."

"Then save the three best," he said, "and they can carry you back to the pyramid."

"Shall I save the elder who died first?"

"No, not that one," Elrick advised. "The ranger earned his revenge."

"If we camp here for a few days, I can raise a few more of them."

"Very well," Elrick said. "We shall encamp by the river and await further orders."

"Seventy-five killed or missing," she reported. "Perhaps Tariq has the heart of the Dockalfar."

"I wonder," Elrick said, "are our hearts any different at all?"

"Oh, don't be silly," Ariana said laughingly. "If you had your way, why, there wouldn't be any more war, and then what would we do?"

"What would we do, indeed."

"The general will not be pleased."

"Andreul foresaw their escape."

"Yes, but I did so much want to prove her wrong."

"If only we could pursue them downriver."

"We have no boats," Ariana said, "unless…"

"Unless we contact the outpost at Grey-Weir Ford."

"My mirror is programmed with that destination!" She then produced her arcane device, and after clicking two forelegs and one hind leg three-times rearward, she soon had the attention of the outpost commander.

"Ah," he said, "Priestess Ariana and Captain Elrick, congratulations on your promotion!"

"Thank you and greetings to you, Captain Drake."

"What can I do for you, Elrick? It has been a long time."

"I am in need of at least five longships. We are encamped at the ruins of Chaos Falls."

"Do you need any additional soldiers? I can spare a company if need be."

"I could use a good squad of marines to help navigate the river from here to the Lost Outpost near the Great Whirlpool."

"Done," Captain Drake said, "I'll send two squads and five fully provisioned boats, enough for you and your battalion. They should reach you within twenty-four hours."

"We are in your debt, Captain."

"Nonsense, anything for a fellow brother of the academy. I will inform you of their departure."

"Hunters, lead the way!"

"All the way."

"Good night, Captain Drake."

"Good night."

Later that night, Captain Drake informed them that everything had proceeded as planned. The longships were on the way. Pacing atop of the bridge, he found the ranger's knife leaning against the rampart, solitary, bloody, and somewhat ordinary. Bending down and picking it up, he wiped the gore from the blade. Finely made, large, and well balanced, it said something about the man who wielded it. Peering over the side of the bridge and into the tumult, he spent time contemplating. Looking at the knife again, he changed his mind. This knife was special indeed. He considered throwing it into the maelstrom, but thought better of it. Tucking it beneath his belt, he resumed his duties. Hopefully the longships would arrive soon.

When they arrived, Elrick wasted no time in boarding his battalion of Orcs, and launching them off in pursuit of his quarry. He doubted their success. The Fermen had an enormous head start, but they were tired. They may even have taken the wrong passage and passed over the Falls of the Damned. Only time would tell.

EFMIEL

Elrin's spy had remained silent during most of the escape, helping when needed and yet mysteriously mute. Shortly after they had cast off, Efmiel approached Leander at the helm. "Two miles downriver, the flow will divide, seemingly slower toward the left passage, but we must turn right. The left passage will lead us to our doom."

"How do you know this?" Leander asked.

"Because Elrin told me."

"Who are you really?"

Gripping the gunwale, she was torn between remaining Efmiel the slave turned spy and revealing the truth about her identity. "I am Efmiel, sister of Tariq, and I may now be the last of the Wood Elven."

"Sister?"

"I have been the Orcs' prisoner since I was a child. Later, I was rescued by a young Dragonian soldier named Vlad Leu Sherroan."

"Vlad!" Kalor said. "I pray that we never hear that name again."

"Oh," Carmen vowed, "we will meet again!"

"She may be his spy," Kur said. "No Elf could have survived for so many years among the Orcs."

"I survived as a slave. When I was a child, I served food to their chief. I was forced to clean their filth and sleep on the ground. When I came of age, they planned my rape and blood sacrifice to their Demon Lord. Their new master arrived that very night. Dressed in black mail, he walked into their midst without the slightest fear. When he witnessed their devilish ritual, he took pity on me. First, he offered the chief a king's ransom in gold and jewels, but the chief had little need for money. His deepest desire was to see me suffer and die at his own hands."

"That's terrible!" Karina said.

"In defiance, the chief ordered the ceremony to begin, dismissing Vlad's offer. Vlad ran him through without hesitation and challenged the Orcin host to battle. Seeing how easily their chief had fallen, the entire tribe swore fealty to him.

"Vlad's brethren were my greatest enemies. They hated me in much darker, more sinister ways, always plotting to kill me the moment that Vlad's power faltered. He made me his personal slave, and by doing so, I gained a safety that I had never before known."

"Such horrors. It is a miracle that you survived."

"I overheard Vlad's fortune teller," Efmiel said. "She foretold that a party of Fermen would break out of the holding cell during the arena match between Kolren and Uzul. Two days ago, Vlad came to me and told me that the hour of my freedom was at hand. He instructed me to drug the prison guards' wine, steal their keys, and lead your family out of the fortress."

"Aye," Moldrin stated, "and she did it well."

"And what of Elrin?" Karina said.

"Don't you see?" Leander said. "There never was any Elrin."

"Clever," Kur said, "but why bother releasing us at all?"

"Vlad is a man of honor," Efmiel testified. "He is a man of purpose, but not a murderer."

"It will take more than this to earn our trust," Kur said. "How can we be sure that you are not his spy?"

"I ask only for fairness," she replied, "but heed my words, if you sail down the left branch, we will all be dashed to pieces over the Falls of the Damned."

"We have to trust her," Carmen said.

"More likely she is leading us into another trap," Kur warned.

"Vlad has used us from the start," Dartin said.

"And I think that it's time for a change," Carmen declared.

"Vlad spoke of a ship," Dao said, "a star vessel. Do you know anything about it, Efmiel?"

"Only his stories," she replied. "He said that he and Darik found it near the heart of the world."

"Oh?" Dao said. "Please do tell us!"

Farad Hoth

The mighty Colosseum was huge, towering, and awe-inspiring, with a hundred rows of benches seating a thousand per row, and on this night, every seat was filled, every aisle and hall overflowing.

It was the night of the Spring Equinox, the same infamous night when the Queen of Dragonia had led her people out of darkness and back into the light. She had been old even then, a mother to twenty-three children, and her firstborn son was the general of her invincible army. Many of her daughters had also heard the sacred call of Lothdea and joined the coven. On that night, five hundred years in the past, the Goddess had urged them to live beneath the sun, challenging all who opposed them. The gods of light had been strangely quiet in those dawning days, and Lothdea's children grew bold. They gave no options save submit or die to the people that they conquered. Their victories were countless, and yet their greatest challenges lay yet ahead. Three continents were yet out of their control, threatening their beliefs and challenging their superiority. They were infidels, nonbelievers, hardly people actually.

Arendal and Shamrun were both lands only recently discovered. Their peoples and customs were mysterious and often dangerous. Dragonia's dealings with them would take time to determine what foreign policy was best to follow: to conquer or to ally, but Fermenor had always resisted. Its people knew the history that had long ago divided them, and their alliances had proven resistant to their military might. They were nonbelievers, infidels, bold, and daring to oppose them, but foolish, for surely such resistance was unavailing. Lothdea had guided them from one victory to another. Moreover, where were the gods of Fermenor? Where were Correleus and the other gods of the Liosalfar? Either he slept or he was dead because the Dockalfar had returned, and they were no longer the weaker race!

Queen Aphra sat in the high seat overlooking the grand Colosseum. Rising slowly to her feet, she straightened herself, and the crowd stilled.

"People of Dragonia!" she said. "Our own past has been full of struggle, strife, and hardship. Our differences were settled on the field of battle, but now our alliances have come full circle. One man may be of Na'Varum blood or Kir-Gil, but ask them what nation they hail from, and they will say Dragonia! Gone are the petty wars of our lands, for now, we stand united! Our people do not starve. They walk their city streets without fear. They say that the fairest maiden can walk from Hoth to Shamrun unattended and yet travel safely, without fear from harm. That is what we have come so far to achieve! That is what it means to be Dragonian, to follow the path laid out for us all by the Goddess.

Ever we must remain watchful. We must always prepare for war to ensure our own peace. This truth has always been and forever shall be. Other nations threaten us. They jeopardize our beliefs and seek to ruin us from without and within. We must look to our own shores and the faraway shore. I speak to you now of Fermenor, a land of infidels, barbarians, murderers, and thieves! It is they who seek to destroy us, filling our minds with lies of other gods. They are blind. Can they not see that Lothdea reigns supreme? We have come out of exile to walk again beneath the warmth of the sun. We have returned in the palm of Lothdea's hand. We have achieved victory after victory, and yet where are the gods of Fermenor?

Verily, the Fermen do oppose us, and with no small skill. They are worthy foes. We have battled them for five hundred years, but never before have we been so prosperous, so united. Our armies are the most powerful on Tempus. Our navy will crash through their ships like the head of a pike through mail. We will deliver our forces to their shores in numbers vast beyond their barbarous imaginings. Every city of Fermenor will submit to our might or fall. We shall create a new world order, where heathens will learn the errors of their ways. Every man, woman, and child will know the divine grace and honor of Lothdea. They will learn what it means to be Dragonian.

It is my honor on this, the anniversary of our escape from exile, to announce our new Declaration of War. I do hereby renew our pledge to defeat the lands of Fermenor! We shall begin a full-scale invasion of their shores by the month's end. The First and Second Royal Divisions of Marines will lead our attack against the Kings of Itzul. The ships of the First Fleet will deliver them. We will assail their lands from the north. We will crash into their west shores, and shatter their east. We shall descend upon them from the sky, upon the backs of dragons, raining ruin upon them from the south, until they no longer have anywhere left to run. Within ten years, the godless Fermen will submit, or fall, by all the wisdom and grace of the Goddess. Do not fear for them, good citizens, for we shall be merciful in our might. If the unbelievers choose surrender and swear fealty to Dragonia and the Goddess, they will be spared. If they continue to oppose us, then they shall fall.

Dragonia shall spread her greatness across the breadth of the world, and all its people will benefit from it. When Tempus is one empire, one great nation, then there will be no more war, and peace will reign among us all. All hail the mighty! All hail Dragonia!

The peoples' deafening roar filled the air, their right fists clenched and held high. The Queen stood before them proudly, holding her fist aloft. Her aged body now held tall, bold, defiant, and powerful.

"All hail the Mighty! For Dragonia and the Queen! For Dragonia and the Queen!"

She was their leader, the most awe-inspiring Queen that any of them had ever known. The crowd was hers, and together, their voices were so powerful that they were heard from one end of Farad Hoth to another. The spectacle in the arena that day rivaled any that had come before it. Those that witnessed it remembered it forever. It was a fitting tribute to the pride and honor that was Dragonia.

THE GODDESS AND THE QUEEN

Kneeling before the altar, in the finest temple ever erected in Lothdea's name, the Queen prayed. She was the most powerful priestess that the Dockalfar had ever known, both in god-given power and station. She spoke frequently to the Goddess, and at times, Lothdea spoke to her, especially when her designs for her people were not proceeding in a manner that she found pleasing. The events of the past season had gone especially badly, and for that reason, Lothdea did not simply speak to Aphra; she appeared.

The Goddess answered her prayers from the second row of pews in the worship hall. "We have a problem," Lothdea said.

Startled, Aphra turned, groveling at the feet of the most powerful deity in her pantheon. In form, the Goddess could appear in any way that she pleased. In anger, she could become a demonic terror surpassing any mortal's greatest fears. Within her church and before her chosen Queen, she appeared as the Dockalfar themselves, and yet her supernatural beauty could spell doom to any mortal bold enough to look upon her. She sat in a nonchalant fashion, relaxed, supremely confident, as if she was a simple patron watching a play in a concert hall.

"My lady!"

"Rise and sit, Aphra," Lothdea said. "You need never kneel before me, child."

Aphra rose to her knees and then stood. The Goddess urged her to sit beside her.

"Vlad has become too powerful to be left to his own designs any longer. He must be killed as soon as possible."

"Ariana is no longer loyal to us," Aphra reported. "She has fallen in love with the man."

"She too must be killed," Lothdea considered, "but we must use her first."

"We will use her to kill the son of Aklon."

"It may take more to kill that one," Lothdea considered, "so I have brought you a new servant to send against him."

"Servant, my lady?"

"Arachnidon has created a new knight, soulless and devastating. In his former life, he was known as Ranvarwen J'Throi."

"He was one of the traitors sacrificed in the arena!"

"Yes, yes, but the Great Spider saw a potential in him, a childhood hatred that he could fashion to our designs. After his soul was consumed, only his hatred remained. Arachnidon cunningly used Ranvarwen's malice, turning it against the son of Aklon."

"But will his power be enough?"

"He is now a knight of Shadow, with the power to walk between worlds as Vlad does. His sword is ensorcelled to destroy both the Demon and the Elf. He has all the powers of a fallen paladin. The only desires that he knows are revenge and the ultimate destruction of good."

"But Vlad will foresee his coming."

"I have stripped Andreul of her sight," Lothdea said. "Now she only sees what I want her to see."

"The traitor will finally pay the price that his father paid, and we will finally be rid of House Leu Sherroan!"

"Witness our Black Knight!" Lothdea said, and Ranvarwen then appeared out of shadow, haunting, invulnerable. Six feet tall, broad-shouldered, and wearing a full suit of spiked plate mail, his helm was round and flat-roofed, with thin perforations in the form of the Great Spider for his eyes and his breath. Sheathed at his left hip was a broad hand and a half sword. A short mace dangled by his right. His gauntlets were forged of the same adamant metal and spiked in the fashion of his armor.

"Remove your helm," Lothdea commanded. "Kneel before your Queen!"

He did so and then rested his arms across his knee, bowing low.

"Raise your eyes," Aphra said, "so that I may look upon your face."

Ranvarwen may have once been beautiful, but many battles had scarred his face, the most prominent one crossing over his right eye and deforming his nose. His eyes were red like blood, his hair both silver and long in order to pad his helm.

"What is your greatest wish, Black Knight?"

"To destroy House Leu Sherroan!"

"Excellent, Ranvarwen," Aphra said, "but we must do it carefully. He must not know of your purpose until it is too late. I will send you to join him at the head of a battalion of marines. In the heat of battle, you will betray him. Destroy him until there is no trace left of Leu Sherroan but his memory, then travel to his house and destroy his servants. We must ensure that no seed of his has been left to take his place."

"I will destroy him."

"You may leave us now, Ranvarwen," Lothdea replied dismissively. "Prepare yourself. Your ship sails at dawn."

"Yes, my lady," he said. "My Queen." And then he was gone.

"The hour of our victory is at hand!" Aphra said with hardly contained excitement.

"We must remain ever vigilant," Lothdea warned. "Prepare your spells. When Ariana next lies with him, she will put knives through his hearts or die."

"And what of the others?"

"Leave them to me," Lothdea said. "I have already planned an ending for them. The lucky ones will be claimed by Arachnidon, but most of them will not be lucky at all."

"I will prepare myself, my lady," Aphra promised.

"Sit with me a while, my child. I still have much to discuss."

And so she did.

Pomp and Circumstance

"Assemble the legions," Vlad commanded. "I wish to inspect the full muster of our garrison."

"Yes, Commander," Elrick said, "I shall disperse the order. Shall we form up on the Plains of Orcseus?"

"That shall prove fitting," Vlad replied. "Let the Orcs assemble before the monument to their god, and there we shall announce the plans for war."

"Shall I send for Uzul as well, Commander?"

"Uzul still rests with the healers," Vlad said. "His mind is not yet ready to resume command. He has suffered his first defeat, and at the hands of his archenemy. It will be a miracle if he recovers enough to assume his former rank and title."

"The tribes are fat and spoiling for a fight," Monica El Far, who was often called the Silk-haired said. "Their population has grown remarkably during the last few years of peace. Except for the army of Lycurgus, there have been few casualties and no deaths from disease."

"How many warriors will they commit?"

"Each tribe has offered two thousand veteran fighters, and three remote tribes to the west have pledged three thousand more. They don't want to miss out on the spoils of this war."

"More than three regiments!" Vlad said, dropping his right fist into his left palm. "It just may be enough to shift the odds in our favor."

"There are rumors," Olak reported, pausing, his face both determined and grim, "that Vremick has assembled an army in order to rekindle the old war."

"He seeks the sword of his father," Draco said. "We nearly killed him with the son of D'Agol."

"It seems unavoidable," Vlad considered. "We will bring war to one front, and it shall strike us on more than two. I will not sacrifice the honor of the D'Agol clan by ordering the surrender of the sword."

"Nor would any of us," Draco said. "We are fighters, and we will fight!"

"And we will finally deal with this Sentien once and for all," Olak vowed. "His mad quest for revenge has always been a threat."

"It is still likely," Vlad said, "that we do not yet have the necessary strength to subdue the armies of Safehaven. Lord Cherek has a mighty garrison at Khan, and his barons can assemble thousands of knights in a matter of days."

"The Queen seeks to rid herself of us."

"The time of our confrontation is fast approaching," Vlad agreed, "but we have a few surprises for her all our own."

"When do we move for the last piece?"

"We must attempt to gain the circlet before we march on Safehaven. Andreul has foreseen a terrible defeat if we should fail to unite the staff before the war begins."

"How soon?"

"After the ceremony," Vlad replied, "we shall inform the army of the campaign, place our field commanders in charge, and prepare ourselves. By the week's end, we must be aboard *Imperium*."

"And what of Carmen's Rangers?" Olak asked. "Are they not part of the prophecy?"

"My spy shall see to it that they know of our plan and the location of the ship. It will be up to them to stop us."

"What if your spy betrays us?"

"Her betrayal is the plan," Vlad explained. "I fully expect her to tell them everything. Besides, Ariana and Elrick will be close behind them to help guide them in the right direction if need be."

"Destiny has become uncertain," Andreul said. "The yarn of Fate is frayed and my power diminished. Everything seems to hang in the balance of our success."

"So your future sight," Draco surmised, "will no longer lead us to victory?"

"It seems," Christoff said, "that you are now free to make your own destiny, maybe for the first time in your history."

"This is our time," Vlad resolved, "when the strength in our hearts and in our minds will be sorely tested. The day is coming when the strength of our character must outweigh the power of the gods themselves."

"Then it is the time that you have all been waiting for!"

"And forever feared," Draco said.

"As always," Olak concluded, "the likelihood of our survival is slim."

"Only if our faith in ourselves should falter."

"We will not fail, Commander."

"Enough of this gloom and doom," Vlad said. "Assemble the legions. I have a speech to give and orders to disseminate. When we return from the Ice Moon, we will lead our armies to victory at the head of the most powerful weapon ever created!"

Four divisions assembled upon the Plain of Orcseus. Twenty-four thousand Orcs, Giants, Goblins, and Dragonian regulars, soldiers all, stood disciplined and organized as their commander told them of the coming campaign.

"The Spring Thaw has come," Vlad began, "with our victory on its heels! Many times, have the Orcs marched on Safehaven, only to meet impregnable castle walls and the swords of Lord Cherek's knights. These are all outdated, blunders unavoidable in the absence of proper planning. Now the Orc is stronger and more numerous than ever, allied with Giants, and Goblins, Dockalfar, and Men, Dragonians all. Together, we will sweep through the lands of Safehaven like a wildfire. We will shatter the gates of Khan Keep and pave the way for a thousand dragon ships to land. With courage, we shall reap the whirlwind! Long live the mighty, long live the brave!"

His army roared. Most of them knew little of Dragonia and its people, but all of them knew him, and he, they would follow to the death.

"Prepare yourselves in the coming weeks," he said firmly. "Test your blades and sharpen your weapons and yourselves. When the Blood Moon rises, we march!"

One-Eyed Jack's

"Leander piloted the longboat well," Kur said, "and led us down the right branch in the river. Our light was like a beacon in the dark, and the shadows chased us from behind as heartily as they fled before us."

"We had no idea what lay ahead of us," Kalor continued, "but for the first time, we knew the face of our enemy, and we were more determined than ever to stop him."

"Carmen must have been devastated," Pauli said. "How could she go on?"

"She was our leader, and she wouldn't let us down. Some part of her must have held on to hope. We never saw Tariq die, but the odds were beyond any man."

"How could you possibly beat someone so powerful?" Eric asked. "He had everything perfectly planned down to the smallest detail."

"And he had everything that he needed to complete the staff," Garad said.

"Oh," Kur replied, "he had all the cards all right, but we had Efmiel."

"And that is a story best told another night," Kalor concluded, "with fresh hearts and minds, because much of the tale is beyond belief."

"The truth," Kur said, "usually is."

End of book 2

The third part is entitled *The Ice Moon* and tells of how the party escapes from Underearth and races against time to reach the star vessel *Imperium*. Battling on the frozen wastes of the Ice Moon, they struggle to stop their nemesis as the war to end all wars begins beneath them.

CHARACTER INDEX

Character Name: (Pronunciation), (Race: H-Human, E-Elven, HA-Halfling, HE-Halfar, DW-Dwarven, G-Gnomish, S-Sentien, D-Dockalfar, DG-Darg, O-Orc, T-Titan, F-Floating Lord, Gn-Goblin, L-Lych, V-Vanir, A-Aesir), (Gender), (Ancestry), (God worshipped), (Land of Origin), (Profession/Skill), (Story).

1. Carmen Elise Anastasia: (Car-men E-leeze), (H), (F), (Daughter of Sir William and Gwyneth, Sister of Lisette, Noreen, Kathleen, and Cynthia), (Vanamoinen), (Safehaven), (Paladin), (Veteran of the Jackal Wars, leader of Carmen's rangers).

2. Kalor Starseeker: (Kay-Lore), (G), (M), (Adopted son of Uldrick, parents unknown), (Knowledge), (Safehaven?), (Illusionist/rogue), (Narrator of the story, Karina's "Little Thief.")

3. Kur Kegporter: (Cur/Ker Keg'-Porter), (DW), (M), (Son of Moldrin and Isa, direct descendant of Baldric, sire of the Mountain Dwarves), (Clangeddeus), (Born in Lord Min's fortress at the heart of the volcano), (Soldier), (Hero of the Stair, Underearth guide, wielder of Korun-Koth).

4. Moldrin Kegporter: (Mole-drin), (DW), (M), (Son of Aldo and Helga, descendant of Baldric), (Clangeddeus), (Born at the heart of the volcano), (Brewmaster/chief/

rogue), (Brewermaster of Kegporter wines and ale, former adventurer, husband of Isa, chief of the Kegporters).

5. Dartin Odinson: (Dar-Tin Odin's Son), (HE), (M), (Son of Gretchen and Odin, Brother of Grondor and Elijah-the Sons of O'Rook), (Odin), (Iconerthra-Ice Fortress of the Northern Elves), (Warrior Priest), (Emigrated from Arendal, veteran of the Jackal Wars, faithful member of Carmen's rangers).

6. Leander Forestborn: (Lee-and-er), (HE), (M), (Son of Llewelyn and Muriel. Lifemate of Robbin), (the gods of nature), (Arendal), (Druid), (Emigrated with Dartin, veteran, lifelong friend of Dartin, follower of Carmen, and teller of tales).

7. Tariq Longstride: (T-a-r-Rick), (E), (M), (Son of Enid and Oswin, brother of Efmiel and Morgana), (Correleus), (Tribal Elven kingdoms of the Northern Reaches), (Ranger), (Expert guide and tracker, sworn enemy of the Orcs, loyal follower of Carmen).

8. Dao Greylinx: (Dow Gray-links), (E), (M), (Son of Gwillym and Isidora, descendant of Athenasius High-elven), (Correleus), (Born in the Enchanted Forest), (Warrior Mage), (Learned in ancient Elven lore, apprentice of Gwillym, lifemate of Karina, loyal follower of Carmen).

9. Karina Greylinx: (Ka-Ree-Na), (E), (F), (Daughter of Yseult and Madoc A'Kiva, descendant of Demetrius Earthborn, Sister of Mia), (Correleus), (Born in the Enchanted Forest), (Sword maiden), (Wife of Dao, Keeper of Sunshine, loyal follower of Carmen).

10. Elrin Von Mathers: (El-Rin), (H), (M), (Unknown), (?), (?), (Wizard of the Blue Cloth), (Disciple of Arunduille the

White, hired the party to undertake a dangerous scouting mission).

11. Arunduille the White: (Arran-Dweele), (E), (M), (?), (Correleus), (?), (Arch-wizard), (High Wizard of the Realm, Advisor to Lord Cherek).

12. Lord Ivan Goliath Cherek: (I-van Go-Lie-ath Cherr-eck), (H), (M), (Son of Khan IV and Anne Marie, descendant of Prince Ivan, founder of Khan City), (Ilmater), (Born in Khan), (King), (Ruler of Safehaven).

13. Grog Anvilhead: (Grog Anvil-head), (DW), (M), (Son of Chief Bjorn Anvilhead and Cara), (Moradeus), (Born under the Volcano), (Soldier/blacksmith), (Secret contact, outfitter).

14. Valon Swiftarrow: (Vay-Lawn), (E), (M), (Son of Gavin and Shona), (Correleus), (Enchanted Forest), (Ship's captain), (Captain of the Fermish Vessel *Waterspirit*, protector of the seas off the coast of Safehaven).

15. Elrin Muldoone: (El-Rin Mull-Dune), (E), (M), (Son of Emma and Dane), (Correleus), (Enchanted Forest), (Wizard), (First mate aboard *Waterspirit*).

16. Simage Ruel: (Sim-maja Roo-el), (E), (F), (Daughter of Conn and Leah), (Correleus), (Enchanted Forest), (Sailor, second mate aboard *Waterspirit*).

17. Kane Tanakuro: (Cane Tan-a-cure-o), (H), (M), (Son of Anton and Gidi), (Poseidon), (Fulracus), (Captain), (The huge red-bearded captain of *Courageous Heart*).

18. Targon: (Tar-gone), (H), (M), (Son of Jon and Maya), (Poseidon), (Fulracus), (Navigator), (Sailor aboard *Courageous Heart*).

19. Efmiel: (Ef-me-el), (E), (F), (Daughter of Enid and Oswin), (Correleus), (Tribal Elven Kingdoms), (Healer/Alchemist/Herbalist), (Vlad's concubine, Elrin's spy).

The Judges

1. Tom Zu: (Tom Zoo/commonly referred to as Tomzu), (E), (M), (Son of Joseph and Jackie), (Correleus), (Northwell), (Wizard), (Wizard of the Blue Cloth, famous for his adventures with Sir Aidan of Handover).

2. Sir Tiernan Frostbrand: (Tier-nan), (Gray Elf), (M), (Son of Muirchatec and Chloe), (Correleus), (Rieuwood Hollow), (Paladin), (Sheriff of Rieuwood Hollow, local hero).

3. Brim Stonewarden: (Hill Dwarf), (M), (Son of Slate and Crystal), (Moradeus), (The Gnoll Hills), (Farmer/brewer), (Brewer of blackberry wine).

4. Sir John Anderson of Monson: (H), (M), (Son of Fredolph and Agnes), (God), (Monson), (Knight of Renown, hero, injured during the Battle of Sissily).

5. Mister Tisno Chiselnook: (Tizz-no), (G), (M), (Son of Rubin and Firefly), (Ilmatar), (Western Hills), (Brewer), (Steward of Chiselnook wines, well known for their burgundy).

6. Mister Duncan Kenworthy: (HA), (M), (Son of Ian and Kate), (Dalla), (Ibbington), (Brewer), (Crafter of fine brandy).

7. Sir William of Laughlin: (H), (M), (Son of Frank and Patricia), (Mielikki), (Northwell), (Bard), (Most talented bard in Safehaven, and possibly the world).

On the Darker Side

1. Vlad Leu Sherroan: (Vlad Loo Sherr-own), (D), (M), (Son of Aklon and Ketura, descendant of the "First Born"), (?), (Centurio-domus/mother died during childbirth), (Warrior Mage), (Master of House Leu Sherroan, commander of Dragonian forces at Drakon Mur'-Falor, captain of Drakkar Noire, Lord of Shadow, and the Master of Plans within Plans).

2. Darik Al Luan: (Da-rick Al-lew-on), (D), (M), (Son of Guy and Paige, descendant of Uriel), (?), (Shantu), (Necromancer), (Lieutenant, second in command, loyal friend and follower of Vlad, inventor of tools of both science and magic).

3. Ariana Queensdaughter: (Ari-anna), (D), (F), (Daughter of Maeve and Tristram, Descendant of Cadwalader, adopted by the Coven of Lothdea and renamed Queensdaughter), (Lothdea), (Kal Zakath), (Priestess/Sorceress), (High Priestess of Lothdea, follower of Vlad).

4. Elrick Du'Raneurden: (El-Rick Do-Ran-er-den), (D), (M), (Son of Oswald and Jasmine, Descendant of Marcius), (?), (Dagon), (War-wizard), (Student of Surface Wizardry/ martial artist, follower of Vlad).

5. Shiran Coldrun: (She-Raan Cold-Rune), (D), (M), (Son of Lyss and Moyra, descendant of Alastair), (?), (Shang Tzun), (Weapons Master), (Follower of Vlad, martial arts instructor for Dragonian forces at Drakon Mur'-Falor).

6. Andreul Do'Nurum: (Ann-Dray-ool Doh-New-Rum), (D), (F), (Daughter of Cuthbert and Hephzibah, descendant of Magnus), (Lothdea), (Farad Hoth), (Psychic/Expert in Secret Night-Fighting Techniques), (Prophetess, loyal follower of Vlad).

7. Dorlin Varul: (Door-Lynn Varr-ool), (D), (M), (Son of Iachimo and Sabine, Descendant of Jan), (?), (Namun), (Acrobat), (Master of the Dragon Style of Kung Fu, hand-to-hand fighting instructor of Dragonian forces at Drakon Mur'-Falor, follower of Vlad).

8. Olak Tempestus: (Oh-Lack Tem-pest-us), (D), (M), (Son of Arturo and Clara, descendant of Kevin), (?), (Farad Hoth), (Expert swordsman/archer), (Loyal follower of Vlad/Alias: Berrick Mornbend).

9. Draco Pertinax: (Dray-co Per-tin-axe), (D), (M), (Son of Thaddeus and Sarah, descendant of Gautier), (?), (Farad Hoth), (Spy), (Expert in all forms of espionage, Loyal follower of Vlad/Alias: Darius Mornbend).

10. Monica El Far: (Monica El-Far), (D), (F), (Daughter of Boldwind and Christy, Descendant of Eleehu), (?), (Shantu), (War-wizard), (Expert in Red Orcin Tribal Culture. Loyal follower of Vlad, sometimes referred to as "The Silk-haired").

11. Lycurgus Vespa, "The Mad": (Lie surge us), (D), (M), (Son of Gregory and Mariam), (?), (Altus Caverna), (Sorcerer/mad scientist/general), (Creator of Beasts both fantastic and foul/leader of the Orc army), (Loyal follower of Vlad).

12. Anselm Der'Marshance: (An-selm Der-Mar-shance), (D), (M), (Son of Ethanius and Flavia, descendant of Morag), (Lothdea), (Kal Zakath), (Swordsman/mage), (captain

of Dragonian forces assigned to the Shattered Continent, arch-rival of Vlad).

13. Queen Aphra Der' Lachalet: (Af-ra Der-La-Sha-lay), (D), (F), (Daughter of Cephas and Helena, descendant of Sholto), (Lothdea), (Novus Castellum), (Warrior/Priestess), (Queen of Dragonia, chosen by Lothdea to lead her people out of exile and on to victory, blessed priestess chosen to hear the voice of the Goddess).

14. Jason Da'Gol: (Dah-Gaul), (D), (M), (Son of Durin and Aurora, Descendant of Hu), (Leu-Raig), (Kal Zakath), (Warrior/Mage), (A new lieutenant of the Drakkar Noire, sent with his company to support the Northern Reaches campaign under Commander Vlad).

15. Sgt. Kala Goldsmith: (K-La), (D), (F), (Daughter of Gavin and Deirdre, descendant of Macklin), (Leu-Raig), (Shantu), (Soldier/martial artist), (A member of Jason Da'Gol's Team).

16. Sgt. Dawn Newmason: (D), (F), (Daughter of Percival and Flavia), (Leu-Raig), (Dagon), (Soldier/Survivalist), (A member of Jason's Team).

17. Sgt. Feldwin Carnage: (D), (M), (Son of Baron Carnage and Teresa), (Leu-Raig), (Kal-Fret), (Soldier), (A member of Jason's team).

Other members of Jason's team: Sgt. Bran McHewn, Sgt. Braidwick, Lieutenant Tulina

1. Christoff the Assassin: (Chris-stoff), (H), (M), (Raised in a brothel), (?), (Assassin), (Joins Vlad's troop and helps to capture a certain all-important hostage/Alias: Madam Minx, and Master Johan Christy of Linea).

2. Louis Pinch: (H), (M), (Raised by Wolves), (Loki), (Somewhere in the mountains), (Bandit Lord), (Controls the mountain passes near Linea).

3. Apex the Floating Lord: (A-pex), (F), (M), (Son of Blob and Lula), (The Great Eye), (Tyrannia), (Floating Lord), (Faithful friend and butler to Christoff).

4. Vremick, Son of Illian: (Vrem-ick), (S), (M), (Son of Illian Psi and Bree, Descendant of Geebu), (The Great Mind), (Yir Psi), (Sentien captain/knight/psychic), (Quests to recover the lost sword of his father, General Illian Psi).

5. Sai Ignatius: (Sigh, Ig-nay-shee-us), (S), (M), (Son of Stalwart and Dreamweaver, Descendant of Freewill), (The Great Mind), (Tu Grin Psi), (Sentien knight/psychic), (Follower of Vremick, survivor of the skirmish at King Rodamon's mine).

6. Dravian O'Blesque: (Dray-vee-an Oh-Bless-que), (S), (M), (Son of Sindian and Warmhearth, descendant of Soulwind), (The Great Mind), (Yir Psi), (Sorcerer), (Chief Sorcerer of Vremick).

7. Uzul: (Oo-zule), (T), (M), (Son of Otto and Shona), (?), (Titania), (Warrior), (General in command of the Orc Legions of Drakon Mur'-Falor under the command of Vlad, Destroyer of the Tribal Elven Kingdoms).

Hill Dwarves

1. Kabe: (DW), (M), (Son of Ross and Lusa), (Moradeus), (Thorn Mountain), (Prospector), (Leads Olak and Draco to the Village of New Hope).

Darg

1. A'Goric: (Uh-Gore-ick), (DG), (M), (Son of Plague Bringer and Wretched Wife), (Abbathoreus), (Grulthank—the Darg's mightiest obsidian fortress), (High Chieftain/Assassin), (Agrees to repay Aklon's debt of blood).

2. Silent Scream: (DG), (M), (Son of Deadeye and Faithless), (Abbathoreus), (Underearth Wildlands), (Vile Paladin/member of an order of evil called "The Hand of Abbathor, and captain of a Darg company), (Leader of A'Goric's war party).

3. Black Bible: (DG), (M), (Son of Cutpurse and Betrayer), (Abbathoreus), (Grulthank), (Priest of Abbathoreus), (Member of the war party).

4. Fell Sorcerer: (DG), (M), (Son of Broken Heart and Soul Deceiver), (Abbathoreus), (Grulthank), (Necromancer/Wizard), (Member of the war party).

Vanir

1. Sheena El-Vanir: (She-nah El-Vain-ear), (V), (F), (?), (?), (?), (Chaos Lord, Psychic, Mage, Dragon Rider, Goddess), (Chaos Maiden, lifemate of Lucidus Rhys El-Vanir, laid the ancient curse that freed the Vanir from their galactic prison.)

2. Lucidus Rhys El-Vanir: (Loo-sid-us Reese, meaning "bright ardor"), (V), (M), (?), (?), (?), (Chaos Lord, psychic, warrior, dragon rider, god), (Lifemate of Sheena, died battling Modrul, prophesized to rise again.)

3. Odin: (Oh-din), (A), (M), (?), (Valhalla), (Greatest Norse god/Sacrificed his eye for the power of the runes), (Husband of Frigga).

BIBLIOGRAPHY

Anon. "A Glossary: Castle Terminology." N.p., n.d., http://www.oldcastleshop.com/glossary1.htm.

Anon. *TSR Fiend Folio: TOME OF CREATURES MALEVOLENT AND BENIGN*. Edited by Don Turnbull. Lake Geneva, WI and US: TSR Hobbies, Inc. and Random House, Inc., 1981.

Anon. *The US Army Ranger's Handbook*. US GOVERNMENT PRINTING OFFICE, 1988.

Cordingly, David. *Under the Black Flag: The Romance and the Reality of Life among the Pirates*. n.p.: Harcourt Brace & Company, 1995.

Fowler, Ramsey H. *The Little Brown Handbook*. Boston, MA, USA: Little, Brown and Company (Inc.), 1983.

Giuong, Phan Van. *Tuttle Concise Vietnamese Dictionary*. North Clarendon, VT: Tuttle Publishing, 2008.

Gygax, Gary. *Advanced Dungeons & Dragons Monster Manual*, 4th ed. Lake Geneva, WI, USA: TSR Hobbies Inc., and Random House, Inc., 1979.

Gygax, Gary. *Advanced Dungeons And Dragons Special Reference Work Dungeon Master's Guide*. Edited by Mike Carr. Lake Geneva, WI, USA: TSR Hobbies, Inc., and Random House, Inc., 1979.

Gygax, Gary E. *Advanced Dungeons And Dragons Players Handbook*. Ed. Mike Carr. Lake Geneva, WI, USA: TSR Hobbies, Inc., and Random House, Inc., 1978.

Hodges, John C., and Mary E. Whitten. *Hardbrace College Handbook*. San Diego, New York, NY: Harcourt Brace Jovanovich, Publishers, 1986.

Kindersley, Dorling. *World War II, the Definitive Visual History*. New York, NY: DK Publishing, 2009.

Lane, Carl D. *How to Sail: A Complete Handbook of the Art of Sailing for the Novice and the Old Hand*. New York: W.W. Norton & Company, Inc., 1947.

Langenscheidt. *Langenscheid's Universal Latin Dictionary*. Edited by CDN, Costa, M.A.B. Phil., and Mary Herzberg, M.A. Berlin and Munich, Germany: Langenscheidt KG, 1966.

Lee, Philip Yungkin. *Periplus Pocket Cantonese Dictionary*. North Clarendon, VT: Periplus Editions (HK) Ltd., Tuttle Publishing, 2003.

Levin, Gerald. *The Macmillan College Handbook*. New York, New York: Macmillan Publishing Company, 1987.

Mayer, Adrienne. *Greek Fire, Poison Arrows & Scorpion Bombs: Biological and Chemical Warfare in the Ancient World*, 1st ed. n.p.: The Overlook Press, 2008.

Melville, Herman. *Moby Dick*. Edited by George Stade. New York, New York: Barnes & Noble Books, 2003.

Naian, Shi. *The Water Margin*. Translated by J. H. Jackson. North Clarendon, VT.: Tuttle Publishing, 2010.

O'Brien, Erik D. J. *Kur's Rage: Part One of the Duaredheim Staff Saga*. Denver, Colorado: Outskirts Press, Inc., 2007.

O'Brien, Erik D. J. *The Drums of Doom: Part 2 of the Duaredheim Staff Saga*. Denver, Colorado: Outskirts Press, Inc., 2009.

Savage, Robert Woosnam, and Anthony Hall. *Brassey's Book of Body Armor*. Dulles, Virginia: Brassey's, 2001.

Terban, Marvin, Steve Otfinoski, and Sue Young. *Scholastic Writer's Desk Reference*. New York, New York: Scholastic Inc., 2000.

The Holy Bible, Containing the Old and New Testaments, New King James Version. Thomas Nelson, Inc. 1982.

The New Testament of our Lord and Savior Jesus Christ with Psalms and Proverbs, Nashville, Tennessee: THE GIDEONS INTERNATIONAL, 1985.

Wales, Jimmy, and Larry Sanger. Wikipedia, the free encyclopedia. n.p.: Wikimedia Foundation, Inc. 2001.

Ward, James M., and Robert J. Kuntz. *Advanced Dungeons & Dragons Special Reference Work Deities & Demigods Cyclopedia*. Edited by Lawrence Schick. USA: TSR Games, and Random House, Inc., 1980.

Warren, Doug; Cagney, James (1986) [1983]. *Cagney, The Authorized Biography*, mass market ed. New York: St. Martin's Press. ISBN 0-312-90207-7.

Webster's Universal Dictionary and Thesaurus. New Lanark, Scotland: Geddes and Grosset Ltd., 1993.

Weigel, James Jr., M. A. *Cliff Notes on Mythology*. Lincoln, Nebraska: Cliff Notes, Inc., 1991.

Whipple, A. B. C. Fighting Sail (The Seafarers). Ed. of Time Life Books, George G. Daniels. Canada: Time-Life Books Inc., 1978.

Whitney, William D. *The Century Dictionary and Cyclopedia*. n.p. 1895.

Zhong, Jin Jing, and Andrew Timofeevich. *Authentic Shaolin Heritage Training Methods of 72 Arts of Shaolin*, 1st ed. Tanjin, USA: Create Space, 1934, 2008.

THE O'BRIEN FAMILY TREE

The Dal Cais Tribe

Oilliol Ollum, Cormac Cas

Mac Cennetig(Mac Kennedy) King of Thomond

Mathgamain, Brian

(Mathgamain was the King of the Dal Cais in 968, who in that year defeated the Viking king Ivar of Limerick, "reducing the town to a cloud of smoke and red fire." (From a 12th Century O'Brien text) He was later murdered through treachery in 976. Brian then assumes the kingship of the Dal Cais, avenges his brother, and assumes the kingship of Munster at Cashel.)

Brian Baru High King of Ireland from 999–1014
(Ended Viking Tyranny and won the Battle of Clontarf in 1014.)
Murchadh, Toirrdhelbhach, Donnchadh
The Descendants of Brian

James O'Brien and Bridget
Richard, Helen, William

The Descendants of Curtin
Jeremiah Curtin and Hanna
David, Ilene, Margaret, Florence, Leona, Hanna(Anne), Jerry

The Descendants of O'Brien
William James O'Brien and Hanna(Anne) Curtin
Kevin, David

Kevin James O'Brien and Lucia Esther Pease
Erik David Jeremiah, Amy Beth, Molly Lee, Emily Lue, Daniel Owen

The Descendants of Pullum
Shelby Jean, Robert(Bob), Thomas(Tom)

David O'Brien and Shelby Jean Pullum
Anna Bernice

The Descendants of Winterson
Finbar Robert Winterson and Debra
Steven

Steven Winterson and Amy Beth O'Brien
Jack Finnbar, Christopher Dana

The Descendants of Costello
Marie Abigail Costello
Ruth Lillian

The Descendants of Farrar
Minnie Fitz
George Rufus Farrar
Harland Winfield

Harland(Bumpa) Winfield Farrar & Ruth Lillian Costello
Ruth Marie Farrar

The Descendants of Gabriel

The Gabriels originated in the Caen region of Normandy, where they were an anciently seated family of great nobility. The name is derived from the given name, Gavriel, which means, "God has given me strength."

(French, Arizona Sioux)
Frederick Gabriel

Frederick Gabriel and Ruth Studer

Frederick Albert Gabriel

Frederick Albert Gabriel and Ruth Marie Farrar

James Morrison, Paul Winfield, Jean Marie

James Morrison Gabriel

James Christopher, Patrick Stewart, Bryanna Lynn, Logan Frederick

The Turner clan was first found in Oxfordshire, England, where they held a family seat from 1066.

James Morrison Gabriel and Laurie Patricia Turner

Chloe Lynn

Paul Winfield Farrar and Molly Lee O'Brien

Zackary Harland Winfield, Kyle Dalton James, Maya Nicole Madison

Jean Marie Farrar

Chase, Troy, Gage

James Christopher Gabriel

James Harland

Leonard derives from the Gaelic "O'Leannain."

They were first found in Galway, where they held an ancient family seat.

The Descendants of Leonard

1. David Leonard
2. Dana Stewart

The Descendants of Umbrianna

1. Peter Umbrianna
2. Karen Mae

Dana Stewart Leonard and Karen Mae Umbrianna

1. Dana Stewart

Dana Stewart Leonard and Emily Lue O'Brien

1. Tara Mae
2. Leah Allison
3. Jeremy Layne

The Paskell Family were anciently seated as an aristocratic family in the seigneurie of Merins in the French Alps.

The Descendants of Paskell

1. Ethyl Paskell
2. Ronald

The Descendants of Lincoln

1. Roy Lincoln and Ethyl Croto
2. Polly

Ronald Paskell and Polly Lincoln

1. Kim
2. Shelby
3. Jennifer Leigh
4. Carla

Kim Fox

1. Robert and Christopher Lefave
2. Austin Fox

Kenan Connell and Shelby

1. Devyn
2. Shealyn

Daniel Owen O'Brien and Jennifer Leigh

1. Daniel Owen Jr.
2. Aiden James

Carla Cason

1. Michael, Samantha

The Gaelic form of Anderson is, "Mac Ghille Aindrais," meaning Servant of St. Andrew.

The Anderson Clan originated in the Lowlands of Scotland in the District of Badenoch.

The Descendants of Anderson

Britta Johnson (Sweden), Mother of:

Molly, Elida, Fredolph, Charles, Herbert, Jack, Amanda, Harold

Fredolph Anderson and Agnes Turner

Evelyn Charlotte, John (Johnie) Elias, Esther Helen, Hazel Sophia, Frederick(Freddy)

The Descendants of Pease

John and Robert Pease sailed to America aboard the Ship Francis in 1634.

Their ancestors came from Essex and Great Baddow, England.

Pease

1. Robert Stebbins, Lina

Robert Stebbins Pease and Leola Bradway

Chester, Rachel, Holton, Lucia

(Lucia passed away at 16 of Spinal Meningitis)

Leola would tell Lucia not to play the piano in the evening until her Father Robert had gone out to do his farming chores, lest he get nothing done!

The Descendants of Chester Pease

Chester(Chet) Lincoln Pease and Evelyn Charlotte Anderson

Lucia Esther

My mother would often play the same music on the same piano at her grandpa's house in Hampden as her aunt Lucia, but her grandma never told her, and how she must have cried inside!

Chet, my grandfather taught me many secrets, one of them was a cure for rabbits sick with a cold or flu. He would only put enough water in their bowls to cover the bottom until they improved. This dehydrated them just enough to help them survive their illness, and usually they did.

Nordin is a combination of *Nord*, meaning "north," and the surname *–in*, meaning "descendant of."

The Descendants of Nordin

Alton(Mack) Nordin and Hazel Sophia Anderson

1. Glen Nels
2. Janet Louise

The Descendants of North

1. Ernest North and Bernice Henry
2. Cynthia Irene

Glen Nordin and Cynthia North

1. Jill Ellen
2. Amy Lynn
3. Kristen Ann (my dearest cousins)

Michael Walulak and Jill Ellen Nordin

1. Kurt Patrick Meslavich
2. Nicole Marie Meslavich

The Descendants of Juneau
Blackfeet Indian Nation, Montana

Benton Juneau and Janet Nordin

1. Jennifer

Jennifer
Zane

Benton was a tall, awe-inspiring gentleman with the firmest handshake that I ever felt.

He once told me that his grandson Zane could run like a "wolf man."

I once told him that my biggest rainbow trout was five pounds. I asked him what his biggest was; he said twenty. I didn't have much to say after that.

The Descendants of Linton

Linten is a village and civil parish in the Maidstone District of Kent, England. It is derived from an Old English word meaning, "Lilla's village."

Elden Linton and Evelyn

1. Jane
2. James

The Descendants of Anderson
Frederick Anderson and Jane Linton

1. David, William (Billy)

The Clan Wright was first found in Berwickshire, Scotland, where they held a seat from ancient times. They are part of the sept of Clan MacIntyre.

David Anderson and Debra Wright
Melissa Kate, Meghan Kara, Mollie Krystal

William(Billy) Anderson and Elizabeth
Kelly Elizabeth

A family tree is so much more than a list of names. It represents a grand circle of life as old as time. It tells us where we came from and hints at where we are going. It is as important in real life as it is in fantasy, and so I have included it here, my family tree. May it live and grow forever.

My Sisters Molly and Emily and I visiting
Uncle Johnie in Monson around 1986.

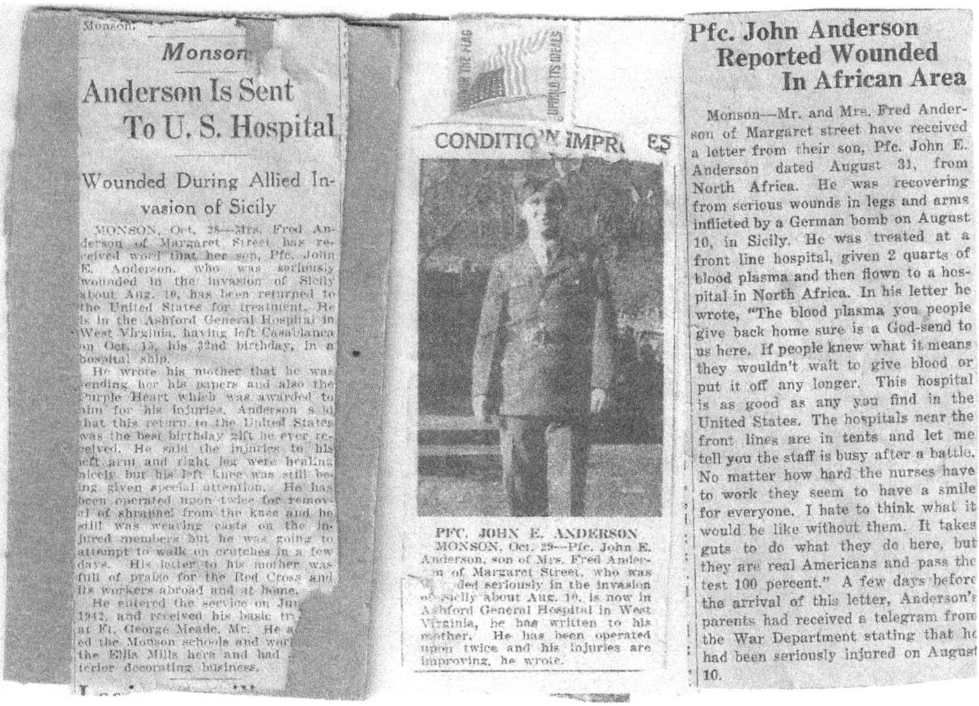

Monson

Monson

Anderson Is Sent To U. S. Hospital

Wounded During Allied Invasion of Sicily

MONSON, Oct. 28—Mrs. Fred Anderson of Margaret Street has received word that her son, Pfc. John E. Anderson, who was seriously wounded in the invasion of Sicily about Aug. 10, has been returned to the United States for treatment. He is in the Ashford General Hospital in West Virginia, having left Casablanca on Oct. 15, his 32nd birthday, in a hospital ship.

He wrote his mother that he was sending her his papers and also the Purple Heart which was awarded to him for his injuries. Anderson said that this return to the United States was the best birthday gift he ever received. He said the injuries to his left arm and right leg were healing nicely but his left knee was still being given special attention. He has been operated upon twice for removal of shrapnel from the knee and he still was wearing casts on the injured members but he was going to attempt to walk on crutches in a few days. His letter to his mother was full of praise for the Red Cross and its workers abroad and at home.

He entered the service on Jun[illegible] 1942, and received his basic tr[illegible] at Ft. George Meade, Mr. He a[illegible]ed the Monson schools and wor[illegible] the Ellis Mills here and had [illegible]terior decorating business.

CONDITIO[illegible] IMPR[illegible]ES

PFC. JOHN E. ANDERSON

MONSON, Oct. 29—Pfc. John E. Anderson, son of Mrs. Fred Ander[illegible]n of Margaret Street, who was [illegible]ded seriously in the invasion of Sicily about Aug. 10, is now in Ashford General Hospital in West Virginia, he has written to his mother. He has been operated upon twice and his injuries are improving, he wrote.

Pfc. John Anderson Reported Wounded In African Area

Monson—Mr. and Mrs. Fred Anderson of Margaret street have received a letter from their son, Pfc. John E. Anderson dated August 31, from North Africa. He was recovering from serious wounds in legs and arms inflicted by a German bomb on August 10, in Sicily. He was treated at a front line hospital, given 2 quarts of blood plasma and then flown to a hospital in North Africa. In his letter he wrote, "The blood plasma you people give back home sure is a God-send to us here. If people knew what it means they wouldn't wait to give blood or put it off any longer. This hospital is as good as any you find in the United States. The hospitals near the front lines are in tents and let me tell you the staff is busy after a battle. No matter how hard the nurses have to work they seem to have a smile for everyone. I hate to think what it would be like without them. It takes guts to do what they do here, but they are real Americans and pass the test 100 percent." A few days before the arrival of this letter, Anderson's parents had received a telegram from the War Department stating that he had been seriously injured on August 10.

HEADQUARTERS SEVENTH INFANTRY
OFFICE OF THE PERSONNEL OFFICER

APO # 3
15 June 1945

SUBJECT: Purple Heart Award.

TO : Commanding Officer, Ashford General Hospital, W. Va.

1. Reference is made to Letter, your Headquarters, dated 15 December 1944, subject: General Orders for Combat and Purple Heart Awards, written to Commanding Officer, Hq Co, 1st Bn, 7th Infantry, relative to Pfc John E. Anderson, 31126170, formerly of this command.

2. A thorough check with medical installations through which Pfc Anderson was evacuated for wound incurred 10 August 1943 reveals that award of Purple Heart was not made during soldier's period of hospitalization.

3. Enclosed herewith two (2) Extract Copies of General Order #200, Headquarters Third Infantry Division, dated 7 June 1944, which may be used as a basis for presentation of Purple Heart to Pfc Anderson. Further requ st that appropriate entries be made in soldier's service record.

For the Commanding Officer:

H. TOLAND,
CWO, USA,
Asst. Pers. Off.

1 Incl:
Extract Copy GO 200, Hq 3d Inf Div
dtd 7 June 45 (duplicate)

R-E-S-T-R-I-C-T-E-D

GENERAL ORDERS)
:
NUMBER 200)

HEADQUARTERS THIRD INFANTRY DIVISION
APO #3 7 June 1945

* * * * E-X-T-R-A-C-T * * * *

Award of Purple Heart. I

I - AWARD OF PURPLE HEART. Under the provisions of Army Regulations 600-45, as amended, a Purple Heart is awarded each of the following named individuals for wounds received in action against the enemy:

JOHN E. ANDERSON, 31 126 170, Pfc, Inf, Hq Co, 1st Bn, 7th Infantry Regiment, Capri Leone, Sicily, 10 August 1943. Residence: Monson, Mass.

* * * * E-X-T-R-A-C-T * * * *

By command of ~~Major General O'DANIEL~~
BRIGADIER GENERAL SEXTON:

CHARLES E. JOHNSON,
Colonel, G. S. C.,
Chief of Staff.

OFFICIAL:

/s/S. J. Rogers
/t/S. J. ROGERS,
Lt Col ~~Major~~, A. G. D.,
Adjutant General.

A CERTIFIED TRUE EXTRACT COPY:

H. Toland

H. TOLAND,
CWO, 7th Infantry,
Asst. Pers. Off.

R-E-S-T-R-I-C-T-E-D

SIR JOHN E. ANDERSON

My hands tremble. I cannot stop my tears. My uncle John was a very special man and the most noble one that I have ever known. I have included the documents that were saved by my family with his Purple Heart, earned during World War II. They speak eternally for themselves.

The following articles appeared in the newspaper following the grievous injuries that he received in Northern Sicily:

> **Pfc. John Anderson**
> **Reported Wounded**
> **In African Area**
> Monson-Mr. and Mrs. Fred Anderson of Margaret street have received a letter from their son, Pfc. John E. Anderson dated August 31, from North Africa. He was recovering from serious wounds in legs and arms inflicted by a German bomb on August 10, in Sicily. He was treated at a front line hospital, given 2 quarts of blood plasma and then flown to a hospital in North Africa. In his letter he wrote, "The blood plasma you people give back home sure is a God-send to us here. If people knew what it means they wouldn't wait to give blood or put it off any longer. This hospital

> is as good as any you find in the United States. The hospitals near the front lines are in tents and let me tell you the staff is busy after a battle. No matter how hard the nurses have to work they seem to have a smile for everyone. I hate to think what it would be like without them. It takes guts to do what they do here, but they are real Americans and pass the test 100 percent." A few days before the arrival of this letter, Anderson's parents had received a telegram from the War Department stating that he had been seriously injured on August 10.

The following article appeared beneath his soldier's photo with the title, "Condition Improves":

> **PFC. JOHN E. ANDERSON**
> MONSON, Oct. 29--Pfc. John E. Anderson, son of Mrs. Fred Anderson of Margaret Street, who was wounded seriously in the invasion of Sicily about Aug. 10, is now in Ashford General Hospital in West Virginia, he has written to his mother. He has been operated upon twice and his injuries are improving, he wrote.

This is the last article in my possession.

Monson
Anderson Is Sent
To U.S. Hospital
Wounded During Allied Invasion of Sicily
MONSON, Oct. 28--Mrs. Fred Anderson of Margaret Street has received word that her son, Pfc. John E. Anderson, who was seriously wounded in the invasion of Sicily about Aug 10, has been returned to the United States for treatment. He is in the Ashford General Hospital in West Virginia, having left Casablanca on Oct. 15, his 32nd birthday, in a hospital ship.
He wrote his mother that he was sending her his papers and also the Purple Heart which was awarded to him for his injuries. Anderson said that this return to the United States was the best birthday gift he ever received. He said the injuries to his left arm and right leg were healing nicely but his left knee was still being given special attention. He has been operated upon twice for removal of shrapnel from the knee and he still was wearing casts on the injured members but he was going to attempt to walk on crutches in a few days. His letter to his mother was full of praise for the Red Cross and its workers abroad and at home.
He entered the service on Jun

1942, and received his basic tra
at Ft. George Meade, Mr. He a
ed the Monson schools and work
the Ellis Mills here and had
terior decorating business.

The above article appears exactly as does the remaining original.

My uncle Johnny told me that he was rescued from the battlefield by Jehovah's Witnesses. They wore bright red robes and carried the dead and wounded back to friendly lines exhaustedly and without fear. He said that their faith was so great that they had no fear of death. He had the greatest respect for their endless courage.

May humankind one day find no more use for war.

—Erik.

John E. Anderson
October 15, 1912–February 20, 2001

Wounded at Capri Leone, Sicily
10th of August, 1943
Awarded the Purple Heart
7th of June, 1945

15th of October, 2008
For exceptional Valor,
Heroism, Character, and Courage,
In the Highest Court of God,

I dub thee, Sir John.

CPSIA information can be obtained
at www.ICGtesting.com
Printed in the USA
BVHW030812080521
606854BV00010B/118

9 781643 455037